BLOOD TRAILS

BLOOD & SHADOWS BOOK 2

BOOKS BY ALIANNE DONNELLY

BLOOD AND SHADOWS
Blood Moons
Blood Trails
Blood Debts
Blood Hunt
Shadow Hawk

DAWN OF RAGNAROK
The Royal Wizard
Dragonblood
Prince of Deceit

THE BEAST
Bastien
The Beast

OTHER TITLES
Wolfen
Virtual
Function: L1VE

ALIANNE DONNELLY

BLOOD TRAILS

BLOOD & SHADOWS BOOK 2

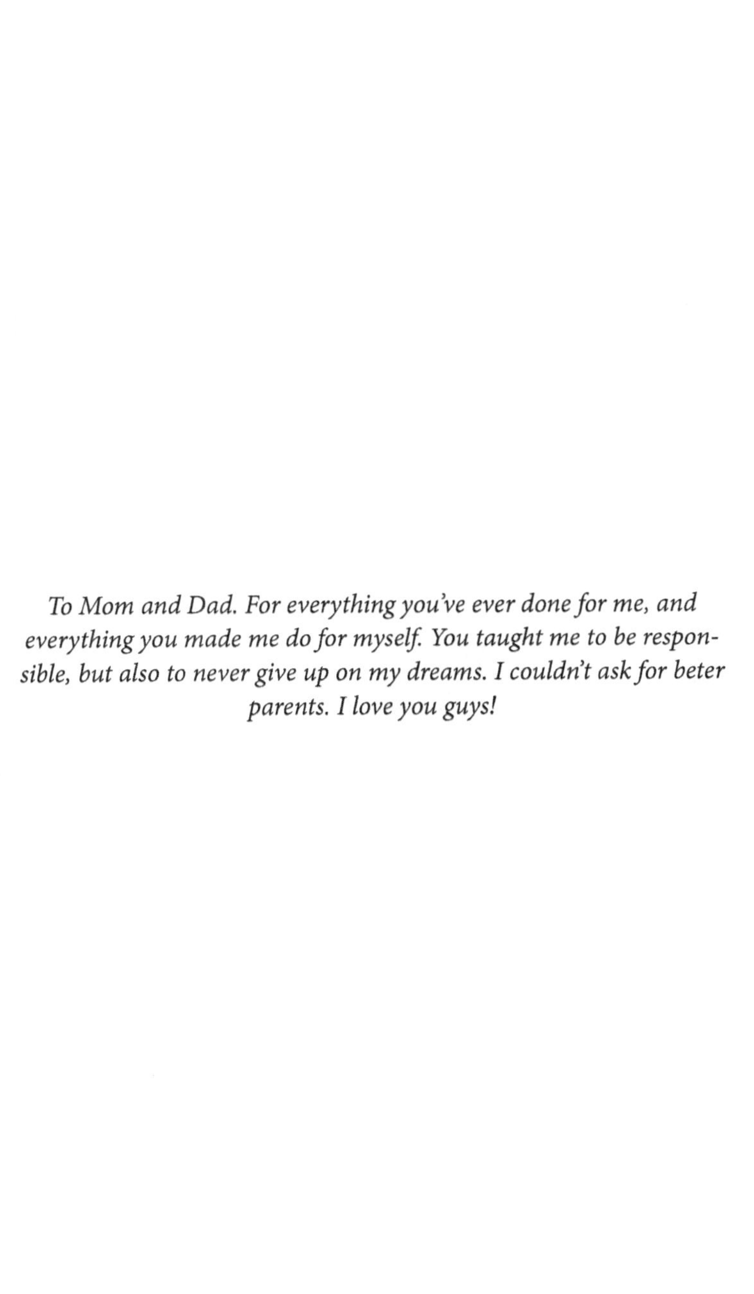

To Mom and Dad. For everything you've ever done for me, and everything you made me do for myself. You taught me to be responsible, but also to never give up on my dreams. I couldn't ask for beter parents. I love you guys!

The loss is a regrettable one. Subject THNA was our last and only hope for the study's success. I'm afraid our chance to create a human-animal shape-shifter has died with him. It is time to accept this experiment as a failure. We are finished.

-Dr. Amelia Chase

Want to bet?

- Hailey S. Chase

– 1 –

So this is what dying feels like…

It's what she would have thought if coherent thought were still possible. It wasn't. With every break, Hailey lost a little more of herself. With every rolling movement of flesh, she screamed a little louder inside her head. Her throat was closed off, choking her. Everything was going so horribly, terrifyingly, *painfully* wrong.

Her bones broke again and again; her lungs contracted, compacted into a different shape. Her spine pulled and pulled, and then her head. *Oh, God, help me!* She was dying. The pain was killing her. Hailey smelled blood—her own. She couldn't even feel the broken glass she was rolling over, the small pricks and cuts lost amid everything else. Flashes of light made her eyes want to roll back in her head, and then there was darkness. For a moment Hailey thought she'd gone blind, but when she opened her eyes she could see again. Brief glimpses that made no sense. Black computer screens flashing light erratically. Data streams mixing, racing over them. They shouldn't be—she'd turned them off.

An overturned table. Glass shattered everywhere. Colorful liquids running together over the floor. Mixing and smoking. The fumes were toxic. Burned her lungs—which suddenly expanded beyond what she used to think was possible.

Images formed and broke up in thin air. She recognized a limb here and there, but even the scanner couldn't make sense of what it was picking up. Then it gave up and shut down. INSUFFICIENT DATA POOL blinked uniformly over all of the screens now.

The lights were flickering red in alarm, while a horrible squealing scream stabbed at her sensitive eardrums.

And the pain. *Christ, just let it be over soon.*

Shouldn't have done it…

Too late for that now!

No regrets. That's what she'd promised herself. *Yeah, right.* Hailey's eyes were bleeding now. She could finally feel the red tears soak into her fur. Her hands were useless to wipe them away, the claws too long; she'd poke her eye out if she tried. But she couldn't move even to do that. Her limbs twitched, still shifting, struggling through the in-between, going the long way around and backwards several times.

But her mind was still so very human. It comprehended every step of what was happening. Could calculate how long she had before she passed out from the pain and how much longer after that until she bled out internally. She'd timed this perfectly, making sure no one would be around to catch her.

The one thing that had worked out exactly as it was supposed to. No one was around—to save her.

For just a moment, her mind seized on the most absurd thing. What would they find when they returned? Would Hailey still look even remotely human? Would she make it far enough to make identification impossible? Would they dispose of her like so much trash?

A horrible sound ripped from her throat, and she couldn't tell if a creature even existed capable of making such a sound.

As if a timer had gone off inside her body signaling the end of what it could stand, her flesh rebelled against the change. Hailey screamed as her body broke and shifted again, reverting to the beginning.

No!

She'd been so close!

And then all coherent thought froze again, drowned out by the breaking and shifting in her skull. Chips and fragments stabbed into her brain, momentarily paralyzing her, blinding her, and causing a seizure in turn. There was nothing to grasp onto. The world around her moved; her senses were completely disoriented, incapable of telling her up from down anymore.

She was spinning, and floating, and drowning, all at the same time, inwardly screaming for help. A tranquilizer, a cure. A goddamn blow to the head. No one could hear her. Any longer and no one ever would again. She would end up as just another statistic. A black mark on the already tarnished record of Dr. Amelia Marguerite Chase.

Except this one really wasn't on her, was it?

Hailey didn't know precisely when her body stopped shifting. The pain continued long after the world settled and the cold of the floor began chilling her bruised bones. Her breaths came in small, fast pants. Her ribs were broken; she could feel the sharp edges grazing her lungs. One wrong move and one of them would pierce through. And then she'd be dead for sure.

Ears ringing, eyes burning, body shaking uncontrollably, Hailey waited for the end to come. Closed her eyes and prayed. When the ringing eased and the sensation of falling returned, she was almost glad. *It's over now...*

~

She couldn't tell what woke her, but something must have. The residual pain still racking her body was nothing compared to the memory of her torture.

"Oh, God!" She heard the horrified whisper from across the lab. She smelled the fear hanging thick in the air. The beast forced one eye open, moved her head to search out the source of the sound. "What have you done?"

The beast remembered that voice. Her neck protested the movement but she managed to tilt her head enough to catch a hazy glimpse of a person standing in the doorway. Blonde hair. White coat. Familiar scent beneath the stench of fear. *Sister.*

The woman stepped closer. "Hailey," she said, her voice shaking. "Oh, God."

Hailey. Is that me? She breathed slow, deeper each time, testing her ribs. Whole. At least whole enough not to kill her right this minute. She flexed her fingers, curled them into her palms. Felt sharp claws pricking her skin.

The woman wasn't coming closer. She wanted to; there was tension in her as if she didn't know whether to run to or from the creature curled up naked on the floor.

The beast tested her limbs, pulled her hands beneath her to push herself up. They held. But her head began splitting like a log, sending her back down. She clutched it, claws digging into her scalp to stop the pounding. Felt her face move and crack, beginning to change again. Somehow it stopped on its own.

The next time she tried to rise, she did it slow. Slinking backwards, pulling her legs beneath her. She was weak. Sitting up hurt. Trying to stand was agony.

The woman was talking, crying, wouldn't come closer. *Good.* "Hailey," she said again.

The beast tested the word in her mind. On her tongue. "*Hey*-lee." *Me.* This woman knew her. Familiar scent. She couldn't place it. *Sister.* Pack? No. Another word. Human word. *Fa*-mi-ly.

The woman stepped a little closer.

The beast snarled, startling the woman as well as herself. She swayed, unstable. Two legs weren't enough to keep her steady. She couldn't walk like this. There was nothing around to offer support. Sharp things all over the ground. They hurt her… feet. She looked at her hands, examining the long black claws. *Pretty.* They retracted then lengthened again.

"Hailey, d-do you know me?"

She looked at the woman again. Her vision was still cloudy and she couldn't shake her head to clear it. Hurt too much. Blonde hair. White coat. Black squares on her eyes. Tears. *Sister.*

The woman touched something on a flat surface, and lights twinkled in front of her. The beast jerked back, startled. "I'm your sister," the woman said as another person appeared between them. But it was wrong. Inside out. All bloody and ripped up. No skin. The woman made a sound of pain looking at that other person, then said, "Let me help you. Please, you need to let me help." Another step closer.

The beast snarled again, feeling fangs lengthen, and dropped into a crouch, ready.

The woman jumped back, hands curling into fists at her sides. "You'll die!" she shouted, angry and still scared. "God, Hailey, I told you no one ever survived this."

A lie. The beast could smell it. A vague memory snared her attention, and she tilted her head. There was another like her. Different, but the same. He survived and has lived through many changes of season with a mate. The woman hid him and kept him secret. Why? He was bigger, stronger, a perfect predator who could protect himself and his mate. Was the woman part of his pride?

The beast snarled again, warning the woman away from a thing with glowing buttons. She was bothersome. Had she come even closer while the beast had been distracted? Hackles rising, she growled low.

The woman jerked back a step. "Damn it, *why*?" she shouted, making the beast bare her teeth in warning. The woman held up her hands. "Okay. Okay, just don't move." She shifted again, slow, deliberate. Not looking away from the beast until the very last second. Whatever she did, it made the wrong person disappear and flat things on the wall glow with moving lights.

For a moment the woman paid the beast no attention. She was watching those moving lights, and the beast was too curious to look away. She merely tilted her head the other way and watched, amused, as the woman's eyes widened.

"A chemical catalyst? Jesus, Hailey. No, no, this is insane. You… from his *blood*?"

Blood. Yes. The beast remembered blood. It was on the floor now, mixing with other things that smelled wrong. Something must have attacked her while she'd slept and brought her to this strange place. Only it wasn't strange. The beast might not know where she was, but there was… a voice. It told her what some of those things were, and where the entrance to this cave was, and it told her to stand up on two legs. She complied.

A dull ache in her midsection made her whine low.

The woman looked at her at once. "Hailey, listen to me. What you did is not stable. It will kill you if we don't fix it. It's killing you already."

Hands behind her back. The beast did not like it. "You know me, Hailey. Hailey Chase, you are my sister. We're family. Let me help you."

Beasts have no ties. Predators hunt those that do. Sister or no, it didn't matter. One of them shouldn't be here. The woman moved like she belonged here. Her territory. The beast didn't belong. No matter; she didn't like it here anyway.

The woman spoke again. "Are you in pain?" Why was she speaking so much? "I can help you if you let me." A hand outstretched, beckoning.

Growling low in her throat, the beast shifted, stepping sideways, careful of the sharp things. The woman turned with her, keeping her in sight.

Another ache, this one sharper. More intense. It made her lose her balance.

"Hailey, please. Let me help you." As her eyes cleared, the beast could see the woman had something in her other hand. Shiny. Dangerous.

The flat things on the walls started screeching, flashing red. Too much. Too loud. Too bright. Her legs cramped, aching to push off.

The woman lunged.

The beast made a run for it, fleeing into the dark corridor, following her nose out into the night.

But it wasn't night. Everything was bright, lights shining all around. Humans everywhere. *Don't let them see you.* She crouched into shadow, watching. Couldn't wait too long.

She took a chance, running on silent feet down the long, flat path, following instinct. She knew where to go. How to get there. Knew it would take her longer if she ran, but she couldn't reach it any other way.

Then she was in that place where her scent was everywhere. Her den. A window was open high up on the wall. She launched herself up, caught the edge twenty feet off the ground. *Feet? What feet?* Pulled herself inside and dropped to the ground for a moment, pain racking her body. She sat there and breathed until it eased. Was she sick?

She went to that place where she could get water into a big white basin. Fiddled clumsily with the water spout until it ran strong, then, following some long-lost memory, she stuffed the hole in the bottom with a silvery thing so the water could pool. She bathed there, crouched in the pool, washing off the blood and dirt. Some would not come off. If she tried to rub harder, it hurt. A wound? Under her skin, marking her.

The water helped to soothe it; it was cold. She used the nice-smelling things to remove the stench of that other place and then crawled out carefully and dried off with the dark red cloth. *Towel.*

She drank from the smaller white basin, irritated that it was so far off the ground, she had to stand on twos to reach it.

When she straightened, something moved in the shiny thing above the basin, startling her. Drawing closer, she watched her own features change, settle, change again, settle, but not the way they used to be. Memories returned slowly, each a sharp dagger piercing through her mind. She remembered things like *minds* and *daggers* now.

Couldn't comprehend the drops of water leaking from her eyes at first. Then understanding returned. The shock. The fear. The grief. *What happened to me?*

Her once beautiful auburn hair now fell in a tangled mess below her shoulders, white as snow. Her eyes had used to be more blue, hadn't they? They were pale gray now, like polished silver. She touched her cheek, gasping when she saw her black nails. Sharp. Not nails anymore; claws.

Hailey stumbled away from the mirror, wincing as her bruised, cut feet touched on the towel she'd dropped to the floor.

It wasn't her anymore. That... creature... looking back at her, it wasn't Hailey anymore. It wasn't the stubborn, curious, happy woman she used to be, the one who loved sunbathing and flirting, and driving her sister crazy.

The thing in the mirror, watching her now with so much horror in her silver eyes was so far from the person Hailey had once been that it couldn't be called human anymore. Her hair white from shock—it would never regain its original color, she knew. Her eyes like an animal's, her senses sharp beyond comprehension. She clutched her ears to block out the incessant loud drumming from next door, but then she realized that it was her own heartbeat.

Her body had changed. It was leaner now, stronger, with defined muscles the likes of which she never would have had the strength of will to attain on her own. Most of her torso was black with bruises, her legs splotchy with them. How was she still standing?

Shock. Had to be. That kind of internal damage was fatal. As soon as her mind caught up with that, she would faint from the blood loss, and if it wasn't stopped, she'd die.

Odd, she didn't seem worried about it. Her reflection's head tilted, studying, curious. She was still standing. She would live long enough to heal. That strange detachment took her away from the mirror into the bedroom. She got into bed, turned a couple of times, and curled up in the messy nest of blankets and sheets, clutching a pillow to her stomach.

She breathed in deep, analyzing the scents wafting in through her window. Curious scents, man-made and strange. Nothing the beast inside her recognized.

The beast inside me…

It wasn't inside her; it *was* her.

Hailey Samantha Chase had indeed remained on the floor of that lab. She'd never woken up.

So this is what dying feels like…

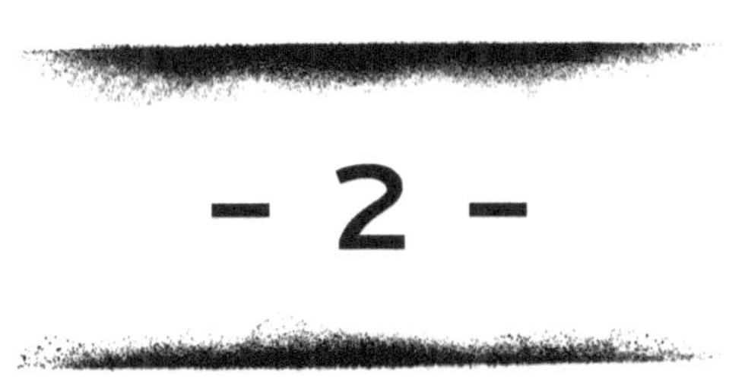

July 17, 3032 – Planet Torrey

Pixie was twirling, her skirts flaring out. She was wearing a replica of some ancient gown, her hair curling and arranged in a net of braids over her head. He didn't like how low the gown was cut. There were too many men around, staring at her. He scowled at Pixie, projecting open hostility toward every male in the vicinity.

Pixie laughed at him. She chose a partner from the multitude and pulled him into the throng of dancers that hadn't been there a second ago. He was about to go after her when Hunt appeared out of nowhere in front of him, an amused look on his savage face. The man shook his head, his eyes glowing.

"Wake up, bro," Pixie called. "Life's moving on without you."

"Wake up, bro…"

Jeremy groaned, recognizing when reality started fading into his dream. Or rather *Pixie's* dream and his personal nightmare. He groaned, turning his face into the pillow. "Pixie," he muttered. "Stay out of my head."

"Okay, but you gotta wake up."

"What time is it?"

"Seven thirty. And is it necessary for you to sleep naked? Ew."

"It wouldn't bother you if you didn't barge into my room so early in the morning," he told her sweetly.

"It bothers me that your clothes aren't permanently sewn into your skin," she replied just as sweetly. Funny, he harbored that same sentiment about her. His little sister was eighteen now. And way past the time when she was a cute little kid everyone gushed over. Now she turned heads for very adult reasons. It was a good thing they lived so far from town. Jeremy was afraid he'd kill the first guy who approached her.

"You wouldn't dare," she said, reading him.

And she didn't seem interested in making things easy on him, walking around in shorts that barely covered her ass and shirts cut low at the top and short at the bottom.

"Hey, those are perfectly respectable clothes, I'll have you know!"

"For who," he shot back, sitting up and pulling the covers over his lap, "the town hooker guild?"

Pixie smiled sweetly. "You would know, I'm sure."

Actually he wouldn't. "Get out of here, will you?"

"Fine, but hurry up. You have a visitor." She wagged an eyebrow. "She's gorgeous, by the way."

The pillow he threw at her thumped softly off the door she closed behind her.

Irrepressible. Sometimes he thought he worried for nothing. That girl wouldn't take shit from anyone, especially a man. But those times were few and far between. His sister was the only family he had left. Protecting her was his job.

—Between you and Hunt, I'll never *get a life of my own,—* she thought him with a dramatic sigh.

He grinned. *—Not until you're too old to do anything about it.—*

A fast-paced song he'd never heard before was playing all through the house by the time he emerged from his room to meet the mystery woman visitor. Pixie shimmied past him on her way out, a backpack swinging from her grasp. "See you tonight," she said.

"What? Wait! Where are you going?"

She danced back, wriggling her butt to the song. "The Hunts are putting on their first ball this weekend. Everyone's invited. Dara needs my help to put it together."

Jeremy winced. Heavily pregnant with twins, Dara could barely walk, let alone decorate a giant, cavernous ballroom. "What about Tristan?"

Pixie twirled. "He's still busy with the bailey."

Jeremy rolled his eyes. "Fine. Call if it gets dark before you're done."

His sister rolled her bright blue eyes. "I don't know why you even bother. There is literally nothing between this house and the Hunts', and even if there was, this is Torrey."

Old habits died hard. Even though they were worlds removed from the gutter that used to be their childhood home, Jeremy refused to let his guard down. He'd seen too much, lived through too much to risk it. So he was a little overprotective. Pixie would deal.

Pixie made a face. "Dara said I could stay over," she offered in grudging concession and danced out the door before he could say anything.

He was still shaking his head on his way to the living room. In the doorway, he stopped in his tracks. "Dr. Chase," he said, dumbfounded.

His guest smiled, but it never reached her eyes. She looked like she'd aged ten years instead of the five that had passed since he'd last seen her. There were dark circles under her eyes as if she hadn't slept in days, and she looked ready to pass out. "It's been a while, Agent Calen."

"Sit, please. Is something wrong? You look…" He trailed off awkwardly.

"Yes," Dr. Chase said, "I know."

The music blared louder. "Music off," he said to stop the noise. "Er, can I get you something to drink?"

"Oh, your sister already provided refreshments," she said with a genuine smile. "She's grown. She's beautiful."

He uneasily made his way to the couch opposite her. Of all the people from his past, she was the last one he'd ever expected to see again. He had a sick feeling in his stomach. This was clearly not a social visit. "What can I do for you, Dr. Chase?"

"Please, call me Amelia," she said. "And I'm sorry to barge in on you like this. I know you're on leave but I just… I had nowhere else to turn."

What about Tristan, he was about to ask, but he already knew the answer. The less contact between them, the safer both of them were. Amelia wouldn't risk exposing what she'd put so much effort into hiding. Besides, Tristan was not about to leave Dara's side any time this century. Especially not now, in her condition. "What about the

Special Unit?"

Amelia shook her head, rubbing the bridge of her nose. "This is a delicate matter. I want to involve as few people as possible. I know you're thinking I should have gone to Tristan, and I did consider it. But given the circumstances his involvement would make matters worse, I think."

Jeremy's brows rose with interest. "What's going on?"

Amelia hesitated. The confident scientist he remembered from five years ago was gone. The woman who now sat before him was scared. If not broken, then fractured by something not easily borne. Amelia had met with some kind of tragedy. And whatever it was, it had left a deep mark on her. She pulled an electronic notepad from her bag, typed in her code—which he tuned out, out of courtesy—and handed it to him.

"It concerns my sister," she said.

A whole lot of medical jargon filled the screen: notes, graphs, charts, and chemical formulas. "You may want to explain a little further, Doc. I can't make sense of this."

"I made a mistake." She scoffed softly, a self-loathing sound. "Another in a long line of them. But this one…" She closed her eyes as if she didn't want to confront what she said next. "I should have destroyed all evidence of Tristan's experiment. But I didn't. What you're looking at used to be my original notes and formulas for the serums administered to him, as well as subsequent treatments. Only they're skewed now.

"Somehow, my sister found my notes and… must have gotten it into her head that she could do better. We never talked about it, I never mentioned anything about the studies; it was all confidential."

Not the whole truth but understandable. Amelia didn't want her professionalism questioned, but she must have mentioned something to her sister; there was no other way she could have found out. "Is your sister a scientist, too?"

"She's always had the brains for it. Used to steal my textbooks during med school for what she called some 'light reading.' I tried to get her to attend at least one class but she refused. No, Hailey is—*was*—a tour guide on Miramar Colony. May I?"

Jeremy handed the notepad back to her.

"She was so very careful. About everything except her own well-being. She made sure no one was around when she did it, and she turned off all security, recording devices, monitors—everything she could find. There were some she didn't. She staked her life on the assumption that her calculations were right."

When she handed the notepad to him again, the screen showed a scanner image of a body that, from all appearances, was dead. The skin layer was removed to show the internal structure. Dozens of red warnings littered the side of the screen pointing to this and that, but it was plain to see the broken bones—was there even one that was whole?—and massive internal bleeding.

"I am sorry," Jeremy said heavily. In his mind he sought Pixie for reassurance that she was all right. Hunt had once asked him what he would do if his sister was ever hurt or in danger. Jeremy had resented the obvious ploy to manipulate him into doing what Hunt wanted, but the truth was he'd resented the subliminal warning or, in Hunt's case, threat. Jeremy didn't know what he would do if anything ever happened to Pixie; his mind refused to even contemplate the possibility that something might. What he knew was that he had the knowledge, skills, and resources to take a very precise kind of revenge.

But he only had to look at Hunt to see where that would eventually get him.

Amelia blinked. "Oh, no. You misunderstand. My sister's not dead."

—*Idiot,*— Pixie returned, sharing her exasperation. —*Wait for her to finish before you start freaking out.*—

Jeremy frowned, ignoring that. "She's not?"

Amelia got that look on her face he knew from before. She was compiling tons of technical data and calculations in her mind, shaping and translating them into something a normal person would understand. "My sister, Hailey, altered my research. Tristan's treatments took a year, given his chemistry, and the fact that we were forced to implement it by degrees. She made it take effect on hers immediately. With just a vial of Tristan's blood, she managed to break a year of research down into its components, alter the proportions to fit her physiology, and make them reactive in series so that they built on each other, with the change agents taking effect last.

"It was a huge gamble. Especially since she changed the animal DNA she introduced into her body. The experiment would either flop, which it should have, or kill her."

"But it didn't do either."

Amelia shook her head. "Hailey discovered the trigger I didn't have back when Tristan first entered the trial. It was a chemical cocktail that acted as a catalyst for the change. But it wasn't a natural byproduct of the body, and it reacted adversely with the rest of the serum she injected herself with." Amelia reached over to tap the screen and what looked like a mathematical formula streamed over it. "It bonded with the regeneration agent and warped it.

"You see, you only need the trigger once to spark the ability to change your shape. Once your body recognizes it, it becomes another mechanism that can be called on at any time, like movement, or temperature regulation. But the regenerative agent is essential to counteract the massive injuries that result from those changes. In Tristan, that also became a part of his system. In Hailey, it didn't. It's disintegrating. Without it, the shape-shifting will eventually kill her."

"How long does she have?"

Amelia sighed. "I don't know. It depends on how often her body needs to regenerate. The more she changes, the more she'll need it, and the faster it will deplete itself. Worst case scenario, another month. Maybe."

Jeremy blew out a breath. This was a whole lot of background information but nothing about what she wanted from him. He had his suspicion but lightly scanned the surface of her thoughts to make sure. "She's missing," he said, rather than asked.

"Yes. She ran away the night it happened. I found evidence that she'd been to her apartment first, but by the time I got there she was already gone."

"And you need me to find her."

Amelia nodded. "I believe I can fix the damage and stabilize her condition, but I need her in my lab to do it." She hesitated. "There's… also something else."

He waved her on to continue.

"It might be completely unrelated, but… I've been watching the news, looking for any hint of her presence. There have been reports of animal attacks. Several in the last few weeks. Mainly young people, teens and early twenties."

"And you worry that Hailey was responsible."

"If you saw her that night—"

"May I?"

She blinked at him. "You want to read my mind?"

"Only with your permission. I would look at that one memory and nothing else."

"Yes, of course. Anything you think might help find her."

Jeremy leaned forward. "Just close your eyes and think of your sister. I'll be able to pick up what you see."

Amelia nodded and closed her eyes.

Jeremy took a second to center himself. He hadn't been just wasting time here on Torrey. Any opportunity to hone his senses was indispensable and he just so happened to live a few miles away from one of the most frustratingly proficient mind readers in existence. Tristan Hunt wasn't just a telepath. When he entered someone's mind, he became that person, without betraying himself to his host. And he could manipulate thoughts in subtle ways, instill fears that didn't exist before, lessen phobias, create dreams—or nightmares.

Jeremy was nowhere near his level of finesse. But the one skill Hunt was teaching him was how to enter a mind without causing pain. He focused his thoughts now on Amelia, dispersing his consciousness into mist that gently fell over Amelia's mind and became absorbed in it.

All at once, he found himself in chaos. He stood in the middle of a series of scenes that went by much too quickly: memories of childhood, of two little girls playing, one blonde, the other dark-haired. They'd done everything together. Laughed, played, studied, cried… until Amelia graduated med school and Hailey didn't.

He saw Hailey grow up, a bright, happy woman with dozens of friends—it was a life like Jeremy imagined life should be; like he and his sister had never had. Hailey's smile, her laugh, was so joyous, it drew people to her, and she always welcomed their company. She was never alone.

This wasn't what Jeremy needed to see. But it was what Amelia needed to show him. He sensed her reluctance to show him what Hailey had become. She wanted him to know her sister as she'd been before this insanity. Wanted him to see her as a person, a human being. Not an animal.

Jeremy gently reminded her why he was there.

The scene changed so sharply he sucked in a breath and nearly knocked himself out of Amelia's mind.

Gone was the sunshine and laughter. He was suddenly standing in the middle of a destroyed lab. Where before the scenes had rushed past him too quickly, this one was almost too slow. A table had overturned, spilling chemicals all over the floor. There was broken glass everywhere and dark liquid, most of it blood. He could smell the pungent odor of the chemicals, the sickening metallic tang of blood, and he felt the stab of pain Amelia had felt at the sight.

Crumpled on the floor was a person. A woman, though her body was curled and twisted, discolored with countless contusions that bled together until her torso was completely black with it. *My sister is dead,* the memory Amelia thought, her heart shattering. He choked with her, becoming her in that moment.

Her tears blurred his vision, but the woman wasn't dead. She moved, glass scraping the floor, looked at Amelia, her eyes glowing in the darkness. She looked unnatural. Her hair as white as snow, her eyes gray like a cat's. Her feet were still disfigured but changing rapidly.

Then the scene cut again and he saw her on all fours, snarling viciously, like a cornered animal. *She doesn't know me,* Amelia was thinking. *Is she still human?* Deep shame suffused Amelia, and Jeremy, at that thought.

All sorts of alarms were going off—loud noises, flashing lights—and understandably, Hailey ran.

Another scene, this one of a bathroom somewhere, with bloody water still filling the bathtub and a towel carelessly thrown on the ground.

—*Was anything missing?*— Jeremy asked.

Amelia jerked in surprise but answered. *Just some clothes, money.* There was relief at that. It meant that Hailey was still human enough to plan ahead. It gave Amelia hope for her recovery.

Jeremy withdrew carefully, leaving her memories unchanged. If he could, he'd lessen the emotional burden they carried. But not even Hunt could do that. Complex emotions like love, grief, pain, could not be altered. Free will seemed to be a universal concept, not just a religious one.

Amelia took off her glasses to clean the lenses. "I checked with the local police. They tracked her making payments for transport off world. They think she ultimately went to Earth but I don't think so. If there is any comparison possible between Hailey and Tristan, she will react the way he did. She'll want to find a place familiar to her animal side. Some kind of natural habitat. Not a concrete jungle and a crowd of people."

"What sort of animal did she… incorporate?" His hands were shaking. He curled them into fists to stop it.

"There wasn't enough data to find out exactly. I was able to narrow it down to feline. Some kind of big cat. Not tiger, though. Knowing my sister, she'd want to be original."

Jeremy rubbed a hand over his mouth and jaw. "It's been what, two months now?"

"A little over that, yes."

A long time to be missing. Jeremy had dealt with enough missing persons cases to know that after this much time the person either didn't want to be found or wasn't around to be found anymore. He didn't tell Amelia that. There were extenuating circumstances here that made trying to predict something impossible. "I'll talk to Hunt, see if we can't put our heads together and come up with something."

"Y-you're not going to follow the animal attacks?" He couldn't tell whether she was more relieved or disappointed at that.

"I have to follow them. If there's even a remote possibility that your sister is behind them, I have to investigate." He shrugged. "But, like you said, it could be completely unrelated. In which case, I need all the input I can get, and Hunt is the best available."

Amelia nodded. Hesitated again. "Agent Calen," she started then hesitated more. "When you find her, she might not be… lucid."

"I know," he said, trying to sound reassuring.

"I don't want her to get hurt even more."

"I'll do my best to honor that."

"And as for payment—"

"We can discuss that once your sister is home, safe and sound."

Her shoulders slumped. "You don't know how much this means to me."

Snow-white hair streaming, half covering a savage face. Fierce silver eyes glowing in the dark. Cornered. Frightened. Hurt. It made Jeremy tense again. He couldn't shake that memory. "I think I do," he replied.

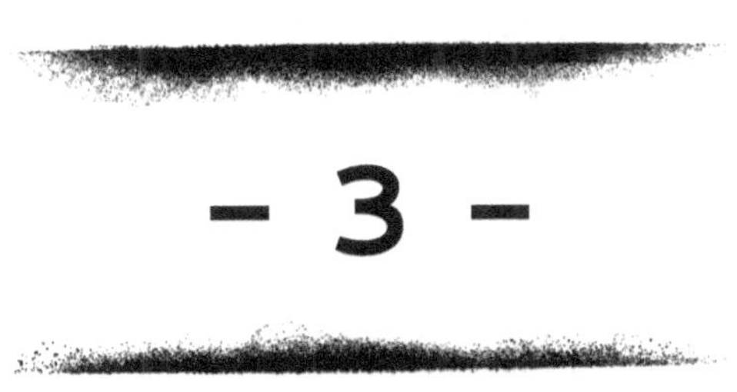

- 3 -

August 1, 3032 – Sapphire City, Planet Jericho

She'd lost the trail. Hailey just prevented herself from growling in frustration. This cat-and-mouse game was becoming tedious. Hunting was one thing. If she went out of her way to stalk her prey, then she wanted the satisfaction of catching it.

Being hunted, on the other hand, infuriated her.

She sniffed the air again, searching for any trace of the scent she'd been following—the one that seemed to be following *her* from world to world. There was nothing left. The bastard lost himself in a crowd as if he knew she wouldn't be able to find him there.

Her jaw ached, fangs itching to emerge. Hailey swallowed the urge, dropped low to the ground to sniff again. It had rained last night, a huge storm she could still hear from miles away where it had moved on. The ground was still wet but it didn't hold a clue to point her in the right direction.

She was vexed. And that was a word she'd never have used to describe herself BC (Before Changing). Losing her patience, she gave up and turned back. She was walking downwind. If anyone followed her, she'd know before they even came into her sight. Hailey wished the bastard would. She was sick of having a shadow. She wanted to finish this.

Her shoes pinched. Hailey had gotten too used to walking barefoot. People—normal people, anyway—tended to frown at that. Gave her strange looks. Better to fit in. The less attention she got, the better.

And the more she clung to her human habits, the less she behaved like an animal. It never left her, though. Hailey went to sleep in a bed each night, but some mornings she woke up on a nest of blankets on the floor. More and more now she wanted to eat with her bare hands and had to remind herself to use utensils.

Clothes felt wrong on her skin. They abraded and confined, making her fur itch when she didn't even have any. She'd started wearing long, loose dresses and a trench coat, easy to put on and take off in a hurry in case she needed to change.

Weird, though. She felt a sense of the cat in her mind, but there was still just her. Hailey. With freakishly altered senses that made her jumpy. She kept her head down to protect sensitive ears. Loose clothing didn't abrade as much. There was that eating thing, but that was just impatience as far as she was concerned. Who didn't eat with their hands every once in a while? Besides, metal tasted cold.

Hailey stepped out of the alley onto the main street. A transport whizzed by, horn blaring for no good reason. It hurt her ears and she hissed. Stupid creatures, drivers. A low growl rumbled in her chest. She bit it back.

Maybe she should have stuck to the side streets.

The planet's two moons would be crossing in a day or two. The gravity fields played havoc on the seas. In this harbor city, people were already taking precautions against a possible flood. There was a lot of nervous energy making her hackles rise. She shook out her head like a wet dog, then glanced around warily to see if anyone noticed.

Her damn stalker was making her paranoid. Hailey flipped her collar up, hunched her shoulders, and quickened her step.

Two blocks from her den—*apartment, damn it!*—she got that be-ing-watched feeling. She was really getting sick of it. A hunter didn't like being hunted. Had a tendency to lash out at inanimate objects when threatened by something unseen. She'd mangled a number of parked transports that way.

Digging her claws into her palms, Hailey focused on the human side of her mind to bring herself back under control. She couldn't. Not until that feeling receded, her watcher gone. Only then did she relax the slightest bit.

The rest of the way Hailey walked slowly, careful with every step she made. Scents filled her nose, both familiar and strange. *Don't think about it. Let it go.* If she didn't, she'd lose it. *Can't do that.*

Three steps from the door.

Hailey scented the air one last time, a security measure. She didn't sense a threat; couldn't tell if she'd been followed, but her stalker's scent wasn't among the many she could distinguish.

Key in the lock. Low-tech, no biometrics. Shady part of town. Bars on windows and doors. A cage she willingly locked herself into. Couldn't be helped. It was as much for her protection as everyone else's.

Door locked from the inside, chain wedged in place beneath the handle.

Only then did Hailey take a full breath.

Her hands were shaking, her entire body humming with the nervous energy of a failed hunt. The beast inside her was restless for a good kill. She could feel it. Fur bristled against the underside of her skin, making her itch all over.

Hailey toed off her shoes and dropped her trench coat, shrugging out of her dress on her way to the bathroom. Blasting the shower all the way to cold, she stepped into the freezing stream. It was the only thing that seemed to work. Maybe it had something to do with her animal. Snow leopards thrived in freezing weather. The cold calmed her beast enough for Hailey to feel human again.

She didn't bother with towels or clothes when she emerged. The longer she stayed pleasantly chilled, the longer she was able to concentrate. And she needed to concentrate. Bypassing the mirror, Hailey padded on bare feet to the one defined room in the shithole apartment, trailing water.

It was empty except for a bed in the middle and a handful of whiteboards. Every available surface she could reach was covered in writing. Somewhere in that unholy mess all over the walls was an answer to her condition. Somewhere in the midst of chemical formulas and complex calculations there was a mistake Hailey had overlooked, a contingency she hadn't accounted for.

The one that would kill her.

Hailey knew her mistake—hubris. She'd been so drunk on her victory, giddy to have superseded years of research in three days, that she'd forgotten one crucial fact: *nothing exists in a vacuum.*

She knew what went wrong: her compounds had reacted to each other. What she didn't know was why. And without knowing the why, she couldn't formulate a solution. The trigger compound hadn't broken down. It was still in her body, messing with other things. She needed to fix that before she could fix the rest.

Hailey looked around at the daunting task before her. She was determined to continue her research but each roadblock and failure disillusioned her a little more.

Amelia had a fully stocked lab and a virtual team of assistants, and she couldn't come up with a trigger. All Hailey had was herself. She couldn't even use a public library computer. Any search she might make would alert someone. That was the last thing she needed. Hailey wasn't a certified scientist; she didn't have the necessary clearance to allow for unhindered research. The chemicals she needed to research were volatile, sometimes unstable, and dangerous in large quantities; just using certain search words would red flag the computer and paint a great big bull's-eye on her back. The government still had tight control over their failing chem-treatment business. They monitored every molecule of chemical elements from production to storage and disbursement.

Hailey wasn't yet desperate enough to pursue black market vendors, but she had no illusion that that was precisely where she was heading. Without hands-on studies, all of her calculations and research were for nothing.

When the cold began to fade, Hailey found a patch of clear wall, picked up a marker, and set to work. *Keep busy. Keep thinking.* Idleness shut down the ego and the id came out to play. She wrote until her hand began to cramp, then wrote more, until the marker fell out of her grasp. By then, her hair was almost dry. She brushed the snow-white tresses out without ever looking at them, until they were as soft as silk. Then she slipped into a nightgown and set to straightening the room up.

Her stomach growled insistently. Hailey had been so involved in her hunt she'd forgotten to eat today. A dangerous thing to do in her condition.

The refrigerator was empty except for a few frozen meals. She took out two of them, perforated the packages with her claws, and heated them. It took less than two minutes to make them ready to eat. When she took the trays out of the heater, Hailey's hand was already reaching for a piece of chicken on one of them. She stopped herself, stubbornly took out a fork, and transferred the food onto a proper plate. There was no table or chair in the kitchen. She usually ate her meals sitting on a big pillow on the floor in her bedroom, picnic style. Tonight was no different.

Hailey liked it that way. It reminded her of her college days when her roommates would come home carrying bags of takeout for the inevitable all-nighter they were about to participate in. She had fond memories of those times. She'd used to laugh. When was the last time she'd laughed?

Back then, she and Amelia had hardly talked to each other. The obligatory phone calls were limited to bare minimums of personal information and a whole lot of weather and school small talk. That was one thing she could always talk to Amelia about—school. They'd compared notes on their respective courses, made fun of professors, complained about the cost. Amelia bought her textbooks, preferring to have them on hand for reference. Hailey had checked hers out from the library.

But the moment their conversations touched on ambition and Hailey's lack thereof, they always ended the same.

Hailey wasn't the star of the family like Amelia, but what she lacked in ambition she made up for in tenacity and stubbornness. If theories and laws were put into context and engaged her curiosity, she was just as good. Hailey had studied because she wanted to learn, not because she wanted a piece of paper that said she was smart. Amelia never understood that. To her, results were everything and if Hailey wasn't going to do anything with what she knew, there was no point in learning it at all.

But that was the past. Dead and gone. No point dwelling on it anymore. Only today was relevant, and the brand-new day tomorrow.

She cut her tongue on her fang while she ate. She barely noticed. The taste of blood didn't make her as sick now as it used to. And the cuts healed by the time she was done with dinner.

She cleaned and put away the plate and fork, then Hailey had nothing else to keep her busy. This was the part she hated. After a full day, before sleep, those few hours in which all she had was herself for company and nothing to do. It made her feel restless and caged. The walls were too thick, the windows didn't open far enough, and those bars. *God, those bars!* Much longer and Hailey would be clawing at the door to get out and run. Just run free. Wherever.

She'd done it before. One time when it got really bad, she'd completely blacked out. One minute she'd been sitting on the couch of some strange apartment, the next she'd been waking up on the beach three hundred miles away, waves lapping up to her waist, and it had been three days later. There'd been people around that time. They'd called the authorities about a confused, naked woman on the beach. Hailey had swum away before they could catch her.

Today was beginning to feel a lot like that. Without a TV or any kind of entertainment system, the apartment was as quiet as a tomb. Fitting, since she was probably going to die here.

No. I'll figure this out.

It was just a matter of time and, although Hailey might not have the lifetime she would have liked, as long as she didn't change too much, she had enough time to fix herself.

Tonight would be another experiment. Another card in her hand, one she hadn't used before, discounting it as outside her capabilities. She didn't have the luxury of discounting anything anymore. It was worth a try. People had been learning and succeeding to control their minds and bodies since the dawn of recorded history. It was a question of discipline. Concentration and meditation. It was a possibility. One more twig to grasp onto and hope it held long enough for her to fight her way out of this quicksand.

Hailey sat on the bed, praying this wouldn't set her back, and closed her eyes.

The beast in her instantly sensed an opening and tested its limits. Her hearing intensified until she could make out the waves breaking on the beach a few blocks away. She matched her breathing to that rhythm, forcing her hands to relax, her claws to retract back to human nails. Or as human as she could get them. Her skin itched everywhere, needing to grow fur. Hailey wouldn't let it. She set the boundaries. She drew the lines for the beast, not the other way around.

A curious thought. It had become a battle; a war between her and the beast. It shouldn't have. Not when the whole point had been to integrate the animal into herself.

A lofty goal.

And look where it got you. Doubt. She hated its voice in her head. *Alone, stranded on a strange planet, without a friend on it. Lost… losing yourself. It* has *to be a battle. And you* have *to win.*

Her claws ached, but remained dormant. *It was my choice,* she argued back to herself stubbornly. *I chose this. I wanted this. And I'd be happy now if…*

If you weren't dying.

Hailey had no comeback for that.

Her beast growled grumpily. It was a temperamental little bitch. Or rather… what was the term for a female feline? Hailey drew a blank on that one.

She shook her head, straightened her spine, and focused on nothing. She cleared her mind of all clutter, even the useful kind. Uneasily she let go of her formulas, bushed back the memories, crowded the beast into the cage she'd constructed for it. It fought her. Hailey fought back. It swiped a paw between the bars, scoring a mark. Hailey could feel soft fur erupt along her spine.

She pushed back, made the walls solid and soundproof. Still, the beast threw its weight against the walls of its prison, and the shock waves reverberated through Hailey's mind. For a moment, she was afraid she'd falter. The walls bulged outward, softening, and she braced herself for the moment they gave and let the beast loose, enraged and out for blood.

But the walls held, and in a minute gradually straightened and strengthened again, with no effort at all. As if the beast just gave up—though Hailey knew it hadn't. She could still feel it, a part of her, fighting to be free. She pushed her fear away and embraced darkness, finding peace where nothing else existed.

Soon the sound of her breathing muted, as did her heartbeat. It was the calmest she'd felt since she'd started on this path. It took no effort at all to stay in that state. With the beast locked away, there was nothing to distract her.

Unreal.

It was almost as if she wasn't doing it at all. Hard to believe, given how wired she'd been lately, that she was capable of achieving such complete peace of mind. But Hailey wasn't about to look a gift horse in the mouth. She needed to catch a few hours of uninterrupted sleep while she could. So she lay down without opening her eyes and let her consciousness fade into that dark, calm pool…

The dream Hailey wasn't like the real one people saw these days. She was the Hailey of a few months ago. Dressed in a barely there bathing suit, her dark hair blowing in the wind, getting in her eyes. She laughed, the sound echoing on the empty beach, and pulled the hair back, loosely braiding it to keep it out of her face.

The sun was setting on a greenish-blue sea, a giant broken moon rising in its place. Hailey closed her eyes for an instant to enjoy the heat of the sun on her face. As soon as she lost sight of the scenery, fierce silver eyes stared at her in her mind's eye.

Hailey gasped and stumbled back, falling onto the soft sand. She looked around frantically for that beast, but there was nothing around her. When she shivered, a large beach towel appeared next to her. She bundled herself up in it, drawing her knees to her chest.

She felt naked without people around, exposed and abandoned.

"Where is everyone?" The sound of her voice was delayed. Her mouth formed the words a lot faster than her ears heard them. It was eerie.

One by one, people appeared. Men, women, old friends and family members, even some strangers. There was music now, but no voices. She saw her friends speaking to her, but couldn't hear them. Even so, when one of them pulled her up to dance she followed gladly, eager to lose herself in something familiar.

He pulled her close to say something in her ear. Hailey closed her eyes and a flash of fangs rushed at her face. She pushed away from the man—far away. He didn't seem to mind, or notice much. He already had another woman in his arms. How easily he'd replaced her...

It wasn't right. None of it.

Don't think, just enjoy.

She couldn't. There was a wild animal on the loose, and Hailey just knew it was coming for her. She spun in a circle, scanning the crowds, the beach, but saw nothing that would pose a threat.

Except a man dressed in a suit, staring right at her from across the crowd. There one second, gone the next.

Hailey shivered. Her hair slid loose, blinding her, but it wasn't her hair anymore. It couldn't be; it was all white! "W-what is this?" *She'd already turned another circle by the time she heard her own words. Something growled, and Hailey got the impression it was pacing, waiting for something; an opportunity to strike.*

Hailey turned and ran.

She didn't get far. The crowd of dancers was all around her now, blocking all paths of retreat.

And there was that man again! In a crowd of people wearing swimsuits and little else, he stood fully dressed in a suit and shined shoes. His eyes were intense, so blue they were nearly black. And they stared at her without blinking, watching and learning. It was like having her soul interrogated.

Hailey blinked and he was gone again.

She fought her way through the crowd, pushing and shoving against sun-warmed bodies, but whenever she looked at any of their faces, those same blue-black eyes stared at her. Hailey couldn't run. She couldn't even move anymore.

The man had his arms around her, keeping her still, only his suit was gone and his arms were made of granite. She was trapped.

The man spoke. His mouth moved, forming words, but she couldn't hear them.

"Let go of me," *she pleaded.*

"You cannot run from this," *she heard him say, his voice as delayed as her own. It was foreign, didn't belong. This was her dream, her world. He didn't belong.*

Hailey fought but nothing would move him; nothing worked until she realized she had a secret weapon. She stilled in his arms, scared, furious. Desperate. She felt the beast stop as well, a coiled spring tensed to go off. Complete silence descended on the scene. The dancers froze midstep, the air stood still; the sea might as well have been made of glass.

The man shook his head. "Don't."

"Try and stop me," she retorted, and her voice was a growl. Her claws dug into his arms and he released her, but she had fangs now and was dying to use them. He'd keep coming back. She had to scare him off.

She let the beast break free…

The snarl woke her, but Hailey was too far already to stop herself. She saw her own clawed hand tear at the locks on the door, and then her body broke and shifted, folding in on itself, tearing her insides apart and rearranging them into something else.

Her paws still hurt when she touched down on all fours, but the pain was nothing now. She was free! Her scream-roar rose to the sky and echoed between the buildings. The leopard took off, running for open space. For the beach.

In the back of her mind, the very human Hailey watched and wept as the beast possessing her body threw caution to the wind.

Nothing would stop her now.

Jeremy sat straight up in bed and had to pound his chest a few times to gasp in a breath of air. He was reaching for his pants before he'd even wrestled free of the sheets, and he hopped to the door, pulling them on, then stabbed his feet into shoes. Without thinking he went out into the night, breathing hard.

Jeremy knew where she was heading. His feet took him after her and he ran, wincing when he tripped on his laces. He stopped only for as long as it took him to tuck them into the sides of his shoes, then kept going, pumping his arms for speed, propelled by a fear he couldn't shake: that Hailey would hurt someone.

He'd fucking blown it. *Jesus Christ! You're not Hunt!* Jeremy shouldn't have even made contact. But he'd just found her again this afternoon after having lost her three times over the last couple of weeks—the woman had some serious stealth—and he couldn't let an opportunity pass him by. Amelia was on Torrey, anxiously awaiting news. He'd wanted to actually have something to tell her the next time he called.

He'd needed to gauge Hailey's state of mind.

What he'd found was a woman on edge. She'd pushed herself almost to the limit. Hailey had been mostly going without sleep, catching only an hour at a time because she was afraid she'd shift in her sleep. Her mind had been so preoccupied that even when Jeremy had made contact, she hadn't noticed. And he'd gotten lost in her thoughts, unable to tune in to her senses to see through her.

Now he knew there was a boundary between Hailey and her animal side, and she had to stay alert all the time to keep the animal contained. Even so, she only managed to suppress its will, not its senses or... personality.

Being in her mind had wearied him so much, he'd felt what she felt. For both their sakes, when Hailey sat down to meditate, Jeremy had helped her along, keeping the beast separate so she could just think for a few minutes.

It had worked, too.

Until Hailey fell asleep and dragged him into her dreams. She must have felt him there, an intruder. Having never done anything like this before, Jeremy's focus had slipped. He'd lost control of himself and the beast he'd been holding at bay, and it broke free with a vengeance.

Coming up on her apartment, Jeremy saw that the security door had closed behind her but her apartment door hung wide open. As he passed, he caught a glimpse of the inside of her room through the bars. He stumbled but kept going, making a mental note to come back here and take a closer look. Had that been writing all over the walls?

Three blocks down, one over, and one more down, and then the streets opened up onto a beach. In this part of town, it was covered in trash, the water murky with something Jeremy had no wish to identify.

There was no sign of Hailey.

It was dark with only the moons' glow to illuminate the beach. He couldn't make out any tracks, and he hadn't thought to bring a flashlight. The sea hissed in and out in big sighs while Jeremy searched the night, catching his breath.

Damn it, where are you?

In his mind, something stirred. It wasn't a thought or a presence, just... a faint sense. He couldn't see Hailey, but somehow he felt her raise her head, ears pricked forward. Had she heard him?

—*Hailey?*— he tried tentatively.

An impression of a half snarl was his answer.

Jeremy pushed for a direction and found himself turning left to go farther along the beach. For all he knew, he could be heading toward a very angry, very hungry big cat. And he hadn't brought anything remotely useful for self-defense.

He studied the animal's reactions as he approached. She was standing still, poised in the darkness, waiting for her prey to appear. She felt a long way off, but Jeremy kept his pace slow. He had no idea how much of him Hailey was picking up and the last thing he wanted to do was spook her.

In another block, street lamps began to illuminate the boardwalk in regular intervals. It was enough to allow Jeremy to see two blocks on all sides of him and twenty or so feet onto the beach. He watched for any kind of movement, but couldn't even see a tail twitch.

The animal stirred in his mind again, turning in his direction.

He stopped.

She stopped, too, but then moved tentatively in his direction. A slinking step, no more.

Jeremy took a step.

The animal mirrored him.

He had no idea how this game worked. His gut told him that having a big cat stalking him was not a good thing. He was relieved she wasn't running farther. Another step, then one more.

The animal slid forward more, then sat up, tail swishing left and right. She was curious. Didn't recognize his shape in her mind.

Jeremy was close enough now that he could better sense where she was. He turned right, stepping off the boardwalk and onto the beach at an angle. There was a pile of jagged rocks up ahead, close to the water's edge. She would be there somewhere.

His shoes filled with sand instantly, but he didn't take them off.

—*Hailey, can you hear me?*—

The animal tilted her head. She didn't understand. She knew words from before but didn't remember what *Hailey* meant.

—*Hailey is your name.*—

He was coming up on the rocks now, but still couldn't make out any movement.

The animal scented his approach. She bristled to have her territory invaded by what she perceived was a dominant male. The small—but feisty, she wanted him to know—female didn't like it at all.

Jeremy couldn't help smiling at that. She was warning him, but wasn't engaging. It almost felt like… flirtation. But he wasn't taking any chances. Most big cats were fickle beasts. If they got bored or irritated, they could lash out without warning. Females especially tended to be fierce around males, even during mating season.

But the males could usually hold their own. Jeremy didn't have their claws or fangs and there was nothing to protect him from Hailey's. He was beginning to regret not having put on more clothes before he'd left the hotel.

The animal became aggravated at his stalling. As Jeremy came closer, a big projectile of white fluff dropped down from the rocks, nearly on top of him. The impact was soft; the animal… strange. Her tail was like a thick, fluffy snake attached to the end of her spine, her paws flat and almost as big as her face. She had white fur, with dark gray spots and patterns. The fur was so thick it gave her the appearance of a fluffy stuffed toy, but her eyes were sharp and intelligent. Some sort of… panther. But one that seemed adapted to cold climates. When she was still, she was nearly indistinguishable from the rocks, and her white paws blended in with the sand. On a jagged, snowy rock face she'd be invisible.

Snow, she thought. She knew snow. Missed it. Too hot here, and she hadn't seen another of her kind anywhere. Her inquisitive gaze looked him over, up and down, side to side. She came close to sniff his pants, making Jeremy go very, very still.

Not like me, she thought. *But close enough.* She rubbed her face against his thigh, then brushed her body against him like a domestic cat; circled him completely. Jeremy wasn't sure he liked where this was going.

When she lay down in front of him, he knew he didn't.

There she lay, tail swishing, waiting.

There he stood, dumbfounded, staring.

She looked over her shoulder at him, impatience written in every spot and line on her feline face, as if to ask what he was waiting for.

Aw, damn. He had to get Hailey out here, ASAP.

The leopard showed him her very big teeth, impatience turning to annoyance. Probably not the best idea to piss off a hundred and fifteen pounds of killing machine. She might be small but Jeremy had no illusions about who would win if this ever turned physical.

He looked around for a distraction, searched the stars for an idea. They had to get out of sight. Fast.

The leopard growled; it seemed to be the loudest noise she could make. The sound was almost more menacing because it was so soft. This creature had no need for overt shows of dominance. She would stalk her prey in complete silence, and it would die never knowing she'd been hunting it to begin with.

No, he would not be pissing this one off.

Jeremy took a step back, keeping her in sight, but retreating. —*Not here,*— he thought to her, projecting a dislike for their surroundings.

She was confused. This felt the most like home to her around here.

His next move would either get them inside or get him mauled. He projected a small wave of patronizing amusement, the sense of a memory. Then he turned and started walking away from her, looking back to encourage her to follow. He would lead her someplace better.

She perked up and after a moment was on her big feet, padding after him. *A den?* her big eyes questioned silently.

Jeremy's step faltered, but he recovered and kept moving. Shit!

He couldn't take her to her place because the security door had shut. He didn't have the key. And the hotel manager would probably frown upon a guest leading an animal into his establishment. What was it that Hunt had said about projecting? *Make them not want to look.*

It was the middle of the night. Surely there wouldn't be that many people around, would there?

Two blocks from his hotel—he'd taken them the long way around, not willing to risk her getting shocked out of this shape at the sight of her apartment—Hailey growled again, showing her teeth. *Many ahead.* She sensed he was leading them toward a crowd. And she wasn't happy about it.

Jeremy sent her gentle reassurance and kept going. As long as they didn't stop, they might have a chance in hell of getting inside soon, before someone noticed a half-naked guy walking a wild beast down the street.

But when they turned the corner, Jeremy stopped dead in his tracks. It looked like the entire hotel was gathered outside on the sidewalk. There was no way he could get them through that crowd. *What the hell happened?* He put a hand on Hailey's head to stop her. She looked surprised at the gesture, but he didn't have time to answer her.

He spread his senses out over the crowd, picking up their surface thoughts like a lint brush. Someone had tripped the alarm, woke the whole hotel, and the staff had evacuated everyone to search for the possible emergency. They'd been standing out there for a while now and so far it seemed to be a false alarm.

The hotel wasn't one building; it was a series of bungalows that took up three blocks on both sides of the street. Jeremy's bungalow was two blocks down. They'd have to go around again.

He looked down at Hailey to let her know about the detour and found her crouched low to the ground, watching the crowd like the predator she was. In a flash, she rolled onto her back, squirming like a playful domestic cat, then rolled onto her paws again, that same sharp look on her face. —*What was that about?*—

She didn't answer, her mind completely focused. Jeremy picked up reflections of his own sense of threat in her thoughts. She'd gone into hunt mode because of him. When he looked for why, her answer was wry, and loosely translated to, "Big male senses threat, female's got to get down to business."

—*No hunting,*— he told her sternly.

A mewling pout was her response. She was still grumbling when he started walking again, but at least she was following. Shaking herself out every few steps as if her fur itched, but following.

Jeremy managed to get them across the street from his bungalow without any contact with the crowd. The last few feet, though, were about to get problematic. Hailey's tail slapped the backs of his knees, nearly making them buckle. That thing was all muscle.

He sent her a reprimand.

Just to make a point, she did it again.

They glared at each other, then looked back toward the bungalow at the same time.

Hailey growled, eyes narrowing on a target. *Move,* she thought, and before he could stop her—as if he could—she slipped forward into the street, keeping low to the ground. She was so quiet no one seemed to notice. They were too busy returning to their beds and complaining about the midnight wake-up call.

Jeremy made himself part of the crowd, turning attention away when he felt someone notice him. He kept his pace slow, kept his gaze away from the ghost-white cat sitting in shadow at his door, but couldn't smooth out the tension in his face. Every time someone's voice rose in agitation, he thought they'd be caught.

The door worked on a biometric lock and opened as soon as he came within range. Hailey preceded him inside, curiosity propelling her to examine and sniff everything in sight. Jeremy closed the door and locked it, posting an electronic Do Not Disturb sign for good measure. *Okay, genius. Now what?*

Hailey was by his bed now, sniffing the sheets that had spilled to the floor, tilting her head curiously. One giant paw touched on it, claw catching the fabric. She pulled, trying to free her claw, and tugged the sheet all the way to the floor. When she was free, she lay down on it and rolled onto her back again the way she'd done outside.

But she lost interest soon enough and jumped onto the bed itself. The sight of her gave a whole new meaning to the phrase *an animal in bed*.

Jeremy shook his head. This was going too far. He picked up the sheet, keeping it close at hand and nudged Hailey's mind to pay attention to him.

The leopard turned to him instantly, big eyes almost feverish, waiting for him to get to it.

"Hailey," he said aloud, hoping his physical voice would register better than his mind-touch. "Can you hear me?"

The leopard huffed and turned away, uninterested.

Jeremy pulled her back mentally and put his hands on her face to keep her still. When her gaze met his again, no matter how uncomfortable it felt, he refused to let her look away. "Hailey, fight this. Come back."

He felt consciousness stirring, lost and confused. The leopard bucked, trying to escape his grasp, but he dug his fingers into her fur and held on.

Jeremy sent out a mental call, creating a beacon for Hailey to follow, and spoke again, guiding her with his voice. "Hailey Samantha Chase. You were born December fifth, 3005, in a big hospital on Earth. You got lost among all the other babies in the nursery. Your sister, Amelia, found you by the noise you made when you cried. You graduated from Westin High School with honors and almost got a degree in biochemistry from Aspen and Ash University."

The leopard reared, fighting him. Claws caught his arm, but stopped just before they pierced skin. *Good, Hailey. That's it.*

Jeremy held on. "How you got into hospitality management, I have no idea but—"

Got bored. Wanted people. Amelia left me, so I improvised. That last was imbued with enough sadness to give him pause, but Jeremy pulled his thoughts back on track, making a mental note to investigate that later.

"Good, that's good," he praised. *—Keep going. Come on, Hailey. It's your body. Control it.—*

The leopard lashed out with its paws again, but at the very last second the claws retracted and all he suffered were minor scratches on his arms. Didn't even break the skin. He knew when the battle between woman and beast began in earnest. The leopard growled loudly and the sound turned into a hiss. Apparently she couldn't roar. Jeremy released her fur and stepped back as she fought herself, pawing at her head and shaking herself out as if to rid herself of something unpleasant.

The transformation was painful to watch. Her fur receded into pale skin but the patterns remained like faint tattoos. He heard joints pop and bones crack and hoped to Christ that she would heal. Her hair was pure white, momentarily obscuring her face, which still had a faint feline shape to it. By the time her body was human again, she was shaking, barely able to hold herself up. The tail was the last to go and by the rough, pained noise she made, it wasn't comfortable.

Jeremy covered her with the sheet. He grasped her shoulders to turn her over to lie flat, but let go immediately when she cried out in pain. Her left shoulder was poking out at an awkward angle, dislocated.

He didn't know what to do, how to help her. "Should I call a doctor?"

Hailey's head was down, her hair hiding her face. She shook it slowly in negation. "Set it," she said, her voice barely above a whisper.

Was she crazy? "I… don't have any medical training. I could hurt you worse."

She looked up at him and the blood tracking from her eyes like tears made him cringe. Her eyes were still silver, cold. And the half-smile she gave him did nothing to soften them. "I'll live," she said. When he still hesitated, she added, "No other choice, right? Unless you get off on seeing women in pain."

Jeremy winced at how hoarse her voice sounded. "Okay. Okay, I'll try."

He took hold of her arm, and she cried out again. Her arm could be broken. "Higher!"

"Right." One hand on her shoulder, the other holding her upper arm, he searched her face. "You ready?"

"God, just do it already," she said, her voice quivering.

He pulled sharply, felt the joint pop back into place.

Hailey screamed, and he pulled her to his shoulder to muffle the sound. Held her while she cried. "Shh," he soothed. "I've got you. It's okay; you're okay. Easy."

He was still sitting there with her in his arms, rocking her like a child and smoothing her hair when she finally stopped crying some time later. He didn't release her; she was the one who pushed away from him. "How are you feeling?"

Hailey pulled the sheet closer around her. "Better." She was still favoring her left arm.

"How long does it usually take you to heal completely?"

"About this long," she said wryly. But when she moved the sheet to show him her arm, it was one giant bruise from her neck down to her elbow.

Jeremy hissed in sympathy. "Let's get you cleaned up. I think I have some clothes that might fit you. Are you okay to stand?"

"I think so."

He kept hold of her good elbow and an arm around her for support as she got to her feet. She was shaking from head to toe, but there was stoic denial clouding her mind, so he didn't say anything. In the bathroom, he sat her down on the toilet and soaked one of the clean washcloths to wipe the bloody tears off her face.

Hailey turned away. "I can do it," she said, holding her hand out for the washcloth.

He wanted to argue, but her mind was already weary. She wouldn't last long and he wanted her dressed before she passed out. Though she didn't seem the bashful kind, he had Amelia to consider and what she would think about him seeing her sister naked. "Okay," he said, relenting. "Don't move from here. I'll be right back."

She gave a wet scoff. "Yeah, like I'm going to be running a sprint outta here any time soon."

He was back in two minutes with a pair of sweatpants and one of his shirts to find her staring dejectedly at the washcloth on the floor. It must have fallen out of her grasp and she hurt too much to bend and pick it up again.

Come on, Ams! Catch up! The childish voice caught him off guard. Jeremy tentatively reached out to her mind and got swept up in her memory. Hailey was running and laughing, calling back to her sister. They were racing toward their parents and the ice-cream cake waiting on the table, but Hailey tripped and fell so hard the memory of pain still made her twitch physically. *There now, see what you did?* Amelia chastised, but she helped her younger sister up, wiped her tears away, and they walked the rest of the way, hand in hand.

There was heartache in that memory. So much that Jeremy found himself rubbing at a sudden hollow in his chest. He was picking up a mere echo of her emotions but if they felt like this to him, what was it like for her?

"I'm cold," Hailey said distractedly, without looking at him.

"I think I can help with that. Here, give me your arm. I promise I won't look." She did as he asked but still wouldn't look at him. Jeremy helped her put the shirt on, bad arm first so he wouldn't have to wrench it later. The sheet covered her well enough that he only caught a couple of glimpses of her nakedness. Thankfully, the leopard patterns over her skin were gone.

Her lack of response bothered him. He talked to her when he guided her feet into the sweatpants and lifted her a little to get them up over her hips. His words fell on deaf ears. If she heard anything, her mind didn't show it.

Hush, you're all right now, the memory Amelia was saying.

Jeremy left the sheet around her for added warmth while he wet a clean washcloth to wipe away the blood. He washed her hands and feet of dirt and sand, looking into her eyes every so often to see how she was doing. If she'd even blinked in that time he wouldn't have known it.

"Okay, let's get you to bed."

She roused enough at that to murmur, "I can do it," but it was clear she was beyond standing on her own. So he picked her up and carried her to the bed, setting her down on the side that didn't have blood on it. She turned onto her good side and curled up at once, but her eyes were slow to close.

Jeremy covered her with the thick blanket, tucked her in as best he could without jarring her bad arm, and turned off the lights. He could still make out her glowing silver eyes when he stretched out on the couch for the night. It was impossible to tell what she was looking at, but the sight still made him uneasy.

Only when her eyes closed did he finally turn away and close his own.

Whether she remembered anything from this night or not, tomorrow morning would be one hell of a wake-up call.

– 5 –

The darkness had substance. It caressed her skin, warm and sure, slipped through her hair, over her eyelids, over her lips. It was everywhere, touching every inch of her beneath the clothing she knew she wore.

Then her clothing was gone and there was only her and the darkness. It was hands now, grasping her wrists, trailing over her taut belly, her breasts and throat. Invisible fingers tilted her head up and her lips parted.

It was lips now, brushing over hers, teasing, but never breaching. She wanted them to. They trailed over her neck and shoulder while those hands played.

It had mass now, weighing her down, on top of her, between her thighs. A body. A man. Faceless stranger with no shame and no hesitation. She felt his lean muscles beneath her roaming hands, felt his hard erection against her thigh. She felt his fingers probing her entrance, and she raised her hips to his hand.

He kissed her, this man who wasn't a man, who had no taste or scent—but she knew him. She'd met him. Why was he hiding?

He brought her knee up next to him, positioning her. She was warm wax beneath his hands. Pliable, malleable. She was his masterpiece and knew he would make her perfect. Her artist was sure and confident; he knew her, too. Knew where to kiss, how to touch; knew things about her body only its owner ever could.

The darkness whispered with strange words. Its voice was low, sensuous. It did not need to be understood, only heard. She shivered, knowing those words to be praise; hot words to stoke her fire, make her feel beautiful and perfect, and everything a woman should be.

It was inside her now, moving slow and deep, invading her, becoming part of her. She opened to it, welcomed it, hugged it to her breast and gave herself up to its spell. Her body wasn't her own anymore. That darkness possessed her, took everything, but gave back so much more. It gave her pleasure, and it gave her peace.

It gave her a beast with silken fur and rumbling purrs, a feline with feral eyes and sharp teeth, and a tail…

It was day. And it was bright. Hailey hissed, rolling over to escape the sharp glare. The nauseating pain in her arm startled her fully awake, and she sat up to take the pressure off her shoulder. It took a couple of minutes for her vision to return and when it did, she stared at her surroundings. Tacky painting on the wall. Carpet on the floor. Worn-out bed with strange-smelling sheets. A hotel room?

And what the hell was she wearing?

She was alone in the room, but that being watched feeling made the soft hairs on the back of her neck stand on end. Her teeth sharpened to fangs but didn't lengthen. This all felt wrong. How did she get here? What the hell happened last night?

Hailey reached up to pull her hair back, offended by the white tresses hanging over her eye. The pain in her arm nearly made her pass out. She had to stop and breathe through it for a couple of minutes more. When it eased, she undid the top buttons of the shirt—a man's shirt—and drew it off her shoulder all the way to her elbow. It bared her left side down to her belly button.

A sound.

Her gaze darted to its origin, but there was nothing, just an empty couch. Still wary, she bowed her head to examine her injury. Her entire upper arm was purple. One would think she'd remember an injury that severe.

Growling low—it was reflex by now—she tenderly poked at her arm, looking for breaks. The last time Hailey had broken a bone, the pain had been excruciating. This was different. She curled her fingers into a fist, squeezed as tightly as she could. It hurt but she'd be able to grasp things at least. It meant that the break wasn't as bad as last time. Maybe just a fracture.

Her shoulder was a whole different story. She couldn't move her arm from its natural position at all or her shoulder joint screamed a delightful symphony of torture. *Do I have any painkillers left?* She couldn't remember. And it was incidental whether she did or not, because *this wasn't her apartment!*

Hailey pulled the shirt back up over her shoulder and buttoned it enough to keep herself covered. She slid her feet down to the floor, gasping at how tender they felt.

Another strange noise drew her gaze back to that couch. It was still empty.

Probably just imagining things.

The door was locked. And it looked to be biometric. If it was, she was never getting out of here until the person who lived here came back, because the stupid door wouldn't open for anyone else. She was about to try a window when the lock clicked and the door opened an inch. She scented the air that rushed in from the outside. Metal, concrete, hint of sea and rain. No human. At least none near enough to open the door. Was it broken?

Hailey wasn't about to test her luck. Tucking her bad arm close, she took hold of the waistband of her sweatpants—which were way too big on her—and slipped out the door, closing it behind her. The pants were long enough and wide enough at the bottom that they hid her feet. No one would notice she wasn't wearing shoes unless they looked close.

Still, dressed as she was, she'd draw the wrong kind of attention. So she kept to the shadows and side alleys, following her nose to find her way back to her apartment. A lot of it seemed déjà vu, but she was sure she'd never come through here before. Not lucid, anyway.

Footsteps sounded behind her, seeming to follow her, but faded quickly and she shrugged it off. She couldn't scent anything, and she trusted her nose.

The beast was silent in her mind, sleeping off a long night. Hailey hoped it had been a good one because she wasn't about to have another. Playtime was suspended indefinitely.

A group of teenagers came out of the warehouse at the end of the block, coming up her way. She could smell drugs on them and about two weeks of dirt and BO. Drawing close to the building, she gave them a wide berth. Even so, when they passed her, they did it side by side, taking up too much space.

The one on the inside barreled into her as if she didn't even exist. He slammed into her bad shoulder, and she was turned by the force of it. Her back touched the building and she leaned on it, stars dancing in front of her eyes, bile rising up her throat. She clenched her teeth, bit back the nausea along with the scream tearing at her chest. The tears were much harder to blink back. For a moment she couldn't even breathe.

Shaking from the effort it took to keep upright, Hailey concentrated on the sound of their retreat, tracking them by it until they turned the corner five blocks up. That was how long it took to regain her balance and risk pushing away from the wall. She stumbled on the first step but recovered and kept going.

Her hopes of a quiet escape crashed and burned when she reached her apartment and found the security door shut. The key was on the countertop inside. Her good arm linked among the bars for support and she touched her forehead to one of them, closing her eyes. She would beat her forehead against it if she wasn't in enough pain already.

"I'm curious about what your plan was once you got this far."

If her good arm hadn't been tangled in the bars, she would have clawed the man's throat open without thinking, on instinct. "Are you suicidal?" she snarled when she extricated herself and turned to face him. Now that she could see him, she could scent him, too. It was the same scent that lingered in the shirt she wore. "Where did you come from?"

He was dressed much like she was, only his pants weren't sliding off him and his shirt was only half buttoned, the sleeves rolled up past his elbows. And unlike her, he wasn't barefoot. She could feel her eyes glow with misplaced interest and was glad for the light of day that disguised it. The man was… In her mind she purred looking at him—*she* did, not the beast. He was tall, his shoulders wide but he wasn't bulky, more athletic like a gymnast. Dark blond hair, shadow of a beard that just looked so damn sexy on this one.

Her dream returned to her in a flash, doing a quick rerun of things that made her sex clench and her knees turn weak. God, she hadn't felt like this in months. Even the beast stirred at this unexpected turn of events.

Hailey remembered a man touching her, petting her; she remembered his breath on her skin and his mouth on hers as if it had really happened. A faceless stranger plucking her strings like a master musician, and she'd sung for him, screamed for him. This man somehow reminded her of that. But how? She'd never seen her dream lover's face.

Had her mind degenerated into full-blown hallucinations? Or was she just so damn horny that any man would do? No, that couldn't be it. The guy seemed familiar somehow. *Was* he her dream lover? She didn't know what was more embarrassing: talking to herself or fantasizing about a stranger when he was standing right in front of her…

…watching her like he knew exactly what she was thinking.

Eyes so dark blue… *they looked black…*

Recognition slammed into her. Because she'd seen this one in a dream before.

And it hadn't been the one she'd assumed.

"You." She hissed the accusation, now regretting not having ripped his throat out.

He just stood there, arms crossed over his chest, glaring at her as if she was the one who'd screwed everything up. "Where are you going, Hailey? Where do you plan to run? You can't even get into your own apartment."

"Do you have," she said, enunciating each syllable precisely through her clenched teeth, "*any* idea what you've done?"

"I saved you," he said easily.

"You're the one who triggered the change in the first place!" A goddamn telepath skulking about in her head. She'd *known* he didn't belong! Even dreaming, she'd known it.

A muscle ticked in his jaw. "Let's start again. My name is Jeremy Calen. I am here on behalf of your sister, Amelia. She sent me to find you." He extended a hand, all angry male struggling to be civil.

Hailey didn't reciprocate. "You found me. You're done. Good-bye."

"Not that easy," he said, dropping the hand. "I'm supposed to bring you back."

She laughed, and it was not a pleasant sound at all. With her voice still ravaged she sounded like a forty-year smoker. "Yeah, I can see that. So what'd you have in mind, Jer, a leash or a kennel?" She didn't wait for him to reply but gave him her back, searching inside her apartment for something she could use.

"At the moment, I am seriously considering a muzzle," he said. "And where I'm from, it's considered polite to look at the person who's talking to you."

"I am being very nice about this," she told him, with just a hint of warning. "But don't push me, Jeremy Calen. Don't provoke me into doing something we'll both regret. One of us more than the other."

Her cat grumbled. It wanted her to do something bad. Just not in the same way Hailey did. Lust sparked in her veins, made her breath come quicker. Deliberately, Hailey filled her mind with thoughts of violence to mask her body's irrational reaction to him.

He moved so fast she didn't have time to react, and she had a suspicion he was manipulating her into thinking that. He grabbed her good arm, twisted it behind her and backed her against the security door. "You mean like this?" his voice rumbled; she could feel it vibrating through the air. He was almost nose to nose with her. "Come on, kitty, show me those claws of yours."

The male's scent made her mouth water for a taste. She could feel the heat of his body on her chilled, traumatized flesh and wanted to take it into herself. Aggression rolled off him, mixed with a dose of lust so potent it made her head spin. This guy wasn't the "as it please you" type. Instinct and the short but vivid preview last night—which she was now almost certain *had* been him—told her he'd be a force of nature in bed.

This one could match me.

The beast's interest grew more, flooding her mind with images she couldn't block out. The more she fought them, the more the beast rose to the fore and it pissed her off, as it scared her.

"Don't," she said, and it came out more of a plea than a warning. Her fangs were aching; her body quaked, tensing to shift. Her bad arm hurt so much she could feel tears pushing to flood her eyes.

Hailey wouldn't let them. She dug her sharp claws into her palms and breathed through it, counting to ten then back to one in her head.

Those blue-black eyes searched hers, and then Jeremy released her without a word, stepping back to the edge of the sidewalk to give her space. "You're not healing."

"Thanks for stating the obvious," she said. It came out breathless.

"You can't keep going like this. It's suicide and you know it."

"It's *my* life! Stay out of it."

"I can help you," he said tightly. He'd gone tense as if he was about to jump her again. "If you come with me, we can get this sorted out. We can find a way to fix you. You didn't maul me last night."

Hailey turned away so he wouldn't see her face turn red. Bits and pieces of her little outing were beginning to come back to her. The beast wanted her to know. Not only had she not mauled him, she'd practically offered herself up on a silver platter. A pretty damn romantic scene: moonlit beach, city skyline lit up in the night… and her furry tail lifted in the air. God, she was never going to live that one down. "A mistake I don't intend to repeat."

"I doubt that."

"To your own peril, then."

"You seriously want to do this on your own so badly." It was a statement rather than a question, but he still seemed to expect an answer.

"Yes."

"Then I would like my clothes back."

She whirled back on him, jaw slack.

All he did was raise an eyebrow and hold out his hand expectantly. He was serious!

Hailey closed her mouth and gave him her back again. Light spilled over her bed just beyond the damn security door. So close and completely out of reach.

Hang on a minute…

"I'm waiting," Jeremy said.

"Give me one minute," she replied, already looking up. What was it, ten, fifteen feet? She'd cleared more before. Except she'd had two good hands. Still…

"Hailey?"

One step back. One more. She needed to see where she was going. "Hailey, what are you…"

Hailey bent her knees and launched herself at the roof. She caught the edge with one hand, had a pretty firm grip on it, too. Concentrating on her feet, she changed her toenails into claws and dug them into the wall for support. It was awkward and it hurt, but she wasn't falling yet. Jeremy was cursing below her; it sounded as if he'd come closer to catch her in case she fell. She didn't intend to.

Digging in her claws above and below she hauled herself one-armed onto the roof. Good thing, too. Her pants had started to slip again.

"Hailey?" Jeremy called from the street. "Hailey!"

She ignored him and got up to try the skylight. It wasn't *supposed* to open but Hailey had just enough strength in her good arm to break through. She'd be landing on broken glass, but it wasn't like she had a choice. *One, two, three.* She jumped down.

Five minutes later she opened the security door on a furious-looking Jeremy and thrust his clothes back at him. She was wearing a beach dress after having dropped the shirt and sweatpants. Good thing he was so much bigger than her, otherwise she never would have gotten out of them without help.

His gaze raked over her, stalling on her breasts—she couldn't put on a bra and she was pretty sure her nipples showed through the fabric—and then on the region of her hips—well, yeah, she wasn't prematurely white *everywhere.*

Hailey cleared her throat pointedly, still holding his clothes. Her arm was getting tired of it.

He looked up at her face, then beyond it to something behind her. He uttered some kind of oath as he brushed past her into her den, staring at her walls and whiteboards. Hailey tried to see it the way he probably would: like a crazy person's asylum cell. But to her, this room was the sum total of her work so far. Every single letter and symbol was invaluable to her. It almost spelled her survival. Almost.

Jeremy touched her formulas on the wall. *She* didn't even do that, afraid she'd smudge the symbols. "Are you a biochemistry enthusiast?" she asked to distract him away from there.

"To be honest, I have no idea what any of this says," he replied. He didn't touch anything else. "Are you close to finding a cure?"

"Yes," she lied.

He gave her an annoyed *truth, please* look.

Hailey rolled her eyes. She'd never met a telepath before but she hadn't been enthusiastic about the idea of one when she'd read about them in Amelia's notes. Now she knew that she didn't like them. It was doubly unnerving because not only could he read her thoughts—or see them, or something—but he could also insert himself into her mind, make her see things.

Like last night.

What was worse, she had no idea when he was doing it. Her dream had felt so surreal she'd never noticed anything amiss. Yet at the same time it had been the most tactile dream she'd ever had.

But then, after months of only herself for company and… other things, *that* didn't really surprise her.

Hailey wasn't the bashful type; she didn't embarrass easily. Hell, he'd given her material enough to fantasize about for months while she… kept her own company. But to have her mind laid out like an open book for him to read whenever he pleased, *that* bothered her.

By the look on his face, he was doing it now. Just great.

Back to the real world.

"I could be one equal sign away," she said in answer to his question. "Or I could be leagues and miles in the wrong direction."

"The chemicals you need change as soon as you take them out of the container. You can't predict how they will react to air, let alone to each other, and you can't move forward without testing them properly."

Hailey's hackles stood on end, making her itch all over. Bad enough she was still reacting to him as if he was the man from her dream—which he was?—but he was completely unaffected. Well… not completely. But he was completely in denial and rooting through her mind to things he had no business touching. "If you already know the answers, why are you wasting my time asking questions?"

"You're afraid you're going to hurt someone. You have no control over the animal's psyche and once it's out, you have no way of even monitoring it."

"And again, with the time wasting." Hailey began gathering her things to keep herself busy. As long as she kept her left arm down by her waist, she managed fine. She'd stayed here longer than any other place before. It was time to relocate.

"You're stubborn, emotional, impulsive, and reckless."

The dress she was folding ripped in two in her hands. "Your point?" she growled through fangs that were suddenly too big to fit into her mouth.

"My point is that you can't do this alone." When Jeremy approached her, she nearly snarled. He took the ruined dress out of her hands and set it aside. "You don't have to like any of this. I wouldn't in your position. But sometimes we don't have the luxury of getting what we want."

"But we can get what we need, is that it?" Now that she'd managed to shrink her fangs to a manageable size, there was nothing to disguise the bitterness in her voice. "Was that what last night was?"

He reared back. But he didn't deny it. And she knew he knew *exactly* what she was referring to. So it had been him after all.

"I'm curious. Whose needs were you seeing to then? Mine or yours?"

"That was... ah... unconscious."

Yeah, she'd just bet. But she let that go for now. "What do you want to bet that the moment I step foot in the same room as Amelia I won't be a human being anymore? What would you wager that she'll have a tranq dart all ready for me before I even walk in the door?"

"She is your sister. She wouldn't do that."

"Yes, *my* sister. Objective scientist, through and through."

His eyes narrowed, and Hailey just knew he was reading her mind, so she deliberately thought of all those times when Amelia had shut down her heart. The times Hailey had watched her cut into corpses to study the effects of some experimental drug, an emotionless automaton, brows drawn in concentration, distracted voice dictating cold, hard facts. She showed him the Amelia her sister became when no one was watching, all compassion set aside in deference to science. Emotion clouded judgment, and her research, whatever it happened to be at the time, required complete objectivity.

Hailey showed Jeremy what he wanted her to do and how it would all end: with her in the lab, in a cage, strapped to a gurney, needles jabbed into her veins, seemingly docile, but screaming inside her head.

Jeremy sucked in a breath, backed away from her. "Stop," he said on a harsh breath, clutching his temples and squeezing his eyes shut. He'd paled, and now looked physically ill.

"Real world too harsh for you, Jer?" she said coldly. "Sucks when your rose-colored glasses don't fit anymore, doesn't it? Can't stomach the possibilities? There are so many to choose from." She showed him her worst fear. The absolute worst-case scenario: Hailey in a pool of her own blood, gasping her final breath. Body broken, unrecognizable. Not human but not animal, either. Limbs contorted, bruised skin visible through a thin layer of pure white fur. Hailey dying, not because she'd failed to cure herself, but because someone somewhere decided to sacrifice her for the good of posterity. An acceptable cost; one life to further science and medicine by leaps and bounds.

Jeremy made a visible effort to get himself under control. Hailey figured he must have made a hasty retreat out of her head, because when he met her gaze again, his blue-black eyes were flat, unaffected by the thoughts that made her want to run out the door and leave her life in the dust. "I prefer to think better of people," he said. "Until they prove me wrong."

"Optimism is a dangerous affliction of the mind."

"Pessimism is a lonely one."

Another flashback took her back to her dream. Not to the sex, but the rest of it. That faceless darkness that still somehow had a shape, a presence. It had been everywhere, around her, inside her, restraining her.

She should have felt caged, trapped.

Instead she'd been… relieved. It had felt safe to be cocooned in that strength, as if it—*he*—could protect her from herself. She'd wanted him to hold onto her.

Now it all felt like one giant manipulative scheme. And damn if that didn't sting. "Oh, that's a good one, Jer. Hit me where you think it hurts, appeal to my emotional female nature. Nice. Very nice."

He crossed his arms over his chest, his patience clearly fraying but he would keep at it. Persistent bastard. "What are you more afraid of, Hailey? Finding out that your sister doesn't care, or finding out that she does?"

"Why would I be afraid of someone caring for me?"

She ought to be tossing him out on his ass, not indulging him with a round of verbal sparring. But Hailey was a social creature by nature; she loved people and company and having a good time. And for the last few months she hadn't had any of that. Hailey was starved for conversation and apparently it didn't matter who with, or why.

It was also completely unfair that the male was so gorgeous. If he wasn't, Hailey would have no trouble at all telling him off and heading out the door. Eventually. But the sight of him like this, territorial male standing his ground, challenging her… it did something to her, and against her better judgment, she didn't want to leave.

Hailey had good instincts about people. She could tell that Jeremy Calen didn't often run around with his shirt undone and bare feet hastily stuffed sockless into untied shoes. He was a man who prided himself on his self-control. It was obvious in the line of his stance, his sharp gaze, even in the first dream version of him, all buttoned up and meticulous on the beach. It was all about control with him, at least during the day.

He was also a gentleman, his "unconscious" indiscretion aside. Somehow he'd found her last night, cared for her injuries, dressed her and put her to sleep in his own bed, but he'd slept on the couch. Even now, when it would be so much more expedient to just knock her out, handcuff her, and drag her back home, he argued. True, he was resorting to dirty, underhanded tactics, but he hadn't laid a hand on her except that one time, or even raised his voice.

He was a complete contradiction. Hailey had a good idea of what to expect in terms of his actions. But beneath the surface, she had no idea what he could be thinking. It awakened her curiosity and she almost wanted him to stick around so she could figure him out.

Had Hailey ever met a guy like him before?

Jeremy shrugged. "Sometimes love hurts. The thought that something you did was wrong, that it was a disappointment. Maybe you think you don't deserve that affection anymore."

Hailey didn't dignify that with an answer. She turned her back on him and resumed packing. Her shoulder ached but the activity kept her mind from dwelling on things that brought out her animal side.

"You may think the best of people," she said, "but I can't afford the risk of being proven wrong. Go home. Go back and tell Amelia you didn't find me. It's the best solution for everyone." It should have come out a lot more convincing than that.

"I don't believe that."

"I don't care. It's not your decision to make."

He handed her a neatly folded dark green dress—the one that had been balled up and carelessly tossed into the corner a moment ago.

She took it without looking at him and stuffed it into her bag.

"What if I guarantee that you will not be harmed?"

Hailey snorted, pulling out her recorder to take pictures of her work. No way was she leaving *that* behind. His statement was completely absurd. *Can't guarantee that. Can't account for the actions of others.*

Jeremy took the recorder out of her hand to make her look at him. "I will give you my word." He said it like some knight of old, so sure he would make everything better. Might as well be swearing fealty and proffering arms in a real my-sword-is-yours deal.

Jeremy's eyebrows rose. "Is that what it'll take to earn your trust?"

She mimicked the face. "Do I suddenly deserve that kind of care?"

"I never said you didn't."

"Right," she said in all seriousness. "Not until I prove you wrong. I remember." Hailey reclaimed her recorder, saved her work, and placed it neatly in her bag's special compartment. Clothes she could replace; this she couldn't. "Look, why don't we cut all the polite crap and get down to it?"

"By all means. Why don't you tell me what you think *it* is?"

From the kitchen, Hailey retrieved her keys and some trinkets she didn't want to part with. From the bathroom, she got her med kit and towels. Everything got tossed into the bag. "Your job is to bring me back. I don't want to be brought back. Now, we could fight about this, get physical, but neither of us would like the outcome. Bottom line is, you did help me out last night. And for that, I am inclined to spare you. Also because I am injured. But don't think that would stop me if you really pissed me off."

"Noted," he said with a nod.

"So the path of least resistance here is for you to step aside and let me walk out that door. If you follow me, I'll know, and I won't like it."

Jeremy seemed to consider it, then nodded again. "Fair enough. Now it's my turn. My job is to bring you back. And I take my job seriously. The real bottom line here is that you're, what, a hundred and twenty pounds, maybe? One thirty-five at most? And you're one good arm short of making a go of it. If I wanted, I could have you subdued and on a shuttle to wherever I chose without breaking a sweat. But that would mean hurting you, which I am *not* getting paid for. So the path of least resistance has changed." He pulled a recorder out of his pocket—*her* recorder!

Hailey gasped, making a grab for it.

She didn't even come close before he moved it out of her reach. How the hell... *when* the hell did he manage to snatch it out of her bag?

"You come with me," he said, "or you walk out that door without this."

– 6 –

Jeremy got them through security and onto the shuttle in record time. Any minute Hailey was bound to discover that he'd fooled her. And if she found out he didn't really have her recorder before they took off, he was in deep shit. Hailey would tear through that shuttle mid-launch and break through the door to get away from him.

He kept her mind occupied, attention warily trained on the rest of the passengers flooding in and through their cabin, until the door closed. If he could have kept it up until they landed, he would have. But as it was he had neither the energy nor the inclination to stay in her mind any longer than absolutely necessary. With the shuttle sealed for liftoff, there was no more immediate danger of her bolting past the flight attendants and making a run for it, so he relaxed his hold on her.

As soon as her mind was free, Hailey dived for her bag. Clothing went flying out, mostly at him, and when a pale blue slip of under-wear landed on his head, Jeremy was glad the flight attendants were busy elsewhere.

Naturally, Hailey found her recorder safe and sound right where she'd put it, and she shot him a vicious glare that warned revenge was imminent. Her face changed subtly as her temper flared, faint rosettes painting over her brow and cheeks like tattoos. Jeremy hoped to hell no one else noticed.

A lesser man would have cowered at the sight, but Jeremy wasn't feeling very apologetic, wearing her thong as a hat and her dress as a blanket. He drew the underwear off his head and held it out to her from a fingertip.

She snatched it from him and growled, "I hate telepaths."

"I'm sure they don't like you much, either."

Hailey snarled.

Jeremy almost laughed. This was as absurd a situation as any he'd been in lately. Even after a five-year friendship with Hunt, he still wasn't sure he'd ever get used to the concept of shape-shifters.

This, coming from a man who can read minds.

It was one thing to alter the abstract; thought was fluid and change-able enough on its own to make that an easy task for anyone capable of tuning into it. But to change the solid and physical…

He kept replaying last night in his mind. Whatever he'd expected, seeing Hailey break and tear her way from one shape to another hadn't been it. She'd been in agony and Jeremy felt responsible, felt like a cad for having been so wholly unprepared for it.

If he'd had even a rudimentary med kit on hand, he could have eased her pain. In hindsight, not having brought one was just plain stupid on his part. If he'd known that forcing a transformation the way he had would cause her to go into shock, he would have found another way to bring her back.

The memory of bloody tears streaming down her face made him cringe and shift uncomfortably in his seat. "Here," he said, reaching for his bag. "Amelia sent this for you. I'm not exactly sure what all it's capable of, but she was certain you'd want to have it."

Hailey took the small computer from him, still glaring. Jeremy held his ground, refusing to be cowed. His brief forays into her thoughts gave him glimpses into her character. She might appreciate a gentle-manly gesture, but she saw a line between courtesy and submission. Hailey wasn't one to tolerate the latter. She grew bored with push-overs, and now with the animal's influence, she was even less likely to bother with anyone too weak to stand his ground. If he was going to get anywhere with her, Jeremy needed to be on equal ground with Hailey as well as her leopard.

So he held her gaze in a staring contest, waiting for her to blink or to look away first. Luckily, as stubborn as she was, Hailey had her priorities. The computer was more important than showing him who was boss. Even knowing that, when she finally tore her gaze away to inspect the machine, he couldn't prevent the tiniest thrill of masculine pride that he'd won this round. "Did my sister happen to send a connector, too?"

"All this high-tech machinery and you still need a cable?"

She gave him a look again. "One would think even someone like you would know that you can't stream without a cable on a shuttle in flight."

What was that supposed to mean?

As tempting as a fight with her might have been, he didn't press it. Just fished the cable out of another compartment in his bag.

The shuttle shook as it took off, and the cabin plunged into total darkness for a moment. Jeremy froze, not wanting to drop the damn thing where he wouldn't ever find it again.

A soft hand grabbed his none too gently and pried the cable from him. *Night vision,* he recalled. Good thing to remember for later on.

The computer fired up, screen glowing to illuminate Hailey's rapt silver gaze. She looked freaky and unnatural with her white hair, but beautiful at the same time. She bit her lower lip as she hooked her recorder up to the computer, and when it slid slowly free, Jeremy felt a sudden urge to lean over and catch her lip between his own. It was a completely male reaction and he wouldn't have thought anything of it, except Hailey must have sensed something. She stopped her rapid typing, turned her head slowly, and narrowed her eyes at him. The slits of glowing silver should have looked menacing. And they did.

But Jeremy found them… cute, too.

She drew her lips back enough to show off one impressively sharp canine.

Jeremy shook himself and looked away before she decided to test her claws on his face. Had Amelia mentioned anything about pheromones? He didn't think so. She should have. Those things were dangerous at the best of times. He made a mental note to research—he speared a quick glance at her thoughts—*Nosy, interfering, son-of-a-bitch mind reader! Gonna tear him a new one as soon as we land. And I know you're list—*

Snow leopards. And how to avoid being mauled by one.

The cabin lights came back on as the captain announced their successful departure from Jericho and rattled off the same information every pilot of every flight always did. Not that anyone was paying attention.

This shuttle was built almost like a train. The cabins held a handful of passengers each and had restrooms attached. For flights this long the seats even adjusted down to narrow beds. Not exactly the comforts of home, but enough to survive fifteen hours in proximity with a seriously pissed off, temperamental shape-shifter.

Not that Jeremy blamed her.

He still couldn't believe they'd actually shared a dream. Or close to it. Jeremy had glimpsed images and sensations of it in her memories. It was as if they'd each had one half of the same dream. Hailey had never seen the other person in her dream, just as he hadn't in his. But he at least had known who it was. Hailey had had a rude awakening figuring it out in the light of day.

Jeremy rubbed a hand over his face. He'd have to ask Hunt about that. It took training to screen out other people's thoughts, but it also took training to project one's thoughts to others. How could he have managed it in his sleep? And why Hailey?

More importantly, why a dream like *that*?

Maybe it was just similar frequencies aligning with each other, the same way twins could finish each other's sentences and sense when one was hurt. Maybe he hadn't manipulated anything. Maybe she would have dreamed it, regardless. The only difference was that across that veil of darkness he'd dreamed exactly the same thing. *Had* he manipulated her dreams? Or had his own mind simply tuned into hers and gone along for the ride?

And, holy hell, what a ride it had been.

Jeremy flashed a quick glance at Hailey again. She looked preoccupied but he wasn't about to chance another peek at her thoughts. Something told him they would not be flattering. Besides, he'd learned long ago that a person learned the worst things about themselves when eavesdropping.

He pushed a few buttons on his armrest to stretch his seat out into a bed, and turn on the warming feature and the ambient noise reduction. The blanket was feeble at best, but he still draped it over him as the pillow beneath his head expanded to just the right thickness and texture. The lights were dimmed low, soft music played, and Jeremy felt exhausted after his mental acrobatics of the day and the night before—intentional and not. Hailey was busily typing away on her computer, so engrossed in her work she probably didn't even notice what was going on around her. It seemed like a good time to get some shut-eye. "Wake me when it's time to leave," he said.

She flipped him off, still typing with one hand.

Jeremy shrugged and closed his eyes.

Hailey cursed the telepath in her mind, using every profanity she knew of and some she made up on the spot. She cursed loudly, hoping he'd hear, but apparently he'd chosen not to spy on her brain activity anymore.

Bastard sonofabitch piece of shit jerkoff.

She didn't feel one bit better thinking it, but maybe somehow all of that negative energy would translate into his brain and give him some seriously messed-up nightmares. Yeah, that would make up for her own.

The computer was a piece of crap. It didn't even have instant stream. Hailey had to upload the images one by one and hope to hell it didn't gank before she was finished. Though she had to admit the little piece of software that extracted text from the pictures was pretty neat. It cut down on a lot of typing.

Hailey kept an eye on it while she brought up the browser to do a little research. It was already preset with Amelia's user name and password, and Hailey was fairly certain it was the same one she'd used before, which meant it was safe to use. Relatively. Feeling like some kind of criminal, she cast a quick look around to make sure no one was looking before she logged in. The telepath was sawing *Z*'s next to her. Looking at him made her feel exhausted and sleepy. She shook her head, ordered a coffee through the seat's console. Next time Amelia sent someone to kidnap her, she was going to demand first-class transportation.

She scowled at the background picture Amelia had uploaded. It was a family photo from so long ago, Hailey couldn't remember it. She was still a baby in the picture, barely sitting upright on her mother's lap. Amelia had her hair up in a big pink bow and she was draped over her father's knees and smiling into the camera. The Christmas tree behind them was lit and sparkling with ornaments, and all around on the floor were piles of wrapping paper.

Was Amelia trying to make her nostalgic? Hailey shook her head. All she felt was annoyed. She changed out the picture for a generic one of a sunset beach and brought the browser back up.

As she began typing in her first query, her vision dimmed to black for a second. She shook her head hard. *What the hell?* She blinked, looking around warily. The person three rows in front of her was watching the news. She could see the headlines on that miniscule screen. The one across the aisle was reading a digital magazine with swimsuit pictures while the woman next to him dozed off. *Pervert.*

But Hailey could still see it; she wasn't blind.

Warily, she went back to work.

A moment later, it happened again. Hailey saved all of her work, backed it up, and shut down the computer. Butterflies fluttered uncomfortably in her stomach. She left her computer behind and hurried to the restroom. After splashing cold water on her face, she checked her eyes out in the mirror.

They were doing that freaky glowing thing in the low light, but her pupils were responsive and she could focus without a problem. What was going on here? Was her condition deteriorating faster than she'd anticipated? How much faster?

A wave of dizziness swept over her with the next blackout, and this time when her vision returned she was… she was…

She was looking at a bombshell version of herself, dressed in skimpy underwear, writhing on a huge bed with satin sheets. It looked like the other Hailey was in ecstasy, moaning and arching, and Hailey's body stirred to life.

Only it wasn't her body…

Lust hit her like a punch to the gut, and she stumbled to that bed, but hesitated.

The impostor Hailey was stunning, all smooth, supple skin and generous curves, but somehow still exuding a tightly leashed, explosive energy. It drew her just like her white hair did, and her lush lips, and that sexy black, barely there lingerie that she wanted to take off with her teeth.

Not me!

The other Hailey opened her eyes, smiling a sly cat smile as if she knew what the real Hailey was thinking, and curled her fingers in sensuous invitation.

Hailey almost fell over the impostor, wanted to so badly, it hurt to not move. But she forced herself to step back. This wasn't right. It's not me…

None of it was her.

But the other Hailey pouted and reached for her, grasping onto—she gasped—something no woman had. And still, Hailey shuddered with pleasure at the touch. Hands so soft, but her grip so firm…

Hailey fisted her hands in her hair and shook her head hard to banish the vision.

She freaking *hated* telepaths!

Her hands felt clumsy as she fumbled with the latch to get out of the restroom. She had to hold onto the seats she passed to get back to her own so she could wring that bastard's neck. If he thought he could screw with her like this, he had another think coming. Her mind was all she had to fix herself. *No one* was messing with that.

He looked like he was sleeping when she got to their seats. Playing possum? That just pissed her off even more. Hailey reached for him, grabbing a fistful of his shirt and…

…found herself tangled in the satin sheets, with the Hailey impostor's legs around her and her impostor hands in her hair. She tugged; Hailey groaned. Not her voice. *She curled her hips up and Hailey grabbed them to hold them still.* Not her hands!

The impostor laughed, tugged her down for a kiss.

The shuttle shook like it had taken a meteor hit, and Hailey went sprawling over the telepath. He woke up, but before he did, a split-second rapid fire of neurons plunged her right back into his dream.

On his/her back, with the impostor straddling his/her hips. She smiled a feral little smile of victory. She had him/her right where she wanted. The impostor ground her hips down, threw her head back and shouted, "Yes!"

She/he/they bucked upward, right into the impostor's orgasm.

"Shit!" she heard before the pervert grabbed her and shoved her off him. Somehow Hailey managed to get back into her seat, nearly sitting on her computer. Dazed, disoriented, pissed off, and so damn close to an orgasm that just crossing her legs would probably send her over the edge, Hailey squeezed her eyes shut and breathed deep.

Her beast was stirring again, eager to come out and play. She felt its aggravation that she wouldn't do anything about that little vision. Oh, but Hailey would. As soon as she got herself under control and could look at him again without wanting to rip his throat out with her teeth—or maybe rip his clothes off and straddle him…

No!

Oh, God, this was so, so wrong!

"What the hell happened?" he snapped.

He was pissed at *her*? "You tell me, Freakazoid," she growled back, still not trusting herself to look at him.

"Oh, *I'm* the freak?"

Her hackles rose, and her spine shivered in anger.

"I was sleeping," he said. "And the next thing I know…" He trailed off, and she could just imagine the look of dawning horror on his face. He swore—at least she thought he did. Whatever he ground out between his clenched teeth, she didn't catch it. When he spoke again, he sounded tired. "I take it you saw?"

She nodded. Saw, heard, *felt*. The reminder made her squirm and she gasped. *Oh shit!* Hailey crossed her legs tightly and clutched the armrest, shuddering through the unexpected climax. Eyes squeezed shut, jaw clenched against the deep moan working its way up her throat, she prayed no one would notice.

Calen did. She could scent his lust, knew he was probably tenting his pants right now, but he could easily hide it with a blanket across his lap. It only intensified her reaction, and for that, she hated him even more. The leopard roared her victory. God, she was going to kill him so much for this!

Calen swore again. "Look, I'm sorry," he said, and she could hear in his voice he was just as embarrassed as she. "I'm not exactly a lucid dreamer. I have no idea how you got dragged into my head." The effort to sound casual was totally ruined by the fact that his voice had just dropped half an octave and he kept it low, as if he couldn't catch his breath enough to speak full-out loud.

Because he felt her coming?

Just what the hell did someone say to something like that? *Thanks for the first orgasm in months that I didn't have to self-induce? You're welcome for having come without actually* coming? And he hadn't ejaculated, she could tell. God, this was so messed up.

"I'll try not to sleep in proximity to you again. Maybe that will help?"

She didn't know what was worse, him having wet dreams about her and not knowing about it, or sharing them. It was a toss-up in her mind between feeling violated and turned on. If her body was anything to go by, she'd happily go for round two, but there was such a thing as boundaries. Where exactly she was supposed to draw them in this situation, though, she had no clue.

Wait… he actually sounded sincere. And contrite. She detected no lies in him, just unease and awkwardness. Yeah, she got that. A stranger having a spontaneous orgasm right next to you on a public shuttle was not exactly the icebreaker you'd think it would be. It didn't lessen her anger any, but she could understand not being able to get a handle on something.

Could it be that he was no more in control of his abilities than she was of hers? She might actually be inclined to forgive him if that were the case. Ironic; he could mess with other people's thoughts, but couldn't keep a rein on his own.

"We don't talk about this. Ever again," she said.

"Deal," he eagerly agreed.

Hailey nodded and retrieved her computer from the floor with a shaky hand. She had work to do. Best get to it, time being of the essence and all.

– 7 –

August 4, 3032 - Reynard Colony

Jeremy checked the locks again to make sure no one except him could open them. This time he'd chosen a hotel in the middle of the posh district, an elegant structure that stretched toward the heavens. The suite he'd requested had two bedrooms, each on either side of a dining room, and a balcony overlooking the gigantic swimming pool oasis, tucked away from the rest of the city behind a living green line of demarcation. But Hailey wouldn't be getting out of it on her own. Not unless she was keen on proving the old adage that cats always fall on their feet. He doubted that would be the case for a fall from the ninety-fifth floor.

"I'll be back in twenty minutes," he told her at the door.

She didn't even look up. She'd been ignoring him ever since his subconscious mishap on the shuttle. He'd never seen a woman shut down so completely. Hailey wouldn't talk to him, wouldn't look at him, wouldn't even acknowledge his existence unless he made it absolutely necessary.

Good thing, too. Jeremy didn't think his raging hard-on would have argued his case. Sweet Jesus, the sight of her—the *feel* of her—coming right next to him on the shuttle refused to leave him. He was an embarrassment of a telepath if he couldn't shield his mind when wide awake. But then again—a bad, bad thought made his mouth twitch to smile—maybe he hadn't *wanted* to shut her out.

Hailey's eyes were reflective in low light like an animal's, but on that shuttle they'd *glowed*. They'd been glowing even when he'd woken up to find her in his lap, and he could still see the glow when she'd squeezed them shut. The sight had short-circuited his brain and his shields had gone down as if they'd never even existed. Jeremy had *felt* her coming as sharply as if the orgasm had been his own. Just how he'd retained his power of intelligent speech was one of those things he would never understand. Jeremy had been one tiny mental filter away from telling her to look at him, selfishly wanting to see everything. He'd caused it, after all. Well, his mind had, anyway.

And the messed-up thing about it was that he'd been angry with her. She'd gotten to finish, while he'd been stuck in his seat with the hard-on from hell because people would notice if he went to relieve himself in the lavatories and the front of his pants preceded him by a considerable amount. They'd definitely have noticed him pulling Hailey back into his lap and working her up so he could make her come again like he'd wanted to.

It had been the most uncomfortable fifteen hours of his life. Once his dick had finally gotten the message that it wasn't getting any action, he'd even considered asking to move to another cabin to give her space, but he couldn't trust her not to bolt the moment the shuttle touched down. As it was, he'd almost lost her in the crowds at the shuttleport. Maybe a leash wasn't such a bad idea.

Good thing he hadn't broached the subject. Jeremy could tell the woman was just waiting for an excuse to knock him on his ass. He was just surprised she hadn't done it yet. Hailey had, for all intents and purposes, given him a tentative break on this. It was unexpectedly charitable of her; a fact she was fully aware of. But Jeremy knew he still walked that razor's edge and she could change her mind any second, which was why he was about to remove himself from her immediate vicinity to give her some time to cool off.

The terrifying thing was that getting her here was the easy part.

To get her to Torrey would be much more difficult. The planet was twenty-six light years away and traveling in the newly redesigned long-distance shuttles required the passengers to be asleep and immobile during the journey to prevent any problems. Would he even be able to get Hailey on the shuttle?

Jeremy closed and locked the door behind him and made his way down to the media room. That was one thing he loved about these fancy hotels. Anything he needed, he got. In this case, the hotel had an entire floor dedicated to just communication with outside worlds for the guests' convenience.

The TVs were all turned on and circles on the floor indicated where one had to stand to hear the audio accompanying the video. Three of the twenty-one TVs were showing news of the peaceful antichem rallies happening throughout the Union. Jeremy glossed over them without paying much attention.

Nothing new there. Since the outing of New Alaska's secret experimentation years ago, the voices speaking up against chem-treatments have gotten much louder. For now, they contented themselves with publishing skewed medical reports and picketing outside of immunization clinics, but Jeremy had a bad feeling this thing would only keep getting worse. Maybe if New Alaska had stayed a secret, everything would have continued on as normal. But once the population discovered how far the Interplanetary Council of Governance was willing to go to control and manipulate its people, everything changed.

All the telepaths felt it—everywhere. No acts of violence, or thoughts of them yet, but there was a definite undercurrent of tension in everyone's minds. The kind of tension that usually grew in silence until it broke in a big way. If he had to guess, he'd say they weren't far off from that point. It would only be a matter of time.

Passing the last TV, Jeremy's step faltered as he glimpsed a different headline out of the corner of his eye. He stepped into the yellow circle to hear the story.

"The police department in Sapphire City is asking the public for help in identifying the animal responsible for the deaths of five teenagers," the announcer was saying while several pictures of sheet-covered bodies flashed one by one, then arranged themselves in a row at the bottom of the screen. *"A description has not yet been released, but similar accounts from other colonies have prompted the officials to declare a state of alarm."*

The chief of police then stepped in front of the camera. He was standing on the boardwalk by the beach. Jeremy recognized the area; he'd found Hailey not far from there. *"We believe that the animal is most likely a stray dog. There have been reports of several large ones wandering the streets. The proper authorities have already been notified, and while a state of alarm is now in effect, we want the residents of Sapphire City to know that there is absolutely no need for panic."*

He was about to say more, but the picture cut back to the news anchor. *"The police department has assigned surveillance teams to patrol high-risk areas after dusk. Residents are being warned not to approach strange animals or lost pets. If you see an animal out of place, the safest thing to do is to notify the police immediately and retreat indoors. In other news…"*

Jeremy left the circle.

The report didn't give dates of attack. It could have happened as early as a week ago and as recently as an hour ago. But it couldn't have been Hailey, could it? He'd kept a close eye on her for two days prior to their meeting and she'd spent the last day and a half glued to his side. She hadn't changed a single time, not even a little. Not with her arm refusing to heal properly; she wouldn't take the chance.

Or was he being too quick to dismiss his suspicions? He'd been tracking Hailey for weeks. Creating a mental map of her movements, Jeremy tried to compare her recent locations to the animal attacks on the news. They seemed to match almost perfectly. With the exception of Sapphire City, Hailey had been in each town at the time when someone was attacked.

There was a neat and perfect trail of blood leading right to her.

No, it couldn't have been Hailey. He'd lightly scanned her a few times during the trip from Sapphire City. Not once had he detected any kind of bloodlust in her thoughts, aside from the brief one directed at him.

But it wouldn't have been Hailey, would it? It would have been the leopard. The two were separate enough that neither had much awareness of the other. The leopard could very well have been the attacker, and Hailey never would have known it.

As soon as he thought it, Jeremy discarded the theory. He hadn't been lying when he'd told Hailey that he preferred to think better of people and risk being proven wrong. As long as Hailey was in his care, he would keep an eye on her. Just as he'd promised he would keep her safe until she proved him wrong.

He was still frowning when he sat down at a screen and established a connection with Torrey. Pixie noticed.

"Something's wrong," were the first words out of her mouth. "What's wrong?" She was wearing some kind of dark green thing, with her hair braided in an intricate pattern.

"Is there another ball going on and no one told me?"

Pixie grinned and stepped farther back to show off her gown. "You like it?"

"Looks very nice." And by that he meant *expensive*.

"I got it for the Baroque Bash in English Village. It's gonna be so amazing! A full month of period reenactment."

"Sounds like fun," he said without enthusiasm. "When's it start?"

"October first." She returned to her seat, arranging her skirts around her. "It'll go the whole month, and end in this huge fireworks thing on Halloween night."

"And you only got one dress." *Hard to believe.*

She laughed. "No, silly. I got the whole wardrobe. Me and the gang"—the gang that consisted of Pixie's hormonal classmates, all of them as nuts as she was but thankfully not a mind reader among them—"are going to rent a cottage in the village."

"Uh-huh. And who will be picking up the tab for that?"

Pixie rolled her eyes. "No one, Jeremy. You don't have to worry about shelling out a single copper penny. We'll be part of the show for tourists. It's a paying gig and all the proceeds will go toward our stay. It will practically pay for itself."

"Right."

"So tell me how the hunt is going." She was eating chips, crunching each piece loudly with her mouth open.

"Uh, good. I found Hailey."

Pixie straightened, her eyes going wide. "You did? Really? Where is she? Is she okay? What's she like? Are you bringing her back to Torrey? Will I meet her?"

"Yes, yes, upstairs in the room, relatively, insane, yes, and no."

She frowned. "What?"

"Forget it. I can't talk long. Just wanted to check in with you and make sure the house is still in one piece."

Pixie pouted. "Okay, but Tristan stopped by, wanted to talk to you. I didn't have a contact to give him, so he left all cranky. And by that I mean all sexy-intense, glowy-eyed, and tiger-striped."

Jeremy glared.

She hitched her shoulders up to her ears. "Just saying."

"I'll call him. And you stay away from him. I don't want you to end up on the news."

"Oh, you saw that, too?" He hadn't told Pixie about the attacks, not wanting to worry her. Apparently she'd found out on her own. "I hope they catch the guy. And soon."

"You're so sure it's a guy?"

"Well, yeah. Call it instinct. A girl just doesn't fit. No. It's a guy. A really sick one, like that one five years ago…" She trailed off, frowning at him. "Unless you think… No. I won't believe that. Didn't you scan her?"

"She doesn't have a grasp on her animal like Hunt does. I could scan her until I'm blue in the face, but I still wouldn't reach the animal. They're almost completely separate beings."

"Trippy," Pixie said. "Bring her over, then. I'll do it."

Jeremy gave her a look.

"Okay, okay. Fine. I won't. Jeez."

"Be safe, sis."

Pixie smiled with genuine affection, and his heart squeezed. She was growing up so fast. "You, too, bro. I'll see you soon, I hope."

"Yeah."

She made smacking sounds at the screen. "Hugs and kisses, darling. Mwah." And then the screen went black.

The next call he placed was to his boss. John MacMurphy greeted him with his signature straightforwardness. "Didn't think I'd be seeing your pretty face so soon."

"Nice to see you, too, John." And it was. He'd missed the old man, and everyone at the Special Unit. They were the closest thing to family he remembered. Some people had Sunday dinners with their grandparents; he and Pixie had had a round of mind games before lights out. They'd taken turns telling bedtime stories from different rooms in the compound.

"So, what do you need? Shot in the dark here that this isn't a social call."

The curt tone made him wince inwardly. He should have checked in before now. "Do we have anyone working Sapphire City?"

"The one on Jericho?" John didn't show any surprise at the question. "Got a couple agents looking into the attacks."

Excellent. "I need everything you've got. Police reports, autopsy reports, witness accounts if there are any. Just send the whole file to my secure account. I can open it anywhere."

John chuckled. "I thought you were on leave."

"Private contract."

"That so? Must be a pretty important contract if you're calling your old friends."

"John," he warned, "don't start."

"Do you know Nell's been keeping your rooms up ever since you left? She keeps expecting you to just show up out of the blue."

He did wince then. Nell was the mother of the group. Every person who came through the door, be it minor or adult, became her adopted child. Whenever Pixie had scraped a knee, Nell had been the one to kiss it better. At the worst of times Jeremy remembered, when the world had started to close in on him and his responsibilities were so overwhelming he was afraid to get out of bed, there'd always been Nell to cook him a warm breakfast and pour him a cup of hot chocolate. He owed Nell a lot better than he'd given her.

"And Rafe and Juliet ask about you two every time I see them." Everyone in the group had their own specialties. Jeremy's was getting to the truth of the matter, making sense of what people wanted to share and exposing what they wanted to hide. Rafe and Juliet were the artists of the group, and Jeremy had envied them bitterly in the beginning. Juliet had trained as a classical opera singer before her mild empathic abilities flared up to full-blown telepathy. She sang what people needed to hear and used her gift to heal them in some small way.

Rafe was DaVinci reincarnated. There weren't many artists around who bothered with canvas anymore, let alone those who could afford it. Rafe was hired by the richest of the rich to paint their dreams and souls. Every day that man went to work, he got to lose himself in fantasies. Jeremy got to scan felons and criminals standing trial.

Yeah, there was a lot to envy.

"The younger ones don't say anything," John was saying, pulling him out of his bitter thoughts. "But they don't have to. It's all over their faces that they miss their brother and sister."

"We're not family," Jeremy said, but the words felt forced. "Pixie is my family, the only one I have left. You know she's my priority." Seven months of living in the streets of a city like Gray Dublin with a toddler sister wasn't something a guy just forgot. There'd been nights when he'd sat up watching Pixie sleep for fear that she wouldn't wake up in the morning. They'd starved more often than not. They'd spent nights in places that most people wouldn't even come near. Jeremy had learned to hate everyone except Pixie. In the winter, when he'd held his little sister close for warmth, praying to whichever god would listen to keep them safe just one more day, he'd watched fashionable strangers pass him by, unseeing, so preoccupied with how they looked to the world that they hardly even saw the world.

Jeremy owed John and the Special Unit his life.

But he would forever hold the memory of nearly losing Pixie's in his heart.

John rubbed a weary hand over his face, and Jeremy knew he was remembering the little girl she'd been—a dirt-streaked little bag of bones with big blue eyes that could see right into his soul. "I'll get you the files," he said. "They'll be in your account later today. I should warn you, though. It's some pretty messed-up shit."

"After Dara's case five years ago, I think I'm immune to *messed up*."

"If you say so."

Jeremy ended the call soon after that. He was left feeling bereft. John and Nell had practically raised Pixie and made it look as if it had all been Jeremy's doing. They'd taken in two kids off the streets, given them a home, a family, and a purpose; a reason to live. But something had changed when he and Pixie had left Gray Dublin. There was a line now that cut between them, marking them employer and employee. As he'd told John, they were no longer a family.

It seemed… wrong, and he didn't know how to fix it.

He considered calling Hunt next but wasn't in the mood to deal with whatever was bothering the guy enough to go visit. Instead, he got back to the business at hand, checked his bank accounts and the shuttle departure times. He hadn't made reservations beforehand, not knowing how Hailey would handle the first trip and whether she'd need time to recover.

Ten minutes later, he was heading back to their room.

He could sense something wasn't right as soon as he stepped off the elevator on his floor. Jeremy cursed. She wouldn't have climbed out the window, would she?

He burst through the door to find every window in the room wide open, transparent draperies billowing in the crossbreeze. Heart in his throat, he charged to one of them and leaned out as far as he dared. His head spun looking so far down. People were little more than dots down there.

There was no sign of her.

Behind him, the door closed, and he froze. *Stupid!*

"Are you looking for paw prints or a corpse out there?"

Jeremy had never been one for teeth grinding, but this assignment was driving him to it. He took his time to turn around. The longer he took, the less he would be tempted to wring her lovely neck.

When he caught sight of her through the draperies, his breath left him, his power of reason fizzled out with a baffled, *Mflaehbnwow,* and he nearly backed out the damn window himself.

That towel had to have been wrapped around her at some point. Now she'd stripped it off to dry her hair. Her head was bent forward so she couldn't see him staring but Jeremy could not tear his gaze away.

Sleek lines, toned muscles, but all woman in all the right places. Wet, her hair looked silvery gray, but old age never once entered his mind. Jeremy tried to close his eyes—he really did—but his eyelids refused to lower even a fraction of a millimeter. He greedily drank in the sight of her, fingers curling into the window ledge to keep from reaching out.

Hailey straightened again, flipped her hair back so hard it lashed at her hips and stuck there. "Ahhh," she sighed. "Much better."

He wholeheartedly agreed. The woman was temptation given shape. And while Jeremy was now certain on some level that her genetic change caused her to emit some sort of pheromone to attract males, that level had shut down the moment he'd caught sight of her.

She rolled her head a little, eyes closed, a smile playing on her red lips, looking like she was in the throes of an orgasm, and his cock jumped to attention. Again.

Hailey opened her eyes then and looked at him, her smile stretching wider. She let the towel slip from her fingers, and it caressed her hip and the length of her leg on its slow-motion way to the floor.

Breathe, you idiot!

He couldn't draw in air to save his life.

Hailey sauntered toward him, hips swaying sensuously. She stepped with her toes first, rolling her shoulders seductively. Smooth, feline… *Dangerous!*

Jeremy dropped his gaze, seeking the floor, but it snared on her breasts instead. Her nipples were beaded, seeming to strain toward him, and his mouth watered for them. *No! Don't think like that. Floor. Look at the floor.* His gaze dropped lower and snared on the triangle of dark curls at the apex of her thighs. He nearly went to his knees.

Hailey hummed. "I can feel your eyes on me," she whispered. "I can smell your need." Her voice turned breathy as she came within inches of him. Nothing stood between them except the damn draperies. "Agent like?" she purred and leaned closer, a breath away from leaning on *him.*

Air exploded from his lungs and on it a hissed, "*Yes,*" and he could finally breathe again.

He gripped the windowsill harder, picking up on her intentions before she did. She leaned her face in and drew a deep breath, scenting him, her eyes closed and lips parted the slightest bit. Jeremy wanted to snatch her up and force those lips wider, taste her just as she was now. Lost in abandon, wild.

Hailey shifted closer and rubbed herself against him, then brought her hands up to touch him through the drapes. She was panting now and her eyes, when she opened them, were glowing. Her foot caressed the side of his leg up to his calf, then her knee brushed his hip and she braced that foot on the windowsill next to his white-knuckled hand.

—*What are you doing?*—

Her unfocused gaze latched onto his in surprise, but it soon faded as her lids drooped and she smiled wickedly. She rose up, nuzzling his neck, his jaw, up to his ear. He could feel her parted lips through the wispy drapes; willed her to turn her head just a little. Just enough for a taste. That was all he needed. A hint of her.

And then all of her.

Hailey took his hand, coaxed it from the windowsill to the curve of her hip. Jeremy couldn't hope to stop his fingers from curling into her soft, giving flesh. Without meaning to, he brought her closer, and she leaned on him, breasts flattening against his chest.

Christ, the woman could tempt a saint.

Which he wasn't. Not even close.

Hailey's parted lips brushed his through the drapes. Her tongue peeked out to touch. Jeremy moved to catch it, but the damn drapes were in the way. He reached for her hair with his free hand and became entangled in the fabric.

Hailey smiled, kissed him just barely, then pulled back.

—*Tease,*— he said, and she laughed low and sweet, tilting her hips to press the core of her against him.

Jeremy sucked in a breath. Whatever his mind could conjure, this was so much more. More real, more intense, more *everything*. He tried to recall his professionalism, but it was like swimming against the current; no matter how hard he fought he couldn't move from his spot, and it would be so much easier to give in and let that current carry him further.

He could smell the generic hotel soap she'd washed with, and on her, it was more enticing than the most expensive perfume. Jeremy wanted to get closer, the way she'd done with him, and find the source of that scent.

He was beginning to hate draperies.

—*What are you doing to me?*— Christ, even his mind-voice was unsteady.

"I thought every man dreamed of an animal in his bed."

It was the one thing she could have said to break the spell.

Jeremy snarled and snatched her shoulders. He cursed himself when he hesitated at the feel of her bare flesh through the draperies. Impatiently, he tugged them aside and reclaimed his hold on her, shoving her back, taking both of them away from the window.

Her eyes lost their sensuous haze, and he hated himself for causing it. But he hated *her* more right now. "You are *not* an animal," he said, his voice harsher than he'd intended. "You want to drop your inhibitions and go wild, fine. Believe me, you'll get no complaints from me. But don't use the cat as an excuse. This is all you, Hailey. Nothing else."

Hailey broke away from him, looking shell-shocked. She backed toward the towel, then fell to her knees trying to reach for it. Without looking, she curled her fingers in the fabric and hugged it to her chest. Not for cover, but for comfort.

He was taken aback by her reaction, about to go into her mind to gauge her sincerity, but her next words stopped him cold.

"You… say I'm not an animal. But you cooled off mighty quick when I reminded you I'm not exactly human." Bitter self-loathing filled her eyes when she raised them to look at him again. "Better than a bucket of icy water."

He opened his mouth to argue, but she cut him off. "Say all the pretty lies you need," she said, picking herself up from the floor. "You can even make yourself believe them. But don't insult my intelligence. We both know that the only reason you're not pinning me down and shoving inside me—and don't even try to tell me you didn't want to—is that there is something seriously wrong with me. Doesn't it just suck when reality doesn't live up to your dreams?"

The barb hit its mark with deadly accuracy. He winced. She *would* bring that up. And he'd given her no reason to think otherwise. Without looking into her thoughts he knew what she had to be thinking: good enough as an idea, but not in reality. "Hailey—"

"I get it, okay?" She wrapped the towel around herself. "You don't have to worry. I won't throw my offensive self at you again."

From out of her mind with lust, to shock, to fury, the transformation was so quick, Jeremy wanted to call her bluff. Sneer and tell her to grow the hell up. Except… she really believed what she was saying. He could see now the change he'd been too distracted to notice earlier, the way her own instincts had caught her off guard, allowed a lot more of her leopard to the fore where it couldn't be so easily controlled.

While anyone else would have buckled or fought, Hailey had used it, turned it into a test—for her. She'd wanted to prove that no matter what the cat made her feel or think, she was still Hailey, and she could own her actions. And in her mind, she'd failed. Jeremy had just reminded her of everything she'd been trying to make herself forget. So instead of berating her, he now felt like punching the wall.

Hailey didn't slam the bathroom door behind her. That would have taken more ire than she possessed right now. What the hell had gotten into her? What could she possibly have been thinking to make her do that?

She knew the answer. She *hadn't* been thinking. Sometime after Jeremy had left, she'd found herself staring at the computer screen with no idea what she was looking at. Text and numbers flashed across, scrolling so fast they were a blur. And all she could think was: *Shiny.*

Not her best moment so far. She'd freaked out so bad that she'd nearly dropped the computer on the floor.

The cold shower had helped, though. Sort of.

But then she'd come out just as *he* had burst in, and it had all gone downhill from there. Hailey groaned and tugged at her hair in frustration. From all appearances, Tristan Hunt was a successful shifter experiment; he could function like a proper human being and the animal inside him only provided added strength and heightened senses. He certainly never lost it on a big scale. He lived his life—*married*, no less, with twins on the way—without a care in the world.

Why couldn't Hailey?

Maybe the difference was self-control. She felt her face heat up. Or her glaring lack thereof. Had to be mating season for snow leopards. Yeah, that had to be it.

She dropped the towel in the corner to be washed and padded to her bag for fresh clothes. Not a dress this time. No, she needed the safety of a confining pair of pants and several layers of shirts. Maybe a jacket. She'd be hot, but at least it would keep her from wanting to rub herself all over an unsuspecting telepath agent.

Hailey brushed the tangles out of her wet hair and braided it tightly so it wouldn't fly all over while it dried. Control, that was the ticket. Maybe if she controlled the little things, the big things wouldn't get out of hand so easily.

All finished with her grooming, Hailey eyed the closed door. She didn't want to leave the room. But she'd left her computer out there.

Just then, Jeremy knocked, startling her. She didn't answer, just sat on the edge of her bed and watched the handle to make sure it didn't move.

Nothing.

Another knock. "Hailey."

She kept quiet. Stealth. Couldn't find fault with it.

She heard him sigh, and it sounded as if he'd leaned his forehead against the door. "I'm about to call down to room service for food. What do you want?"

Meat, was her first thought. Hailey squeezed her eyes shut and forced herself to think about it a little more. Meat, yes. She could go for a nice steak. And this time it wasn't a thoughtless growl in her mind. It was a genuine preference to a type of food. To that, she added a baked potato, a fruit cup, and fresh fruit juice. Mango.

Her mouth watered at the thought of freshly cooked food. She'd bet they had top-notch chefs in the kitchen. How long had it been since Hailey had had a meal that hadn't been nuked into existence?

Ever since I'd grown fangs at the sight of steak tartare in that restaurant on Earth.

So, about two months.

She checked her teeth. Nope, no fangs yet. She was proud of herself and it made her want to smile. "Did you get all that?" she called.

"Got it," he said, and she heard him move away from the door. A few minutes later, "They said fifteen minutes to half an hour."

"Got it," she replied and let herself fall back on the bed with a contented sigh. Food. *Good.* Food was yummy. She liked food. It made her strong and helped her think—about something other than stripping down and rolling around in the snow, or stripping down and rolling around with the telepath…

That was good, too.

Or it might be if she wasn't a freak and he wasn't so painfully aware of just how much of a freak she really was. If he was anything like the man in her dream, Hailey might just risk embracing her animalistic needs and jump him.

But then he'd probably run screaming…

Not good.

Hailey shook herself and darted for the door. She needed a distraction and right now her computer and the telepath were all she had. It would have to be one or the other.

– 8 –

She was melting. She was… *Oh, sweet God,* she was dead, and this was heaven. Hailey hadn't seen such bounty in months except from across a windowpane. She wanted to roll around in it and stuff her face with her bare hands and make a giant mess.

She glanced warily at Jeremy to see if he'd caught that, but he wasn't even paying attention to her. Just to be sure, she narrowed her eyes at him. "Exactly how often do you let yourself into other people's minds?"

He raised an eyebrow, finally looking up at her. But instead of answering, all he said was, "Eat, Hailey. I can hear your stomach growling from here."

Oh, she wanted to. Room service had brought what she'd asked for and so much more. There was a mountain of food spread out over the long dining table and she didn't trust herself to behave like a lady. Her mouth was watering like crazy, her teeth ached, her hands were curled on her thighs under the table.

If it had been just her, she wouldn't have cared about manners. But apparently, she'd retained just enough humanity to feel self-conscious with someone else in the room. She always made a pig of herself the first few meals after a full change. And that was cheap, prepackaged deli food. *This* was *real* food that she didn't have to force herself to chew and swallow.

This is amazing!

"Did you change your mind about that steak?"

Hailey blinked at him, then stared blankly at the juicy piece of meat on the plate in front of her. It was perfectly cooked, on a clean white plate, with some sort of heavenly smelling dark sauce drizzled all around and one single leaf of lettuce as a garnish. Short of picking it up with her hands and biting into it like a savage, she was at a loss as to what to do with it.

"Here," he said. He wiped his hands and mouth on his linen napkin and moved his chair closer to hers. He took her utensils and began cutting the meat into small, chewable pieces. Hailey nearly swooned at the sight. The meat was beautifully brown on the outside and succulent pink on the inside.

"I-I can do it," she said, and even to herself she sounded as if she was in a trance.

The knife stopped mid-cut and all she saw was his hold on it loosening and moving aside so she could take the handle from him. Her hands shook a little when she assumed possession of the utensils.

Easy now. Start slow. Just one bite. Simple enough, right? Just push the fork into that small piece there… or maybe that bigger one over there, and put it in your mouth.

The instructions she gave herself helped. She speared a piece of the steak and slowly brought it to her mouth. Her eyes rolled back in her head when it touched her tongue. Hailey made herself chew it for a long time to savor the taste before she swallowed the morsel. Only then did she fork another one.

"Good?" Jeremy asked, watching her with a small smile playing on his lips.

"Uhh-hhmmm."

He grinned bigger. "I'm glad."

He kept talking, presumably to keep the conversation going, one-sided though it was, but his voice sort of trailed off into a hum. Hailey didn't see or hear him anymore, her focus trained on the food and the food alone. Thankfully, she kept her hands curled safely around the utensils, which kept her from reaching out with her bare hands.

The more she ate, the better she felt. More like herself again. If it turned out that all she'd ever needed to keep the animal at bay was good food, she might just hurt somebody.

The steak and baked potato were followed by half a plate of greens, then the fruit cup. After that was gone, she spotted a dessert platter farther down the table. As if by magic, it floated up and settled in front of her. She ate two tiny raspberry cups and three of those delicious chocolate mini cakes. There was ice cream, too.

Finally sated, she leaned back in her seat with a sigh and her tunnel vision cleared. She blinked at the table, her hands, and the linen napkin in her lap. No mess. Not even a bread crumb anywhere.

Baffled, she looked to Jeremy for confirmation.

"Feel better?" he asked.

There was no word to describe how good she felt. Content was too tame. Human was too trite. Happy—given that she was still about to die, that one was going a bit far. She felt like smiling and dancing and going out among people to just *talk* to them. Not smell them, or snarl at them, or skulk in shadows. "Thank you," she said, and that seemed too weak a phrase to fully carry her meaning.

Jeremy graciously inclined his head. "My pleasure."

Hailey drew the napkin from her lap and dabbed at her mouth. It came away clean. Another miracle.

"By the way," Jeremy said, "your computer beeped while you were eating. There was some sort of message on the screen, but I don't have a clue what it is so I didn't touch it."

Hailey was on her feet and darting for her computer before he'd even finished talking. The screen was flashing green and the message was a Code 2319.

"So what's it mean?" Jeremy asked from behind her.

"It means the formula has finished aggregating," she said, not trusting herself to okay the message and actually look at the results.

"Well? What are you waiting for, then?"

He had a point. Hailey acknowledged the code, and the green flashing disappeared. A clear white screen appeared, with a long formula that took up several lines. It was the same one she'd been working on all this time, except this one had integrated all of the variables and compounds compatible with her two DNA strands—the last unknown she'd needed.

But her eager smile faded as she read the results and the notes generated on the side. Like a cooking recipe, it gave her the end result—the formula—and the sequence of activities needed to achieve it—the notes on the side.

"Something wrong?"

Hailey tried not to sound disappointed when she answered, "It's pretty much what I expected." In order to fix what was broken, Hailey would have to obtain a small volume of the original compound she'd injected herself with in the beginning. It was part of the solution, and she wouldn't be able to fix herself without it.

The only problem was, there was only one place she could find that compound, or recreate it. She'd really been hoping to avoid having to go back.

Whether he'd read her mind or just guessed at what was bothering her, Jeremy said, "It won't be as bad as you're imagining. Things rarely are."

"So what's your guess? Cage, leash, or just a straight-on tranq dart?"

"How about none of the above? Isn't that an option?"

Hailey twisted to look back and up at him. "You really *haven't* known my sister long, have you?"

Jeremy glared. "Should we start packing?"

She turned back to the computer screen. "Not yet." She saved the formula, backed it up a couple of times to be sure, and then turned the computer off. "I'm not ready to move into a lab just yet."

"Hailey—"

"It's *my* life. And I'll live it as I see fit. Tonight, I want to go out." She looked him over and almost felt pity for him. "From the looks of you, you could use some downtime yourself."

Jeremy kept a respectable distance from Hailey as they walked, but he stayed close enough to be able to take her hand in his and steer her another way if need be. She'd dressed in a pair of black leather pants and a shimmery silver strappy top… thing, both so tight as to be nearly nonexistent. Her high-heeled boots brought her almost to his height and did some amazing things to her legs and ass.

She hadn't even needed to think about what to wear. Just pulled out the first items that met her fingers when she'd reached into her bag.

And *damn*, it was a good look for her. He'd tried to get her to put on the trench coat, hoping that he wouldn't notice her so much if she was all covered up, but she'd refused. It was summer here, and Hailey, or rather the animal side of her, overheated easily. Understandable in a creature meant for cold, harsh climates. But that didn't make this any easier on him.

The streetlights in this town shone bluish white, which made her hair gleam like snow. She'd also done something to it to make it shimmery to match her top. It should have looked strange; instead, Hailey looked otherworldly, ethereal. Stunning, and utterly untouchable.

They should have stayed at the hotel.

But as soon as Hailey stepped foot outside, her super-hearing picked up something in the distance, and she headed toward it without a backward glance. Quick footsteps, as long as she could manage with her heels, just short of breaking into a run. And the closer they got to the source of the sound, the more Jeremy resigned himself to his fate this night.

They were headed toward the Midnight Parade, as the locals called it. A procession from the beginning to the end of Main Street, with live music, dancing, and lots of scantily clad individuals. There were bound to be drugs and alcohol passed out freely to the crowd.

It was the kind of thing Jeremy usually went out of his way to avoid. Crowds were not a comfortable place for a telepath to be. Yet he only had to look at Hailey's smile growing brighter with every step to know she needed this.

"Look!" she said, pointing forward.

Yep, there was the river of people. Jeremy scowled. Most of the ones he could see were nearly naked. Oh, this would be fun…

Hailey looked at him with something akin to sympathy. Or maybe it was pity for his impending doom. Then she laughed excitedly and picked up her step even more. Jeremy had no choice but to follow along, or risk losing her in that madness. For both their sakes, he stayed close.

In that throng, the music was deafening, and he quickly gave up on trying to talk or listen to what others were shouting at him.

"*Come on,*" Hailey yelled. He only saw her mouth move; the words never registered in his ears. He caught her hand in his before she could slip away, and held on for dear life.

The procession went on forever. Jeremy got squashed, shoved, groped, tripped, and he was pretty sure there had been a proposition or two. He touched body parts on strangers he never wanted to feel again, but the sight of Hailey in complete abandon, carefree and *happy*, made it all worth it.

She looped her arm through his and hugged it to her side; people around them eased away. Hailey touched his shoulder to get his attention to show him something, and instead of being horrified by what he saw, he felt at ease with her next to him. Or as at ease as he could feel in this crush of drugged-out minds. When she smiled at him—well, laughed at him, really—he wanted to laugh with her.

She danced, and space cleared around them as if by magic. She pulled him into the moves, and he felt like a part of everything, instead of apart from it. Jeremy knew that was because of her. For some reason he couldn't fathom, she wanted him to feel included. Against all odds, he was actually having fun.

At one point, she put her free hand onto his waist and leaned into him to say something in his ear. He didn't hear her voice, but the idea made it through his mental shields: *Is this your worst nightmare or what, Agent Serious?*

Jeremy grinned and put his arm around her because he couldn't *not*.

Hailey stiffened and drew back, meeting his gaze. Her eyes were wide, shocked. Her head whipped around to scan the crowd, and Jeremy could feel the tremor that went through her.

"What is it?" he asked, already knowing she wouldn't hear him. —*What is it?*— he repeated, making it a thought in her mind this time.

She turned back to him, still with that same look in her eyes, only this time, he could discern a mixture of fear and anger. Hailey opened her mouth to say something, then seemed to change her mind. Her fingers curled, sharp claws digging into his side. Not enough to pierce skin; just enough to let him know something was wrong.

She'd perceived some sort of threat.

Jeremy didn't waste time on questions. Keeping his arm securely around her, he pushed and shoved his way out of the crowd, then pulled her away from the commotion and down a quiet side street. It was darker here, and the farther they got, the fainter the blaring noise of the procession became.

His ears were ringing and everything sounded wrong.

When they were far enough away, he pulled Hailey around a corner and stopped underneath a streetlight. There he took both her hands in his to examine her claws. They hadn't receded. And her eyes were glowing now as she scanned their surroundings.

"What the hell is going on?" he demanded.

"Nothing. Let's just go back to the room. I think that was enough excitement for one night." But she wouldn't meet his gaze, and her voice was too high-strung to even give a convincing impression of the truth.

"Hailey, I can't help you if you don't tell me—"

"I don't want your help!" Now *that* was definitely the truth. "Let's just go, okay?" *Have to get him out of sight.*

"What?"

"Nothing. Stop snooping."

"Tell me, or I'll find out on my own, and then we'll both be sorry." No way was he taking them back. He could tell she was planning something. The moment he lowered his guard, she would slip away and do something stupid. "Why do we need to get out of sight?"

Hailey pulled her hands free to examine them herself. She curled her fingers into fists, pressing those sharp points into her palms. Eyes closed, she breathed in deep, ragged breaths.

"Hailey," he said, keeping his voice low, soothing. "Stop, you're hurting yourself." He could already see crimson drops seeping out from between her fingers.

She didn't react.

"Hailey," he tried again, reaching for her hand.

"Back off!" Her eyes snapped open, glowing and furious. Her teeth were sharp. Not full feline fangs, just enough to make her a threat. She'd knocked his hand away, but at least hers had uncurled. Her claws were even longer now, raised to strike.

Jeremy held his hands up in surrender. "I can help. But you have to let me."

He caught only the trailing end of a thought:...*could die...* She wasn't thinking it about herself. Images and impressions forced their way through his shields. She didn't mean to, but she was projecting everything she felt. He saw dozens of images flash past too quickly for him to make them out. Suspicion tinged every perception, bordering on paranoia, but it wasn't. He had her memories of a strange scent, one that followed her from place to place. The sense of being watched. Not paranoia; a predator's sense of a threat.

A stalker?

Someone dangerous. Someone who knew what she was.

Be good, or the Shadows will get you. She shivered at the thought, but even she didn't believe they existed. The Shadows were a children's story, a dire threat to behave, or else. No, the one who stalked her was worse—he was real.

Someone who watched her, waited for the perfect opportunity to strike.

Not her, though. Never her.

Just... people.

People she'd met, people she'd just passed on the street. People she'd looked at.

She'd learned not to look anymore, but still more kept...

There was that scent again!

It made Jeremy's hackles rise. *He* wanted to snarl and warn the presence off, whoever the hell it was. He wanted to hunt it. Be rid of the thing. Establish his territory and protect it.

He was feeling what she felt.

Hailey met his gaze. She knew he was picking up on all of it. She didn't say anything, but her mind echoed the same question over and over again: *How does he keep finding me?*

Some noise he couldn't hear made her gasp and whip her head in the direction of the crowd they'd just left. "We need to get back," she said, not looking at him.

"Okay. We'll go back. Come on, it's this way."

Hailey shook her head. "We go around."...*could die...*

Around meant the long way, probably circling a few times before entering the hotel. "All right, lead the way."

Because she was too close to the edge, he kept a few steps behind her, eyes and ears sharp. He was no longer following the carefree girl who'd left the hotel earlier. This was a predator in fight mode. Anything could set her off, and another full change might very well kill her. And she led him as she would a cub, always checking behind her to make sure he was there, scanning the shadows for any threats. Jeremy felt her unease, her single-minded focus to get him out of sight. It took precedence over everything else in her mind. Hailey was protecting him? From what?

Her hands were bleeding, dripping as they went. She noticed and brought each palm to her mouth, licking the wounds to stop the bleeding.

"Here," he said, pulling a handkerchief out of his pocket. He shook the square out and ripped it in half. "May I?"

She looked at her hands blankly, then nodded.

The fabric was big enough—or her hands were small enough—to wrap around her palm twice and knot securely. At the very least, it would slow the bleeding until they got to the med kit he now kept with his belongings.

When he finished, he took one of her hands in both of his. "Are you doing okay?"

Again she nodded blankly.

"Good. Let's keep going, then."

It took them over half an hour to even get close to the hotel. Then another half-hour of aimless wandering before Hailey allowed him to head for the hotel lobby. By then, her teeth were back to normal, but her eyes were still glowing and her claws were still sharp. The fight had gone out of her, but the uneasiness remained. His step became heavy with the weight of it in his mind.

Back in the room, it was déjà vu all over again, with her sitting on the toilet in a daze and Jeremy washing her hands of blood. Was this what her life would be like now? Once he escorted her to Amelia and officially finished this assignment, would she even have anyone to do this for her?

When he finished bandaging her palms, she caught his hand before he pulled it away, and met his gaze. Her eyes were now back to normal but so lost and confused it made his chest ache.

Jeremy brushed her hair back over her shoulder, cupped her cheek with his free hand. Her eyes closed, and she leaned into the caress. He nudged her forward a little, met her halfway to brush his mouth over hers.

He'd meant to pull back after that. A small kiss to offer comfort. But he found himself going back for another, and another, and then one more, a real kiss this time, not a peck. Her lips parted, and he caught the lower one, flicking his tongue over it. But he didn't deepen the kiss. He didn't press for more.

When he pulled back, she looked better. A little color had returned to her cheeks and her lips were red again. God, he wanted another taste of them. Instead, he cleared his throat. "Come on, let's get you to bed."

Jeremy led her out to her room and turned his back while she changed out of her clothes into a nightshirt of some sort. He tucked her in bed, feeling her eyes on him the entire time. When he said good night, she caught his hand again.

"Don't leave," she said in a small voice. "Please. Stay." *Please live.*

"You know I can't."

Hailey dropped her gaze, let go of his hand, curled into a ball, and closed her eyes.

Boundaries, he reminded himself as he left the room. Whether she liked it or not, he had to preserve some professional distance between them. She was his assignment, nothing more.

That would have been far more convincing if only he didn't see her naked in front of him every time he closed his eyes.

But there were more pressing issues to think about now than his persistent case of blue balls.

Someone was following Hailey. There was something about this whole mess of a situation that just didn't… fit. Jeremy was missing a major clue.

Back in his room, he fired up the courtesy com console and set up a secure connection to the only person he knew who could give him some much-needed answers.

Amelia answered almost immediately. She was wrapped in a big green towel. What was it about the Chase women and showers? "Agent

Calen? What is it? What's wrong? Did something happen? Where is my sister?"

He waited for her to fire all of her questions at him, but instead of answering, he asked one of his own. "Who else knew about Hunt's study?"

She looked taken aback by the question. "Uh… my superiors at New Alaska got the gist of it, but they never knew Tristan was able to successfully change his shape. Some of my colleagues had a vague idea about where I was headed, but we didn't share our research. Umm… I had some lab assistants, but they only knew the bare minimum, and no one else had access to my files. Except, of course, Hailey."

"What about your lab at home? Could someone have gained access to your files?"

She frowned. "No," she said vehemently, then added with more hesitation, "I don't think so. Everything was under lock and key. The physical facility has biometric security *and* password protection, my files were all saved and backed up, the originals were stored in a bank vault, and the copies were in a hidden safe. No one could have gotten to them."

"Your sister did."

She smiled, like he'd just made a joke. "My sister is a freak of nature whose favorite pastime is pissing me off."

Her tone gave him pause. Another piece of the puzzle. He'd promised Hailey that her sister would welcome her with open arms and treat her like family. Had he been wrong about that?

Amelia continued. "The only reason she even went looking for anything was because I told her not to. She broke into the safe to prove that she could, to spite me."

"And what do you think was her reason for picking up where you left off with the study?"

Amelia blinked, clearly at a loss for words.

"That's beside the point," he continued. "The fact that Hailey had gotten past your security would indicate to me that it was insufficient. My question is: who else could have gotten in? Who else do you know; who would be interested in your work or its results? An enemy maybe, or a rival; anyone come to mind?"

"N-no. No one knew. Why steal research that's supposed to be a failure?"

"The night Hailey... changed herself. You were the first to find her, correct?"

"Yes."

"Did you notice anything out of the ordinary?"

"Besides my lab being in shambles and my sister lying in a pool of her own blood? No." Her tone was cutting now. She was getting defensive. It was Jeremy's fault; he hadn't done his due diligence. He should have asked all of these questions the day Amelia had come to him with this case. He hadn't, because there had been no reason for it.

Well, there was reason now. "You had video feeds from the lab. Were there recording devices outside the lab? In the hallway, or outside the building?"

"Yes, some."

"Have you reviewed all of them?"

Her mouth compressed into a tight line. "The ones Hailey didn't shut off? A dozen times. What is this about, Agent Calen? Are you suggesting that this was somehow my fault?"

"I'd like to review the feeds from that night myself."

"Well, you can't. The system reboots and refreshes every month, unless someone overrides it. I did it once, to preserve the feeds in case you needed them, but then I forgot. They're gone. Wiped."

His fault again.

"Now what the hell is going on?" she demanded.

"I have reason to believe your sister is in danger, besides the effects of the serum she injected herself with."

"And what reason is that? She told you?" Amelia rolled her eyes, and her exasperation grated on Jeremy's nerves. What the hell kind of reaction was that? "Agent Calen, she's manipulating you. Can't you see? She's painting herself as a helpless victim so that you'll do what she wants."

That just pissed him off. Sister or no, Jeremy wanted to put her in her damn place. The woman had no idea what Hailey was thinking. Who the hell did Amelia think she was, making accusations like that? "It occurs to me," he said, striving for diplomacy he honestly didn't think was deserved, "that this was a mistake. You're not the one I need to talk to about this. I'm sorry to have alarmed you."

"She's dying," Amelia said quickly, just as he was about to close the connection. Jeremy bit his tongue to keep from telling her to piss off. "The computer I gave you for her… it's linked to my systems here. I can see everything she's doing. I know she finished the formula, and I've already synthesized several doses. They will not work."

"Why?" he asked impatiently, suddenly feeling as if *she* was manipulating him.

"Her base, the constant in her equation, was the original serum she used. But that's not what's in her system now. It's degraded, changed. This *cure* will most likely kill her and without it she doesn't have much longer. You need to bring her back." There was genuine concern on her face now. "Please, the only way to save her is to bring her to me."

"What will you do with her?" *Cage, or tranq dart?* The image of Hailey strapped to a table, immobile but awake while Amelia stood over her, flashed across his mind. It wasn't his creation. He glanced over his shoulder to see Hailey standing in the doorway.

You know what she will do, she thought to him.

"I'll need to run some tests. A series of them to determine how quickly the compound is changing inside her. Whatever solution we come up with, it will have to be timed perfectly. Depending on the speed of transformation, probably down to the minute. This is not something she can do on her own, no matter what she tried to make you believe."

Ever the good old Ams, Hailey thought bitterly. *Take whatever you can, sis, and give back only as much as you have to. Just enough rope to hang myself with.*

Jeremy rubbed his forehead, making an effort to block out her thoughts. He didn't need another bias. "You will stream your findings to the computer you sent for Hailey," he said. "*All* your findings. Your sister will want to verify everything you just told me."

You're taking my side?

—There are no sides here.—

Then that's your first mistake. Thinking that there is no wrong in this case. There is. The sooner you figure out where, the better off all of us will be.

"You're setting the terms now?" Amelia asked.

"Look, Dr. Chase," he said, ignoring Hailey and her gloom and doom. "You want your sister back, and I want to help. But do you think she'll come back when she knows you're withholding information?"

"Then don't tell her," she snapped impatiently.

"He doesn't have to," Hailey said, loud enough for Amelia to hear.

"God, is that her?" Amelia's eyes had gone as wide as saucers. "Hailey, is that you? Oh, honey, are you okay?"

"Ugh, spare me the sentiment, Ams. We both know how genuine it really is."

"Go to sleep, Hailey," Jeremy ordered, putting as much compulsion behind the command as he dared.

She just raised an eyebrow. "I can't. You tucked me in all wrong."

"*What?*" Amelia screeched.

Hailey grinned. "Come do it right," she purred.

"Hailey!" Jeremy snapped.

She laughed as she spun on the balls of her feet and strode away.

"Is there something I should know?" Amelia asked through gritted teeth. "About you and Hailey?"

What the hell did I get myself into? "Listen, Dr. Chase, you hired me for a reason. You can't get Hailey back on your own. I can. And I already told you what I'll need in order to do that."

"You won't get my sister, I promise you that."

It took him by surprise that the first response that came to mind was, *Want to bet?* "I'm good at what I do because I take my job seriously," he said, wondering when the hell reason had left the building. "I can get your sister to you. But once that's done, the rest is up to you. I can't make her stay with you if she doesn't want to, and I'm thinking you won't be able to either. Think about that. I'll be in touch."

He cut her off mid-sentence when he closed the connection.

"Are you beginning to get the picture?" Hailey asked. She was once again in the doorway.

"I think I am," he said. "This is some sort of punishment for my past life misdeeds. That has to be it. I can't think of a single thing I've done in this lifetime that would make me deserve this."

She grinned with true amusement, and Jeremy caught a glimpse of the woman she used to be. "The boy learns."

Jeremy chuckled. "He does, indeed."

Her smile softened with something like affection. He really needed to get some sleep. All of this excitement was getting to him. "So," she said, "are you going to tuck me in or not?"

"*Out!*" he commanded, and in the privacy of his own mind added, *Or I just might.*

Hailey shook her head slowly. She came forward as silent as a ghost. "Poor, sad Mr. Calen," she said, and he couldn't be sure if she was mocking him. She reached out a hand and raised it as if to caress his face. "Who will be there for *you*, I wonder?" Both of them noticed the bandages at the same time. Hailey's hand dropped back to her side before he could catch it and press it to his cheek. Backing into the doorway, her gaze still on him, she said, "All these long, trying days; who will be there at night to cushion your weary head in her lap?" She shook her own head again and slowly retreated into the shadows of the dark main room. Her voice followed her exit. "Poor, lonely Mr. Calen."

– 9 –

"So do you have everything you need?"

Hailey was shaking her head, reading through the huge data file Amelia had sent. "Short of my own lab, yeah, I guess." She shot him a crooked smile. "Thanks for this. Remind me to call you in for all future negotiations with my sister."

He groaned. "I'd rather you didn't."

Hailey felt her smile soften. He was ready for the day, dressed in another perfectly pressed shirt and slacks, but not quite the perfectly controlled agent he liked to pretend he was. His feet were bare and his shirt wasn't tucked, the top three buttons undone, the cuffs left open and loose. His dark blond hair was mussed, and he hadn't shaved yet. Hailey wanted to purr.

This was the kind of domestic tranquility she'd never gotten to experience. Not even with her parents. After they'd divorced, Hailey only remembered her mom always looking haggard and stressed. She'd aged prematurely taking care of two young girls on her own. And she'd died prematurely, too. People shouldn't just die out of the blue at age thirty-nine. They shouldn't be wheeled off from their home in a black body bag, never to be seen again. People should have time to say good-bye and grieve. To gather with their loved ones and remember the life of their deceased.

Hailey's dad had never even responded to the message Amelia had left for him that the mother of his children was gone. By then, he'd been remarried to some hot young thing, probably not even thinking of the people he'd left behind.

Yeah, so she was a little bitter about that. Only once had Hailey come close to reestablishing contact with her sire. Years after her mother's untimely death, desperate for some kind of familial connection, she'd sought out the only family she knew of besides her sister. She'd gotten as far as to find him at his new address. But she'd stopped just short of approaching him when she saw him with his infantile wife, acting like he was twenty-two instead of his obvious forty-nine and change. No kids, but the woman he was with seemed just childish enough to make up for the lack.

Hailey had never told Amelia about that.

She was by no means an expert on domestic bliss. But even she could tell that was wrong. The real question was: what was right?

Was this what it should be like between husband and wife? Hailey could almost picture it like a scene playing across her mind. A leisurely morning waking up, padding around the house barefoot, a casual breakfast together, and a slow kiss at the door before they both headed out for work.

She sensed the solace, the depth of comfort in that vision, and she was so close to feeling it. Here, now, the only thing marring the scene was a set of unfortunate circumstances. There she was, the loving wife, sipping her morning coffee while she checked the updates on her computer. There was Jeremy, the doting husband, hovering close by because in her fantasy he preferred to be near her, even though he'd be much more comfortable sitting at the table by the window.

Any minute now he might check his wristwatch and announce he was late, give her a quick kiss and a wink, then rush out the door, only to come back again for his shoes and his briefcase.

He would make a wonderful husband. Just look at the way he was taking care of her, a stranger. Basically a bounty to cash in. Happy would be the woman who got to have him look at her with his whole heart in his gaze. She would never want for anything. Hailey almost wished it could be her.

Hailey sighed, a bit regretfully. She suddenly felt old and disillusioned—and what did that say about her? Put any other woman into her shoes right now and she'd probably be gushing over the handsome prince charming who'd come to her rescue. Play the helpless damsel in distress, appeal to his chivalrous side. Not Hailey. Agent Serious must have lost some universal bet to get stuck with the one woman who was his polar opposite in every way possible. Sure, opposites attracted, but only in magnets. Other things tended to spontaneously combust.

Last night, she'd had another of *those* dreams. She was starting to feel as if she was having an illicit affair with the telepath. It was a welcome change from her recent stint of celibacy, she had to admit. But it would have been nice if he could have kept it simple. Instead, the whole time she'd felt conflicted. Drawn to him, but wanting to keep a certain distance. Feeling protective and vulnerable at the same time. At his mercy and his master all at once. They'd touched without any barriers between them, but every kiss was complicated with a messy knot of emotions that made her want to slap him, and crave him to hold her and tell her everything would be all right.

Damn him for torturing her like that and putting ideas into her head! Shy, she was not. Nor, however, was she a porn star, no matter what he dreamed. Sadly, not even a cold shower had helped her libido after that dream, and she'd been forced to come out to breakfast cranky and surly, eyes glowing like stars in the night.

Interestingly, he'd looked just as bad and wouldn't meet her gaze. Hailey almost wished she could read his mind to know what he was thinking. Was he embarrassed? Was he regretting turning her down?

What was it her psych professor had said? Dreams were the mind's way of consolidating thoughts collected throughout the day while conscious thought could not process it. Exactly how much time did Calen spend thinking about her during the day if she was still on his mind at night? A ponderous development.

"Stop looking at me like that," he said.

Nocturnal indiscretions aside, Hailey had more of that amazing food in her stomach and a boatload of information from Amelia, so she was feeling a lot better. Maybe even playful. She fluttered her eyelashes innocently. "Like what?"

He scowled. "Like you're hungry and I'm dessert."

Hailey grinned. "Dessert, huh?" So he hadn't read her thoughts. Or maybe he had, but just wasn't admitting it. Either way, she appreciated the illusion of privacy.

Calen crossed his arms over his chest. Playtime over. "How long do you think you'll need to go over all that?"

Agent Smooth getting back on track in one sentence. *Stupid track.* "Not long, why?"

"Amelia held up her end of the bargain. It's time I held up mine." So now he was a businessman, too? "We need to get you back to Torrey."

"Torrey? Amelia moved?"

"No, but we both agreed that you would be… uncooperative if we tried to get you back to Amelia's lab. Think of Torrey as a neutral meeting ground."

"Very diplomatic. Think it'll help?"

He shrugged. "You tell me."

"I still believe what I told you will happen."

"And I still stand by what I told you. Amelia will not put you in a cage. I won't let her."

Hailey smiled slowly. "Been a long time since I came within a thousand miles of chivalry." Come to think of it, she'd never come across it in person. And books didn't really count, did they?

"I know, I know. I'm full of surprises. Now get back to work. This hotel isn't cheap, you know."

She shrugged. "So what? Amelia's picking up the tab anyway, isn't she?"

"What if I said no?"

"Then I'd say you got majorly ripped off on this job."

He made a valiant effort; she could see it in the way his face strained not to laugh. But his eyes were already shimmering with mirth, and his mouth twitched. Finally, he gave a short chuckle, which was more amusement than he'd ever shown before. He padded back to the window, shaking his head.

Hailey tilted her head, watching him go. As nice in the back as he was in front. She sighed wistfully. Such a waste to put a perfectly biteable ass like that on a guy who didn't flaunt it one bit.

Jeremy fumbled with a coffee cup and spilled the hot stuff on his hand. He cursed and hissed, shaking his hand out to cool the burn.

Hailey smiled. He'd *definitely* heard that thought.

About damn time he got as discomfited as she was around him. The guy wore cool and in control like armor, and it just irked her all the more that she was so *out* of control. It was all his fault. If it weren't for his *dreams* somehow making their way into her head—and he had yet to talk himself out of that one—she wouldn't be walking around with a female leopard equivalent of blue balls.

So not fair!

Here was a guy who knew what she was and still hadn't run screaming. Well… he wasn't exactly jumping her bones yet either, but she could work with that. Calen was a guy with that rare combination of classical good looks and a whole lot of mystery in his dark eyes, who made her want to use any and every kind of sensual torture to make him spill… everything. A guy, she was beginning to understand, who rarely met her gaze because when he did, he couldn't seem to decide whether to kiss her or back away and find a tranq gun.

Add to that the fact he couldn't stop dreaming about her in all sorts of naughty scenarios and there was no wonder she couldn't keep her thoughts clean around him—who could?

And she couldn't do anything about it because he insisted on preserving their professional agent-target relationship, which came standard with two miles of personal distance.

Grr. Just… *grr.*

Frustration of any kind, but especially sexual, was not helping her situation. Lately, it seemed like Hailey was swimming in it. She had to get her head back in the game.

Amelia's care package wasn't exactly good news. Based on everything she'd read so far, Hailey could theoretically live a normal life for its average duration. *If* she didn't change even a little. Not likely. Even something so seemingly small as changing her nails to claws was gradually killing her. It was impossible to tell exactly how long she had, but Hailey's best estimate was a week, maybe two, barring a full physical shift.

After that, it was mutilation and gruesome death galore. Fun stuff to look forward to.

But she still had some options. Once she had a lab at her disposal, she could do a lot more than theorize. It would take time, but she could find a way to cure the glitch in her system. And if not, there was always the option of synthesizing a protein block that would prevent her from ever shifting shape again. Hailey didn't relish that option. She hadn't come this far, endured so much, only to throw it all away now and pretend it had never happened.

"So, what's on the agenda today?"

"What do you mean?" he said, without facing her. He sounded gruff.

"I mean, what do you plan to do while I work?" When he didn't answer, she twisted in her chair to face him. "You're not just going to sit there and watch me, are you?"

"That a problem?"

Hell yeah, it was a problem. Bad enough she had all the self-control of a horny teen with a sugar high; she didn't need him tempting her with his eyes. Just his proximity was making her hormones go haywire, and after that dream last night, she was a bomb primed to go off if the wind blew a certain way. Yeah, she'd told him she'd keep her hands to herself, but come on! There was only so much a woman could be expected to endure.

"Actually, I have some paperwork to catch up on, myself."

Phew. But still… physical proximity. "You *can* leave me on my own if you need to go somewhere. I'm a big girl, you know."

"Yeah, we tried that. Not about to repeat the experiment, thank you."

"You're going to hold that against me? Do we need to talk about your *dreams*?"

"No need," he said quickly, flushing a deep red. Oh, but she wasn't about to let him off the hook so easily this time. He didn't get to use her in his fantasies and then slap hers in the face, so to speak. If sex was the game, he wasn't the only one who was going to play.

She waited for him to brave facing her and braced her foot on the table. The dress she wore slid down her thigh almost to her lap, baring a whole lot of leg. Shapely, she wasn't too modest to say.

His gaze heated again, and she wanted to smile. She liked that look in his eyes. *Touch me,* she silently willed, not sure whether or not she wanted him to hear.

He must have, given the sound he made, a sound she felt in her core.

Without tearing his gaze away, he said, "You make it really hard to—"

"Do I?" she cut in, feeling wicked. The more time she spent with him, the less she wanted to stay professional. It was ridiculous. She should hate him for practically kidnapping her, had every right to be as nasty to him as she wanted to be. But somehow she just couldn't dredge up all that much resentment. Hailey had never been one to hold a grudge, except when it came to her sister. And really, Calen was just the messenger here; the real culprit was Amelia.

Good thing, too, because it would have been too mortifying to fall prey to the clichéd Stockholm Syndrome. As far as abductors went, this one was definitely Stockholm-worthy. Just his scent could make her go into a tizzy of head-spinning lust. The insanely powerful mix of her own desire and the beast's was something she'd never felt before and had no defense against. Hailey knew he wasn't doing it on purpose, but just his presence, his closeness, sometimes even the thought of him, affected her.

It was becoming a new instinct she had acquired. Sharp senses, predatory impulses, and wanting to jump the telepath. This was one she couldn't justify having to fight. Jeremy made her feel more animal than she ever had, but through it she felt more human and alive than she had in months. She craved that feeling. Might even consider doing something extremely ill-advised to get more of it.

Already her skin was heating and her breaths quickened the slightest bit. The toes she'd braced on the table curled, muscles tensing, needing release. The kind she knew Jeremy could deliver with expert precision. A miniscule mewling sound escaped her, and she swallowed hard, hoping he hadn't heard how desperate she was getting.

His hands curled and uncurled at his sides, eyes fixed on the length of smooth skin she'd bared. She could see his jaw working overtime, muscles jumping. Her sensitive nose picked up on his lust, and she firmly kept her gaze on his face and chest. She would not look lower. If she did, it would be all over.

"Hailey…"

"Yes?" He was seconds away from crossing the distance back to her. She could feel it.

And then…

A low-pitched beep announced an external call. Jeremy shook himself and answered it on a handset. "Calen," he said. Hailey couldn't hear the other side of the conversation, but she could tell it was bad news when his face masked over and he turned away, murmuring a tense response before hanging up.

Disappointment made her foot drop to the floor. "So I take it you won't be hovering today." Or doing anything else to her.

"I have to go for a while," he said. He wouldn't even look at her when he disappeared into his room.

"Whoa, wait. What's going on?"

He came back out fully dressed, buttoned up and official. "Just stay put. I'll be back as soon as I can."

"Oh no, you don't." Hailey was faster and reached the door before him.

Jeremy let out a frustrated breath. "Move."

"No. Not until you tell me what's going on."

"Do you *ever* just do as you're told?"

She considered that. "Once. But then I realized it was stupid, so I did what I wanted instead."

"Brilliant," he muttered.

"God, what is it? Wha… Are you trying to shield me, or protect me, or something? You think the little woman can't handle it? As if I'd care—"

"The police found another mauled body a block away from where the parade happened last night."

Hailey's foot moved back on its own, bringing her flush against the door. "Oh." Her body cooled in a hurry, so much so quickly that she shivered, suddenly chilled in the warm suite.

"Yeah, oh."

"D-do they know the time of death?" she made herself ask.

"Nothing conclusive yet. Now will you please get out of the way?"

"I want to come with." Hailey surprised herself as much as him.

Whatever else he'd been about to say, he didn't. "*No.*"

"Just give me two minutes to get dressed. I won't get in the way."

"I am *not* taking you to an active crime scene. Forget it."

"You take me, or I find it on my own."

He wanted to toss her aside; she could see it on his face. Either that, or shove her back against that door and kiss her senseless. For a moment she just stood there, waiting for him to make up his mind. Part of her wanted to get physical—part of him obviously wanted that, too. But Hailey already knew he wouldn't. Damn it.

His patience was running out, and if she were a man, Jeremy would not be wasting all this time talking to her. Her rational mind told her that. Her animal senses, though, picked up on far more underlying nuances. There was tension in him, and she could scent the slightest hint of fear. His posture was dominant, assertive in the way a male lion stood over the females of his pride. Protective, not aggressive.

He raised his fist to his mouth, then opened his hand to make a rough staying motion. "I can't take a civilian to a crime scene. End of discussion."

"I could be useful," Hailey offered. She had to see this. Might be her only chance to get a close-up look at what was happening.

Jeremy threw his hands up in the air. "What is this really about? Do you think you're responsible? You were here all night long. You didn't leave, you didn't change—"

"You wouldn't have known if I did."

"You underestimate me."

Hailey considered her words, chose carefully what to reveal. "I… don't always have control over when I change. And it's not a pretty process to go through when it happens. But I always have the leopard's senses and stealth. I've shadowed people before, walked up right behind them, and they'd never shown any signs of knowing I was there. If I wanted to—if the animal in me wanted to—I could have snuck out without you knowing."

"You would have shown signs this morning."

"Not necessarily."

"If you changed—"

"I don't need to change completely to do a lot of damage. All I need is claws and fangs."

For a moment, he looked as if he would believe her. Then that chivalrous streak kicked in again and he shook his head as if he couldn't believe he was even wasting time on this nonsensical argument. "How would you even get out of here? The door will only open for me."

"Oh man, you need to read up on snow leopards."

He raised an eyebrow. "You're telling me that you could have left this suite at any time. Through the window." He was blatantly disbelieving now.

Hailey raised an eyebrow to mirror him and crossed her arms over her chest. "The balconies are evenly spaced, the walls have decorative features I could use for hand and footholds, no ice to make them slippery, and a convenient pool at the bottom. Five minutes to ground level. To get back up, about fifteen. But then, I never did like going uphill."

Jeremy stared at her. "It's not… a hill. It's a sheer building."

She shrugged. "Not sheer enough, obviously."

"You know, the only thing keeping me from daring you to prove it is that I think you actually believe you can do this."

When he just kept staring at her and didn't say anything else, she got impatient. "So do we do this your way, or mine?"

Hailey imagined she was a telepath in that moment. His thought process was so clear on his face. Take the dying mutant, or not? Risk whatever psychological issues she had flaring up, or risk her plunging hundreds of feet to her death? Risk her wrath, or her sister's?

That last one amused her the most. The boy was between a rock and, well… her. With no easy way out, and he knew it.

But Amelia wasn't here. Hailey was.

Decision made.

Hailey smiled a little.

Jeremy glared. "You have exactly one hundred and twenty seconds."

She was gone before he'd even finished. And ninety-four seconds after that, she was back, dressed and ready.

He glared even more. "I could really hate you sometimes."

Hailey beamed.

Jeremy was a levelheaded, reasonable sort of guy. He'd been able to argue his way out of trouble since age ten. He could charm his way into anyone's good graces in minutes if he wanted to, and he could arbitrate disputes between telepaths like a pro, which was a feat.

The only one he could never get around was Pixie, and that was only because she knew him better than anyone and could anticipate his every move like a chess champion. When she'd been ten, she'd dragged him into a pet store because she'd wanted a puppy. Jeremy had had his arguments neatly lined up, the logic unquestionable: they couldn't afford a dog, couldn't keep one where they were living, and Pixie was too young to take care of it anyway.

After two hours, they'd walked out of the store with a cute little furball neatly stowed in an open-top box carried by a befuddled Jeremy. The dog had lasted three weeks and then one of the other kids had taken pity on Jeremy and took it for himself.

Arguing with Hailey was nothing like that. She didn't know his strategy and she didn't have one of her own. She just made stuff up on the spot and that made her completely unpredictable. He had no idea how to deal without predictions. Hence, ten minutes after receiving the call, they were exiting the elevator in the main lobby and heading toward the transport he'd rented. He thanked God for the divine intervention of ID lock technology, which linked the transport's navigation to him alone so she couldn't talk herself into taking the wheel.

Driving to the police station with Hailey in the transport was like trying to give a cat a bath. She couldn't sit still for two minutes at a time. She fiddled with the windows, changed the radio stations, poked around in the computer system and navigation. Then she crawled into the backseat—and nearly caused him to drive them off the road—and crawled back again.

It didn't take a telepath to see she was anxious.

But the moment they got to the station house, she grew unnaturally still. She hesitated getting out of the transport and took a full minute before stepping away from it toward the front door.

"You can stay here if you want," he offered. It usually didn't take much more than that to get an unwilling person to turn back.

Of course Hailey didn't act like a regular unwilling person. Oh no. That would be too easy. Too normal and predictable. "No," she said. "I'm fine."

At least it got her moving.

They met the police chief at the front desk, and he escorted them to a quiet room to go over everything pertaining to the case.

"Are you an agent, too?" he asked Hailey.

"She's a third-party consultant in my investigation of this case," Jeremy said before Hailey could get them both kicked out. The lie had come out of nowhere, and for a split second, he didn't know where he was going with it.

Chief O'Reilly looked iffy. "She got all the necessary clearance?"

"As far as you're concerned, yes." What was the matter with him? Pulling rank was the best he could come up with? He sent the chief a mild compulsion to let it go. It was a risk, but the alternative was having Hailey wait outside. Lesser of two evils.

Hailey struck a defiant pose, but thankfully the chief decided to ignore her and focused on Jeremy. "Don't want to get in trouble, you know."

Jeremy was about to reassure him, when Hailey chimed in. "My expertise in this case is mainly medical. I don't really care about the files, but I will need access to the body, if at all possible."

Damn it. Chief O'Reilly swung his gaze back to her, no-nonsense eyes flat. He'd seen Jeremy's credentials, but not Hailey's. Jeremy had planned to pass her off as a civilian, not in any way involved before the lie slipped out. Maybe as his charge or girlfriend who refused to stay home. He could have passed her off as a consultant, too, even without credentials, if she'd just kept her mouth shut. The chief had just been about to take Jeremy's word for her status.

That was out the window now.

"You said your name was…?"

"Chase," Hailey said, flashing him her ID with the first name conveniently covered by her thumb. "Dr. Chase."

The chief typed it into his computer. Jeremy monitored the results through him as he scanned the readout to make sure there were no red flags. There weren't many people with that name in the database he'd pulled up, and without her first name, the chief found her sister's file to verify her credentials. "Fair enough," he said. There was no photo attached to Amelia's file.

Thank God.

And that was all the checking O'Reilly was about to do. Jeremy made sure of it.

For the next hour, Hailey sat in relatively patient silence while they went over every detail of the ongoing investigation. Jeremy got a first-hand look at the techniques used when vastly different jurisdictions were involved. The chief traced the murders from the presumed first victim to this last one. There were a handful of eyewitness accounts, mainly interviews with people who'd found the bodies. The police psych consult had put together a profile of the killer, the details of which Jeremy insisted on reading rather than discussing.

None of it fit what he knew about Hailey.

The police had theories about the perpetrator using trained animals to kill. The victims suggested crimes of convenience. Easy targets to take down for no other reason than being in the wrong place at the wrong time. Possible motives were listed as some sort of political statement for animal habitat conservation or—and this was the one that chilled Jeremy—"Because he could." One theory said that the animals were still in training, being taught to kill on command. Government involvement also made its way into the *Maybe* column. The frightening truth was, this was just the sort of thing the government might do if they knew about the viability of creating shape-shifters and were attempting it.

When Hailey leaned over to read, he moved so she couldn't see. No reason to alarm her yet. The Special Unit had managed to keep details about their unique abilities off government radar this long despite intense curiosity aimed their way, and they would continue to hold their ground. There was nothing in their charter that said only telepaths were eligible candidates. Hunt was already an honorary member—only because he was too… Hunt to join officially. For their aid five years ago, both he and Dara were under the Unit's protection. Jeremy would make sure Hailey would be, too.

If she survives.

She would. She had to.

Jeremy put the file back on the chief's desk more roughly than he'd intended, earning strange looks from both O'Reilly and Hailey. He cleared his throat. "I think I've seen all I need to here. With your permission, we'd like to see the body now."

The chief nodded, still frowning. "Follow me."

The walk down to the morgue was tense. Jeremy let the chief lead the way and kept pace with Hailey. She wouldn't look at him and ignored every attempt he made to get her attention.

A short talk with the medical examiner was all it took. They were given disposable garb and a menthol ointment for the smell. Once again Hailey hesitated, but made herself move forward. Jeremy could feel the effort it took her.

—*You don't have to do this,*— he told her.

She ignored him. One of these days he would have to explain to her that not every suggestion he made was a challenge to be met and answered. She was fighting him needlessly.

The criminal morgue was relatively small for a metropolis like this. There was only one wall of metal drawers and two autopsy tables. Everything was gleaming clean, but the faint stench of death was ever-present. It was more psychological than physical. This facility was state-of-the-art, so their air filtration systems would be, too.

The ME led them to almost the end of the room and opened one of the compartments. When he pulled out the drawer, the body on it was covered with a white cloth. Jeremy was used to seeing things like this.

Hailey wasn't.

She slapped a hand over her mouth, and he heard her swallow hard. She took a couple of deep breaths and pulled her hand away again, taking on the persona of a professional scientist. "Sorry," she said to the ME. "I'm getting over a bad case of food poisoning."

The ME gave her a commiserating smile and said nothing else.

Jeremy had to admire her ability to think on her feet.

He thought she'd lose it again when the white sheet was drawn back, but except for clenching her hands around the drawer's edge, she remained outwardly calm.

"If you need anything, tools or something, let me know," the ME offered congenially.

"T-tools?" Hailey said. "Umm, no, thank you. That won't be necessary. I just need some space, please."

"Of course." The ME left them there alone, but Jeremy could sense him just outside the door. The man was curious, he could tell. Outsiders didn't usually take such an interest in dead bodies.

Jeremy positioned himself to shield Hailey from sight. She looked green. "Are you okay?"

Hailey shook her head.

"Great. What do you need?"

The body was of a nineteen-year-old female. She used to have blonde hair, but it was now dark, stained with blood. Her skin was white, ghostlike, and not at all like a live human being's. Blue tinged her lips, around her eyes, and the tips of her fingers. She'd been dead long enough to look it but not to start decomposing.

Her neck and torso had been ripped open. The file said the injuries were consistent with an animal attack. The injuries were attributed to a large breed of dog, but the scratches were too large and too deep for a positive ID. The findings were inconclusive because of it.

Hailey stared at the body as though in a trance. Jeremy didn't like the look on her face, or that she was so quiet. For long moments, she didn't move. Then she raised a gloved hand and spread her fingers to trace the claw marks, keeping an inch away from the ravaged skin.

Four claw marks, straight and deep. Jeremy could tell where the tips had grazed the skin and where they'd hooked in to tear. Hailey's hand shook over the girl's body, and she pulled it away. "The spacing is about right," she said.

"But you can't be sure."

She shook her head. "I'd have to take impressions and make a model to be sure, but…" Her eyes were haunted. Jeremy didn't have to look inside Hailey's mind to know she was thinking about all the ways she could have done this. Innocent until proven guilty was his policy. Hailey's seemed to be the opposite. She was staring down at the grisly aftermath of a vicious attack, and in her mind, that was evidence of guilt.

Hailey believed herself to be dangerous, and the scientist in her wouldn't let her accept anything less than cold, factual proof to make her change her mind. Jeremy couldn't give her that. All he could do was play devil's advocate and make her see the other side.

"Let's think this through," he said, when he probably should have kept his mouth shut. He couldn't stand the sight of Hailey the way she was now, as though she was drowning. She looked as much a ghost as the dead girl on the table. Jeremy wanted to shake her up, make her angry, make her fight. Anything but this meek acceptance.

It had been a mistake to bring her. She never should have had to see this. He should have stuck to the plan and taken Hailey directly to Torrey.

Stupid.

And reckless. Because what he really wanted to do was shove the drawer back out of sight, take Hailey into his arms and tell her everything would be all right. He wanted to kiss the color back into her lips and feel her breath return. His job was to bring Hailey back to Torrey, not to be her caretaker. He told himself it was all just a pretense to calm her down so he could get her onto the shuttle.

Except it was becoming difficult to see where pretense ended and reality was supposed to begin. Jeremy cleared his throat and dragged his gaze away from Hailey's downcast eyes to the matter at hand. "This girl is five feet, seven inches tall, about a hundred and twenty pounds—"

"It doesn't matter," Hailey said. "It doesn't matter how tall she is, or how much she weighs; whether she knew karate, or had a weapon. She never would have seen it coming. Doesn't take much to take prey down. And once you get that far, it doesn't take much to keep it there." Her voice was hollow as she spoke. She still wouldn't look at him.

Jeremy pulled the white sheet back up to cover the girl's face and break Hailey's stare. "How do you know that?"

Hailey tapped her temple. "It knows. So I know."

"Instinct," he guessed.

Hailey nodded. "Or memory." She put her hand over the girl's forehead. "I remember seeing her. She was wearing a green glitter wig and four-inch platform shoes. She winked at me. Said she loved the hair."

Jeremy took her hand and pushed the drawer back into the wall. "Look at me," he said.

"What if I killed her?" She was losing it; her mind starting to shut down. He had to break her out of it somehow; this was killing him.

"Stop," he ordered. "Look at me." If she went into shock, he'd never get them out of here before someone started asking questions.

She slowly raised her gaze.

"You sensed something last night. Do you remember that?"

Hailey frowned. "Vaguely." That blank look began to fade. It wasn't much, but it was a start. Still not enough; she was still too close to the edge. Jeremy pushed.

"Try harder. Think back. It was something you recognized." If he could just get her to focus on something else…

"I guess. What does it matter?"

He wanted to probe more, ask the things that had been bothering him about this case for a while now. But the window of opportunity slammed shut when he felt the ME decide to butt in. Jeremy let go of Hailey's hand and put a step more distance between them when the morgue door opened. "Everything in order?" the ME called.

"Yes," Jeremy answered. "We're done. Thank you for your time."

"Of course," he said. There was curiosity in his mind. He wanted to get in on whatever Jeremy and Hailey were doing. When neither of them volunteered any information, he said, "If you're ready, I believe the chief is waiting for you upstairs."

"I'm afraid we can't stay," Jeremy told him. "We are expected back at our HQ. Our flight leaves this afternoon."

"It does?" Hailey said, sounding dazed.

"Yeah, I got the message this morning." He took her hand again to lead her out past the ME. "Thanks again," he told the man. "Please convey our gratitude to the chief."

He had them out of the building and into the transport within minutes, and on the road seconds later. Hailey was still as pale as death, even in the light of day. He was starting to worry. "Are you still with me?"

"Where are we going?"

"I'm missing something," Jeremy said. "Can't see the big picture this close to the ground." And he had to. Nothing about this was adding up. Hailey changing Amelia's research, bolting off-world the second she realized she wasn't dead, the attacks, Hailey refusing to come back. For the first time, he didn't believe it was all random. Hailey leaving might have been a knee-jerk reaction, but she wouldn't have kept running unless she had a reason. She wouldn't have avoided Amelia's lab, knowing it was her only chance to save herself.

Damn, he couldn't think! He was becoming too invested in this case. His objectivity was faltering, and it was clouding his judgment. Jeremy didn't care. His instinct told him Hailey was in danger, and he wasn't about to ignore it. The sooner he could get her to Torrey, to his playing field where he knew the surroundings and could control security, the better.

"Can we go to where they found her?"

"What?" Taken aback, he ran a red light and swore. "Why would you want to?"

Hailey looked out the window. She'd pulled her hair back into a ponytail before stepping into the morgue. It was still like that, but he could tell she wasn't comfortable, even with that little constraint. "Maybe if I saw it, I could remember."

"There's nothing to remember."

"You don't know that," she said. "And until I see that place, I won't either."

The transport picked up speed, and he had to make himself ease off the gas. Probably not the smartest idea he'd had, to drive manually when he was this worked up. "What do you expect to find? A sign written in blood on the wall: 'Hailey was here'?"

A pause.

Then, "Maybe."

"And if it's not there, then what?"

Hailey sighed. "Can you please just drive there?"

"Fine," he growled. "It's on the way to the shuttleport. We'll go to the hotel, pack up, and check out. We'll have some time to stop in the alley before the flight."

"Fine," she said and fell silent again.

It was one of those times when Hailey wasn't one hundred percent alert. She'd been having a lot of those lately. And she knew she'd be kicking herself for this one later. A lot.

Jeremy led her across the lobby, civil and accommodating, as if he was trying to project the image of a happy couple to the outside world. He even opened the door for her, and later in the elevator put his arms loosely around her.

All the while he didn't say a word, appearing calm, but Hailey felt the tension in him; knew he was scanning everything and everyone around them. He seemed to have all the bases covered so she just… checked out for a little while. Let her mind shut down briefly to consolidate and process everything. If she didn't think, she wouldn't have to see the dead girl in her mind's eye. She wouldn't wonder if she could have been responsible.

And it wouldn't bother her how her beast was so completely unconcerned and uninterested in all of this. It was bored; annoyed that Hailey was wasting her time and emotion on this when there were so many other, more pleasant things she could do. The animal had no compassion, no remorse, and no guilt.

Hailey shook her head and focused on the screen above the elevator door. It was showing a documentary of some sort. There was a beautiful beach, completely empty and free of human pollution. The water was brilliant in the sunlight and so clear Hailey could see fish swimming in the sea. What she wouldn't give to be there right now.

The elevator dinged, the door opened onto the ninety-fifth floor, and Jeremy guided her down the hallway to their room, one arm around her waist.

The door opened as soon as he stepped up to it, and he closed it behind them right away. "Better get packing, then," he said and headed for his own room. It was such an abrupt change from the close contact earlier, it left her a little disoriented. *Men.* With a philosophical shrug, she turned for her own room. Might as well get to it. No reason to dally.

Shouldn't take too long, anyway; Hailey didn't have all that much to pack. Her riches, jewels, and precious memories were under lock and key in a bank on Miramar. All she had with her were necessities, easily stored and easily gathered in a hurry. She was packed in minutes, but took a few more to just admire her room. This truly was a nice hotel. Hailey might actually miss it. Especially the room service and the delectable food. *Yum.* Just thinking about it made her stomach growl.

Maybe they still had time for one last meal? It would be a shame to miss out on the likes of her dinner last night, or her breakfast this morning. And wasn't another meal included in the price of the room? It'd be rude not to let Jeremy get his money's worth after he paid for all this.

She took her bag to the door and dropped it next to Jeremy's. Where had he gone? "Jer?" she called.

No answer.

Too much to hope he was calling in an order with room service? Hailey sighed. Probably. Agent Starched Underpants didn't seem the type to stray from his schedule once he'd set it, and they had an appointment with a crime scene—*gulp*—and a flight to some backward nowhere planet to catch. "Hey, Agent Calen!" she called again, tamping down her disappointment. "We got places to be, remember?"

Nothing.

What was his deal?

Her senses kicked in too late.

Hailey's lips drew back in a snarl. Her head dropped a little lower, eyes sharp, but there was nothing to see. Goddamn telepath back at his tricks again. Had he left her? She scented the air, but they'd spent too much time in this room. Both their scents were all around her and she couldn't tell if they were fresh or not.

The floor squeaked the tiniest bit, and she whirled around just in time to feel the sting of the tranq dart in her chest, rather than her shoulder.

It was a strong one. Hailey's head swam even as the curses she thought up slurred in her mind. Jeremy caught her against him when her knees gave out.

"I'm sorry," he said against her temple. Did he just kiss her head? "I can't risk you going to that alley." Her eyes closed, but his last words still reached her halfway to dream world. "It's not about what you might find, but what you might not." Then there was nothing.

– 11 –

August 10, 3032 – Planet Torrey

She was dreaming again. Jeremy swore and poured himself another drink. He'd been doing that a lot ever since he'd passed security on Torrey and drove them to a hotel. Hailey had changed far more than even she realized. The tranquilizer he'd used to knock her out back on Reynard Colony was the same one Amelia had used on Hunt more than once. It had knocked him out cold.

Hailey wasn't completely unconscious. He doubted even the sedatives they'd used on the both of them on the shuttle had rendered her that way. She was just… sleeping. Curled in a tight ball on the bed, with her head bent over her hands, breathing in rapid, short pants, sleeping.

And dreaming.

And for some reason he couldn't block those frequencies from invading his mind. Just like every other time one or both of them had dreamed, the images and sensations leaked through whether they wanted them to or not. He couldn't reason it out even as he analyzed his own mind and the strange connection he seemed to have with Hailey.

It was similar to what Dara had described about her connection to the murderer five years ago, in that it seemed to have sprung out of nowhere. But unlike in Dara's case, Jeremy wasn't wholly aware of the link. It wasn't a connection to conscious thought he could easily perceive and control. It was on a completely different level and not at all... concrete.

It felt like the makings of a connection. The building blocks were all in place but not arranged cohesively. Subconsciously, he could only get close to Hailey through it, not actually touch her thoughts. If he were sleeping now, he'd probably catch glimpses, maybe feel a fraction of what she was feeling.

Because he was awake, his mind automatically tuned into those frequencies and did what he'd trained it to do—sorted through everything, gave it meaning and context. Which in this case meant that he might as well be in her dream with her. Except he was still *here*, too.

Nothing he did helped. He'd tried turning away from her—out of sight usually meant out of mind for him. He'd tried leaving the room. He'd gone to the bar downstairs and when he got there, one of the images in her dreams was so graphic, he'd ordered a bottle and resigned himself to riding this storm out to its bitter end.

She was dreaming about her transformation. The study that had gone into creating the serum, the wait until Amelia finally left the lab. The near-lethal injection and the horrific pain that had followed. He saw a rerun of Amelia's memories, only this time, they were from Hailey's perspective.

Pain. Confusion. Blood everywhere, and a strange female speaking to her of things she somehow understood but didn't want to hear. The flashing emergency lights confused and frightened her. She reacted like a cornered, wounded animal.

His heart beat double time; his breaths came short. Jeremy felt as though it was him in her place in that lab. Panic attack tempered by a brief outburst of instinct and aggression. Self-preservation winning the battle over fear. His hands shook, and he rubbed his chest to relieve the ache inside. He knew that whatever Hailey had gone through, she'd done it to herself with full knowledge of all the repercussions.

But that didn't stop him from wanting to get in that bed with her and pull her against him, somehow shelter her from the frantic storm of her nightmarish memories. Hailey was singularly the bravest, most reckless and brilliant person he'd ever met. Most people glowed. Hailey shone bright like a star. She put her whole self into everything she did, put everything on the line, taking tremendous risks.

And she didn't even seem to realize how vulnerable she left herself.

Jeremy reached down to pet her hair. He wanted to help her through this somehow. Even if it was just to offer some small comfort. "It's all right, Hailey," he murmured. "Just a dream." He'd entered her dreams before, with disastrous results. This time, he let them play out, remaining a detached observer. "You're safe now, baby. I'm here." He sat at the edge of her bed, sifting her snow-white hair through his fingers. "You're not alone."

She calmed for a moment, a stray image fluttering like a butterfly across his vision. He saw himself, that night in the procession, dancing and smiling. His arms were around her and she felt… felt…

His vision split again, plunging him back into her dreams.

The run to her den was excruciating on her hands and feet, yet she didn't even notice, the pain just one more among many by that point. Jeremy saw what came after that, too. The shock of her own reflection, the need to flee from it, to go somewhere far away.

He saw the places she'd been. The things she'd seen… It was as if she was reliving the past few months, only none of it was in any kind of order. Just trying to make sense of it all was making his head pound.

Jeremy found himself going to the door again in a daze.

But when he opened it, Hunt stood on the other side.

Ah, shit.

The result of the first successful genetic alteration. A real live shape-shifter who thrived. Tristan Hunt had adapted so well to his animal side that he now resembled it. He was tall, larger than Jeremy remembered him being at their first meeting. His hair was now streaked all the time, and when he got mad, his green eyes changed to glowing gold, and his skin became tattooed with tiger stripes.

He was also a telepath, a much stronger one than Jeremy.

Hunt stared him down, his massive arms crossed over his chest. He shrugged one shoulder an infinitesimal amount. "You don't call, you don't write… and then you drag another shifter to my territory."

It wasn't usually wise to piss this guy off. He took his role of protecting his mate very seriously. If he judged Hailey to be a threat, he wouldn't hesitate to take her out. "It's not your territory," Jeremy retorted, not in the least bit cowed. "It was my home before it was yours."

"Some would say might makes right."

"And others would say fuck off."

Hunt's mouth twitched. "Touché."

"Good. Glad we got that straightened out. Bye-bye now."

When he tried to close the door, Hunt splayed one big hand on it to stop him. "Aren't you going to invite me in?"

"Clearly, no."

"You know I'm coming in whether you want me to or not, right? I mean, you *are* inside my head right now, aren't you?"

Actually, he wasn't. Hunt had mental shields Jeremy wouldn't be able to penetrate with a tank firing atom bombs, so he'd stopped trying a long time ago.

But apparently Hunt had no such problems with entering his mind. He made a disappointed *tsk-tsk* sound. "You're slipping, Jer."

"Don't call me that."

Hunts eyebrows rose slowly. "I think I'll have to meet this female." And then he let himself in. Out of a sense of self-preservation, and because there was really nothing he could do to stop the man, Jeremy stepped out of the way. Hunt actually stopped in his tracks and hesitated for a moment when he crossed the threshold. He tilted his head to one side, then muttered a gruff, "Interesting," and continued on straight to the bedroom where Hailey slept.

He paused again in the doorway, studying her for a few seconds. "She's cute," he said, and he sounded surprised.

Hailey was so much more than just *cute*. She was beautiful. Stunning. Jeremy hadn't known her before her transformation, but there was an innate grace to her that her animal had merely enhanced. Hailey was a sensuous creature and it was so much more alluring because it wasn't manufactured to fit the occasion.

"Now don't start going all poetic on me. You know I hate that."

Said the man who built a *castle* for the woman he loved. Literally, a castle with stone walls, a bailey, stables, Jeremy didn't even know how many rooms, an armory, and a dungeon. The last two, they used as wine cellars.

Hunt glared at that.

"Can you at least *pretend* you don't know what I'm thinking?"

That seemed to genuinely confuse him. "Why? What would be the point?"

Jeremy groaned. "Never mind."

Hunt shrugged and turned to Hailey. Then he looked back at Jeremy. "So you and her…"

"Me and her… what?"

Hunt snorted and shook his head, silently mocking him.

When he took a step toward Hailey, Jeremy started forward on instinct. "That's close enough."

"Try to remember, Jeremy, she's the animal here, not you."

Jeremy wanted to kill him.

Hunt dropped down into a crouch to put his face level with Hailey's and sucked in a sharp breath. "Christ, how does she stand it?"

Still seeing her dream memories flitter across his mind's eye, none of them pleasant, Jeremy had a good idea what Hunt was talking about, but he asked anyway. "Stand what?" *The desolation? The complete disconnect from humanity? The loneliness in knowing she was the only one of her kind on the planet—whichever planet she happened to be on? Or the fear and shame that she could, and might already have, hurt people in horrible ways?*

"The cage."

He frowned. "What cage?"

Hunt shook his head. "It's not something I can explain. I'd have to show you."

"Oh, no thank you."

Hunt glared at him. "I am inviting you in. It's okay to look. You *have to* look so you know what you're dealing with."

Jeremy just crossed his arms over his chest.

"For Hailey," Hunt said.

Son of a bitch. "Okay, fine. Where do you want me to look?"

"Just look. It'll be obvious."

Jeremy dropped back into the seat he'd left before and closed his eyes. He let himself into Hunt's mind, making the trip as short as possible. As soon as he was in, Hunt's growl-voice reverberated all around him. *—You have all the subtlety of a stomping elephant.—*

—I wasn't trying to be subtle,— Jeremy retorted. Subtle took time. The last thing he wanted was more time in Hunt's head.

There was more grumbling but it was wordless, more animal than human; a sound of displeasure.

Jeremy ignored it and opened his mind's eye to look around. He remembered this place; it was the forest where Dara had gotten lost. It was different than he remembered it; softer somehow, more defined and detailed, if that was even possible. This was the tiger's den. There was a soft nest in the middle of a circle formed by giant tree roots. Bugs hissed, birds sang, sunlight streamed in through the treetops like laser beams. Very picturesque for someone who claimed not to like poetry.

—It's home,— Hunt said. *—And it's not just for me.—*

Of course. This was the den for his mate and soon for their cubs, too.

Jeremy blinked and he was somewhere else. Now, there was sunlight everywhere; he was in a meadow, with a big glittering lake off to the right. The forest was behind him; a huge dark stain on the scenery. *—What am I supposed to be seeing?—*

—This,— Hunt replied, and appeared in front of him as a man. The man then transformed, becoming a tiger, then the tiger became a man again. *—Freedom.—*

Jeremy was expelled from Hunt's mind so quickly, it made him dizzy. "I don't get it."

"She lives in a cage," Hunt said.

"*You* lived in one for years, and you turned out just fine."

Hunt looked at him like he was stupid. "You really *don't* get it. A cage in body. Never in mind. That's the one thing I never gave up. The freedom of my thoughts. I embraced the tiger because I wanted to. I was curious about it, and it was curious about me."

"Hailey didn't do that," Jeremy finished as understanding dawned.

Hunt shook his head. "She did something different. It's like she split her mind, tried to keep herself separate from the animal. But she did it wrong. It's unstable and it's hurting her. Both of them, actually." For the first time Jeremy saw pity in the big guy's eyes.

"She's doing all right."

"Is she?" Hunt turned and sat on the floor with his back propped against the bed. "Let me guess. She has no control over the animal. She changes even in small ways when her emotions are too strong, and the more she changes the less she remembers. Am I right?"

"So what? You change when you get emotional, too."

"But the difference is, I never check out. I'm always there, and I know what the animal is doing every step of the way. Hailey… it's like flipping a switch. And you know that, because when you look into her mind, all you see is her or the beast. Never both at the same time."

"But Hailey remembers bits and pieces of the leopard's memories. She is aware of its presence."

"The cage isn't solid," Hunt explained. "It's like two beings on either side of iron bars; they can see through, can reach out and touch each other, but can never cross."

"So what do you suggest?"

Hunt pushed to his feet. "I suggest we leave the room. She's waking up, and she's not very happy with you, Jer."

"I told you not to call me that."

"Whatever. Unless you want carnage, we should go."

The moment they closed the door, Jeremy felt her become fully conscious.

"You should really consider putting up some boundaries," Hunt said.

"Like you do with Dara?" Jeremy shot back.

"That's different."

Hailey was sitting up now, looking around. Another unfamiliar place, more lost memories. At first the desolation, the disappointment in herself hit him like a kick to the stomach.

"Oh? How so?" he said to Hunt, keeping up the thread of conversation. But both of them were staring at the door, waiting for Hailey to burst through it.

"She's Dara," Hunt said simply, as if that was reason enough for everything.

Jeremy knew the exact moment when Hailey remembered what had happened. There was a crash—the liquor bottle shattering against the wall—and a string of loud curses.

"Damn," Hunt said. "If I didn't know better, I'd say she hates your guts."

"But you know better."

"Yeah. Right now, she hates way more of you than just your guts."

She was going to kill him. Hailey was going to let the leopard have her merry way and rip him to shreds. And she'd do it with glee and joy in her heart and damn the consequences. Dying would be worth it if she managed to dispatch *him* before she kicked the bucket.

That goddamn piece of shit bastard mind reader had knocked her out without giving any thought to what it might do to her. He could have knocked out her human side and triggered a full shift. He could have killed her!

He simply had to die.

He'd probably lived a full life. Seen things in other people's minds as if he'd lived them himself. Who knew what kinds of adventures he'd had without ever leaving a planet? There would be nothing to regret. Not like he would be missing out on anything. It was his time.

As far as she was concerned, that was the danger of living more than his fair share of life. He'd exhausted all of the possibilities prematurely, so Nature—meaning Hailey—would be shutting him down. Now. This very minute.

Him, and the son of a bitch he'd dragged to her while she'd slept. She scented another. A male. What the hell was this? Would he make a paying circus attraction out of her now?

Bastard was sooo going down.

Ugh. And she was still wearing the same clothes from, what, a day ago? Two? She actually *smelled.* What the hell!

"Where are you, you asshole?" she yelled. "You better start praying!" Funny, though, she wasn't going all leopard claw. Not even a hint of fangs. Did he think he could manipulate her now? Fine. She'd just kick his ass the good old-fashioned human way.

Hackles standing on end, hair wild, she followed her nose to the door that led out of the room. When she tore it open, the bastards, both of them, stood there without a care in the world. "You"—she pointed to Jeremy—"are a dead man." To the other one she said, "You can wait your turn."

The stranger actually laughed at her. "Oh, I like her."

It set her teeth on edge. "You wanna be first? Fine by me."

His easy smile turned into a snarl. Were his eyes glowing? "You don't want to mess with me, little girl."

"Back off, Hunt," Jeremy said.

Hunt? *The* Hunt. What the hell was he doing in her room? She tilted her head to one side. "So you're the boy who lived. That makes us practically family. Guess it's true you can't pick your relatives."

Hunt snorted. "You should be so lucky. I'll bet you would have preferred me to that deadbeat you call a father."

Her eyes widened. No way...

Hunt tapped his temple with a couple of fingers. "Amazing what the mind can do."

No way! "Are you kidding me?" she yelled. "There are more of you? And who the hell gave you permission to snoop around inside my head?"

"Oh, she's prickly."

"I said back off, Hunt," Jeremy said. "Just get out. I can handle this."

"*Handle* this?" Hailey repeated.

"Oh yeah, I can see you're a real pro," Hunt deadpanned.

Hailey snarled and attacked. She didn't care which one of them. Both were going down, so what did it matter?

Hunt didn't even let her get close. He did something—and *Holy shit!* she didn't even register what—and she went flying back against the wall. The picture frame shattered behind her, glass shards digging into her skin before both she and the glass dropped to the floor. *Ow!*

The pain infuriated her more, and she felt the leopard mirror her. It would take over soon, and for once, Hailey wanted to let it. Finally she felt fangs in her mouth, and her claws lengthen and dig into the floor. But when she set her sights on Hunt again, he wasn't even looking at her.

Probably because Jeremy had a gun trained on him, a twitchy-looking finger on the trigger. *Shoot him,* she thought to him. If he dispatched Hunt, it meant less work for her. Then she'd just have to kill one of them.

"*Shut up,*" he snapped. At her. What the hell was this? Hailey was the only one in this company with any right to be pissed off. He didn't get to rain on her ass kickage. Claws dug deeper into the floor, scratching long grooves.

"She's losing it," Hunt said calmly, and she knew he was saying it for her benefit. They were both telepaths. Whatever they had to say to each other, they didn't have to say out loud. "If you delude yourself into thinking you can deal with this, she'll kill you before you can blink."

The male was catching on.

"Leave, or I shoot," Jeremy said.

Hunt's hands changed, claws lengthening. His were bigger than Hailey's. Of course. He had to be all fancy and have a beast that was the largest big cat in the animal kingdom. But her beast was still prettier. That was why she'd chosen it.

"She needs to be controlled," Hunt said. "It's obvious she can't do it by herself."

"*She*," Hailey repeated, her voice deeper, more like a growl, and her words hissing between her fangs, "has your scent now, asshole. *She* can track you back to your den. And whatever *she* finds there, will bleed."

The next few seconds were a blur. Hunt snarled and charged her; she pushed up to retaliate; then the gun went off and they froze, each looking at the other for injuries. Hailey's back was bleeding from the glass shards, but she didn't feel any other pain. Then again, given the state she was in, she probably wouldn't feel a bullet through her lung.

Jeremy stepped between them and shoved Hailey behind him, gun trained on Hunt again. "Touch her again, and I will kill you."

"You helped save Dara," Hunt said, his voice a low growl somehow formed into syllables. "That is the only reason why I'm not ripping both your throats out right now. But if she comes near me or mine again, I *will* kill her."

"Noted. Now get the fuck out."

Hailey couldn't see past Jeremy, but she heard the growl and then the door slamming shut. It was a feeble barrier against a man like that, she knew, but it still made her feel a little braver, and she stepped out from behind Jeremy to go after Hunt.

He caught her arm in a bruising grip and snatched her back to face him. "Are you suicidal?" he yelled. "What the hell is wrong with you? How could you even think of threatening his mate like that?"

His hand on her was shaking, and he looked absolutely furious, but there was fear in his eyes. Hailey broke away from him. "You still have yours coming," she told him.

"Grow the hell up. I'm getting sick and tired of your hissy fits. In case it escaped your notice, I just saved your life. Any time you want to thank me for that, feel free. Otherwise, I wouldn't mind a little peace and quiet."

Wow. He got sexy when he was mad.

Oh, now where had *that* come from?

That tranq was seriously messing with her head. Or maybe the adrenaline spike was causing her to get stupid. Either way, she itched to get physical and she didn't particularly care how. She could go after Hunt, or beat the hell out of Jeremy, or tear his clothes off and screw his brains out. None of the options were mild, or gentle, or ladylike. She felt wild, out of control, and at the same time it was as if she had a clear goal. *Work off the steam.*

And she still smelled, and now she had blood on her. That miniscule part of her still capable of disgust made her shudder. "I'm going to go take a bath," she said in as reasonable a tone as she could. "It would be in your best interest not to be here when I come out."

"Why? So you can go after Hunt again? I don't think so."

"Such deep concern for my welfare," she said, her tone cutting. "If I didn't know any better, I'd think you actually care about me." It was the perfect opening to either trigger a confrontation—which, given all of the angry sparks crackling in the air between them would lead to the kind of sex that left you utterly boneless—or shut her down with a single, well-aimed verbal arrow.

Jeremy didn't do either.

He backed away and turned to stare out the window as if he was pretending he was out there instead of in here with her.

Apparently he didn't need words to shut her down. "Good thing I know better," Hailey said, for some reason disappointed with his non-answer. She spun on the balls of her feet and silently padded to the bathroom.

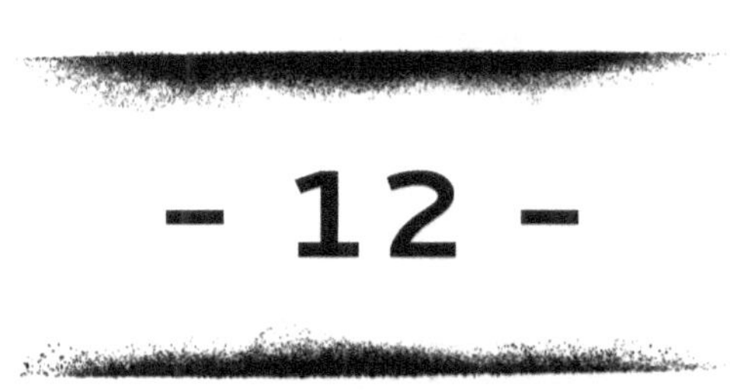

- 12 -

What the hell just happened? One minute he'd been watching Hailey sleep, and the next he'd been shooting at the ceiling and getting between two seriously pissed-off shape-shifters, hell-bent on ripping each other to pieces. Real smart.

How the hell had his life come to this? It couldn't all be coincidence. One decision to accept a case did not just spiral into chaos by accident. There had to be some kind of force out there with a grudge against him. Something wanting to screw with his life.

Jeremy leaned his forehead against the cool glass of the window. Oh, there was a force with a grudge, all right. Only it wasn't out there, it was in here, and it had a name.

Hailey.

He tried to remember the last time he'd had this much trouble keeping a situation under control. Then he realized something he'd been in denial about for weeks now. This particular situation had never been under control to begin with. It was a perfect storm of trouble. Everything was wrong, or going wrong, or about to go wrong, and apparently there was not a damn thing he could do about it.

Like Hailey.

From the moment he saw her, his mind had gone haywire. He couldn't corral his thoughts worth a damn around that woman, could barely keep a civil tongue in his head, and he might as well forget about using his mental tricks to win her over. He kept getting dragged over to her side instead. Willing or not. *Conscious* or not.

What the hell was it about her that made his higher intellect shut down and take a vacation? He was a telepath, for Christ's sake. He ought to be able to look into her head, find out what she wanted, and deliver. Easy.

Wrong. All wrong. From beginning to end, that process failed again and again.

First, getting inside that woman's head was like beating his own against the wall. Either she knew what he was doing and confused the fuck out of him with her portents of doom, or she didn't and confused the fuck *into* him with thoughts a nun would flail herself for in penance for a year. It was getting to the point where his dreams were tame in comparison.

Never had he met a female who needed to get laid more. *Jesus.*

Second, finding out what she wanted was impossible. *She* didn't even know. Hailey was so entrenched in her I'm-dying-alone mentality that her needs and wants were going haywire. Like a woman condemned, she wanted everything and nothing at the same time. She wanted to live her last days out loud, and go slink away to die in private. She wanted to be tough, stand on her own, face the consequences of her actions, but she didn't ever acknowledge that she might need something or someone else in the process.

And as for delivery, well, Jeremy had a proven record of pissing her off like nobody's business.

Damn frustrating woman.

He ought to be escorting her to Amelia's lab right now. He had a job to do. Find Hailey and bring her to Amelia. Simple. Straightforward. An assignment like any other.

Not.

There was no staying professional and detached with Hailey. Everything about her drew him like a moth to the flame. He could see it burning, felt the scorching heat of it all over his body. Knew for a fact that it would eventually reduce him to ash. And still he kept going, kept reaching out to that flame, willing to burn if it meant he could, if only for a second, be warmed by its glow.

Hailey had no idea what it cost him to keep his distance. Every time he saw her eyes cloud over with resignation and he somehow stopped himself from putting his arms around her and kissing her until her eyes glowed liquid again, a crack formed in the walls he'd built for himself to give structure to chaos. There were hundreds of those cracks now. Sooner or later those walls would shatter. What happened after that was anyone's guess. Maybe Jeremy would end up being the one strapped to a table with needles stuck in his arms.

Hailey kept chipping away at his control, stealing it piece by piece. What surprised him was how easily, how willingly he was parting with it.

Even now, when he should be in total damage-control mode, making arrangements to keep Hailey away from Hunt and his family, his head wasn't in the game. *He* was feeling like an animal. Wanted to mark his territory and warn others away.

It was the adrenaline.

No. It was the sight of Hailey going toe to toe with a male twice her size and easily five times her strength.

It was the thought that she was in the shower right now, hot water soaking her, making her body relax and her eyes close as she tipped her head back to rinse her hair.

It was how damn much Jeremy just wanted to be in there with her right now. Wanted it to be his hands rubbing soap into her skin, massaging sore muscles; his chest she leaned against, instead of the cold shower wall.

He wanted *her.*

As if his thoughts had summoned her, he heard the bathroom door open behind him. She didn't make another noise until she cleared her throat from two feet away, but he sensed her approach like a static charge intensifying against his skin.

"What is it?" he said without turning around.

"Look, I wouldn't ask, but there's a piece of glass stuck in my back and I can't reach it to take it out."

Glass? *What?*

What the hell had gone wrong this time? Or rather, what had gone even more wrong?

He turned around to ask and his words died in his throat with a very loud *gulp*. Hailey was holding a towel to her front, her wet hair streaming soft and smooth over one shoulder, her back obviously bare. She looked wide-eyed and hesitant, as if she expected him to yell at her. At the moment, yelling at her was the last thing on his mind.

Her skin was as smooth as silk, so damn inviting, he had to stop himself from reaching for her. The vision of her naked and seductive was still fresh in his memory; he doubted he'd ever get rid of it. Combined with his most recent train of thought, that and the sight of her now, caused a reaction he couldn't hope to disguise. "Turn around," he said, his voice more gruff than he'd intended it to be.

Hailey turned, presenting him with her bleeding back.

Jeremy sucked in a breath and tore his gaze away from her to look for what had caused her injuries. He spotted the giant broken picture on the floor where she'd fallen. She must have slammed into it when Hunt had tossed her back like a rag doll. Anger made his blood run hotter. *I'm going to fucking kill him!* "Why didn't you say anything?"

She shrugged and the small action made one of the deeper scratches emit a fresh drop of blood. "Thought I could handle it on my own."

As usual.

She seemed to have done an impressive job cleaning up most of the cuts, but there were two still bleeding and one, as she'd said, had a small piece of glass still embedded. He firmly kept his gaze above the hollow at the small of her back and the lush curve of her ass barely covered by her pants below it. She'd pushed them as low as she could to keep from getting blood on them. "Go sit down," he said. "I'll need the med kit."

She held it up in her free hand and the towel slipped from her just enough to reveal the side of her breast. Jeremy swayed on his feet. He snatched the box from her quickly before she could see his hand trembling. *Bleeding cuts. Focus on that.* "Sit," he said again.

Hailey picked a chair and straddled it, leaning forward. Jeremy had to kneel to get to eye level with her back. She smelled like hotel soap and heaven. A drop of water trickled down the back of her neck and spine, tempting him to catch it on his tongue and trace its path back up.

Bleeding back, he reminded himself. He was starting to get sick of this stay-detached song and dance. The woman he lo...

He drew back. What. The. Hell… There was something wrong with him.

The woman he cared for… no, that wasn't right, either.

The woman *in his care* was hurt and he'd allowed it to happen. Yes, that's what it was.

Hailey twisted to look back at him. "Something wrong?"

Jeremy shook his head hard. "Face forward."

Hailey rolled her eyes. "Yessir!"

When she did as he told her, her back wasn't just straight, it was the slightest bit arched. It accentuated the groove of her spine and the swell of her ass on the chair. He should have had her sit on his lap.

Focus!

He did. On the fact that he was so close he could feel the heat of her skin through his own clothes. On the slight hourglass curve of her torso and the shape of her legs where her pants stretched taut over them as she sat.

Hailey shivered as if she could feel his gaze, and he kicked himself for it, even while he wondered whether her nipples had beaded against that towel, whether he'd feel them through it if he cupped her breasts. Christ, he wanted to. So damn much.

Bleeding back. Bleeding back!

He cleaned the wounds as best he could with the limited kit. Took his time about it, too, holding the alcohol swabs just right so that his knuckles grazed her skin with every pass, and smoothing the bandage ointment over her skin with exaggerated care.

The one piece of glass he left for last. The shard was about as long as the pad of his pinky, with only a glittering sharp edge peeking out. No wonder she couldn't get it out herself. "Hold still," he warned before he pulled it out and pressed gauze to the wound to stop the bleeding. She didn't even twitch.

Jeremy had to keep pressure on the wound for a moment before he could clean it. While he waited, he imagined his hand skimming the line of her shoulder, down her arm to her side, then slipping beneath that towel to her waist. He'd pull her against him and claim a kiss, a real one, long and deep, until she squirmed and begged for him to touch her.

Hailey shivered again.

"Are you cold?"

She shook her head. Had she seen it? Had he been projecting without realizing it?

"You're being awfully quiet."

"Got nothing to say," she said.

Jeremy shook his head to corral his wayward thoughts. He cleaned the last wound and bandaged it, then washed the last of the dried blood from her back. "All done," he said.

"Thanks," she replied and moved to stand.

Something, some idiot impulse made him stay her with his hands on her bare sides, just below the swell of her breasts. Probably the same idiot impulse that then made him lean forward and brush a kiss over the worst of her wounds.

"What are you doing?" Hailey said. She sounded breathless.

"Kissing it to make it better." He followed that by slowly making his way across her back to all of her wounds and giving each the same attention. The last one was in the hollow at the base of her spine. From there, he trailed his mouth all the way up her back to her nape.

She was panting now, the sound of her breaths loud in the silent room.

Jeremy brushed the sides of her breasts with his thumbs, and with his mouth against her skin, said, "Are you hurt anywhere else?"

Hailey nodded with enough eagerness to make him smile. "I hurt my neck," she said, leaning her head to the side.

"Oh, that could be serious." He pressed an open-mouthed kiss to the spot where her neck met her shoulder, then trailed his mouth and tongue up to her ear. "Anywhere else?" he whispered.

She turned her head a little, then a little more, until their mouths were a breath apart. "I, uh…" Her tongue darted out to moisten her lips. "I bit my tongue when I hit the wall. It really hurts."

It wasn't that he reached forward. It was that Hailey leaned back. All the same, she felt his hands brush her breasts beneath the towel, and her belly tightened, yearning for him to touch her lower. Yearning. She was *yearning*, for crying out loud.

Jeremy didn't kiss her as soon as she said it, as if he wanted to give her a chance to take it back. But when he did kiss her, it took her breath away. His lips brushed across hers, gentle but sure. He caught her lower lip, licked across it, nibbled and let it slip out from between his teeth. Then he was back, teasing her mouth open, but she only felt the tip of his tongue across her teeth. Her entire body tensed, and she held her breath for him to delve deeper. Clutching the towel with one hand and the back of the chair with the other, she waited.

Another teasing lick, a gentle kiss, and then he pulled away. "That better?"

"No." She pouted. "I think it'll need a lot more attention than that."

That must have been his cue because he pulled her flush against him and kissed her hard. No more measured seduction, no more taking it slow. Hailey tasted pure, unadulterated need, and she loved it. She let go of the towel and brought her knee up, intending to turn around and face him, but he wouldn't let her.

With one arm around her waist, he hoisted her up out of the chair, then sat in it himself with her in his lap. His knees spread, taking hers along with them, and her back arched in response, pressing her harder against his erection. Hailey sucked in air, eager to feel him inside her. Jeremy hooked his ankles around hers to keep her in place. She was practically immobile from the waist down but Hailey could reach back, and she did, greedy hand searching, needing to touch him. She mussed his hair, scratched his neck and shoulder, and with her free hand took one of his and brought it to her breast. She felt him groan and it elicited a sympathetic shiver from her as he filled his hands with her flesh, squeezing and caressing, brushing across her nipple just barely, making it pucker and strain for more thorough attention.

Her mind flooded with images. Hailey had always considered herself a woman of the world. She'd never been the shy type, and she'd enjoyed her life to the fullest while it had still been normal. But what she now saw in her mind's eye was beyond even her imaginings.

In that place she knew couldn't possibly be real, candlelight danced all around her, casting intricate shadows that moved. The shadows reached out to her, caressed her, brushed into her hair, leaving not an inch of her untouched. It was like her dream, except this time, she knew exactly who was with her. Jeremy's face took shape among those shadows. He smiled, then dipped his mouth to her skin, kissing and licking until she was out of breath, gasping his name.

He was everywhere, all around her, the most solid thing in this world. His touch was ecstasy; his kiss beyond words. But no matter how hard she tried, she couldn't touch him in return. Hailey's hand slipped through him as if he were no more than mist. In return, his fingers found her clit, and she nearly screamed at the exquisite touch. His mouth came down on hers, tongue teasing her lips apart, slipping between them. She matched him but tasted nothing but air.

Jeremy made her feel amazing things while letting her touch nothing. She was at his mercy, completely possessed by his will, and his alone. She felt him searching through her thoughts like a warm caress. He zeroed in on what she needed, amplified it, intensified the craving, until she wanted to claw herself out of her skin.

And then he gave her exactly what she needed, how she needed it, and more. God help her, she loved it.

She was on fire. She was dizzy with want so intense she trembled. Everything he did to her here only satisfied her mind, while stoking her body's craving into a frenzy of heat. He kept her on that razor's edge, letting her come so close to an orgasm but holding it just out of reach. The illusion was just that, but the mind believed what it wanted to. It was like a wet dream, only the reality matched it this time. Hailey was really there with Jeremy, and his hands were really touching her, amping up the pitch to impossible heights.

He pinched her nipple lightly in that shadowy place inside her mind, matched the action in the physical world, and she cried out, arching into his hand. The shadows formed into a hand and it slid and slipped over her clit, down to her entrance, teasing back and forth… back and forth… stealing inside her and stroking so slowly, filling her just so much, but still not enough. Not nearly. He was tormenting her on purpose, compounding the illusion with physical touch, confusing her mind so that all she could do was feel.

In and out—she moaned.

Back and forth—she clutched the chair for balance as the world tipped around her.

In and out while his mouth played at her breast.

Back and forth while she went out of her head, straining ever closer.

The sensations merged and melded until she couldn't tell the difference between illusion and reality anymore. She felt Jeremy everywhere, stroking her, teasing her, building up to a single blinding moment of overwhelming pleasure. Finally, he allowed her to reach it.

Hailey came so hard, her back arched away from Jeremy and her claws dug into the chair. The illusion gave way in that moment, and Hailey was back in the hotel, on Jeremy's lap, with one of his hands still cupping her breast, and the other between her legs, on the *outside* of her pants, barely touching her sex.

Jeremy stood with her. As soon as her feet touched the ground, she spun around and jumped him, hooking her legs around his waist and squeezing tight, relishing his groan of pleasure. He was hard against her. Hailey licked her lips, eager for a taste of him. Any taste. For now, she settled on his mouth. His step faltered, and he paused to savor the kiss, letting her set the pace, then guiding her to his own rhythm.

This one could match me, she'd thought when they'd met. Now she knew it for certain. It made her kiss that much harder, her touch that much more, feeling as if this was a game, a contest she had to win. Yet every time she thought she'd proved herself, Jeremy did something that undid her. His hand caressed up her spine to cup her nape, his finger brushed across it, and her kiss gentled, calmed. This wasn't a fight, and he wasn't about to compete with her.

In that moment, she felt so utterly vulnerable, tears stung her eyes. Jeremy groaned and kissed her deeper, the hand at her nape dropping down to the curve of her ass and she was back, straining for more, urging him on until he moved again toward the bedroom. His shirt was all buttoned up and with every step he took, she bounced, and the fabric abraded her nipples.

They were kissing like there was no tomorrow. Like they couldn't live without their lips touching. Hailey didn't want to break the contact even to take a breath. Finally standing by the bed, he set her down again so he could take his shirt off. He didn't bother with the buttons, just ripped them off and discarded the now useless rag. Then he pulled her back against him, skin against skin this time, and just held her like that for entire seconds, without moving at all. Just feeling.

Nothing Jeremy had imagined could compare to the real thing. Hailey was molten heat, wrapped in silk and velvet. He'd watched her come. In her abandon, the faintest rosettes had bloomed along her skin; leopard markings there one second and gone the next. It was the most erotic thing Jeremy had ever seen, and he couldn't wait to see it again.

He picked her up again and laid her back onto the bed. She was writhing, eyes unfocused, a thing of beauty.

Jeremy kissed his way down her throat to her breasts. It seemed like he'd been waiting forever to suckle these. She had the most beautiful breasts. Full and round, with perky, dark pink nipples, eager for his touch. He lavished each with attention, licked and sucked and nibbled until she was moaning so loud, he thought the neighbors would complain.

She was wearing linen pants. No zippers or buttons; just one tie. Easy to put on and oh-so easy to slip back off. He tossed them over his shoulder, and they floated down on top of his ruined shirt, creating a neat little pile. He'd be adding to it soon.

But first…

Ah, now this was a stunning sight. Auburn curls crowning God's most amazing creation. Jeremy smoothed his hands over Hailey's thighs, felt her muscles jump beneath his touch. He gently guided her mind fully back to him, directing her focus to the physical sensation of touch. He wanted her feeling everything he was about to do to her with fullest intensity.

Hailey felt Jeremy's touch and purred. He kissed her, and her back arched off the bed. "Oh. My. God!" He kissed her like he'd kissed her mouth, licking up her elixir and coaxing more from her, and then he sucked her clit while he thrust his fingers into her. In. Out.

Merciful heaven…

In. Out.

Oh fuck…

In. Out.

She writhed against his mouth, and Jeremy ground his hips into the mattress, licking in bliss.

Hailey's nails were claws, tearing the bedsheets. She was losing it, her skin erupting in leopard patterns she no longer could hold back. *Beautiful.* Wild and exotic; he couldn't look away. She wore the markings as if they had always been a part of her. He thrust two fingers inside her, raising his head to watch her face when she came. He wasn't sharing her mind now. If he felt her come again, he'd spill instantly. Just the feel of her squeezing his fingers still deep inside her eroded his iron will.

Jeremy released her and rested his forehead on the crease where her thigh met her body. "I think I just found my new favorite hobby," he said.

Hailey laughed huskily. He relished the sound. Pressed a kiss to her sensitive abdomen, making her twitch. He couldn't stop touching her. "Sounds like fun," she said. "I think I'll give it a try."

His cock shot impossibly harder. She was already imagining it, and Jeremy could feel it—her breath on his shaft, her hands squeezing the base, the heat of her mouth on the head. And—*ah, Christ*—her wicked, wicked tongue. He almost lost it before he even entered her. Hailey could bring him to his knees with just a thought. And this one was *eager.*

He growled. Before she could even sit up to take charge, he was on all fours over her, pinning her in place. "Oh no, you won't. I plan for this to last a good long while."

"You know what they say about the best laid plans," she teased, reaching for the waistband of his pants. Her feet were almost at the edge of the bed. If she got enough leverage she could slide down before he could stop her.

With a pained noise ripped from his core, Jeremy caught her wandering hands. "Don't worry, you'll get laid plenty well," he promised.

Hailey heaved a dramatic sigh and let her arms fall wide of her body like a willing sacrifice. "Oh, fine. Have it your way. Main course before dessert."

"Your enthusiasm is overwhelming," he said dryly.

Hailey raised her head. "Hey, I had plenty of enthusiasm. It got shut down." And to demonstrate, she gave him a thumbs-down and blew a raspberry.

Jeremy chuckled. "Just shut up and kiss me."

Now *that* she was more than willing to do. She threw her arms around his neck and locked her legs around his waist again. He had to either fall over her or rise up to sit on his heels. He went up. She could feel him hard and heavy through his pants and couldn't stop herself from rubbing against him. Jeremy groaned into her mouth and caught her hips to make her be still.

Hailey stopped, but only because she had to in order to get his zipper down and his cock free. She wanted it inside her. Now. They fought over who would do it, hands and fingers clashing, but ultimately Jeremy had the best access so she rose up to let him undo his own pants, then lowered back down, taking his cock in as deep as she could.

He filled her completely and she wriggled her hips the slightest bit to savor the feel of him inside her. He broke the kiss and made her look him in the eye as his hands guided her hips up and down his length, again and again.

Jeremy held her so tightly she could feel his heartbeat against her chest. It was as erratic as hers. His hands caressed her hips, her back, up to her shoulders, and down the center of her spine where she was sure that downy soft fur had sprouted down the center of her back. If anything, it seemed to excite him even more, and he thrust up each time she came down on him.

There were no more illusions. No manipulation or confusion. Looking into his eyes, Hailey felt to her core that this was real. And everything she felt was so sharp and poignant, no illusion could ever hope to surpass it. Here and now, with Jeremy looking at her as if she was the most amazing thing in the world and all his, Hailey glimpsed a little piece of Heaven.

Pleasure built and built inside her again, and he sent her over the edge with one deep, lingering thrust. Hailey let her head fall back on her shoulders and felt the world spin when he leaned over her, laying them both back on the bed. Amid the ringing in her ears, she thought she heard him shout her name.

Jeremy pumped his hips again and groaned into her shoulder as he came, too. She felt him spurt hotly inside her and too late remembered to worry about birth control. But only for a moment. This was as close to true happiness as she'd come since this whole mess had begun. She wasn't about to let anything spoil it.

He didn't lower his weight fully on top of her. Instead, he hooked her knee over his hip and rolled them to the side. "You know that new hobby I mentioned?"

"Mm-hmm?" she purred.

"I think I just found a new one."

Hailey chuckled. "*Finally*, something we have in common."

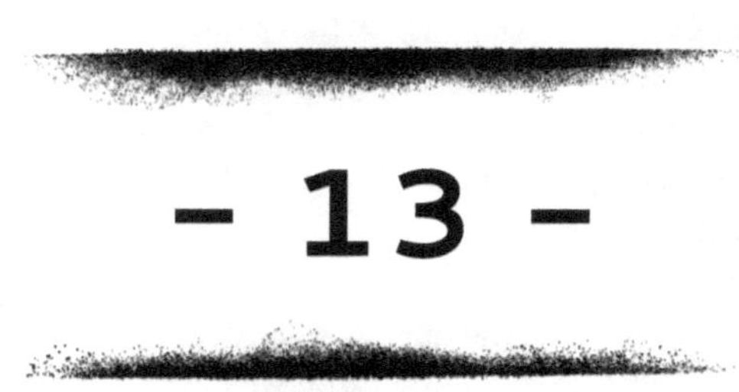

– 13 –

It was raining outside. The romantic kind of rain that fell softly to the ground and sent lovers scurrying for cover under a tree. Except it was nighttime, so it was more the kind that usually lulled people into the best sleep of their lives. Hailey listened to the gentle hiss and the tinkle where the rain dripped onto a metal awning over the windows. Her body was sated, her beast purred, and her mind drifted. Her eyes wanted to close, and still she couldn't sleep.

Wouldn't let herself was more accurate.

Jeremy was sleeping next to her, the sound of his breathing as hypnotic as the rain. He looked so peaceful. Everything around her was so tidy, and ordered, and… normal. It just didn't fit.

Hailey tried to insert herself into the scene, pretend for a moment that she was just a normal person falling asleep in her lover's bed. It would be so easy to forget everything and just let go for a few hours. She was almost certain that if she just closed her eyes, she'd sleep through the night. Peacefully.

But it just didn't fit. It wasn't who she was anymore. Hailey was the failed experiment. She'd damaged herself, most likely beyond repair. Looking at this as anything resembling a lasting phenomenon was pointless. She'd be dying soon. If she shifted, it would be even sooner.

She'd known this for a long time. That she'd lasted this long was astonishing. Hailey wasn't feeling sorry for herself. She'd known the risks going into this, and she'd do it again even knowing what awaited her. That wasn't the point. The point was...

The point was that she'd dragged someone else into this, something Hailey had had no right to do. Jeremy wasn't like her. He looked at the world through knowing eyes. Whatever he didn't know, he made a point of learning. Whatever he was unfamiliar with, he studied. He left nothing up to chance and thus wasn't the type of person to *take* a chance. He dealt with certainty. Hailey wasn't even sure she knew what that word meant anymore.

Oh sure, he said he believed in people until they proved him wrong, but those were people who were part of his job. People he met on a job, socialized with for its duration, and then forgot about once the job was done.

Hailey had glanced at his open wallet. Okay, fine, she'd snooped through his things and *accidentally* dropped his wallet so it would fall open. She'd seen pictures of a young girl; a pretty, doe-eyed redhead who resembled him. It had to be his sister. And from the looks of it, she was a big part of his life.

Jeremy wouldn't take a chance because it wasn't just himself he had to think about. Anything he allowed into his life would affect his sister, too. And so he wouldn't risk taking a chance on Hailey unless he believed in her.

Unless he believed she was safe, in every sense of the word.

And that was one long, roundabout way of saying that Jeremy had slept with her because he believed this thing between them would be going somewhere. She'd bet her last penny that the phrase *one night stand* or *a condemned man's last meal* had never even entered his mind.

A shame, for both of them, because that was all she had to offer. Hailey didn't have a future to consider spending with him. For her, there was only now. And that was A-OK with her. She'd always lived for the moment long before the moment had become all she had left.

But looking at Jeremy, she felt a stab of regret. What could have been? What might have been? If she'd never opened Amelia's files, never changed herself, would she have even met him? And if she had, would she have even bothered to slow down long enough to truly look at him?

Probably not. Living life to the fullest, always surrounded by friends, people who sought her out for a good time and left again until there were more good times to be had, she wouldn't even have seen him except as part of the scenery she was moving past at the speed of light.

Just then, Jeremy opened his eyes. Her night vision was exceptional, but his irises still looked more black than blue. He closed his eyes again, as if everything was the way it should be and then, with a sigh, stretched toward her and pulled her closer. "Something wrong?" he asked, and though he looked as if he was about to fall asleep again, Hailey knew he waited for an answer, and would go looking for one if she didn't give it.

"Just thinking."

"'Bout what?"

"Stuff," she said, then added, "Private stuff. So don't go snooping in my head again."

He cracked one eye open to glare at her. "You're unhappy," he said. "Enough that you woke me from a pretty damn happy dream."

"Really? What did you dream?"

Jeremy smiled against her shoulder. "I'll show you."

The bedroom faded in front of her and she slowly entered into a vision. It wasn't a construct. At least not at first. It was a dream, all muted images blending one into the next without coherence except what his mind could connect. She saw… herself. It was almost a rerun of his earlier dreams about her, except this one was somehow more real. Hailey was no longer a top-heavy bombshell with a saucy smile playing on her red lips; she was herself, complete with—*oh damn*—leopard markings in intricate swirling designs appearing and fading over her skin. Was that what she really looked like?

Had to be. And what was more shocking, Jeremy seemed to *like* it. Even more than his earlier version. She sensed the adoration in him, mixed with a hefty pinch of lust as he looked at her.

It was definitely not a tame dream. What his subconscious had conjured for him made what they'd done earlier seem almost boring in comparison. Hailey saw every detail of it through Jeremy's eyes, sometimes even as an observer. The erotic scenes made her breath come faster and her thighs squeeze together. She saw herself in the throes of what looked like the most amazing orgasm of her life and *felt* the pleasure it brought Jeremy to have wrought it from her. But there was no triumph in his vision. No sense of pride in his sexual prowess. Just… awe. Happiness. Almost relief. A sense that nothing could ever be as perfect and complete as that moment.

And that was one more reason she shouldn't be here right now.

He let the vision fade, returning them both to the here and now. The dreamy feeling of contentment stayed with her, mixed with her own roiling emotions.

Why was it that people were offended to get the *It's-not-you-it's-me* speech? Better question: why had people used it so much it had become an insult? Now, even in cases when it actually applied, the words just sent a completely wrong message.

"I'm sorry I woke you," she said, the best she could come up with under the circumstances. "Do you want me to leave?"

He groaned into the pillow. "No, I don't want you to leave. What's wrong with you? I think the last few hours fully demonstrated just how much I don't want you to leave. I want you to talk to me."

That was something she'd never heard a guy say before. Not to her, and definitely not this late at night, after everything they'd done together. Hailey shrugged. "It's nothing. Just the usual stuff."

Jeremy raised his head to look at her. The window was on her side and whatever light filtered in backlit her so he couldn't possibly see more than a shadowy outline. Still, she felt as if he was looking right into her eyes, and beyond them.

"Stop it," she said. "I told you, no snooping."

"Shut up for a second and let me try something. Come here."

Against her protests, he propped himself up on a mountain of those hotel-issued pillows and pulled her to lie against him with her head on his shoulder. He kept an arm around her and stroked her hair with his free hand as if she were a child. Though it felt awkward, it was really nice, too. She couldn't remember the last time someone had babied her like this. The sane Hailey felt like a helpless idiot. The feral Hailey, otherwise known as the snow leopard alter ego, wanted to arch into the caress and demand a belly rub.

"Now close your eyes," he said.

Arguing appeared to be pointless, so with a big, dramatic sigh, she obeyed.

At first there was darkness. The sound of the rain lulled her; the beat of Jeremy's heart reassured her. She felt heavy and weightless at the same time. But she fought the pull of sleep, afraid of dreaming and of what tomorrow might bring.

The darkness gave way slowly. Hailey found herself in a thick fog, and when it gradually melted away, a vast land was spread before her. She was standing on the ledge of a jagged mountain. There was snow, but she didn't feel cold. The ground was hard rock but her feet, though bare, didn't ache.

As she stood there, the sun slowly came up, illuminating a world she'd never seen before. Mountains, forests, lush valleys, and small villages were all around her. The sky was so blue, it hurt to look at it. The forests were so thick, she could only see a canopy of branches. The houses were quaint and picturesque, like something out of a storybook.

But up here, everything was stark and bare and perfectly still. The mountain stretched much higher above behind her, and right in front of her was a cave. It was completely black, but Hailey knew what was inside.

"Go ahead," Jeremy's voice said, and she turned to find him standing next to her. He wore his suit pants but his feet were bare. His shirt was untucked and halfway unbuttoned, his hands in his pockets. The wind stirred his hair, but he gave no sign that he felt any cold.

—I don't want to,— she said, somehow voicing the words without opening her mouth.

"I'll go, then."

Fear momentarily froze her in place as she watched him casually stroll toward that cave. But when he reached out to the darkness, nothing happened. He put his hand on it as if there was an invisible barrier, then pushed through it with effort. Once his arm disappeared up to his elbow, it seemed the barrier became nonexistent.

Jeremy crouched down, his arm moving in that darkness, and she felt... peace. He was petting the beast in the cave. It couldn't come out and Hailey couldn't go in, but Jeremy could at least reach out to both.

Yet she knew that the beast was a fickle thing. "Come away from there," she called.

He looked over his shoulder at her and smiled. "All right. We'll go somewhere else."

The scene changed. Now they were down in a valley, looking far up at the cliff they'd just come from. Hailey stood in calf-high grass, with a clear, glacier-blue creek running past her feet. Just by looking at it, she knew it would be freezing.

They were on the other side of the forest that cut the mountain off from the valley. In front of her was a path that would lead to a village. The creek continued on, far into the distance. Here, it was still pristine. This was as close to its source as she could get. And even though it was winter and snow covered the mountains, the grass was bright green at her feet, dotted with miniscule wild flowers. It was breathtaking.

"Where are we?"

"Heaven, as far as I'm concerned," *Jeremy replied.*

"You're just trying to trick me into falling asleep."

"Yes," *he admitted unabashedly.* "And it's working. This isn't an illusion, Hailey. It's your dream. I'm just visiting."

"And if I want to wake up?"

"Decide not to want to," *he replied with a shrug.*

"That defeats the whole purpose of wanting to wake up."

"Exactly."

Hailey glared.

Jeremy grinned.

He wouldn't let her leave here, and what was more, she didn't mind it. In fact, Hailey decided that while she was here, she might as well enjoy it.

So she jumped him.

~

No one ever noticed the unassuming little person in the back row. With hunched shoulders and his eyes turned toward the window all the time, he was little more than a shadow darkening the shuttle. He couldn't afford passage on the new shuttle line. On the old ones, everyone stayed awake the entire way. And it took ten hours longer.

But it had one advantage: fewer people on board. In fact, on a shuttle that comfortably seated three hundred passengers, there were only forty. Entire rows were empty and many people had taken advantage of them to stretch their legs. It was almost like lying on a lumpy bed.

The man in that back row, wearing a brown jacket with the lapels turned up against the chill of the cabin, didn't do that. Instead, he watched the lights pass them by and worried his jacket sleeves. His leg was jumping, and he had to consciously make it stop time and again.

He was nervous. Who wouldn't be? The woman he loved had left for a new world, one he'd never even heard about. He was following already a few hours behind, and then a few more because of the lag in speed.

She'll be all right, he told himself. *She is strong, a fighter.*

But that was precisely what worried him. His ladylove was a fighter and didn't shy away from anything. She dived headlong into foreign places and dangerous situations, not caring one bit that she might come to harm. She had an amazing spirit. And it would get her hurt one day. Or, God forbid, killed.

His leg started jumping again. He slapped a hand over it to make it stop. *Don't think like that. She's a survivor. She'll be all right for the day it'll take you to get there, and then you can look after her again.*

His lady needed him. He was her caretaker. Her guardian angel. He did what she couldn't. Someone had to do it.

The stewardess passed by again. That plastic smile was still firm on her tired face and, though she walked slowly, her shoulders were still proudly pulled back. She almost made him overlook the dark circles under her eyes. Another woman in need of a protector. It couldn't be him. He already had a damsel to look after.

The stewardess made her way to the back of the cabin then forward again, checking every passenger. She missed him. Didn't even see him in the seat. He was a ghost. Nobody. If it wasn't for the security feeds at shuttleports, he might have gotten on board without paying.

Unfortunately, he wasn't *that* invisible.

Finally, the captain announced their approach to Torrey. Passengers were instructed to take their seats and strap in—redundant; he'd been in his seat and strapped in the entire time—and the stewardesses disappeared into their own curtained-off section.

The shuttle shook as they neared the ground, but as soon as they touched down, it was a smooth ride to the terminal.

His eyes nearly fell out of their sockets as he gazed out over Torrey. What was this?

Over the last few weeks, his love's travels had taken both of them to amazing places. Bustling cities filled with architectural marvels and droves of people who flooded the streets day and night. Those crowds were a godsend to people like them. Necessary, even. Both needed crowds to get lost in. Anonymity had been their name.

Torrey didn't have architectural marvels. It barely had any buildings. From high above, all he'd seen were rolling green hills, forests, and quaint villages that defied description.

Now, all he could see was the shuttleport. And beyond it, nothing. *My God, was that a castle on that hill?*

Where were the high-rises? Where were the gleaming towers to the heavens, the smooth, paved roads? The *people*?

This had to be a mistake. He must have misread the board back at the other shuttleport. She couldn't possibly have come here. Why would she? Was this place even populated yet? His stomach did a sickening dive as a hideous suspicion took root in his mind. This looked like just the sort of place where a wounded animal would choose to come to die.

No!

His distress grew even more as he disembarked with the rest of the passengers. An audio played on loop overhead, exalting the wonders of Torrey. Newly established, it was being touted as Eden.

The cheerful female voice praised Torrey's natural beauty, acres and acres of untouched territory where all manner of flora and fauna flourished. There was pride in that voice when she informed the passengers that the only form of automated transportation available to visitors in this place was a shuttleport-to-village transport service. From there, Torrey provided several options to get around: bicycle, horseback, or wagon.

"Enjoy this one-of-a-kind journey into the past! You'll never want to leave."

He hadn't even gotten off the conveyor belt yet and already he wanted to turn back.

In the arrivals lobby, several pretty women in shuttleport uniforms were greeting the passengers and giving each something out of large woven baskets. When it was his turn, the pretty blonde handed him a shiny red apple. There was a welcome note attached to it with a string knotted around the single green leaf, which said the apple had been grown naturally, without the use of chemicals or growth agents, right here on Torrey.

As if he cared.

Sweet Christ! How was he going to find her now?

Out in front of the shuttleport building, some kind of hovering vehicle was already waiting to take the new arrivals to the village. It didn't have a driver whom he could ask for help or directions. It made the trip to the village and back, over and over, and that was it.

Worse, it hovered over what looked like a large patch of stomped dirt. Was that supposed to be the parking lot? Around it was an unbroken border made of jagged gray stones, and beyond that, grass and flowers. Not even arranged in any kind of design. Just… chaotic. Wild and untended.

He had no idea what to think about that. Mutely, he took a seat at the front of the hoverbus—the best term he could think of to describe it—and listened to another voice talk about the tourist attractions of the village he was about to go to. Three hotels. *Three?* An authentic marketplace, hiking trails, skiing in the winter months, caves for exploring, lakes for swimming, and castles for touring.

There were more damn castles than there were theaters, the latter of which only featured live plays. How did people live here? But live here they did, he saw as the hoverbus entered the village. There were people around. Nowhere near as many as he was used to seeing, but they were there. And all of them had smiles on their faces and seemed to know each other. They greeted each other, stopped to chat and laugh. They couldn't possibly be that happy. It had to be some sort of elaborate reenactment.

The hoverbus stopped in front of a stout little building with uneven white walls and a slanted wooden roof. The sign on it read: Home & Hearth Tavern and Inn. This was the one and only stop the vehicle would make. He was afraid to get out.

The others hopped down to the ground without a problem, looking tired from the trip but still somehow eager to see what was around them. This type of transport wouldn't move until all passengers had exited, so he had no choice but to follow the others.

"Welcome!" some old guy in strange clothes shouted. "Well, come on then, don't be shy. The ticket you paid for included a complimentary three nights' stay at our fine inn. All the arrangements have already been made, Mr. Arthur Glenn. Your room is ready, and you're in luck." He leaned in as if he was about to impart some great secret. "You got the mountain view room."

Arthur knew some kind of response was customary in these situations, but all he could do was stare at the man's giant white mustache. It covered his mouth completely. Arthur caught his upper lip with his lower one to make sure they were still accessible. "Uh, thanks?" No, that wasn't right. It shouldn't have been a question. *Try a smile.* He smiled, but it didn't feel genuine.

The old man chuckled, resting his hands on his beer belly. "This is your first time here, I can tell. Oh, you're going to have yourself tons of fun. Don't you worry. Now come on. Let's get you settled." He took Arthur's bag and carried it inside.

Arthur followed, growing more horrified by the second. Inside, the building was dark, cramped, and filled with wooden furniture and what the innkeepers probably considered decorations. The lights were little flames in glasses attached to the wall. In the staircase, it was almost pitch-black, and he nearly broke his nose when he tripped on a stair that was slightly higher than the others and pitched forward.

Thankfully, the staircase emerged on a wide, open hallway with giant windows. This had to be the top floor. Above him, he could see the gleaming wooden beams that supported the roof.

"Here we are," the man said and opened a wooden door. "Enjoy your stay, Mr. Glenn." And with that, he left Arthur in a small room with wooden furniture, a miniscule bathroom with hand-operated water spigots, and no idea of how the hell to light a candle.

Arthur prayed Hailey was staying in a better place than this.

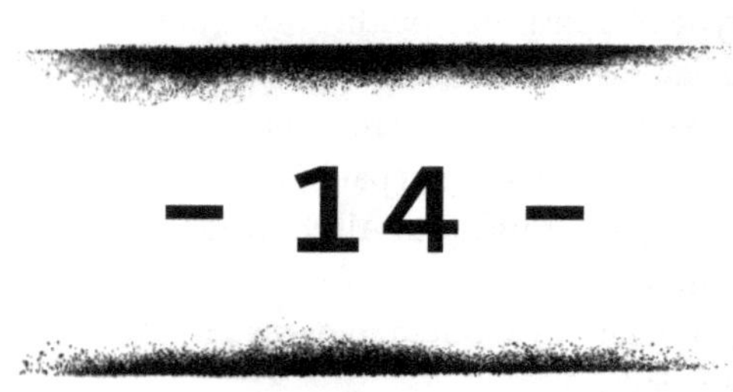

– 14 –

August 11, 3032

Life was good. Nothing better than to wake up smiling after a night of the best sex Hailey had ever had. The sun had just popped up and the air outside was cool with remnants of last night's rain; she was warm and so relaxed, she wanted to laugh. Jeremy was snoring softly into his pillow next to her. She almost blew a raspberry into his neck to wake him, but decided against it. He'd given her a beautiful dream and Hailey knew it must have cost him some sleep of his own.

Deciding to make them an amazing breakfast, she slipped out of bed silently and stretched as far as her muscles would allow. She barely ached at all.

Now to find the kitchen. Hailey knew there was one; this hotel room was more of a studio, fully equipped with all the amenities, looking so quaint and cute, she could just eat it up. She padded barefoot and naked past the bathroom, briefly sighing at the view from the windows.

Aha! The kitchen. A cupboard full of cutleries, heaters and a stove, one pan, one pot, and no food to cook. There was only a basket of fresh fruit, which looked amazing just the way it was. Hailey wondered if there were any stores nearby. She wasn't exactly a stellar cook, but she felt just giddy enough to try her hand at something.

Her lover had sated her well last night. She wanted to reward him.

Butterflies fluttered in her stomach, making her want to laugh. She was still grinning from ear to ear when she ducked into the bathroom for a quick shower. A warm one. There was even a little steam when she came out to dry herself. Humming a little tune, she scrubbed her hair as dry as she could, then twisted it and knotted it on top of her head.

The bags were right next to the door. She reached for hers and dug out a clean set of underwear, then contemplated Jeremy's bag. With a sappy smile, she dived into it and commandeered one of his shirts. It was huge on her. She had to roll the sleeves up so much they weighed the open neckline down until the shoulder seam was hanging almost at her elbow. But it smelled faintly like laundry and Jeremy. From now on, she wasn't sleeping in anything except his clothes. Or naked. She could totally do naked when he was around. It'd cut down on a lot of prep time.

Thus decided, she returned to the bathroom to pick up the towel she'd dropped onto the floor. She hung it neatly on the towel rack and smoothed it out to dry faster. Then she got up on her toes and executed a tight pirouette, turning a circle and a half…

…to wind up facing the mirror.

Whatever color had been in her cheeks bled out in an instant as she beheld her reflection. Her hair, wet, looked gray. Her eyes were silver, not shining but sort of… glittering in the morning light. All the tension that had left her for a brief moment returned full force.

With the exception of that brief, distracted glimpse in the shuttle lavatory, Hailey hadn't really *looked* at herself in months. For good reason. Hailey raised a quivering hand to her cheek. She was a freak. A ghost. No color to her at all. But that wasn't the worst of it.

Hailey kept her distance from that mirror. But she didn't need to get close to it to see every miniscule detail of her face, the faint markings that got darker the longer she looked. A leopard wearing a human skin. Hailey closed her eyes and breathed, willing the faded rosette tattoos away.

When she opened her eyes again, the marks were gone, but she could still feel the beast just beneath her skin, thick fur rubbing against her, making her itch. Making her want to shake herself until that fur grew out and didn't tickle her anymore.

Hailey dropped her gaze and turned away. For a moment there, she'd forgotten. *Better than a bucket of icy water.*

Who was she trying to kid with this game of domestic tranquility? Breakfast in bed? Wearing Jeremy's shirt? As if any of that would change the fact that *she was dying.* Hailey looked down at the white shirt she wore. She ought to take it off. It did her no good to pretend that life was anything but short and painful.

Rainbows and butterflies might do it for some people. Hailey didn't have the luxury of pretense and self-delusion. Every moment she spent ignoring her circumstances was a moment she was never getting back. She could have been working on a cure for herself last night. Instead, she'd given in to her inner cat and wasted precious hours on useless instant gratification.

Hailey grasped the hem of the shirt, ready to pull it off over her head. Her arms would not follow through. It hadn't been useless. And it hadn't been a waste. Hailey pictured Jeremy sleeping in bed and wanted so much to slide back under those covers with him. Snuggle up as close as she could, squeeze her eyes shut and keep on pretending.

Maybe in another time, another place, they could have been truly happy together. But not here. Not now.

She released the shirt and let her arms drop back to her sides. It was all she had now. One more fragile thread to grasp. One more miniscule link to the life she was fighting for so desperately. It would have to be enough.

It was a disillusioned, bitter Hailey who came back out of the bathroom. She hardly glanced at the man still sleeping soundly on the bed. She stepped with her bare toes now, silent as a ghost moving through the apartment. The com system was in a little nook between the kitchen and what probably passed for a living room. She sat down and spoke a name into the directory. Her voice shook enough that she had to say it twice to be understood.

Hailey counted thirty seconds before the connection was established, and Amelia's face appeared on the screen. The moment she saw Hailey, tears of pity filled her pretty blue eyes and her chin quivered. "Oh, honey," she said. She might as well have been delivering a eulogy.

I'm not dead yet! Hailey wanted to scream. For the sake of civility, she made herself smile instead.

~

Jeremy woke holding a pillow instead of Hailey. It wasn't the "Good morning, lover" he had in mind, and he scowled. Out of habit, he looked for her mind, relieved to find her in the next room. At least she hadn't gone far. But why had she left? Frowning, he got up and pulled on a pair of pants.

Hailey was sitting on the windowsill, one foot braced on it, the other swinging carelessly out the open window. She was wearing one of his shirts, and the sight of her in it did funny things to the inside of his chest. Her head leaned back against the wall; she gazed out over the scenery, eyes half-lidded. She looked content, even dreamy, but he sensed unrest in her.

"Good morning," he said.

She didn't look at him. "This is your home."

Jeremy raised an eyebrow. "No, actually, it's a hotel room."

Silence.

He came closer to see what she was looking at. Nothing special going on as far as he could see. The sky was clear today, which meant a cold day on Torrey. Summer was changing to autumn, and here that meant brilliant colors everywhere. Trees turned from green to gold and red, showering the ground with their dry, vivid leaves. In the evening, the sun set in a blazing red glory; and in the mornings, it rose slowly, casting the entire world in gray and white through the mist. The rain last night had prevented mist this morning, but it was still pretty damn chilly. Hailey didn't seem to notice.

From this window, they had a view of the lake at the foot of a mountain range in the distance. Snow already dusted the very tops of those peaks; a hint of things to come. They were at the edge of the village with only a cottage or two across the street, and then nothing but nature. The way Hailey was looking at it... Was she even seeing it?

"See anything interesting?"

Hailey raised her head and looked at him, seeming startled to realize he was there. "It's... charming." In her thoughts, she added, *Peaceful.*

A quizzical smile made his mouth twitch. "What's wrong?" he asked, coming closer. He wanted his good morning kiss.

Hailey jumped as if he'd goosed her. She got off the windowsill and put more distance between them. He frowned. "Did I miss something?"

She fidgeted, looking everywhere except at him. It didn't take a genius to see what the problem was. And damn if it didn't sting.

Last night had been amazing. And not just the sex. Well, the sex had been mind-blowing in and of itself, but he'd never felt with anyone the way he'd felt with Hailey afterward. At peace. As if all the problems of the world had just disappeared and life was perfect the way it was. He'd slept better than he had in years, and he knew it was because he'd sensed Hailey with him the entire time.

Ironic that he'd been sent to bring her back to the life she'd had, and somehow she'd managed to bring him back instead—when he hadn't even known he was in need of it. He hadn't even realized how much he'd been missing, how big of a burden he'd carried every day until Hailey had banished it. Jeremy felt like he could take a full breath for the first time since the day Pixie had been born with a mental cry that had shaken his mind, and before his mother had patiently explained to him that they were both different.

Being with Hailey was the best thing that had ever happened to him. He'd known he could never tell her that, and the secret had, until a few seconds ago, made him feel like a lovestruck teenager, giddy with excitement and impatient to see her and touch her again.

Clearly, she didn't feel the same. He reined in his misplaced enthusiasm and pushed the insidious sting of hurt disappointment aside. "Did I do something wrong?"

She pulled on the sleeves, which were crumpled as if she'd chewed on them, and so long on her they dangled past her fingertips. "I called Amelia," she said. "She's expecting me this afternoon."

"*Us,*" he corrected. "Right? She's expecting *us* because I'm supposed to escort you to her. That's still part of the job." He didn't have to look into her mind. The answer was written as plain as day on her expressive face. "You were just going to leave?" Ice settled in his gut.

She said nothing.

"You were going to leave. After everyth—even after last night." Everything in him screamed in denial. She couldn't possibly be that heartless. Even if she didn't share his epiphany over their night to-gether, it must have meant something.

"I was going to give you a clean out."

His jaw nearly dropped to the floor. "*Excuse me?*"

Hailey's shoulders dropped with exasperation. "Don't do that. It's not like I was trying to bust your ego bubble or anything."

"Oh, this just gets better and better." *Keep it together. She's upset.* And he had no idea why. He resisted the impulse to just pull the answer out of her head. No matter how pissed off he was, last night *had* been special. Invading her privacy like that now, when she so obviously needed to preserve it, seemed wrong. "So what *were* you trying to do?" He crossed his arms, waiting for her to answer.

Hailey looked absolutely miserable. *Would have been easier to burst his bubble,* she thought loudly enough, strongly enough that he heard. Easier for him, she meant. She could have disappeared at any time during the night if she'd just wanted to be gone. She'd stayed to say good-bye.

Jeremy wanted to shake her. It made no sense. He knew for a fact that she hadn't just been using him. He knew with absolute certainty that she'd enjoyed what they'd shared as much as he had. Still, she was so desperate to get away from him, and he couldn't understand why.

"You don't need people like me in your life," she finally mumbled. "You don't need to see what's about to happen."

"What the hell are you talking about?" he snapped, irrational anger making him careless. "I *brought* you here, remember? And, oh, yeah. I vaguely recall something about you not wanting to go along. What the hell changed between then and now?"

"I… just realized this is the only way to save myself, that's all."

"Uh-huh. *Or* you're just pulling my dick and the moment I let you walk out that door you'll disappear again."

The corner of her mouth twitched. "Trust me, when I pull your dick, you'll know."

And that was enough to make it rise to the occasion. Shit.

"That's besides—that's not what I—damn it, Hailey!" He would *not* be charmed into letting this go.

She was there in an instant, pressed against him close enough that all he had to do was lean his head down a little and capture her lips. Her hands played at his waist, dancing and skimming, but never resting fully. "Last night was… it was great," she said. "But I don't want you to start expecting something from me. Like a future."

Because she didn't expect to have one?

"A bit self-engrossed, are we?" he said, hardly blinking at the cruelty of his words. Because he *had* been expecting something from her. If not a happy future, then at least more than *this*. "Hate to burst *your* ego bubble but you're not as irresistible as you think you are."

"Really?"

Jeremy shrugged. "Like you said. Last night was great." *Spectacular. Amazing. Best sex I ever had, and damn you for writing it off so easily.* "But I don't recall ever asking for anything more."

"I know that," she said, but instead of relaxing, she stepped back and put more distance between them. "I also know people. And as far as people go, you're not the love 'em and leave 'em type."

"But you are?"

She hitched her shoulder up almost to her ear and smiled crookedly as if he'd just made an awkward joke. "I don't have anything else to give."

Jeremy didn't even bother addressing that load of crap. "So what's the plan, exactly? You leave, presumably releasing me from my contract and my promise, you go to Amelia, and then what?"

"Then… I start working on a cure."

"And when you find it?"

"Go on with my life."

"Just pick up where you left off, is that it?"

"Yes."

"You really think you'll be able to put all this behind you so easily? It's not like the cat is going anywhere—ever. You'll just be buying yourself more time."

"Everyone has issues."

"What if you *don't* find the cure?"

That seemed to set her back. Hailey looked surprised that he'd even bring it up, as if curing herself was all she'd ever considered. He knew it wasn't. Hailey knew full well what would happen if she failed. She liked to remind him often. But apparently she'd perfected the art of making others face uncomfortable truths for her. Instead of her.

She blinked. "Whatever happens or doesn't happen, it's not your concern."

His foot made an involuntary step back. Not his concern?

For a moment his mind refused to move past that. *Not my concern?* Jeremy still had the memory of her changing shape in front of him, *because* of him; of him cleaning blood from her hands, not once but twice, of feeling her fear, her stubborn refusal to give up, her passion and love of life. The memory of last night, what they'd done together, to each other, was something he'd never in a million years allow himself to forget. And afterward... holding her while she slept...

After all that, she thought she didn't matter? That he could—or worse, *wanted* to—look away and let her face this alone? *Not my concern?* He wanted to throttle her. To kiss her until she melted against him. To crawl inside her and make her care. To tie her to the damn bed so she could never run from him again.

"You're right," he said dazedly. "You're absolutely right." A handful of days, no matter how life changing they felt to him, were nothing in the grand scheme of things. He'd learned so much about her, shared her life through her memories, touched her dreams. He knew her fears and her fantasies; he knew what she hoped for, and what she only thought she wanted.

He was a telepath. Hailey wasn't.

Whatever he'd felt, however intensely he'd felt it in the time they'd spent together, she hadn't. Jeremy had spent so much time around people like him, he'd forgotten the cardinal rule of reciprocity. In order to get, one first had to give.

Weariness replaced the hurt and anger. Jeremy was a telepath. He'd carried the weight of other people's thoughts all his life. The one thing he never thought he'd have to carry was unrequited love. It was... dispiriting.

He hurriedly tamped down the feeling on instinct, knowing that if he didn't, it would destroy him. Brain shutting down, logic booting up. It was an assignment, nothing more. He'd done his job. It was time to walk away.

And yet...

"Tell you what. I want to get paid. If I don't walk you through the door, that implies I haven't done my job. So I'll make you a deal. We go see Amelia together, I hand you over, and then walk out of your life forever." *Lie.*

"Just like that?"

"No complications, no strings. Job done." Shut down the link. Redirect somewhere else. Telepathy wasn't something one could just turn off. It wasn't voluntary. Like eyesight, even with eyes closed, some light always got through. Jeremy directed his senses outside the window. Whispers and ghostly images passed through him like mist. He acknowledged them in passing, but did not dwell on any one of them.

Until he heard Hailey's name.

It drowned in a wave of frantic misery. Someone so lost in this world they could not find themselves. A person who sought an anchor in hopes of finding reason again. He'd seen it many times when telepaths got overwhelmed by their abilities. It took complete isolation for them to regain equilibrium again.

But this was different. This was not someone who was everywhere at once. This one was barely in the place where they—*he*—stood. Someone lost in the world because he wasn't, and somehow could never make himself part of it. Lost, because he had no sense of self. He defined himself by others. By what they did, thought, and said. He liked what others liked because he had no preferences of his own. He perceived the world like a play, a vibrant bustle of activity only to be viewed from the darkness of an audience seat.

At times it gave him a sense of belonging. But there was also an awareness that the feeling was completely one-sided. He noticed everything and everyone, but no one ever noticed him. It was amazing, the contrast between Jeremy's own mind and this one. The things the man saw... things others missed because they were so busy focusing on themselves and what others thought of them.

Hailey snapped her fingers in front of his nose, jarring him. "What the hell is wrong with you?" she said irritably. "Are you off your meds or something?"

He caught her hand and kissed her knuckles. When she would have pulled away, he held fast. "What time is our appointment with the good doctor?"

She yanked on her hand and Jeremy had to release her. He knew he was letting go of more than just her hand. Hailey was free now. Completely. If she never turned to him again, he couldn't make her. It was done. And the pain of that was as sharp as it was unexpected.

"As I was just saying," she said, fuming, "there is no *our* appointment. I don't want you to come with me."

"Why do you even bother to lie to me?" he asked with genuine curiosity. "You're terrified of stepping foot in that lab. You'd give anything to avoid confronting your sister, let alone do it on your own. You don't want to leave this room at all. Although"—he bit back a grin—"that's for a different reason." He gave her facts. No emotion. No reason to run. He gave her something she needed desperately, the only gift she'd ever accept from him: something to fight. An enemy she could see, one she could confront and defeat. Something that made her forget her own helplessness, drown it out in anger, at least for a little while.

Hailey's eyes started to glow, even in the brightening light of a new day. A bad sign. "The next time you let yourself into my brain without express invitation, I will bite your throat out and shove it up your ass."

"You have such sweet pillow talk."

She snarled. Actually snarled, showing off her sharp fangs. Another bad sign. But better her anger than that sickening, desolate emptiness from earlier.

"Look. I have some business to attend to this morning, but after noon we're heading the same way. I don't see any reason we can't go together. And all of your reasons are irrational. So, for once, we do this my way."

Hailey gaped. "When have I ever had things my way with you?"

Jeremy shrugged. "You should be getting used to it, then."

"I *hate* you," she said through gritted teeth. Her nails were claws now, curling at her sides, as if she imagined ripping off his face. He didn't look too deeply at that thought.

"Keep telling yourself that."

He left her standing there and went back to the bedroom to get dressed.

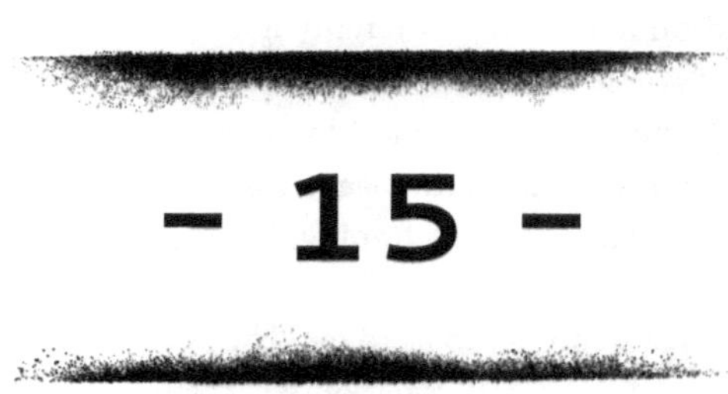

– 15 –

Jeremy didn't lock her in this time. His sudden trust left her baffled. Did he think that she wouldn't try to leave, now that Amelia knew she was here and had arranged to see her? He'd been inside her thoughts. He had to know that she was a master at disappearing without a trace.

Even as she let herself out of the room, Hailey thought it didn't make sense. The way he'd changed, as if he'd just flipped a switch and shut down. One minute, she'd thought they'd have a fight, that he'd try to argue that she should stay with him, and the next, he'd been all aloof agent man just going about the business of escorting his charge to her final destination.

Hailey had wanted this. Jeremy was doing what she'd planned on, anyway—restoring the professional distance between them so that they could walk away without injury. So why did she feel as if he'd just kicked her in the gut?

It felt like he'd given up on her. She would have preferred it if he'd locked her in the room. Even though the windows were near enough to the ground that she could jump down from them easily, that tiny little thing would have restored some balance between them. Instead, he'd just walked out and left her to her own devices. Like he didn't care anymore. Like she didn't matter one whit.

Like she could do whatever the hell she wanted—run away, jump and land on her head, dance naked through the streets—and he wouldn't spare her another thought.

This feeling *sucked*.

She was one hundred percent in self-pity mode all the way to the lobby. Until she got down to the reception and the young man smiling behind the antique-looking desk greeted her—by name. Shocked, Hailey gave him her best attempt at a smile and hurried away. Outside on the street, four more strangers greeted her as if they were old friends. What was this?

The last one, a short, busty old woman with round, red cheeks and a cheery smile even went so far as to offer her a pear out of her basket. For nothing. Just to be nice.

"Thanks," Hailey said awkwardly and took the pear, because the woman wouldn't let her not take it. What the hell had the telepath done? Recruited the whole town to keep an eye on her? "Where am I?"

The woman scowled and shook her head grumbling, "I'll turn that boy over my knee, I will." Then she took Hailey by the elbow and steered her to a quaint little water well. Anywhere else she'd have called it purely decorative. Here, it was actually functional.

"You are on Torrey, girl," the old woman said. "This town is called Amberley. Just over there"—she pointed down the street, far into the distance—"that's English Village."

Hailey looked at the little scattering of dark dots the woman referred to as a village. "Are you sure it's not just an amusement park?"

The woman chuckled. "You get used to it. I'm Mary, by the way. I keep an orchard just outside the town. Lovely little bit of land. Made of sunshine and goodness."

A man with a strange hat resting crookedly on his head and carrying a wooden box approached them. Hailey smelled what was inside even before he pulled back the dirty-looking gray cloth to show them. "Some fish today, Mary? Fresh from the lake." He was all smiles, eyes glittering with mischief.

"Oh! Your timing couldn't be better, John. I'll need three. The children are coming for dinner." The two of them ignored Hailey for a minute, making an art out of choosing just the right fish.

Hailey used that moment to slip away. She was frowning, looking at her feet, and the stomped dirt she walked on, rather than her surroundings. Could it be possible that she was still dreaming? *Anything is possible.* Except she remembered waking up. In more ways than one. And when she dug her dull nails into her palms, she felt it. Not a dream. This place was real.

It seemed to her like walking through a fairy tale. There was no hum of traffic here, no suffocating crowds, no buildings tall enough to obscure the noonday sun. Hailey stared at the pear Mary had given her. It looked… not as pretty as the ones she sometimes bought in a store. But, God, it smelled so much better.

She took a bite. It was so juicy, a drop trickled down to her chin. She'd have been embarrassed if it wasn't so damn good. Three huge bites later, the pear was gone and she was at the edge of the town.

Between Amberley and English Village was a vast open space. The first couple of miles were just green with grass and a scattering of trees. Beyond that, square plots of fields. Some were brown, others golden. It was beautiful to her, but somewhat intimidating to the beast. The leopard was curious but confused. A creature made for harsh mountains and winter climes wasn't used to so much color and… plant life.

Hailey wanted to go see this English Village. She wanted to walk so she could take her time and look around properly. There was an occasional wagon passing between the two towns and the drivers also seemed to know each other. They waved or saluted in passing but never stopped. The road was too narrow; they'd block it if they stopped side by side.

And the horses! Hailey had never seen one in person. They were gigantic. Lucky she was spry. Also lucky that they seemed to want to give her a wide berth. One horse, tethered to a pathetic-looking wagon, pulled sideways to get away from her as he neared. The driver yanked on his reins to get him in line and, timid creature that he seemed to be, the horse obeyed. But his brown eyes were wide open in fright as he passed. Hailey took pity on him and backed away toward an alley.

She made her way to the other side of town, which, though she walked slowly, took her all of twelve minutes, and waded into the hip-high grass. She climbed the first tree she came to, went as high as she could go to get a good view of her surroundings.

Here in blessed solitude she breathed in deeply of the clean air and turned her face up to the sun. Hailey had never felt out of place before. City after city, world after world, no one had ever bothered looking at her unless they wanted something or she approached them. She hadn't realized how accustomed she'd become to being invisible.

Everywhere else, people were a hodgepodge. Blue hair, green skin, yellow eyes, people changing their bodies to make a statement and stand out. All they did was blend in that much more. In a rainbow of colors, one specific hue could never stand out.

Here, people looked at Hailey and actually saw her. Because there was no one here like her. She was a woman in her twenties with hair as white as snow. People noticed that. She felt them notice. They looked and then looked away. They didn't stare or point but they saw. And what they saw was difference.

All of these people had probably come here to get away from the chaos of city living and from crowds of people like Hailey. It didn't take a genius to realize she didn't fit in.

Yet Hailey somehow knew that these people were unlike any she'd ever met before. They were not going to judge her based on her looks but her actions. She didn't know whether that was a good thing or not.

She saw Jeremy approaching from a distance. He was dressed casually and had his hands in his pockets; just a man out for a stroll in the early afternoon. He took his time, too. As if he had all the time in the world.

Hailey didn't like the look on his face. Too serene. He was planning something; she just knew it. Instead of waiting for him to get to her tree, she launched off the branch to jump down. Mid-flight, face-first, she remembered she wasn't a cat. *Oh shit!* She tried to get her feet under her, but it was too late.

Hailey dropped with a thud onto her hands and knees and a split second later down to her elbows and chin. Her entire body was jarred by the impact. Her knees burned—she'd probably skinned them—and her wrists felt broken.

Jeremy's running footsteps stopped half a foot from her. It figured he'd be the one to witness how pathetic the leopard could make her look. "Are you okay?" he asked, and there was no hint of amusement in his voice.

"Ow." Hailey rolled onto her back, rubbing her chin.

"What the hell was that?" Jeremy demanded.

Hailey glared at him. "What are you doing here?"

"Looking for you," he said, just as irritated now. "What do you think I'm doing?" He took her hand and pulled, which made a grenade filled with needles explode in her wrist. Hailey gasped in pain and raised herself up just to relieve the pressure. Jeremy swore and transferred his hold to her elbow instead to help her stand. "You're such an idiot sometimes," he muttered.

"Not like I did it on purpose!"

"Yeah, the launch looked real accidental from where I was standing. Here, let me see that." He reached for her hand again.

"Don't touch!" She twisted to face away from him, cradling her hands against her chest.

"Looks like we're going to see the good doc a little early. Come on."

God, was there no justice in the world? Was this her punishment for trying to mess with Nature's design? Bad enough that she was living with a ticking bomb inside her; did she have to keep embarrassing herself, too?

Jeremy didn't touch her again, just waited for her to fall into step beside him. He kept his hands in his pockets and his gaze shifting between the ground and her. He seemed to know the way by heart. Not that there was anywhere to get lost. "You know, it's interesting."

"What is?" she asked, dormant fangs aching in agitation.

"I've dated a lot of women in the past." He pulled up short. "I mean… That's not what I mean. Er… What I meant to say was—"

"Get to the point."

He pointed a finger at her nose. "*That* is the point. In my experience, a woman finds out I know everything she's thinking, the first thing she does is demand that I tell her what *I'm* thinking too. You?" He shook his head. "You just get mad that I waste your time with questions I already know the answers to."

Hailey said nothing.

"Thank you for proving my point," Jeremy said dryly. "You're not big on this whole sharing thing, are you?"

"I like to think of myself as a private person."

"But you weren't always."

"Were you one? Ever?"

From the corner of her eye, she saw him frown.

Then all of a sudden…

The village was gone and she was in a dark, wet alley at night, hiding behind an overflowing dumpster. It reeked of rot and death. Garbage hung like streamers at her back. She was shaking all over, trying to hide it from the little girl between her and the wall, even though it was useless. That little girl knew more about what was going on than Hailey ever would.

She cried out, squeezing her eyes shut to rid herself of the illusion. But it wasn't in the physical world; it was in her mind, and closing her eyes did nothing. Backing away, she tripped and went down again. Jeremy caught her and sat her down. She couldn't see him, just heard his voice cut through the scene playing out—the scene *she* wasn't supposed to be part of.

"Don't fight it," he said. "I promise you nothing bad will happen to you. Just look."

"W-what the hell is this?"

A pause. She felt his hesitation, how unsure he was. "My past."

Then she heard no more, except the thoughts of a sixteen-year-old boy and his baby sister.

Hiding. Always hiding. Either that, or running.

He was so sick of it! Those damn social workers were always on their case with their fake smiles and their disgusting sugarcoated words that always left a sour taste in his mouth. Fucking bastards.

—Mom would spank you for talking like that.—

—Mom is dead!—

Killed for being who she was. For knowing too much. No one had ever told them why or how she'd died. But both of them had known the moment it had happened. Every. Last. Detail. How do you explain something like that to a three-year-old girl?

They didn't need social workers. All that would get them was lifelong counseling and a team of assholes in white coats poking at their brains.

He looked out from behind the dumpster, gagging at the sight of a bloody rag hanging right in front of him, obscuring his view. The alley was empty, but he could still sense that guy a little up the main street.

Emma yanked on his sleeve.

He brushed her hands away, focusing on that guy. The one who'd found them in the safe house, two kids in the middle of a hundred of them, all huddling together for safety.

Emma yanked on his sleeve again.

—Not now!—

—He's not going anywhere!—

Oh, he was going somewhere. Home, to the hospital, or to the gutter. Either way, Jeremy was getting his sister back to that safe house so she could get her doll and then they were out. Out of Lexington. Out of the state. He doubted they could make it off-world but, hey, a guy could dream.

—Jer!— *The sleeve yanking continued.*

—What?— *he snapped.*

—Talk to him.—

No way. They weren't going anywhere near that guy. Jeremy had a bad feeling about this. It was like staring at a poised trap. His mouth might water for the goodies inside, but his brain knew that if he got caught, he'd never get out. He couldn't do that to Emma. All they had was each other.

—I'm hungry,— *she said tiredly.*

His heart broke a little more. What sort of man was he if he couldn't even provide for his little sister?

Emma curled her little hands in his sleeve, hugging his arm. He kissed the top of her head. "Just a little longer, sis. Just hold on." She had to be cold. Jeremy pulled her into his arms, tucking her close to share what warmth he could. His blood felt as if it would boil, but his skin was cold. Fear did that to a person. Heart pumping, blood rushing, but never where it was needed. Always just circling between heart and brain. Heart and brain. The first to nurture that fear, the second to tire itself out futilely trying to come up with a solution.

Jeremy looked down at his sister. She was so small… like a pixie child.

And she was right. The man wasn't going anywhere. It was as if he knew they were trapped; that if he just waited, they would eventually come to him. He knew, because he was like them. A mind reader.

Emma was so small…

—All right, pixie.— *The words were heavy with regret.* —You win.—
She smiled, hiding her face in his shirt. She liked that nickname.

Jeremy held her close when he stood. His knees were shaky; he hadn't eaten in days. But he made his way to the mouth of that alley and stepped out with his shoulders back.

The man was waiting a few feet away, coat unbuttoned, hands in his pockets, hat sitting crooked on his head, and a cigarette puffing smoke. He extinguished it against the wet wall as Jeremy came closer.

"I know what you are," Jeremy told him boldly. "You think you can use us? Think again. I'll kill you before I let you hurt my sister."

The man studied him for a minute in silence. Then he reached under his coat. Jeremy flinched, expecting him to pull a gun, but what appeared in his hand was…

Emma's doll. The man gave it to the pixie without a word, even smiled. It was a sad smile, filled with pity, but at least it was genuine. "Come on," he said. "You can stay at my place tonight."

"Why the hell would we fall for that?" Jeremy demanded. His arms were tiring holding his little sister, but he was not about to back down.

The man shrugged. "Come or not," he said. "It's not my sister freezing and starving to death out here."

Bastard!

The man tilted his head at that. Jeremy hadn't exactly been subtle thinking it. "If it makes you feel better, my wife and kids will be there."

"You don't actually expect me to believe you, do you?"

The man tapped on his temple. "Just look."

Just what Jeremy had been waiting for. He shoved himself into the man's mind, wreaking havoc, flying everywhere at once. He looked at everything, past and present, real and imaginary. He saw what the guy wanted him to see, and much more. He forced his way into corners so dark, they hadn't been visited in years. What he found there made him shudder and nearly drop Emma.

By the time he emerged, John MacMurphy was leaning against the wall, and Jeremy was on his knees, clutching Emma. And he knew two things as clear as night.

The man was honest; he meant them no harm. And they had no choice but to go with him.

– 16 –

The walk back through Amberley was a slow, somber one. Hailey didn't say a word about what Jeremy had shown her, and Jeremy didn't try to find out on his own. She'd tell him when she was ready.

He kept his arm around her as they walked, holding her elbow for support. She was loosely hugging herself, switching arms every so often to take the pressure off the bottom arm for a little while. He'd checked her wrists while she'd… visited. They didn't seem broken, just banged up. They might hurt like hell for a while, and she probably wouldn't be able to pick anything up, but she'd heal quickly.

People smiled and greeted them as they passed. He was known here. Although his house was miles away near the lake, this was where he and Pixie came for supplies. Jeremy loved the easy camaraderie here. This was what he'd always wanted for Pixie.

The girl took to Torrey like a fish to water. She made friends easily; she was known here, and liked. She never walked past the baker without him giving her a pastry. The weaver and blacksmith were her favorite people to visit, and even the tanner had warmed up to her eventually. Jeremy never had to worry about her getting hurt here; he wasn't the only one looking after her anymore.

Casting a sideways glance at Hailey—which she reciprocated with a suspicious one of her own—he could imagine his life here. His little house by the orchard, a wife, maybe children. Beautiful little girls and brave boys. He could see himself growing old, one of those people who always had a smile on his face and candy in his pockets.

Walking hand in hand with his love of countless years whose smile was the reason he got up in the morning with a spring in his step.

You'd think such simple dreams would be easy to attain.

"Are you not talking to me now?"

Hailey shrugged and switched her arms again. "Got nothing to say." *Nothing worthwhile ever came easy, he reminded himself.*

They were about to go through the marketplace. This time of day it was crowded with merchants and visitors. It wasn't just fruit they offered. There were stalls for painters, clothiers, and basket weavers, among others. One man even sold raw stones and crystals. At a glance they looked ordinary, but all it took was a little time and attention to transform them into beautiful sparkling gems. These mountains were rich with them, and it was as much an adventure to find them as it was to uncover their inner beauty. Much like other things in life.

Jeremy pulled Hailey closer so she wouldn't be jostled so much.

"I'm not an invalid," she growled.

"What makes you think I'm doing this for you?" he returned. "Maybe I just like holding you." And he did. She looked up at him uncertainly, and Jeremy half expected her to pull away, but she didn't. Was it his imagination, or had she eased closer?

They slowly made their way through the marketplace, and Jeremy could feel Hailey's relief when they neared the other side. He'd arranged for a taxi to take them to Amelia's compound. He'd have ordered a wagon just to see Hailey riding in one, but the trip would have taken them three hours. With the taxi traveling at top speed, it would be about twenty minutes.

When they were clear of the crowd, Hailey finally relaxed. And it would have to be right at that moment that someone careened into them. Hailey was turned around and jostled out of his hold. He heard her hiss in pain, and in his mind, he heard her leopard wake angrily.

The man responsible gasped.

Jeremy winced when he saw Hailey's eyes starting to glow as she turned around, and he stepped between the two for both their sakes. "Easy," he told Hailey. "It was an accident."

"It's you," the man said.

Jeremy glanced over his shoulder at him, frowning. That voice sounded so familiar. "Hey," he said in greeting. "Morgan's brother?" he guessed.

The man ignored him, his attention rapt on Hailey. And the look on his face! Such relief and… adoration. "You're here," he said as a big smile spread across his face.

Jeremy turned back to Hailey. —*Friend of yours?*—

Hailey frowned, watching the man. Jeremy felt her searching her mind for a memory. There was nothing she could connect him to. Not a friend. "Do I know you?" she asked him.

The man's smile faded. "Know me?" he said in a small, hurt voice.

Jeremy's instincts screamed an alarm. He took Hailey by the elbow again and steered her away from the guy. "We'll be late," he told her. She went along with little more than a shrug, dismissing the stranger without another thought. Jeremy happened to glance back as he helped Hailey into the taxi.

The man was still standing where they'd left him, staring at Jeremy now with murder in his eyes.

The drone of the engine drowned out most of the noise immediately around her and the unfamiliar scents of horses and people were too thick in the air to make out subtleties. Still, something about that chance meeting struck Hailey as wrong. Damned if she could put her finger on it, though. And not just because both her wrists and hands hurt something awful when she moved them. *Har har.*

In the taxi, she could finally rest her hands in her lap. The directions were already programmed into the console and this thing didn't exactly follow the road. It had a destination and took the straightest possible route to it, which meant that aside for swerving around a tree or hill, it didn't deviate from the path it had chosen.

A few minutes later, the ground beneath her window changed from green to black; not asphalt but smooth rock. A moment after that, the taxi came to a stop, and Hailey looked up from the ground at the building standing on it.

"Hard to believe she got this done in a month."

A month?

The behemoth in front of her was an entire compound, two stories high and sprawling over a hell of a lot of land. Knowing Amelia, this place wouldn't be just bare walls on the inside. No way; Dr. Chase liked to work in style. She would have pulled all the strings she could to fill this place with state-of-the-art equipment and supplies.

Jeremy helped her down from the taxi and then pushed a button to send it back to wherever it had come from. Once it was gone, Hailey was left with the stark building in front of her and the picturesque countryside behind her. A strange contrast, but she should probably start getting used to it. She'd be spending a lot of time here. Maybe the rest of her life. However long that might be.

"Are you ready for this?" Jeremy's hand rested on her lower back. It was a comforting gesture.

"I'm glad you came," she said.

He got a strange look on his face and nodded in answer. Whatever that meant.

When they approached the door, it opened from the inside, and Amelia came rushing out. "Oh, thank God you're here!" She launched herself at Hailey and hugged her so tight, it hurt.

Hailey couldn't breathe. "Hi, sis," she squeaked.

Amelia drew back and caught Hailey's face in her hands. She looked overjoyed, but her heart was racing and her hands were trembling. Amelia was nervous. Her hair was shorter, cut in a puffy bob that ended just below her shoulders. It was cute; it tempered the Doctor of Doom vibe her glasses and lab coat gave off.

"You look good, Ams."

Amelia chuckled. She caught Hailey's hand and pulled her along. Hailey winced in preparation for the pain, but the worst of it had ebbed. "Come on. Everything is set up and ready."

Before they could get through the door, Jeremy caught Hailey's other arm and pulled them both to a stop. "Wait," he said.

It was his tone more than anything that made Hailey look over her shoulder at him. He was furious. Aggression poured off him in waves that made her dizzy. Her beast raised its head, scenting for threats. The muscles in Jeremy's jaw were jumping and he looked just about ready to beat the crap out of someone. But his hold on Hailey's arm was ever so gentle.

Amelia faced him, too, the two of them standing on either side of the compound, one in, the other out, and Hailey in the middle. "Something wrong, Agent Calen?" Amelia said. She wasn't smiling anymore, and her eyes held that signature Don't Piss Me Off attitude she usually reserved for people in her field.

"She's not going in there," Jeremy told her.

Hailey gaped.

"Excuse me?" Amelia said, raising a perfectly groomed eyebrow.

Jeremy met Hailey's gaze and spoke to her, rather than her sister. "I gave you my word."

"What word?" Amelia demanded. "What are you talking about?"

What if I guarantee that you will not be harmed?

Can't guarantee that. Can't account for the actions of others.

I will give you my word.

The conversation came back to her as if they were having it all over again. Funny, for a second there, seeing her sister, Hailey had forgotten all of her fears about coming here in the first place.

What's in there? she asked in her mind, the question directed at him. *What did you see that made you change your mind?*

"You know," Jeremy said to Amelia, but he kept holding Hailey's gaze, "I like to believe the best of people. I thought Hailey's fears were unfounded, that the bond between siblings meant a hell of a lot more than some science experiment. Now I realize my judgment was clouded by my own experiences." Then he met Amelia's gaze dead-on. "See, I would die for my sister. I thought you would, too."

His words tugged at Hailey's heart. She hoped to God she didn't look all doe-eyed just then. That would be embarrassing. When he met her gaze, he gave a little squeeze on her arm, and his thumb brushed back and forth once. In assurance? Her knight in shining armor, coming to her rescue. Even after she'd spurned him.

—*I'll always come to your rescue,*— he said in a tone that said she should know this by now.

Why?

Before he could answer, Amelia cut in on their private mental conversation. "Are you accusing me of something?"

"You should know better than to try to hide something from a telepath," Jeremy told her.

"I'm not hiding anything, and this is none of your business. Your job is d—"

"Why is there a tranquilizer in your pocket?" he cut in. "What is the cage for?"

Ah, so it was both, then. Hailey had figured one or the other. Should have known Amelia wasn't one to take unnecessary chances.

Hailey's sister looked between her and Jeremy, her mouth compressed in a thin line. "Tristan came by yesterday. He said Hailey was unstable, possibly a danger to others and herself. He told me in no uncertain terms that he would not tolerate her so close to his home and mate."

"God," Hailey muttered, "what an asshole."

Amelia glared at her. "He's just doing his job as the protector. His wife is pregnant."

What about you? Hailey wanted to say. *Are you doing your job as my sister?* Had Amelia even argued her case? Or had she taken the shifter's word without question? Hailey leaned toward Jeremy. He stepped up closer at the same time. *He'd* take her side. He already had.

"His wife isn't anywhere near here," he said.

"Do you think that matters?" Amelia crossed her arms over her chest, visibly uneasy. "Who knows how fast or how far Hailey can run when she changes? We know she can do damage. We all saw the news reports."

Hailey flinched. *Jesus.* She grasped the doorjamb for support. It was one thing to have suspicions. But to have them confirmed, to have Amelia, the only family she had left, blatantly throw them in her face like a well-known fact…

"Y-you really believe that?" It was nearly impossible to say the words out loud, to acknowledge such betrayal. And that was exactly what it felt like. Even though Hailey and her sister didn't get along. Even if they rarely spoke. Even if Hailey had screwed things up royally with her.

—*None of that should matter.*—

Jeremy said it. But he made her want to believe it, too. She should deserve better. She did.

—I'm here,— Jeremy said.

Amelia's shoulders slumped. She had that look on her face that doctors used to tell patients they would die. "I have to take into account every contingency. You said yourself you have no control over the leopard once it's out—"

"So you think you'll control it for me?"

Her sister drew herself up. "Wouldn't you want me to? Isn't that what sisters do? Clean up after each other's messes?"

Hailey backed up all the way outside, her step perfectly synchronized with Jeremy's. "Who are you?" she said, staring at the stranger who called herself sister. "God, Amie, is that what this is all about? Is that why you sent an agent after me? To *clean up*?"

Amelia and Jeremy exchanged a look. A *meaningful* one. The kind that was usually accompanied by a conversation no one else could hear.

Hailey felt as if someone had ripped her insides out. She looked at Jeremy, and the answer was plain as day on his face. "No…" She shook her head a little, afraid that any sharp movement would make her shatter like brittle glass. "Tell me you didn't."

"Hailey…"

How could she have been so stupid? Of course Amelia wouldn't give a rat's ass about whether or not Hailey recovered. She only cared about the casualties being left in the wake of her screwup sister's antics. She just wanted to hide any trail that might lead to her.

And Jeremy!

Oh, God…

His big monologue about believing in people, all that crap about standing by her, taking her side. All a lie. One giant mindfuck, psychology and telepathy at their best. To make her cooperate. To get her here.

—You don't believe that.—

"Shut up!"

God, how well it had worked! She wanted to retch, remembering the speech she'd given him just this freaking morning about how *she* needed to break things off. He'd made it all seem like her idea. He'd turned her animal instincts against her, made her want him, and then so valiantly offered himself up like some great sacrifice for the good of the mission. And then he'd left it up to *her* to end it.

All this time she'd worried about hurting him. *Idiot.*

Claws erupted, fangs sharpened. The cat was pissed. Itching to do damage. To show them just how much of an animal she could be.

Jeremy reached for her.

Hailey hissed and pulled away. "Don't you touch me." *None of it meant anything at all.* How he must have laughed.

Her cat made a low, whining sound of pain.

Jeremy swore, reached for her again.

Hailey lashed out with a snarl. Not to hurt; just enough to scare him.

It worked. He backed up, hands in the air, splitting his attention between her and Amelia.

It worked on Hailey, too.

Shocked at herself, at how damn much she hurt and wanted to do damage—*she* did, not the cat—Hailey stared at her claws, blinking back tears. Maybe they were right. Maybe she was a danger to others. Other women might want to scratch their men's faces off for hurting them, but Hailey could actually do it.

"Hailey, look at me," Jeremy said urgently. "You didn't hurt me."

No, but she could have, so easily. She wanted to.

She closed her eyes. *Take away the emotion.* Amelia did it all the time. It couldn't be that hard. Hailey removed herself from the scene. She made herself a neutral observer, watching the dilemma of three people locked in a stalemate.

She knew without looking that Amelia had a tranq in her hand. She knew without seeing that Jeremy was doing his psych mojo to defuse the situation.

Remove the emotion. See the facts.

Fact: Hailey was unstable. She couldn't do anything on her own, except die.

Jeremy swore. She ignored it.

Fact: She was dying. She needed to be here. She needed a lab and her sister's expertise to find a way to fix herself.

Fact: They might be right to worry.

—*No! Don't…*—

Hailey shook her head to dislodge Jeremy's voice. *Remove the bias.*

She felt herself shut down. The pain ebbed, the disgust faded, the tears dried. Calm settled over her as cool as an autumn lake. When she opened her eyes, she could look at Amelia without the hollow in her chest burning her insides. She could face Jeremy without the sting of humiliation making her twitchy.

Her claws receded, teeth dulled. Hailey sighed.

"Hailey?" Amelia said cautiously.

She met Jeremy's gaze, and he flinched. She didn't.

"Hailey."

"Thank you for getting me this far," she said formally. "Your job is finished, Agent Calen. Well done."

"Hailey, don't do this. Just let me explain—"

"If I know my sister, your payment will be processed with utmost expedience."

Jeremy speared his fingers into his hair as she spoke. That muscle in his jaw was jumping again.

"To hell with the payment!" he snapped, and would have said more, but Hailey cut him off again.

"Now, if you'll excuse us, my sister and I have work to do."

- 17 -

August 13, 3032

Hailey negotiated a truce with Amelia. It was tentative and frail, and it rested on one assumption: that Hailey could control herself. Hailey would sleep in a room with barred doors and windows. Any other time she was free to roam the compound, but as soon as she felt herself start to lose it, she had to either lock herself up, or tell Amelia to do it.

Hailey had her suspicion that one morning she would wake up and the barred door just wouldn't open, so she'd taken precautions for that contingency. She'd stolen a key card. *Fooled me once...*

The first round of tests was grueling. They needed blood and tissue samples as well as extensive body scans to measure the damage. The second round would be the same to compare data and measure the speed at which the compounds degraded in Hailey's system.

The one thing Hailey was grateful for throughout this process was the fact that Amelia wasn't a gabber. She didn't ask about why Hailey had done this, where she'd gone, what she'd done there, or why she hadn't come back before now. All of her questions were direct and relevant to the work at hand.

Which meant that Hailey got to play music. The audio system in this place predated the apes by a hundred years, but it was good enough for blasting rock music throughout the entire compound.

The heart of the main floor was a central lab with a lot of computers and screens where everything came together. Scans and test results were all routed to this central room, and this was where Hailey and Amelia spent most of their time. At their own separate stations, but in the same general area.

Hailey didn't ask how Amelia had managed to bring all of this together. She really didn't care. All she wanted to do was cure herself so she could get the hell out of Dodge again. All of this family together time was bad for her peace of mind.

It didn't help that Jeremy hadn't visited once since he'd left two days ago. No calls, no messages, no overt gestures of apology, or even covert ones. Hailey was almost certain Amelia knew something about his whereabouts, but she wasn't sharing, and Hailey was not about to ask. But it bothered her. Like an itch she couldn't reach to scratch, she kept thinking about everything that had happened between them.

Hailey didn't know how to deal with that. There was something missing, left undone between her and Jeremy. It felt as if they'd skipped over a major step before parting ways. Conflict. Closure? Mind-blowing breakup sex.

Hailey frowned, looking over her instruments. Then she realized that grumpy-sounding rumbling noise was coming from her. She scowled and went back to work.

She hadn't even dreamed about him since Reynard Colony. It bothered her that it bothered her. And it shouldn't... bother her. She shouldn't even be thinking about it. All those dreams had been just another part of his grand manipulation.

Or had they?

Whenever the topic had come up, he'd seemed genuinely confused and embarrassed. Could he have faked that? She hadn't sensed any falsehood. Then again, he'd already proven beyond a shadow of a doubt that he could manipulate her senses, make her see—or not see—anything he wanted. And it was all too neat, too convenient. Why would the dreams have stopped after she'd slept with him?

Not that she missed them or anything.

Hailey stifled another growl and fidgeted in her seat. It was just this place playing havoc on her mind. The last time she'd been in a lab like this, she'd almost died. This time, she probably would die. That thought never left her, and the more time she spent here, the more edgy she became.

Just two days since she'd entered this lab and already she was starting to feel she had to get out. She was under surveillance twenty-four hours a day, with cameras set up in every room and hallway. Hailey had destroyed the ones in the bathroom. She needed at least that much privacy. Well, that wasn't *all* she needed, but it wasn't like she was getting the rest of it.

She needed to stretch her legs. Hailey pushed away from the microscope, defiance giving her enough strength that she propelled herself in the chair on wheels to rebound off the cabinet fifteen feet away.

Amelia flinched at her station. So jumpy.

"I'm going out," Hailey told her. She wasn't about to ask permission.

The building abutted a mountain. The kind of mountain her beast felt at home in. Hailey couldn't decide whether Amelia had chosen this place to soothe the leopard, or to test it. Either way, Hailey was going to be exploring it today.

"Oh, okay, sure," Amelia said. "Just be careful."

Hailey could swear she heard her sister's sigh of relief from down the hall when the music stopped and the compound fell silent as a tomb.

She took a running start out of the building and headed straight for the jagged rocks. Her shoes were slippery and couldn't get traction on the gravel. After five minutes, she just took them off and tossed them down to the parking lot.

Ah, much better.

It was easy going after that, felt like this was what she'd been born to do. Up here, the air was cold and crisp. She could *smell* the rocks. Heaven.

Hailey found herself a nice flat surface to stretch out on and catch some rays. She wanted to purr. Well, not really. Because having all of this freedom to frolic was making her horny, and it just so happened that her social circle currently included only her sister. The one truly screwable guy she knew had turned out to be a backstabbing liar who deserved to be beaten bloody.

Bastard.

But even as she had that thought, her thighs squeezed together, missing him between them. She was tempted to go on a little fantasy spree in hopes that he would pick up on it. Show the telepath what he would never have again. But that was ultimately a bad, bad plan. If he saw and didn't respond, Hailey would know forever that she'd been cruelly played. If he did respond, she wasn't sure she wanted him inside her head again. Of course, he might not see anything at all.

Either way, she'd just end up making herself miserable, which was extremely counterproductive. Instead, she imagined all of the things she'd do to him once she was cured. Booby traps galore. The man wouldn't be able to get out of bed in the morning without something screwing up his life. She'd make his existence hell. She'd pay him back with interest for what he'd done to her.

"I'd think you would have more serious things on your mind at a time like this."

Hailey snarled, but didn't move to acknowledge the other half-animal. "I warned one telepath off already. Didn't think *you'd* come crawling back."

"Didn't have to read your mind," Hunt said. "Your pheromones carry for miles."

Oh, hell no! She got up so fast, rubble rained down on the tiger man. "So what, you came running? You just turn your tail right around and shoo, kitty."

He made a disgusted noise. "As if, woman. I found my reason for living in my mate. Wouldn't look at you twice if I didn't have to."

Amazing how casually he said that. He had to love his mate very much to admit so easily just how much power she had over him. The man didn't strike her as the type to give up power to anyone without a fight. For that, she was inclined to overlook the insult he'd just delivered.

"Besides," he said, "you wouldn't know what to do with true, honest-to-God interest if it dragged your sorry ass across the universe to save you."

Hailey snarl-hissed at him.

"That guy you are so eager to take revenge against would put his life on the line if it meant sparing you a moment of unhappiness. Although don't ask me why." He gave her an appraising once-over.

"You're seriously damaged goods."

Her hackles rose. She bared her teeth at him. How dare he even broach that subject? "Keep talking," she dared.

Hunt laughed at her. "You're such an idiot. You say you want to live. You're so focused on restoring the pathetic life you had, that you won't even consider that you might have something so much better if you'd just stop chasing it away."

Now he was seriously pissing her off. He was on a level below hers, surefooted for the moment, but not exactly a mountain goat. This wasn't his type of terrain. Hailey was surprised he'd even bothered climbing up here. "You need to leave." Perched on her rock, head canted down, hair flying everywhere, Hailey had to look like a gargoyle. And she wanted to swoop down and see how well she could play one. "This has nothing to do with you."

"See, that's what you don't get. You think you live in a bubble and your actions affect only you. If they did, I'd be wishing you jolly good luck and moving on. But you're fucking up the harmony of *my* life by blaming *my* friend for everything that's wrong. Wake up. Or I will make you."

"He manipulated me."

"And you've never done *that* to anyone in your life, right?"

Hailey blushed. She wasn't exactly an angel, but she'd never done anything that huge. She'd never led anyone on, made them think she cared when she didn't.

Hunt rubbed a hand over the back of his neck. He'd get a crimp in it soon, looking up at her the way he was. "Your judgment is clouded. You're projecting your own fears onto him. And if you weren't so preoccupied with your abandonment issues, you'd see that."

"I do *not* have abandonment issues!"

He gave her a *Who are you trying to kid?* look. "I'm not saying you don't have reason," he said, somewhat more rationally. "But you can't assume everyone you meet is out to hurt you and leave you." That almost sounded kind. Until he added, "First of all, not everyone gives a shit. And second, you'll end up as alone as you always feared you'd be."

Hailey scored the rock with her claws. "Why did you come here?"

Hunt surveyed the rocks, probably couldn't see an easy way up, and gave up with a frustrated sigh. It couldn't sit well with him to have to look up at her. Well, she wasn't about to make it easy on him. "I thought," he said, "that we could talk once you'd calmed down. Shifter to shifter."

Hailey pushed to her feet, as graceful as a ballet dancer, and stood up straight and tall.

And he had to look up that much higher. *Shifter to shifter, yeah right.*

"I gotta admit, I didn't expect you to be this unreasonable. Especially with me. We're on equal footing, you and I. I might be the only one who will ever understand what you're going through."

Highly doubtful. "Do you know," she said, making her way to a boulder on the side, "why snow leopards never go into the jungle and tigers never go up a mountain?"

He actually rolled his eyes at her. Asshole. "Enlighten me."

She hadn't been planning to do it. At his words, she changed her mind.

Hailey hopped up onto the boulder, braced one foot on it and the other on the cliff wall at her back. "In each other's territory, they are *never* on equal footing." And she pushed against the wall, dislodging the boulder. As it rolled down, missing Hunt by inches, Hailey hopped back to her platform, smooth and graceful. "Now then." She crouched back down and canted her head to the side. "What was it you were saying?"

"I'm not known for my patience, girl."

"Really? I read otherwise."

Hunt bared his teeth, launched himself up and landed on her level, right in her face.

Hailey fell back, but righted herself and sought higher ground. There was none. Behind her was fifty feet of sheer rock. There wasn't another platform or even easy hand-or footholds nearby. And Hunt was cutting off her access to the edge.

She was trapped.

"Now that I have your attention," Hunt said, "let's talk."

~

Everyone noticed the furious-looking man forcing his way through the crowd. They gasped or yelled when he shoved them out of the way, backed off in a hurry when he looked at them. They saw him. And he saw no one.

He didn't see the whispering groups he left in his wake or the parents who shooed their children inside. He didn't even hear them, not past the thrum of noise in his head.

Voices. Echoing over and over and over, always repeating the same thing, making him crazed. Livid. Wanting to hurt something and make it last.

Do I know you? Do I know you?

Knowyouknowyouknowyouknowyouknowyou…

It got louder and louder until Arthur thought his head would explode. He clutched his temples, squeezing his skull to keep it contained. He felt like screaming. But that last little bit of sanity that remained kept him in check. It told him to run.

Arthur wasn't a runner. Just the fifty yards out of the village made his knees shake and his lungs burn. He was wheezing, but still managed to draw enough breath to scream.

And scream.

He screamed himself hoarse, and still it wasn't enough. When his knees buckled, he didn't even try to stop them. He pounded at the earth with his fists, tore at the grass, dug at the dirt until a fingernail tore off his finger. Arthur never felt the pain.

Do I know you?

Every word was a dagger through his heart and soul.

He'd failed her.

All this time he'd kept his beloved safe, protected from her demon. And now this. A split second of indecision. A missed flight. Two days away from her. The demon had won. It had ripped into her mind and wiped away her memory of him.

And he knew who was to blame.

Arthur had made a mistake, true, but he wasn't the one who'd provoked the demon out of its sleep.

It was that man.

The one he'd seen her with just two days ago. Arthur had seen him before, but hadn't thought he'd stick around.

It was him. *He'd* done it. Somehow he'd forced his way into Hailey's life, probably filled her head with lies, played the hero. The *gentleman.* The word was as foul to him as this entire damn world. The way he'd touched her, helped her into the transport. So accommodating. It sickened him.

"Hey, sir, are you all right?"

The voice pierced Arthur's rage, but just barely. Normally, it would have made him uncomfortable to be addressed so directly. Now it only added fuel to his wrath. Arthur picked himself up off the ground and took deep, shaky breaths. "I'm… fine," he said calmly.

"Are you sure?" the intruder asked, all false expression and fake concern. People could not be trusted. *No one* could. Only Hailey. She was the only source of sincerity in the world.

"Yes," Arthur said. "I just lost my head there for a moment." Just boiled over. That was it. Two days he'd been holding that in. Ever since he'd watched Hailey dragged to that taxi.

Oh, but now he had a purpose. Now he knew where to focus his attention. These people knew the man. Arthur could use them to find him. It wouldn't take long. Hell, he could probably start with the guy talking to him right now. But not in the state he was in.

Arthur composed himself the way he always did—by thinking about his first meeting with Hailey. A fated one.

No one ever noticed the thin, awkward man making his way through campus. They walked right into him, as if he were invisible. Thrice he had his books knocked out of his hands by some stupid jock hopped up on testosterone and booze. And they never even said a word in apology.

I am no one, he thought, kneeling in the middle of the walkway, braving the foot traffic to pick up his scattered books and notes.

And then a strange hand reached for the same book he did. Startled, he looked up into the face of an angel. A smiling beauty with sunshine in her eyes and a heavenly voice. "You okay?" she asked. "You're taking a beating out here. Here, let me help you."

Arthur was smitten. She helped him pick up his books and walked with him to his classroom.

And the most amazing thing happened. People actually noticed him.

Or was it her they saw? The crowds parted as if by some divine power, and… everything just seemed so much brighter. "Take care," she told him and waved good-bye when she left to her own class.

He'd fallen in love with her that day. Had never stopped loving her. Watching over her.

He'd seen her at her best and her worst. Been there to watch her seduce a crowd with just a wink and a smile, and to see her cry over a heartbreak. He'd have killed the bastard who'd hurt her if he'd known who it was. But back then, he hadn't learned to pay attention yet.

He'd watched her that night, months ago, stealing into a locked laboratory being watched by soldiers in the shadows. He'd watched for them to strike, for the police to come rushing in, ready to distract them if need be. Anything to help his beloved. He'd known that whatever she'd gone in there to get, she needed.

But then he'd seen her run back out. No longer his Hailey, his angel, but a beast with feral eyes and sharp claws, covered in blood.

Red blood, white hair.

The police had never come.

The soldiers had taken one look at her and backed off, writing her off as dead, or soon to be.

And Arthur had never felt such fear.

His beloved was possessed. A demonic beast inhabited her body, tormented her soul. It demanded of her things that would damn her for all eternity, if she gave in and obeyed. But the beast's power could be defused, diverted elsewhere.

Hailey didn't know how to do that.

But Arthur did.

"Well, hey, listen," the man said. "If you need anything, just let me know."

He did it for her. All for her. To save her, he damned himself.

"My name is Sam Nunez. I'm… here to help."

She was worth the sacrifice. She was his light.

And she didn't even know who he was.

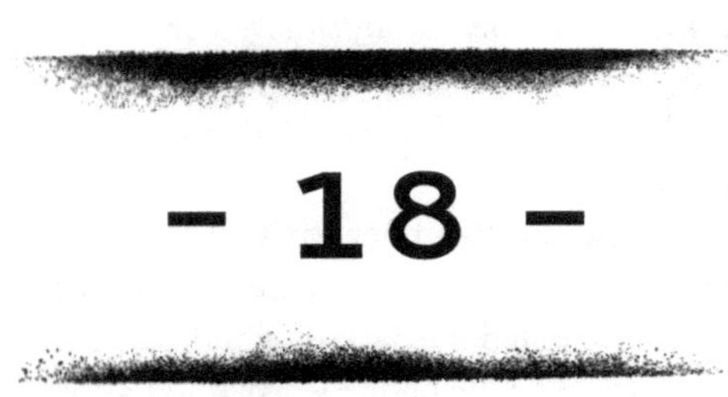

– 18 –

The bass solo was actually pretty good. Jeremy leaned back on the couch to listen for a while. His eyes needed a rest from all the not-reading he'd been doing. He had a stack of files on his computer to go through, but every ten minutes he found himself looking out the window at the mountain in the distance with no idea what the last page and a half of data was about.

He must have read the same thing twenty times by now and still he had no clue.

The song ended. Jeremy typed another title into the miniconsole on the coffee table and more hard rock music blared through the house. It would have been easier to just choose a bunch of songs by genre, but he never knew what the next song was supposed to be until the first one was almost over.

"You are pathetic," Pixie said from the doorway. She was wearing normal clothes for the first time since he'd come back. Her red hair was loose. No medieval gown, no intricate hairstyles.

"Thanks ever so, sis," he said. "So what's this getup called?" She'd named her costumes based on what they looked like. At last count there was a princess, a maid, a wench, and a gypsy.

Pixie twirled to show off. "You like it? It's called 'my jackass brother is giving me a headache because he doesn't have the balls to go after the woman he loves.'"

"That is way too long to fit on a name tag."

"Ya think?"

"And anyway, I'm not in love, she doesn't want to see me, and I'm not playing the music to give you a headache. I'm just… in the mood for drums and bass guitar."

"Because that's what *she's* listening to."

Jeremy snorted. "Whatever."

Pixie just raised her eyebrows.

"No way," he said. "On my best day, I don't have that kind of range."

"Have you learned nothing from Hunt? When it comes to forces of Destiny, range becomes totally irrelevant."

Jeremy pointed an accusing finger at her. "You've been reading too many romance novels again."

"And *you* haven't been reading enough. Of anything. Read the signs, man. The universe is talking to you. The least you could do is listen."

Another song ended. Jeremy didn't know what to play next. For some reason, it bothered him. "I don't have time for this, Emma." Usually the use of her given name ended a discussion instantly.

This time it failed. "Yeah, I can see that. Wouldn't want to get in the way of all that woolgathering you've been doing."

Jeremy glared.

Pixie glared right back.

"What will it take to get you to leave?"

"Oh, I wrote down a list of demands," she told him. Then she actually pulled out a printed list and started reading off item after item. "Number one, you will stop that godawful music. Number two, you will shower and shave. You look like hell, brother. Number three, you will call Dr. Chase for an update on Hailey. Addendum to number three, if Hailey is there, you will talk to her. If she isn't, you will get up off your ass and go see her."

Enough. "Stop. You don't know what you're talking about, so just stop."

"See, that's where you're wrong." Pixie folded the note and stuck it into her back pocket. She came to sit in the love seat kitty-corner with what had now become Jeremy's couch, and tapped on the computer. "I know that file inside and out now. Read it ten times through you, and the funny thing is, you *still* don't remember what you read. I know that you haven't slept for two nights, because you keep me up with your tossing and turning. I know you haven't shaved or showered in two days, and I haven't seen you do that since… well, ever. And before you ask, no, I don't know what you are thinking. I don't look. Whatever *you people* did together is none of my business, but I do know you've spent more time in the past than you have in the present since you walked in that door."

He was forced to admit the truth in that. All of it. He didn't sleep, because he kept reaching for Hailey, expecting her to be there, and when she wasn't, he woke up instantly, searching for her, thinking she was in trouble. It was pathetic. They'd spent one night together in the same bed. Just one night. A few measly hours. Hardly enough to be memorable under normal circumstances. And yet every night he didn't have her to hold, he couldn't sleep.

Pixie was right about the woolgathering, too. Jeremy kept seeing Hailey's face when she learned how little her sister thought of her. She'd been hurt. Just thinking about it made his chest ache. He still didn't know how he'd gotten dragged into it, but he knew that Hailey now believed everything they'd shared had been a scam. And there was nothing he could do about it, no way he could explain and allay her fears.

Because she wouldn't let him.

He'd gone for a walk yesterday and had found himself within range of Hailey. Unable to help himself, he'd reached out to her. She'd been completely engrossed in whatever scientific task she'd been performing, one hundred percent focused. It had worked like a shield over her thoughts. She'd meant it when she'd said they were done.

Damn it, he missed her. And not just her nearness or her touch. Jeremy missed *everything*. Her temper, her catty comebacks, the way her eyes glowed with strong emotion, the way she slyly looked him over when his back was turned. He even missed fighting with her. And it had only been two days.

—*Try telling me again how you don't love her,*— Pixie said in his mind.

He glared at her.

"Any questions?"

"Yeah, a couple," Jeremy said, resigning himself to her wisdom. "How did you get to be so smart?"

Pixie smiled, and even though he was still miserable, he wanted to smile back. "I had a great mentor," she told him, and Jeremy drew himself up a little with pride. Then she said, "John MacMurphy."

Jeremy tossed a pillow at her. She dodged it, laughing, and threw one back at him.

"So what's your other question?"

Jeremy sobered. "This one's important."

"I think she's good for you. That's what you were going to ask, isn't it? What I thought of Hailey?"

"Uh… no, actually." He loved his sister dearly, but he was not about to ask her permission to date or not date someone. If he wanted Hailey to be part of his life—and, damn her temperamental shifter hide, he did—she would be, whether Pixie liked it or not. But her blessing, so easily given, was a relief. Now he just had to convince Hailey that they fit together.

"Oh, then what is it?"

"What I was going to ask is… what the hell is in that file?"

Pixie grinned. "You better get comfortable, 'cause it's a doozy."

~

Nothing like a long, cold bath to soothe the body and mind. Hailey was bruised. A lot. She hadn't even realized what the rock face was doing to her feet until she'd come back down and realized she was trailing blood. And her scuffle with Hunt hadn't helped.

In her own defense, prefacing a profound pearl of wisdom with, "You're an idiot," wasn't the best way to get her to listen. Hailey now knew that there was no way she could defeat Hunt in a fair fight.

Good thing she didn't fight fair.

He might have tossed her around a bit, bruised her up, but she'd scored some marks, too. The guy would feel those for days to come.

Hailey gingerly stretched in the metal tub. She was in the dressing room for the exercise lab. The tub was specially made larger than ordinary tubs, so she could submerge completely. But while it was heaven on her body, her mind was still tense.

Hunt's words still weighed on her, and even though she wanted to say, "What the hell does he know?" and move on, what he'd told her was starting to make sense.

"You were at death's door two weeks ago. You were a leopard the first time you met Calen. Tell me, how many times have you shifted since then?"

The answer was none. Not once.

"Why do you think that is?"

She hadn't had an answer for him on that one. Not even her usual "Fuck off, asshole."

Then he'd said the thing that still bothered her, hours later: "You may not be able to control what happens to you *when* you shift, but you can control *whether* you shift. It's all in your mind, Hailey. All the power in the world, contained in thought. If you can't handle that, then you have no business living. And it seems to me you had yourself a damn effective anchor to keep you grounded before you let him get away. A woman smart enough to find a way to do this to herself should also be smart enough to get him back. Amelia can't save you if you won't save yourself."

Asshole.

Couldn't even let her be mad for a few days. So what if she was blaming the wrong person? (She hardly even flinched at that, hardly at all.) Hailey would have figured all of that out eventually. Once she'd calmed down, she would have seen that her emotions had gotten the best of her and she would have been able to look at the situation differently. Even if by then Jeremy wanted nothing more to do with her—she did flinch then, and drew her knees up to her chest—she would at least have confronted it on her own terms.

Hunt was an asshole who apparently liked to poke and prod into other people's problems.

But could he be right about the anchor thing? She'd felt the leopard stronger than ever since meeting Jeremy. But in her mind, not her body. She'd thought like the leopard, reacted like her, but hadn't looked like her. Claws and fangs didn't count. They couldn't kill her. An elongated spine or a crushed skull, on the other hand…

Hailey growled her frustration and submerged herself completely, holding her breath underwater to test how long she could last. Theoretically, her lung capacity should be greater. But her beast didn't like water. It fought Hailey, trying to get her to surface again.

All in the mind, Hunt had said.

Hailey was willing to test that theory.

She closed her eyes and concentrated on the sound of her heartbeat. She imagined herself in the dreamworld Jeremy had created for her—the valley with the stream. In her mind, when she spread out her arms, she felt the gravel of the stream's bed and banks. Without opening her eyes, she knew the exact shade of the bright green grass and the flowers scattered everywhere. They had tall, thin stalks and drop-shaped petals that seemed barely attached, and so heavy, Hailey thought they would blow away in a strong breeze.

The leopard raged up above in that dark cave, trapped and angry.

Shut up, Hailey told her from underwater. Air bubbles escaped her lips and were swept away by the water's current.

But the beast heard her. She threw herself at the darkness, swiping out a giant paw. Even from so far, Hailey felt the scratch on her thigh.

Hailey snarled and scratched back. She heard the leopard whine and retreat to lick her wound. There was still grumbling and complaining, and Hailey could almost understand the sentiments. Not in words, but images and sensations. Emotions.

The world around her settled into tranquility, and she relaxed. The only thing missing was Jeremy…

Metallic drumming snatched her out of that world, back to reality. Hailey surfaced and gasped for breath, her heart racing.

"Figured you'd put an end to your own suffering?" Amelia asked.

Hailey glared. "I was," she said between gasps, "testing my lung capacity."

"I see. And how long did you last?"

Long enough to score a small victory. That, in and of itself, was worth celebrating. Only Amelia didn't look very happy. "What's wrong?"

Amelia adjusted her glasses. Never a good sign. "Get dressed," she said. "We need to talk."

What did I do now? Hailey wanted to whine, the way she always used to do when they were kids. But Amelia was already walking out the door. She'd never been one to waste time on pleasantries.

Hailey shrugged and got out of the tub. She toweled herself dry, knotted her wet hair atop her head, and dressed in a pair of loose pants and sweatshirt. She left her feet bare even though they still hurt, the cuts relatively fresh.

Amelia wasn't in the central lab. Okay, what was this, hide and seek? "Ams?" she called.

"In here," came Amelia's voice from another room. Hailey followed it to a place she hadn't been in before. It was like a hothouse oasis. There were plants everywhere and it was so humid, Hailey didn't want to go past the threshold. She couldn't even see Amelia in all this greenery.

"Where are you?"

"Over here. By the window."

Hailey made her way on the tiny path between bushes and giant ferns to a window that took up the entire wall and overlooked the valley. "Nice view," she praised.

"Sit, please," Amelia said.

"So what's up?" Hailey dropped into the bowl-like seat lined with a giant fluffy pillow. It felt like the inside of a fist. She squirmed and twisted to find a better position and eventually gave up and slid down to sit cross-legged on the floor.

"I got the test results," Amelia said. "The compound is completely decomposed. All that's left is the separated components. They should filter out of you harmlessly over time. But as of noon today, you no longer have any special regenerative capabilities."

Hailey had figured it wouldn't last long. "Okay, so what now? We do it again? Now that it's gone and the DNA is already integrated, there shouldn't be any more cross-reactions, right?"

"It's not that simple, Hailey. The serums you put together were unstable to begin with. I don't even know how the two DNA strands managed to incorporate without killing you. But the one thing the regenerative agent seems to have done is make your body develop an immunity to the original virus. If we injected you with it again, your immune system would just fight it off as an infection."

"So we use a different virus. No biggie."

Why did Amelia look like she was about to cry? "It's a biggie, Hailey. There is no other virus. The one we used took decades of careful engineering to develop. We… we've run out of options."

Hailey just stared. "If this is some kind of joke, I'm going to kill you."

Amelia shook her head. "No joke. No tricks. You have no idea how much I wish there was another option. But there isn't."

Hailey frowned, fingers curling into the fabric of her pants. "Bullshit."

Amelia ignored her. "Even the smallest change can do major damage now. Claws could potentially tear up your nail beds beyond repair. Fangs could fracture your maxilla and mandible. If your eyes change, you could go blind."

"*Bullshit!*" Hailey shoved to her feet. She was shaking, scared. Couldn't catch her breath. This wasn't happening. It couldn't be right. *Nonononononono.* There had to be a way.

"Hailey—"

"There has to be another solution. You used people as guinea pigs for years. Don't you dare tell me you didn't come up with anything new in all that time."

"I did," Amelia said, her tone sour. "And then you went and bastardized my work."

Anger and helplessness were an explosive combination. Hailey wanted to tear her hair out, to break things. By some miracle she kept herself barely under control, knowing that Amelia might lie about her options, or might be in denial, but she was right about the consequences. If Hailey lost it, she was dead. Period.

So she paced, working out her jaw when her teeth wanted to clench until they cracked, and racked her brain for ideas. "That just means you've got one more guinea pig to test your theories on."

Amelia looked aghast. "I'm not testing potentially deadly viruses on my own sister."

"You don't have a choice, Ams," Hailey snapped, temper flaring. They should be in the lab, researching, not wasting precious minutes arguing. She hadn't come this far to give up now. "Either you do, or I do. And we both know my science experiments tend to go boom."

"You can't even comprehend what you're asking of me."

"I'm asking you to save me!" Hailey shouted at the top of her lungs. The wilderness around her stole her voice and swallowed it without ever giving back an echo. It was eerie. "Isn't that what you've always wanted? Huh? To save your little screwup sister? How long have you been after me to come home? Well here I am, sis. And I'm not leaving until I get this fixed."

"Hunt could train you. You could learn to live without—"

"To hell with Hunt! This isn't something that will go away with a few hours of humming and yoga. Don't you get it? Every goddamn minute of the day I have to remind myself I am a human being. Now you're telling me that if I slip up, even the slightest bit, I could end up a cripple, or worse. How can you even ask me to live like that?"

"I can't do what you're asking of me," Amelia said tightly. "I refuse."

Soothing cold settled over Hailey's bones. Impasse. Fear ebbed; anger drained out of her. Hailey sensed helplessness in Amelia so strong it choked her. She accepted her sister's resignation, but she couldn't let it rule her. Hailey let it die along with any lingering sentiment, leaving herself empty. Steady. Curiously detached.

She held Amelia's gaze; a stupid staring contest neither of them could win. Hailey wasn't about to budge. And she couldn't sway Amelia. *Stalemate. Game over.* "Then you're not my sister anymore."

"I haven't been for a long time," Amelia said, mirroring Hailey's deadened tone. "You wouldn't let me."

Something above beeped low. An automated voice announced, "Incoming call from Jeremy Calen."

Neither of them moved.

The computer beeped again.

Then one more time.

"Take a message," Hailey snapped.

A different kind of beep. "Recording."

And then Jeremy's voice came through. "Hailey! Where are you? Pick up. Come on, you have to hear me out." A sigh. "Okay, I have to see you. I found something in the animal attack files. You need to see it for yourself. Meet me tomorrow, two p.m. at the Patio in Amberley. Can't miss it, there's only one." A pause. "I... miss you." *Click.*

"Documenting appointment for Hailey," the computer said. "Tomorrow. Two p.m. Amberley Patio. Scheduling call to confirm. To-morrow eight a.m."

Damn, she should have stopped the computer before it did that.

"Sounds like you have a date," Amelia said.

"Yeah," Hailey replied. "A shame I might not make it."

She left Amelia there to brood, or mourn, or whatever it was she felt she had to do. Hailey had work to do. This lab was equipped with everything she could possibly want or need. Machines, chemicals, a plethora of bacteria and viruses, diseases from all over the universe, and from Earth throughout history. There was no way Hailey wouldn't find one that worked on her.

She would find a solution if it was the last thing she did.

Hailey just hoped that thought wouldn't end up being prophetic.

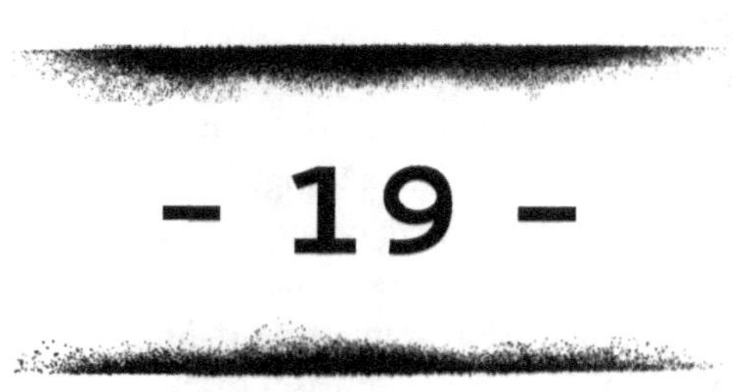

– 19 –

August 14, 3032

The recorder engaged. It wasn't the worst piece of equipment in the universe, but Hailey had seen five-year-olds with better ones. Which was why she was glad that there was nothing to interfere with the acoustics—she was the only one in the lab. Amelia hadn't come out of that green sauna since Hailey had left her there. She didn't let herself think about that. If she did, well… bad things happened.

For once, the cat in her went along with the program. It had to sense Hailey's drive and fear. It kept silent, hidden, and didn't even try to touch Hailey. Small blessings counted for a whole hell of a lot now. Hailey thanked God for each one.

"Here we go," she said. The microphone was a tiny thing attached to her ear. "This is Hailey Chase. Location… somewhere on Torrey. I don't actually think this place has a more direct address. Date is August 14, 3032, but just barely. Time of recording is three fifteen in the morning." She was typing as she spoke, getting the details in writing as well as on video. This might very well be her final legacy. She wanted it properly documented. A cautionary *Do as I say, not as I did. But if you do as I did, here's how you can fix it. Or try, anyway.*

"Statistically, a sister virus strain, a mutated version of the virus originally used, would have the best chance of being successful. Similar enough to perform the same function and just different enough to avoid an attack by the subject's immune system. Apparently the subject has developed a defense against the original virus, so I had to improvise. And, hey, it only took me fifteen hours to come up with a workable serum. Tested it and everything this time. The newbie learns fast, no?"

Hailey paused in her typing and looked directly at the recorder. "You can skip the next two minutes or so if you're not interested in the technical crap." And back to typing. A small sense of pride tickled her as she described the process of creating the serum, giving enough detail to explain but not enough to make it re-creatable. The last thing she wanted was for the wrong someone to get their hands on this and pick up where Amelia left off. No, there were enough shifters in the universe.

Hell, just attaching her face to this was a huge risk she probably shouldn't be taking, but it wasn't as if Amelia was there to look over her shoulder and correct her work. If anything went wrong, her sister would need to know exactly what she'd done. That was assuming she'd bother to do anything about it in the first place.

Hailey shook off that unpleasant thought and resumed her narration. "I have cleaned the isolated, rare strain as much as possible. Given the time frame I am working with, it would be ridiculous to try to fully remove all its harmful effects. That would take months, maybe years. Quite possibly longer. Besides which, there is a limit to how far I can take it before it starts to degrade and becomes useless for my purposes. As is, the virus is aggressive enough that it should spread throughout the subject's entire system easily. Double DNA shouldn't cause any problems whatsoever, as the virus attacks animals as easily as humans."

She saved the typed file and fully turned her attention to the recorder. For the sake of thoroughness she had to consider as many contingencies as possible in case they happened. Again. But she was hesitant to even admit their possibility to herself.

"This is… a risky procedure. At best, the subject will become infected with the regenerative agent and some of the virus's indicators. At worst…" This was where she hesitated. In mind and recitation. If this worked, it would be a miracle. If it didn't, she might wish she'd died instead. "At worst, the solution contains a cell or two of the full, live virus, in which case introduction into the bloodstream will mean immediate infection. The subject will feel lightheadedness and nausea, followed by paralysis of the legs, spreading upward. Bleeding from orifices, even pores in the skin, difficulty forming sentences, then words. The brain will lose function in proportion to the paralysis—fifty percent paralysis correlates to fifty percent loss of brain function. In thirty-six hours, the paralysis reaches the lungs and heart. If by some miracle life functions can be continued artificially, in forty-eight hours the internal organs will be damaged beyond repair. Fun stuff, this virus."

Hailey uncurled her hands. They were shaking. "Each consecutive injection increases the risk of infection by twenty-five percent. I'll need three to fully incorporate the regenerative agent into the subject's DNA. Easy math, there. It will need to be timed precisely. The disease can be stopped and even reversed in early stages, but once it reaches a certain point, game over. I need to allow enough time for the virus to carry its load to every cell and then stop it before it does irreparable damage to the subject's system."

Hailey would have to inject herself at precise seven-hour intervals. The final injection had a time-released antivirus component. She'd double- and triple-checked it to make sure it would not activate until the virus had done its job.

"On a brighter note," Hailey said, giving her best attempt at a smile, "I have a date today." With a bracing breath, she sobered again. "Okay, here we go." She put on gloves and rolled up her sleeve. The three syringes were already prepared. She could have used an injection gun but, call her crazy, she was a classicist. "Time of injection, three twenty-two." Hailey jabbed the needle in her arm. "Computer, set alarm, new reminder. Ten twenty-two. New reminder, seventeen twenty-two."

"New reminders. Set," the computer announced. "Ten twenty-two and seventeen twenty-two. Today, August 14, 3032."

"That's great," Hailey said and pressed gauze to the injection site. "I'm going to bed." If anything went wrong, she'd know in the next two hours. She took an injection gun with the antivirus with her just in case.

Nothing to do now but wait. She'd be going crazy if she wasn't so damn tired. Pulling all-nighters used to be a cakewalk. With some caffeine and standard issue neural stimulants, she could go two or three days without sleep, cram for a test, ace it, go celebrate, and then return to her normal sleep cycle as if nothing had ever happened.

Ah, those were the good old days. The best club she'd ever been to, she'd been half zombie when she walked in at the trailing end of three days without sleep and her usual pharmaceutical help. But stepping into that club had been like getting hit by lightning. She hadn't left until the early morning hours, still flirting with the DJ to play just one more song. He'd played a slow one and danced with her before he escorted her to the door.

Hailey missed those times when she could do whatever the hell she wanted and her body actually obeyed. She was beat from having to fight so damn hard for every little thing. Each victory felt the same as a failure. Each took a little more out of her. It was exhausting just keeping her mind focused so she wouldn't go into spin cycle and curl up in some dark corner to bawl her eyes out.

It was tempting, so tempting, to just let herself fall asleep and never wake up.

But Hailey had never been one to give up without a fight. She still had some left in her.

When she came out of the lab, she found Amelia sitting on the floor in the hallway. Hailey's jaw nearly dropped. The aloof scientist was a mess. Amelia's hair was mussed, her eyes red, her clothes in disarray as if she'd tried to sleep in a chair and ended up tossing and turning all night. She looked like she was heading into the worst wave of DTs, all shivery and staring off into space—and was that dirt on her hands?

"I should have scanned your brain more deeply," she said. "Maybe I would have found some anomaly to explain why you're so determined to kill yourself."

"I'm tired," Hailey told her. And it was true. She was drained. Not enough left in her to worry about herself or her sister. Or to give a shit about what Amelia was saying. Now Hailey wasn't just a screwup anymore. She was damaged. Touched in the head. Funny, Hunt had said something similar to her yesterday. She couldn't be bothered to come up with a reply. Amelia had already delivered her death blow.

Everything after that was overkill.

Amelia pushed to her feet. "You could have jumped in front of a bus. Could have asked Hunt to throw you off that damn cliff. Hell, if you'd told me a few months ago that you wanted to die, I could have put a bullet through your head!"

"Big talk for someone who refused to inject me with a virus." There was no heat in her words.

Amelia compressed her mouth into a thin, offended line. She wanted to hit Hailey, that much was obvious. But she was restraining herself. As if it mattered. "A bullet is more humane," Amelia said, seething. "What do you expect me to do now? Sit by your bedside and hold your hand while you fall apart?"

"No," Hailey said. Despite what had to be Amelia's best attempt to rattle her, Hailey wasn't rising to the bait. And that had to drive her sister crazy. Hailey didn't care.

But hey, if Amelia needed to vent her frustration on a dying person, if that's what helped her sleep at night, it wasn't as if it made a difference to Hailey one way or another. Either she would die, in which case she wouldn't care one bit, or she would recover and say good-bye to Amelia—forever this time. In which case… she still wouldn't care one bit.

It was a strange feeling to willingly cut oneself off from someone like that. There was a hollow in Hailey's chest where some sort of emotion should have been. Anger, grief, pain… something. But there was only the smallest smidgen of regret, that faint whisper of a question: *What if? What would have been?* Not enough to make her dwell on it. Not enough to go back and do something about it. Just enough to serve as a reminder that at some point there had been something.

Hailey was worn out so completely she couldn't dredge up another ounce of emotion. She took out her earpiece microphone and pressed it into Amelia's hand. "I expect you to do what you always do best. Be objective. Be the scientist, Dr. Chase. I'm going to sleep."

Jeremy should have done as Pixie had told him and gone to see Hailey instead of calling her. He was almost sure that she would show tomorrow, but that still left hours of waiting until then. Pixie had gone to her friend's house for a sleepover, saying she couldn't take it anymore. Without her to distract him, Jeremy was about to go crazy.

He paced the house for a long time then went to bed, tossed and turned for what felt like hours. Every time he closed his eyes, they just wanted to open again. He needed to see her.

The clock on his nightstand read 4:05. In an hour or so it wouldn't be so bad if he just showed up at the lab. Lots of people had guests at five in the morning.

Jeremy punched the pillow. It didn't help. He tossed it to the floor.

Great, now he didn't have a pillow. What the hell was wrong with him? He was going to see her in a few hours. If not at the Patio, then at her lab. He wasn't going another day without talking to her. That should have put him at ease.

But something felt off. Jeremy was exhausted and restless at the same time. He wanted to sleep but couldn't because he had that annoying sense that he might have forgotten something important.

He hated that feeling.

Frustrated, he sat up, but couldn't stand off the bed. His legs felt weighed down with lead, his head spun, and his eyes slid shut. It took a lot of effort to open them again.

This wasn't him. Jeremy was wide awake, his mind working over-time. This was something else.

Could it be…?

No.

But maybe Pixie was right…?

It didn't matter. Even if she was, Jeremy didn't have the mental prowess to test his range right now. Clearly he was picking up on something, but to tune in to it and trace it to the source would take more concentration than he was capable of at the moment.

He wondered how Hailey was doing. Had she found a cure yet? Had it worked? Was she sleeping now? He wanted to see her dreams. It was the only connection he had with her, and maybe, just maybe, it was strong enough to hold across a distance. Hell, it was worth a try. It wasn't as if Jeremy had a plethora of other things to keep him occupied, and he'd already accepted that sleep would not be forth-coming tonight.

The one thing about that connection was that it was effortless. It sucked him in whether he tried to enter or not, whether he wanted to or not. *Just close your eyes and sleep. Nothing to it.*

He closed his eyes.

And sucked in a shocked breath when the darkness in his mind's eye brightened rapidly into a world he knew.

Mountains of pale gray stone, green fields, lush flowers… a crystal-clear creek winding its way through the valley.

Was he dreaming? No way. He couldn't have fallen asleep that quickly. And his mind was too sharp, too active to be asleep. What the hell was this? Pixie could have dosed him with something, except he hadn't eaten anything and he never let her pour him anything to drink anymore. Not since that last time she'd poured absinthe in his juice just to see what would happen.

So… this was real?

She appeared out of nowhere on the other side of the creek.

It wasn't the Hailey he knew, but the one she used to be. Shiny, auburn hair billowed around her in the breeze. Sunlight picked out the red in it, making it stand out like flames. She was wearing a strappy top and a wraparound beach skirt. Every time the wind tugged at the fabric it revealed the lush length of her leg up to the top of her thigh. A pair of flip-flops dangled from her fingertips. She was smiling, but her eyes were sharp.

"Hailey?" What was this? The vision felt real. He could feel the ground under his bare feet, the warmth of the sun on his shoulders. He felt the breeze stir his hair, and he smelled the flowers all around him. It could be manipulation of some sort, someone making him see and feel this. Except even Hunt couldn't create one out of scratch like this and make it complete in just a blink of an eye. He was as uneasy as hell that he couldn't figure it out. "What's going on?"

Hailey dropped the shoes and turned in a circle. "You like?"

"Where are we? Is this my mind or yours?"

She shrugged. "If I had to guess, I'd say we're somewhere in between."

"Come on, be serious for a minute. You have no idea how easy it can be to get lost in a mind. It's dangerous." And he could already feel his grip on reality slipping. He no longer sensed the mattress beneath his head or the covers over him. He'd left the window open, but though he knew it had to be cold with the breeze coming in from the lake, he felt nothing but the warmth of this world. Jeremy looked around for some kind of anchor and found nothing. There was no inconsistency here, no rip or seam in the surrounding scenery. Nothing to tell him what was real except the knowledge that this wasn't.

Hailey rolled her eyes. "Talk, talk, talk. Boring. Why don't you come over here and kiss me instead?" She opened her arms to him, beckoning.

And still he didn't cross that creek. He rooted his feet, even though every cell of his body wanted to go to her. Touch her. Taste her. He hadn't even realized how much he'd really missed her until now, when she was standing in front of him, a spirit of the sun, made to thrive in it, bright and beautiful and so alive. He wanted to feel that strength in her, to take succor from it.

But it wasn't strength. It wasn't beauty. It was an illusion, and her eyes betrayed it—they were wary; her smile never reached them. Those blue-gray eyes said—screamed—so much more than the image she was trying to project. Something was wrong here. This wasn't his Hailey. This was a stranger, someone who didn't exist anymore, if she'd ever existed to begin with. This was who Hailey thought she should be. He didn't want this. "Stop it," he said. "Show me the real you."

She blinked, and her arms lowered to her sides. "Why? I thought you'd like this."

"I want the real you. Who you are, not who you think you used to be." He wanted her so much, he was sick with it. Could she feel it? Sense it somehow? "Why the big show?"

Something changed in her expression. She came forward to cross the stream, and as she did, her appearance faded like a mirage into something else. Now her hair was brilliant white in the sunlight, glistening like snow, and she wore a flowing white dress. Gray eyes looked up into his, almost desperate when she came to him. She looked and moved like a ghost; her feet never disturbed the surface of the creek. The haunting image made his gut clench. "What would you do with your last day in this world?" she asked.

It was her tone that undid him. She was everything he'd ever dreamed of and so much more, standing right in front of him, and still somehow completely out of his reach. *Wrong. So wrong.* "Jesus, Hailey, what did you do?"

She didn't answer. "If you knew the world would end tomorrow, what would you do with your final hours?"

I'd spend them with you. Holding you. Loving you. I'd put an entire lifetime into a kiss and take my last breath in your arms. The answer was instantaneous in his mind; he didn't even have to think about it. Jeremy had spent his entire life analyzing every thought, every decision and action, always searching for a reason or explanation.

He let all of that go, accepted the world around him, gave himself up to it. Instead of fighting now, he simply acknowledged and accepted. *I love her.*

In such a short period of time, he'd managed to fall in love with the most beautiful, stubborn, complicated, pain in the ass female he'd ever met. A few months ago, he would have laughed it off as ridiculous. It took years to truly get to know a person and appreciate them for who they were, let alone love them for it.

But when it came to Hailey, rules of the universe didn't seem to apply. Everything around him was proof of that. An impossibility that somehow became possible. Just for them. To bring them together when it seemed as if they'd be torn apart. Jeremy needed this, needed her.

He looked at Hailey and couldn't imagine the rest of his life without her. She was in every picture and fantasy his mind conjured. At every crossroads and major event he could imagine from now until the end of his life; even in the ordinary, everyday moments, he saw her with him.

The thought that she might not be there made him desperate to freeze time somehow, to keep her forever.

Because he knew her question wasn't an idle one. It wasn't random musings or some new need to discuss philosophy. Jeremy looked into her eyes and saw fear. Something had happened since they'd parted ways. Something had shaken Hailey enough that she truly believed she would be dying. Very soon.

Had she failed?

She wouldn't tell him, of course. The way she was looking at him—

desperate for something—if he pushed, made her confront it, she would disappear, and Jeremy knew he'd never find her again. In this world, or the real one.

"Tell me you're okay," he said, silently pleading for reassurance.

Her smile was sad. "Answer the question."

No words would ever be enough to answer her, so he showed her instead.

He kissed her, putting all of himself into that small gesture. It should have been momentous. Instead, it felt so pathetically insignificant. A kiss. The exchange of breath; something romance novels forever touted as one of the most important, most telling events in any budding relationship. In reality, or at least this version of it, it could never be enough.

Jeremy didn't just want Hailey's breath. He wanted all of her—her soul. He snatched her up in his arms, desperate to hold on to her even while he felt her slipping away. Jeremy kissed her in a frenzy of need, and the small sound she made, almost a sob, tore at his heart.

She touched him softly. Brushed her fingers through his hair, gently. Where before she'd clung to him, scratched and demanded her due, now she was still in his arms, caressing him almost as if to soothe him. When she was the one so hopeless, so in need of solace and safety.

Jeremy realized then that was exactly what this world was.

Her sanctuary.

Where she needed to be so desperately, where she was safe, and warm, and loved.

Jeremy broke the kiss, touched his forehead to hers. "Christ, baby, don't do this. Don't leave me."

"I'm right here," she whispered. *For now.* She didn't say it, didn't want to acknowledge it, but it was there, all around them, an hourglass turned upside down, sand quickly trickling away, time running out.

Jeremy drew back. "How long do we have?"

Again Hailey smiled sadly. "All the time in the world."

"Then let's make it count."

– 20 –

Hailey felt the lie all around her. She embraced it, gave herself up to it. The strap of her dress slid off her shoulder. She pushed the other one down as well, letting the garment slide to the ground at her feet. She was bare beneath it. Exactly as she was, flaws and all.

Because that was what Jeremy wanted: her.

Not an illusion of her, not some airbrushed model, just Hailey.

She felt his gaze on her skin, and it made her shiver. Faint rosettes bloomed all over her body, a scattering of spots she'd used to hate. In his eyes she saw his reaction, and softened. They were beautiful, because he thought they were.

"Ah, Hailey," he breathed, almost like a prayer.

Hailey choked back tears. "Touch me," she whispered. If tomorrow never came, she wanted, *needed*, to have at least this night.

Jeremy came to her slowly, put his hands on her with reverence. He didn't treat her as if she was fragile. He touched her the way every woman should be touched. As precious, and worthy, and beautiful. He brushed her hair back over her shoulder, sifted his fingers through it and watched it glimmer in the sun. It was like snow, or angel wings, shimmering with magic. She'd never looked at it like that before.

With suddenly nervous fingers, she set to work on the buttons of his shirt. Jeremy didn't rush her. He let Hailey take her time while he nuzzled her hair and caressed her skin. He was close, always touching her, and with each pass of his hand, Hailey felt herself relax a little more.

Finally his shirt fell away. His pants followed, and then he pulled her against him skin to skin and kissed her deep. Hailey clung to him, matched her tongue to his, gave herself up to it and let him oh so slowly stoke her passion.

This wasn't anything like their last time. Where before they'd been wild for each other, now every touch and kiss meant so much. The sheer intensity of it stole Hailey's breath away. When Jeremy looked at her, she felt on fire. When he touched her, he left trails of molten lava in his wake.

The world spun as he laid her in the soft grass, the sun above blinding her; but then Jeremy was there, shielding her from it, kissing her, stroking her. Hailey trembled, eager to go faster but somehow knowing he wouldn't allow that. He'd meant it when he said they'd make this time count.

She brought her knee up to cradle him, and Jeremy rocked against her, teasing. Hailey could hear his heart beating faster. He wanted this as much as she did. Why was he stalling?

She braced her foot and pushed until they rolled over and she ended up on top. She smiled down into his eyes, the color of dark sapphires in the sunlight. "This is my dream," she said. "And in my dream, I want to play."

Jeremy blinked, uncomprehending until she wriggled down his body to settle between his legs. His shaft pulsed, hot and hard. Just looking at it made her mouth water for a taste and her body clench to feel it inside her. Jeremy said nothing, but when she grasped him and squeezed, he cursed on a groan, and his head thumped back on the ground. He was up a second later, watching her.

Hailey liked his gaze on her. It made her feel wicked. She licked the underside of his cock from base to crown and then swirled her tongue around the head before she sucked it into her mouth. His hips shot up, but she held on to him, pumping her hand and using her mouth at the same time. Another string of harsh curses made her laugh around him, eliciting a deep moan of pleasure.

He tunneled his hands through her hair, guiding her movements. She felt the growing tension in him, knew he was close even before he bit out, "Hailey, you have to stop."

But this was her dream. Her rules. Hailey took him deeper, and his hands fisted in her hair but not to pull her away. Jeremy hesitated just long enough for Hailey to do it again. He shouted her name when he came, spurting into her mouth. She lapped at him, taking all of him, any way she could. Hailey was greedy for this man.

In the next instant, she was on her back again, Jeremy's eyes scorching her. She gasped when she felt him hard against her again. "It's my dream, too," he informed her.

Jeremy never wanted to wake up. Hailey smiled at him in challenge, wrapped her legs around him, and tilted her hips up in invitation. But if she got to play, he wanted to, as well. He matched her smile with a devilish one of his own. "Turn around," he said.

Her eyes flashed silver, and she slowly unlocked her legs, taking every opportunity to touch while she did as he told her. Jeremy leaned back to watch her pull her knees under her and lift her ass up in the air, back arched like the cat she was. His cock throbbed to get inside her.

He gripped himself with one hand and the swell of her hip with the other, coming up to kneel between her thighs. Hailey made a mewling sound when she felt him, reaching back to make him hurry. *Oh, no.* He wanted to take his time; wanted to tease her, drive her out of her head with lust.

He wanted to see that incredibly soft fur he'd felt along her spine before, wanted to rub his face in it. She'd never be this open, this free with anyone but him, he vowed. Jeremy would be the only one who ever got to see her in such wild abandon.

Hailey turned her head to look at him askance. The flicker of silver in her eyes nearly made him spill again. He teased the head of his cock against her entrance and shuddered. "So wet."

Hailey hummed in answer, rocking her ass to try and coax him closer. Jeremy resisted. Just barely. Reaching around her to her front, he stroked through her folds to her clit, reveling in the sounds she made. Jeremy leaned over her and kissed her spine, pushing slow and deep. He felt her tremble and, *Ah, God, yes!* There was that downy fur, the rosettes standing out stark against her pale skin. Not everywhere, but in swirling patterns. Artwork worthy of a master.

Hailey arched her back more, pushed against him, drove him with silent commands to go deeper, faster. He couldn't resist if he wanted to. He thrust into her, skin slapping against skin, feeling her squeeze like a fist around him. It felt more real than anything else outside of this illusory world.

She cried out, her words muffled against her arm. Shock made him still, deep inside her. "What did you say?" It couldn't be.

Hailey pushed back against him insistently. And she said it again.

Hell no! Jeremy pulled out, flipped her onto her back and fell over her, bracketing her face with his hands. "Look me in the eye and say it."

She was panting, eyes unfocused, too far gone into her lust to guard her words. Even while her body strained again for him, she gasped out, "I love you."

He could have happily strangled her. "You're only saying that because you think you're going to die."

Hailey met his gaze, an inferno blazing in her liquid silver eyes. Instead of answering, she pulled him down and kissed him hard. No holds barred, no tender touches; it was all tongue and teeth, wild and hot. And so clearly a stalling technique.

Jeremy broke away and buried his face in her shoulder. The scent of her clean, hot skin made him dizzy with want and he couldn't keep from rocking against her. He wanted to believe her. Was desperate for her to mean it. "*Fool is he to love the wind,*" he quoted from an obscure text he'd found years ago. "That's what sucks most about this, you know."

He raised his head to watch her face when he pushed into her again. He wasn't gentle. "I love you so much, it's all I can think about," he growled and thrust again, even harder. "I wake up and you're there, even when you're not. I look out the window and wonder if you'd like the view. I play music and wish you were there to hear it, too." His words were punctuated with each slam of his hips, and she gasped. "But to you, I'm just a last-minute hot fuck." One more time and she cried out, clutching his shoulders, claws digging in. "Well, you get what you asked for this time, babe."

He fucked her exactly the way she wanted him to, took out his frustration on her, but never hurt her. Even if this was a dream, he could never hurt her. She might wake up in the morning and recall nothing more than a hazy illusion, just like all the other times. She might not even remember she'd said those words to him. But he would.

And for that, too, he wanted to make her pay.

Hailey matched him, took his aggression, reveled in it, loved it. She'd wanted this and wasn't shy about enjoying herself, thoroughly oblivious to the arrow she'd just shot straight through his heart. He felt her near her peak, then reached between them to stroke her clit and send her over. She screamed, claws scoring his back and making him follow right along with her.

Jeremy hated her for making him feel this way. For making him love her, and despise her, and want to take care of her, and punish her all at the same time. She was driving him insane and there was nothing he could do about it.

"Thank you," she whispered, tunneling her fingers through his hair.

Jeremy tightened his arms around her, furious, terrified that he'd already lost her. Even now, with their minds entwined so completely that he couldn't tell where one began and the other ended, he couldn't shake the feeling that none of it had mattered. Deep in his gut, he somehow knew he might never see her again.

Resentment coiled in his stomach. She'd never promised anything, had gone out of her way to let him know this was all she would ever allow him to have of her. His own fault for not listening. He'd chased this storm, let it sweep him up and give him wings, heedless of the wreckage it left behind. And the pathetic thing was, even as he crashed down, watching the storm move on, he still wanted to get up and chase after it again. Just to feel the wind beneath his wings one more time. Jeremy was sick of it.

The sky began to bleed like a canvas doused with water; blue rained down onto the green grass; colors mixed and swirled, diluting and darkening, pulling them apart. He didn't fight it, let the illusion crumble with a morbid feeling of satisfied relief that it was finally over and he could let his shattered heart die. He didn't even look at Hailey again until it was almost gone.

She was crying, her quiet good-bye.

And he felt like his soul just got ripped out of him.

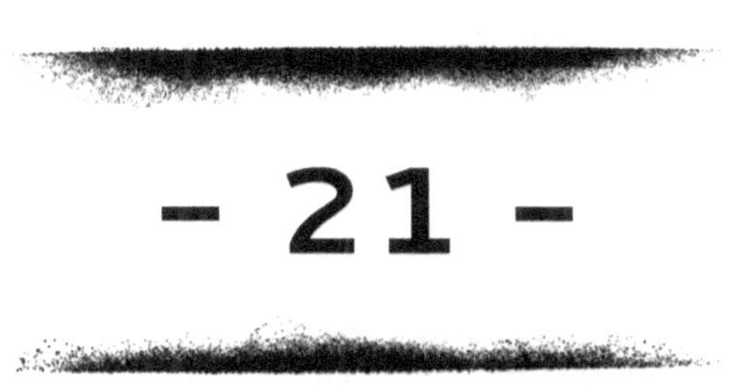

Hailey was shivering when the alarm woke her. And it had nothing to do with the curl-your-toes, turn-your-world-upside-down erotic dream she'd just had.

God, if only.

She was freezing and the chills came in waves, sweeping though her body deep into her bones. The temperature in her room was seventy-five degrees. It was a bad sign. Hailey reached blindly for the syringe on her nightstand, nearly dropped it, her hands shaking too much to get a good grip on the small thing. She jabbed herself in the arm and collapsed back on the bed. The ceiling was spinning. It made her queasy to look at it, but closing her eyes was even worse.

No regrets, Hailey had told herself a few months back. Then, as now, she'd been holding a syringe to her vein. *No regrets*. Such a simple concept and still she couldn't wrap her brain around it.

No regrets?

She'd changed her body past the breaking point—literally. She'd completely altered the course of her life and it wasn't exactly for the better. Maybe Amelia had been right about her all along. Maybe Hailey really was a reckless idiot for doing this to herself. It wasn't as if she'd done it for some noble cause, for the betterment of humanity or some such crap.

She'd done it to prove that she could. To show Amelia once and for all that she wasn't in any way special, or better than Hailey. All through college, when Amelia had been working on her MD and Hailey had been living life to the fullest, beach hopping and sampling local brews, it had been so obvious to Hailey what a disappointment she'd become to her sister.

Squandering her potential. Not taking responsibility for her life. Being the lazy, good-for-nothing brat who never worked for anything in her life.

And Hailey had let her think that because she'd always known one day all of it would change. One day she would do something so phenomenal and amazing—*without* Amelia's help or support—and then maybe she would regain some modicum of respect.

Was it too much to ask for her sister to not judge her lifestyle? The fact that she'd been "squandering her potential" meant there was potential to squander. But somehow Amelia had never managed to see Hailey's past her own. She'd been living in the spotlight for so long, it had blinded her to everything outside of it.

So who was the bad one?

Hailey sighed and sat up. It didn't really matter in the end. Truth was, both of them had screwed up majorly. Amelia might have a stellar career, but she was a hermit because of it. If she had any friends, Hailey didn't know about them.

And Hailey…

Well, her current state was testament enough as to how messed up she really was.

She wrapped the blanket around her when she stood and went to the bathroom. The floor was so cold it felt like stepping on ice. She turned the shower on all the way to hot, something she hadn't done in months, and stepped into the spray. Hailey had to touch the wall to steady herself. She wasn't leaning—yet—but the contact helped to anchor her, otherwise she'd sway on her feet and probably bust her head open on the tile.

Hailey waited to see whether her condition would worsen. It wouldn't get better until she got the last injection, but if it got drastically worse, it would be in the next few minutes.

Nothing happened.

Not quite progress, but she would take anything at this point.

At least the hot water stopped the worst of the shakes.

Hailey dried herself and dressed in layers of clothing; it was the best she could do here. She put on three pairs of socks, but didn't bother with shoes. She liked feeling the ground beneath her feet.

"Startup medical equipment," she said. The computers here were all voice-activated.

"Medical equipment ready," the automated voice replied. Strange; it usually took a few minutes.

"Locate. Dr. Amelia Chase."

"Locating. Dr. Chase is in the chemical lab."

"Is she messing with my stuff?" She'd better not be.

"Dr. Chase is in the chemical lab," the computer repeated. It did that when it didn't understand the question.

"Yeah, I got that, thanks." Hailey headed in the opposite direction to the kitchen. She wasn't hungry at all, but she had to try to eat something. *All the power in the world, contained in thought,* Hunt had said. Maybe if she just told herself she wouldn't get sick, it would work.

Amelia came to her there just as Hailey was sitting down with her bowl of fruit salad. "How are you feeling?" she asked.

"Never better," Hailey said. Ask a stupid question…

"I went over your notes."

"Oh, God, here we go. You couldn't have waited until I finished eating? As if I'm not sick enough already?"

"I was impressed," Amelia said.

Hailey almost dropped her fork. She stared up at her sister, waiting for the punch line. There would be one any second now.

Any second…

"May I sit down?"

"Uh, yeah." What was this, some kind of trick?

Amelia sat and adjusted her glasses. "Listen, I'm… really sorry about yesterday. I handled the situation badly. I just… I got scared. But I want to help, Hailey. Any way I can."

Hailey put her fork down carefully. "Why? So you can put it in one of your medical journals?"

Amelia nodded. "I deserved that. No. I want to help because you're my sister and I love you."

"Well, that's great that you had this epiphany, but you were right yesterday. There's really nothing you can do."

"That's not true. You haven't finished the course of injections. We can still alter the last one."

"To do what, exactly?"

Some of Amelia's enthusiasm faded. "I haven't really thought that far ahead. The truth is, you actually did a really good job with the virus this time. Under the circumstances I don't think anyone else could have done better."

"Amazing how a death sentence can motivate you."

Amelia blew out an exasperated breath. "I am trying to make amends here. It would be nice if you could meet me halfway."

Okay, that did it. "*Meet you halfway?*" she repeated. "Where the hell have you been since Mom died? I've tried for years to reach you. I invited you to every outing I went to until I moved out. You never even *looked* at me. You just kept on typing on your computer and told me to go and have a good time. And now suddenly when I'm dying you have a change of heart and *I'm* supposed to meet *you* halfway? There is no *way* between us anymore, Ams. You burned all the bridges a long time ago. You left me on my own because you couldn't deal. Well, I can't be there to console you now. I'm too busy fighting for my life."

The tirade got her heart racing, but instead of bracing her, it just made her more dizzy. It took Hailey a moment to focus enough to see the tears glittering in Amelia's eyes. And she felt like shit. Even though she knew she was one hundred percent right.

"Everything you said is true," Amelia said, duly subdued. "I guess I haven't been there for you much. It was just easier to deal with strangers. It didn't hurt me when they were in pain." Her composure cracked. "I'm sorry," she sobbed. "I don't want to lose my sister."

I will not cry. No crying here. I will not *cry.* Her chin wobbled. *Aw, damn it!* She gritted her teeth against the tears. "It won't change anything now," Hailey said.

Amelia wiped her nose on her lab coat sleeve. "I know," she said. "But I still want to try."

It was just fear talking. If Hailey died, it wouldn't make any difference anyway, and if she didn't, the two of them were too different to get along for any extended period of time. In a month or so, they would be back to fighting and not talking to each other. So it made no sense to keep up this pretense now.

Still, it was kind of nice to have a sister who cared, for once. "Well, then maybe you could turn the heat up in this joint and put some music on."

I play music and wish you were there to hear it, too…

Hailey shook her head hard. Where the hell had that come from?

Amelia laughed. She got up and hugged Hailey where she sat. "Eat up and then meet me in the lab. I think I can do something about the side effects without changing the virus."

I love you…

But to you, I'm just a last-minute hot fuck.

"Yeah," she said, dazed.

You get what you asked for…

"I'll be there in a minute."

~

Someone here didn't belong.

Tristan was standing hidden in the shadowy doorway of the butcher's house, a predator looking out over the crowd filling the marketplace. He recognized almost everyone, their minds as familiar to him as their faces. He knew their memories as well as his own. They were friends, or they were visitors.

One of them wasn't.

One mind in that throng was different enough to attract his attention. It made him uneasy. Not because he sensed a threat, but because he couldn't… pinpoint it. Whoever this person was, it was almost as if he barely existed. Tristan sensed his presence but nothing about him. A blank slate. A mirror reflecting the world around him but retaining nothing.

His fur itched beneath his skin, and he wanted to pace. An intruder on his territory. The other shifter was one thing. She would be dead in a day or two, or she would be gone. But this one… he didn't like it.

Tristan pushed away from the door to seek out the owner of the unpleasant mind.

He stopped midstep when a sharp pain pierced his abdomen. Fear made him sway on his feet. *—Dara?—* he called.

Silence. Strain.

He turned toward his castle and pushed his way through the crowd. *—Dara, talk to me!—* She was veiling her mind. Not blocking him out completely, just hiding her thoughts behind a curtain. She never did that. *—Dara!—*

He was about to force his way deeper when she answered.

—You better come home,— she said, and even her mind-voice sounded worried.

She drew back the curtain and let him merge with her mind completely.

Tristan stumbled as his abs tightened painfully. Heart in his throat, he changed directions again and ran for the doctor's house. He could still sense the young man there, about to go out into the market. Tristan caught the doctor a few steps from his doorway.

The ready smile dropped from the doctor's face in an instant. "Is something—"

"You're coming with me," Tristan told him.

"O-okay," the man said. He was timid and so damn young, but he was the best doctor on this world next to Amelia. And he had experience with birthing babies, something Amelia lacked.

—Tristan, don't scare the man.—

—I'm not,— he replied, refusing to look at the frightened doctor's face. *—How do you feel?—*

—Like two watermelons are fighting inside my stomach to pass through a hole the size of an orange,— she said. *—How about you?—*

—Like I'm about to kill someone if they don't get out of my way.— Anyone else would have cowered to hear him say that. Dara just smiled. He loved that about her. He loved everything about her. She was the sole reason for his existence. If anything ever happened to her… "Move it, Doc. We don't have much time."

"Then may I suggest a taxi?" the doc said, and pointed far right to the hovering transport next to the fire station.

"Genius," Tristan praised. He dragged the man to the transport and all but tossed him inside. Then he got into the front seat and reprogrammed the navigation to his address and maximum speed. "Hold on," he warned.

When the taxi took off, the doc fell back hard against his seat with a yelp. He'd be bruised, most likely, but he would live.

He'd better.

Tristan's mate was going into labor, delivering two children of a very large shape-shifter. He'd be jumping for joy if he wasn't so damn scared for her.

—It'll be fine,— Dara told him, even as another contraction nearly made her pass out.

Tristan punched the taxi's console. *—Hang on, baby, I'm on my way.—*

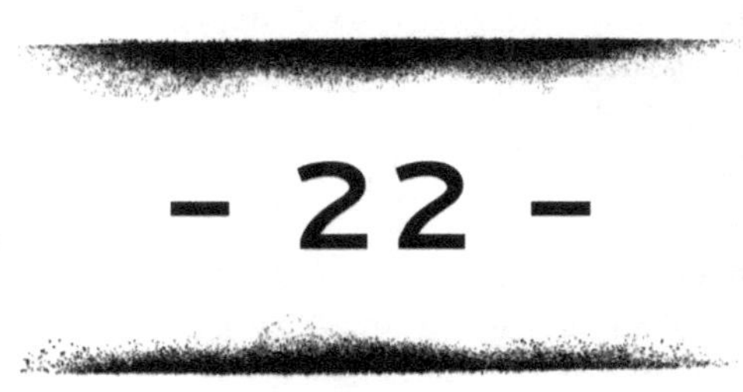

– 22 –

She hadn't come back. And no one would tell Arthur where the bastard had taken her. No one fucking *knew*! With every hour that passed, he worried more and more. Was she okay? Was she hurt? What had been done to her? All sorts of horrible imaginings filled his mind. She was alone and helpless in this place. She didn't know anyone here, just like Arthur, and without him, she had no one to watch over her.

All these people here were like bees, always buzzbuzzbuzzing around, always something. *Good morning, Mr. Glenn. How are you today, Mr. Glenn? Would you care for a biscuit, Mr. Glenn? How about a fish?*

What in the name of all that was holy was he supposed to do with a fish?

Arthur had eaten premade meals all his life. Now he was in a place where they only had "fresh" and "real." He was forced to either eat things raw or go to a restaurant. And there the volley of questions came from all sides.

But he'd managed to get a few answers, too. He was learning. Adapting. It was okay to talk back and respond here. People expected it. That was how things worked. People talked, and then Arthur was supposed to reply.

It was an interesting way to exchange information. He now knew the name of the man who'd taken his lady: Jeremy Calen. He also knew that the only way to get her back was to force this man to tell him how. Only he hadn't come back, either. There was no doubt in Arthur's mind that Calen was keeping her captive somehow. He must have learned something or seen something, and now his Hailey was trapped with that monster somewhere, and Arthur couldn't fucking get to her!

He had to switch hotels. That wooden shack was starting to feel like a coffin. He found a slightly better one on the other side of town. It was still quaint, but at least it had electricity and room service. Not that anyone ever came when he called. Unless there was a problem, people tended to forget he was there. The one drawback of being invisible was that he had to keep reminding the front desk of his presence, otherwise they'd try to rent the room out to someone else.

That had happened to him a few times in the past, too.

"Ah, Mr. Glenn!"

Arthur cringed.

The little old woman was dressed in something that defied description. Her waist was cinched, and the skirts looked so heavy he didn't know how she could breathe or walk. She was smiling at him as if he was her favorite person in the world.

"Uh… hi," he said, backing away from her. He might know the mechanics of conversing with people, but that didn't mean he had to like it.

"Well, don't be shy," the woman said and linked her arm with his, pulling him into the streets that were quickly filling up with more and more people. Normally, he would have loved getting lost in a crowd. Here, it was impossible. People saw him here. They smiled and greeted him as if he was some kind of idiot who needed that kind of affirmation.

He didn't need any of them.

He needed his Hailey.

"Listen, I really should be going. Lots to do today."

"Nonsense! No one is working today. Everyone will be at the faire. Whatever business you have will have to wait until tomorrow."

"Everyone?"

"That's what I said. We're celebrating the tenth anniversary of our town today. There's all sorts of fun things planned. Can't miss it!" She stopped and looked up at him. "Say, you were looking for our Jeremy earlier, weren't you?"

That Calen bastard! "Yes, I was." *Don't ask questions.*

"Oh! Well there you go," she said. "I heard Mr. Clark tell Mrs. Johnson that the boy reserved a table at his bistro for later today. Seems he's bringing a lady friend." She winked at him. "About time that boy found a good woman."

He recognized the care in her voice. She fretted over a bastard so undeserving, like a mother hen with an adopted son. Why would she bother? Calen wasn't related to her or she'd know more about him—and she didn't. No one knew anything except that he came here regularly for supplies and lived somewhere outside of town. They'd offered to take him there, but Arthur didn't dare make the trip. Who knew what circle of hell he'd be stepping into?

But the situation was approaching a point where he might not have a choice anymore. The longer Hailey was away from him, the more she was at risk. It was better for Arthur to brave the monster's lair than for his Hailey to do it on her own.

Now this woman was telling him he might not have to. Hope flared, making him almost tremble with the need to do something.

Arthur grabbed her arm to stop her when she turned to start walking again. "What time? Where is this… bistro?"

The woman blinked at him. "It's just over there on the Patio."

What the hell was a patio? He looked where she pointed to a slightly raised, giant wooden platform. It was bordered by some kind of low wooden fence that had flowers growing on top of it. There were two long tables with benches for seating, and along the fence little round tables with actual chairs.

"Are you sure?" he demanded. He couldn't take the chance that she might be wrong, or thinking of someone else. "Jeremy Calen"—*the bastard*—"made a reservation there?"

"Y-yes," she stammered. "Agent Jeremy Calen. The detective. Do you know him from Gray Dublin?"

Arthur looked at her, unable to disguise the animosity in his expression. He had no talent for it; he'd never had a need to hide what he thought. It used to be that no one noticed.

She did. She gasped and tugged at her arm. "You're hurting me, sir." She was looking around now, probably for someone to help her, and her hand shook when she tried to pry his fingers loose. "Let go!"

Fear. About time someone else felt what he felt. "I can't do that," he told her. "I'm afraid you'll fall if I release you. You're looking very pale. Maybe we should get you out of this crowd for some air."

She was wheezing now, shaking her head but unable to form words.

"It's all right," Arthur told her, smiling, though she would take no comfort from it. "Nothing to fear in this world except for demons. And I am just a man."

~

Jeremy had forgotten about the celebrations today. By the time he got to the town square, he had to push his way through the crowd to get to the Patio. It was packed, every table occupied, and a line of people waiting to be seated. They kept eyeing the one lone empty table by the edge with a view of the market, but the maître d' wouldn't let anyone sit there.

She'd better not; that table was reserved for Jeremy and Hailey.

It was almost noon.

He was a little early. But it was better to be out here, watching the parade and performances, than sitting at home and staring at the clock. He'd debated going to the lab to pick Hailey up for their date, but he'd already left a message for her to meet him here. It was bad manners to show up unexpected.

Still, any much longer without some kind of distraction and he'd do it anyway.

The people in line for the Patio didn't want to let him through to the front. They were mostly tourists, strangers who didn't know how things worked around here. Jeremy doubted any of them had ever had to wait for anything in their lives.

Here, nothing was rushed. It was rare for anyone to get asked to leave, even if they'd been sitting at the table for hours, doing nothing. That was all part of Torrey's charm.

Jeremy waved at the maître d' from the back of the line. Her name was Julia. She was a young girl, fresh out of college with a lot going for her. When she saw him, she smiled brightly and waved him forward.

"Excuse me," Jeremy said, trying to get the people to move.

"Wait your turn," someone had the gall to say. "I've been waiting for that table over there for thirty minutes."

"Yeah?" Jeremy replied. "Well, you've wasted your time. I reserved it for the day."

"Bullshit, man," the guy said, and grabbed Jeremy's arm to stop his progress. "There's no such thing as *day* reservations. Now, I want that table, and you're not taking it from me."

Jeremy speared him with a hard glare and pushed into his mind. The guy had only been here one day after a really long flight, disappointed as hell by what he'd seen so far, and frustrated because he couldn't get a flight back out for another week. He was about ready to snap, and Jeremy had just provided him with an easy target.

Or so he thought.

Jeremy moved some thoughts around, skewed his perception a little, amped up some paranoia, and pushed the violence to the back of his mind. All so he could shake off the guy's hand and say, "Don't mess with me. Not today."

It worked.

The guy shut his mouth and backed up a half step, as much as the limited space would allow.

Jeremy held his gaze a little longer to make his point, then looked at the others to see if anyone else felt like objecting. They didn't. He made his way to the maître d's podium, where Julia already waited, watching with her mouth hanging open.

"Nice day we're having," he said in greeting.

"Dude," Julia said, "that was the coolest thing I've ever seen!"

Jeremy wanted to grin. This was the first time he'd ever used something other than diplomacy to solve a problem. Apparently, Hailey was a bad influence on him. He couldn't wait to tell her. "Thanks," he told Julia, feeling like a rock star.

"Seriously," she said. "You just stared at him, and he backed off like he got dunked in cold water. Can you teach me how to do that?"

"All in the attitude." Plus some telepathic sleight of hand.

Julia took him to his table and gave him a menu. It was in Italian. If someone didn't understand, they could either take their chances, or ask a waiter.

"I should warn you, we got fresh apples today," Julia told him. "Bushels of them. The boss went nuts, so there are apples in every dish on the specials menu. Plus we have like five different apple desserts to choose from."

"You know, apples sound like just the thing today," he said, feeling restless and impatient, already scanning the crowds for any sign of Hailey. "I think I'll have the apple chips while I wait for my date."

"Ooh, a date, huh?" Julia waggled her eyebrows. "Anyone I know?"

Jeremy grinned. "All in good time."

"Must be serious. I've never seen you here before with anyone except Pixie."

"She's… one of a kind." Jeremy wondered if she remembered anything from last night. He did. Not everything, but enough that if she wasn't there in the next half hour, he'd be heading for the lab. He knew she probably hadn't meant it, but he still got that weird, funny feeling in his chest recalling her declaration that she loved him. *Wonder what it'll take to make her say it again…*

"Hey!" someone yelled from the line. "How long do you expect us to keep waiting? There's two tables empty already!"

"Keep your pants on," Julia yelled back. "I'm coming."

"Busy day?"

Julia's shoulders slumped dramatically, and she turned her gaze to the heavens. "You have no idea."

When she got back to her station, a waiter brought him a cold glass. "Courtesy of *il capo*," he said.

"What is it?"

The waiter grinned. "Apple juice."

Some kind of commotion across the square caused everyone to jump up and cheer. The Patio was raised three feet off the ground, but Jeremy still had to stand up to see over the flailing arms to the stage. The town's mayor was arriving in a fancy horse-drawn carriage. Both carriage and horses were decked out in flowers and ribbons, and the mayor wore a wreath of them on her head.

She was dressed in a historical costume and a translucent veil that was so long it flowed over the back of the open carriage and almost touched the ground. It looked like she was standing, but even with the mildest horses that wouldn't have been safe or comfortable for a woman of her years. There was probably a stool of some sort hidden by her skirts.

The carriage circled the gathering so everyone could get a good look, and then stopped by the stage. The mayor got down and waved to her people, then took a seat on the throne that stood ready for her. "Oh, Dunworth!" she called. "Dunworth!" When no one answered, she looked to her people. "Where is my master of ceremonies?"

A young woman whose costume seemed to be made of colorful ribbons and tiny bells danced her way onto the stage. "He's busy," she announced. In the past few years, this performance had changed actors a few times. The mayor and this Mistress of Misrule were the only original members of the cast.

"Busy?" the mayor repeated. "Doing what?"

The Mistress of Misrule shrugged. That was her only answer.

The mayor huffed. "I suppose we shall have to replace him…" She smiled. "Let us have *Mrs.* Dunworth!"

The crowd cheered as the troubadours called for Mrs. Dunworth to take her husband's place. They had to keep calling after the cheers died down to make themselves heard. But after a few minutes, when Mrs. Dunworth still hadn't appeared, the actors started exchanging worried looks. The mayor whispered something to her Mistress of Misrule, and the girl nodded and ran off.

"I suppose we can guess who is keeping Mr. Dunworth busy," the mayor said, but her heart wasn't in it. She looked worried.

Frowning, Jeremy left his table and went down into the crowd. It was humming around him like a nervous beehive, people whispering and murmuring, complaining about the delay, and pitying the actors who were so obviously unprepared for this.

There was so much noise, he couldn't make out the mayor's thoughts. He took the long way around to her throne, taking his time so as not to draw any attention from the already restless visitors. As he drew nearer, he opened his senses and screened through the chaos, looking for the mayor's consciousness. It took him a while, but the impressions became clearer the closer he got.

This was not part of the performance. The mayor had meant to honor Mrs. Dunworth for her services to the town. It was supposed to have been a surprise, which Mr. Dunworth should have played into. But for some reason, Mrs. Dunworth wasn't there.

Jeremy was ten feet away from the stage when the Mistress of Misrule screamed bloody murder.

The crowd turned into a stampede toward her, and Jeremy didn't have a hope in hell of following. He just stood aside and let them through.

On her stage, the mayor rose from her throne, but whatever the actress had found was too far to see. She worried her sleeves, waiting for someone to tell her what had happened.

Jeremy went closer to try to calm her, but he hadn't gone two steps before someone grabbed him from behind. An arm came around his neck, cutting off his air, and a hand covered his mouth. Jeremy was pulled off balance by the shorter attacker and couldn't get enough leverage to fight back. He was having a time of it just staying on his feet as he was dragged away from the square into a side alley.

Jeremy was trained for this sort of situation. He let himself go limp, even though it put more pressure on his throat. The man had to either carry his weight or drop him. At the same time, he forced his way into the guy's mind to gain control of the situation.

The moment he was in, chaotic emptiness swept him into a strong current he couldn't fight. There was no substance to latch onto and pull himself out. Only thoughts. Instantaneous; there one moment, gone the next, as if nothing ever… stuck.

For a moment he froze, fear warring with indecision as he sank deeper and deeper with that riptide. Anger swirled with excitement, a monstrous wave that crashed on top of him, driving him down into anxiety, and a feral, almost rabid isolation. There was weight without substance, heat without a source, and darkness that no amount of light could overcome; darkness so all-consuming Jeremy was losing himself in it.

Jeremy felt his eyes roll back in his head. He felt himself getting lost and wished to hell the guy knocked him out at some point because that was the only way he was ever getting out. He couldn't hope to sever the connection on his own—he didn't even know where it was anymore. Still he fought, grappling his way through the current of images and sounds, trying to find some sort of anchor, blindly flinging himself this way and that, at times falling through a mirage, at others being battered by one. None of it amounted to anything tangible. Those thoughts could destroy him if he let them. But Jeremy couldn't influence a single one.

Inside that thick vortex of nothingness, his overstimulated mind caught on an idea. If there wasn't an anchor, he had to create one. A single point of solidity would be enough to launch himself out of there. It had to work; it was the only hope he had.

Jeremy took hold of anything he could. Some thoughts slipped through his fingers, others dissolved into mist. But those he caught, he slammed together, forcing his captor to dwell on them.

Ten thoughts. Twenty. Fifty. The mounting confusion around him slowed the current almost to a standstill, yet even so, thoughts around him kept changing. They winked out of existence as new ones formed. His plan wouldn't work if those thoughts couldn't stick together. Already some were fading. Jeremy redoubled his efforts, added more thoughts, and the more of them he put together, the steadier the whole became.

The more of them he got, the clearer the picture became. It was like putting tiny pieces of a mosaic together and he couldn't distance himself enough to see the entire image.

But he felt it.

He touched the grooves and contours, and felt the design. It was so much bigger than Jeremy; bigger even than the man himself. It dwarfed them both, this idea that held more importance than anything else in the guy's mind, including himself.

Hailey.

Everything this man thought or imagined, no matter how brief or seemingly insignificant, centered on her. She was the reason for all of it, the grand design that gave meaning to his life. She was his god, his fate, his entire world. She was his savior, and he'd appointed himself hers in return. And everything he did, he did for her.

Jeremy was horrified at the depth of this obsession. It had managed to penetrate the guy's madness and give it focus, had altered the pathways just enough for him to latch onto Hailey as the only thing of interest in the universe. He defined himself by her and rarely even thought of his own name. But he had one…

Arthur Glenn.

Jeremy braced himself on the mural he'd created and used Arthur's mind, everything he had at his disposal, to send out one signal like an atomic explosion. He prayed it would reach someone who would know what to do with it.

Arthur screamed from the pain of it, opening a bright window into the outside world, and Jeremy launched himself toward it. Arthur's voice, louder than the blast of a foghorn inside his own mind, became completely lost among those of the crowd outside of it. Those who had found poor Mrs. Dunworth's lifeless, mutilated body.

Almost there. Almost out.

The window shuttered, plunging Jeremy back into darkness as a furious wave swept him sideways, away from his salvation. It was consciousness turned inward. Focused, yet still perceiving the world outside. Jeremy had no more strength to fight it.

Arthur raised his arm and clubbed him over the head with something hard and heavy. He felt the pain as if from a distance.

Jeremy had never been so relieved to pass out.

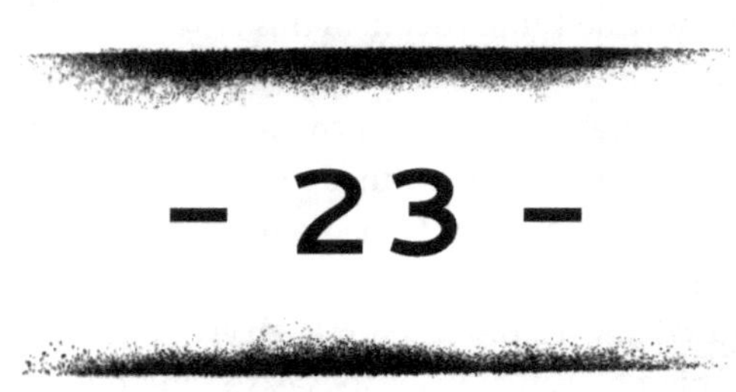

– 23 –

It was classical music day. Normally a snoozefest, but today a balm on Hailey's ears. Much easier to deal with than the brain-pounding rock she'd tried to put on earlier. That didn't work at all in her current condition.

And the classics made Amelia all happy, too. She hummed along while she checked Hailey's vitals, swaying to the rhythm as if she was imagining someone dancing with her. Hailey wished she could compartmentalize like that. Here they were, the good doctor Chase administering to her dying patient, and she was smiling. For the first time since Hailey had entered this lab, Amelia had a gentle, dreamy smile on her face as if she was somewhere completely different.

Let's see, where would I go? The beach. Or maybe a really great party.

Or more likely to a clearing at the foot of a mountain range with a freezing cold creek and a smoking hot telepath.

Hailey sighed grumpily and dipped her head a little farther into the blue, waterlike solution she was floating in. Just enough for it to cover her ears and dull the worst of the drums. Any small upset to her inner ear now made her feel like she was drunk and trying to drive a shuttle that hadn't been tuned in a decade.

To you, I'm just a last-minute hot fuck. What the hell had that meant? Though bits and pieces of last night's dream had been coming back to her all day, she still only had a vague recollection of what had happened. The harder she tried to remember, the more futile it became.

And why did she remember that Jeremy had been pissed at her, but not why? Had her mouth run away with her again? Had the cat done something to embarrass her?

She had no idea.

It was probably just nerves getting to her. It wasn't as if she always remembered her dreams in perfect detail, especially when the telepath was involved. But there was an annoying suspicion that worried her. Maybe it wasn't just the normal way of dreams. Maybe it was her brain starting to shut down little by little.

Hailey wiggled her toes to make sure she still could. She felt them moving, but without looking, she couldn't tell how much. She didn't dare look.

An electric shock passed through the solution, making her muscles twitch. That happened every few minutes now and seemed to help with the dizziness. Sort of… rewiring her brain a little. Who knew electroshock therapy could actually be helpful? Now if it could help her remember, she might consider making it a daily ritual.

"Okay," Amelia said. "A couple more minutes and we can get you out of there. How's your stomach feeling?"

Since she'd thrown up the fruit she'd had for breakfast? "A little better." Actually, it was in knots from the electric shocks and growling for sustenance, but the thought of food made her nauseated. Amelia had her on an IV for some nutrient cocktail, which was fine for a human, but the leopard inside her salivated for a chunk of raw meat to chew on.

Major ick.

The song ended, smoothly segueing into a soft aria as Amelia helped Hailey out of the minipool. Hailey felt as if she were leaving her spine in there. She dried herself off and put her clothes back on. The temperature in here was now ninety-five degrees. Amelia was working in her tank top and shorts, her lab coat hung over the back of her chair.

And Hailey still shivered.

The computer on the right beeped and a drawer unlocked. Amelia took out the tray and brought it to the gurney where Hailey sat. She wasn't weak enough yet to have to lie down, but she figured it was better to reserve what strength she had and not stand around needlessly.

"The patches are ready," Amelia said. "Lift your hair up."

The patches were thermochemical. Something new Amelia had just cooked up that would probably make her rich through retail sales. They were small, round bandages that adhered to the skin and, through some scientific mojo Hailey wasn't bothering to comprehend, regulated the body's temperature.

Meaning, if someone was in fifty degrees below zero, they could slap on a couple of these babies and be nice and toasty for twenty-four hours. And if someone had a fever, the patches would bring it down to a safer temperature.

Hailey was the first guinea pig for them.

Amelia peeled one small white circle off the tray and placed it on Hailey's nape, right at her hairline. The next one went lower on her spine, between her shoulder blades, and the third at the small of her back. Within seconds Hailey felt the patches warm as they sucked the heat out of her. Her body cooled by degrees until the room's temperature began to feel about right, and then even more until she was feeling hot in her jeans and long-sleeved T-shirt.

Both of them watched the portable monitor for any signs of distress to the body. Hailey's fever was down, her chemistry remained unaltered, and when Amelia checked Hailey's back, she concluded, "No sign of skin irritation. The patches seem to be working."

Another one for the record books.

"How's my blood looking?" Hailey asked. One of the computers was running continuously, extracting information out of the blood sample Amelia fed into it every half hour. Hailey had so many pinpricks on her fingers, she'd stopped counting them.

Amelia typed a few commands to display the results. "Looks like your white cell count is a little high, but that's to be expected. I don't see any degeneration of the red cells; that's a good sign."

"And the virus?"

Amelia shook her head. "It's too early to tell. We won't know if it worked until you get your last injection."

"But it should already be doing something, right?" she persisted. "I mean, I haven't had the full dose, but some changes should have already occurred if it worked."

"Possibly," Amelia said. "The trouble is, we don't know which parts, and to what extent."

"Then let's test it. I can change my toes and if they don't fall off, great. If they do, well, I just won't wear sandals."

Amelia glared. "*If* something changed, and I'm not promising that it did, there's no reason to think it would be your toes."

"But missing toes are much easier to conceal than missing fingers," Hailey said reasonably.

"You're not going to risk missing anything. We do it by the book this time. You wait until after your final injection. Once you stop feeling sick from the virus, we'll see."

The computer beeped again, and Hailey winced. Sharp noises felt like needles through her eardrums now. "I thought you programmed the stupid thing to stop doing that."

"Appointment reminder," the automated voice said. "Appointment for Hailey at Amberley Patio. Two p.m. Current time. Twelve thirty p.m."

"I didn't program *that*," Amelia said. She was smirking.

"What is this, third grade?"

"Hailey and Jeremy, sitting in a tree," Amelia teased. When Hailey glared, she cleared her throat. "You're right. I should go fix that."

Hailey sighed and pushed her sleeves up to her elbows. "You can also turn down the heat while you're at it."

Amelia waved from behind the console.

Three seconds later, a high-pitched screeching sound resonated through the lab. It brought Hailey to her knees, screaming and covering her sensitive ears. It didn't help. It was as if the sound was inside her head.

"Oh, God, what did I do?" Amelia yelled, frantically pushing buttons and typing commands.

Finally, the noise stopped. Hands shaking, Hailey pulled herself back onto the gurney. "What the hell was that?" Whatever it was, it had just ripped ten years out of Hailey's already troublesome life span. She was not amused.

"I don't know," Amelia said.

The noise started again, a chainsaw cutting Hailey's head open and rearranging her brain. "Turn it off!" she screamed, but couldn't make herself heard. Her ears felt like they were bleeding. She would kill somebody.

If she ever recovered enough to stand up.

Amelia ran to the doorway and broke the glass covering the fire alarm. Everything shut down, all the doors opened, and the rooms flooded with cool mist. It contained a fire retardant that was strong enough to douse a fire, but gentle enough not to destroy the equipment.

Blessedly, the noise stopped. By then, Hailey was so shaken all she wanted to do was lie down and sleep.

But in the darkness, she heard running footsteps in the hall.

She didn't have time to warn Amelia before someone ran into the room yelling, "What the hell took you so long!"

Hailey saw Amelia feel around the wall for the fire alarm again. The same button restored normal functionality. The lights came on a second later, and both Hailey and Amelia stared at the teenage girl with red hair and wide, bright blue eyes. She was panting and sweating, sickening fear rolling off her. Hailey breathed down a wave of nausea. She had nothing left to throw up, and dry heaving would just hurt too much.

"I've been trying to call you forever!" the girl said, bracing her hands on her knees to catch her breath. She was unsteady, clearly worn out and running on fumes and adrenaline.

Why did she look so familiar?

Wait… "Pixie?"

Jeremy's baby sister, now much older than the tiny little girl Hailey had seen in her vision, turned on her and grabbed her hand. "Come on, we have to go."

"Whoa," Amelia cut in. "She can't go anywhere."

"No choice. Jer's in trouble."

"She can hardly stand!"

"Listen, Doc," Pixie yelled. "I don't have time for this. Dara's in labor, Tristan won't budge an inch from her side, and a psychotic killer has my brother! I need Hailey's senses to find him and you're not stopping me from taking her."

Hailey's head spun. "Back up. Who has your brother?"

Pixie pulled. "There's no time. *Move!*"

Hailey cast Amelia a look and ran out, pulled along by the redheaded teenager. She sensed the girl's weakness. There were no hovering vehicles or horses around when they came out of the lab; she must have run the whole way. "I need you to tell me what happened."

"I don't *know* what happened," Pixie said. "One minute I'm trying on a dress, and the next I'm on the floor with a jumbled mess in my head. I dropped the dress, ran here."

"Did you see who took him, or where?" It was far easier to run over grass than over hard rock, Hailey decided. Even if her knees buckled every few steps from the strain. She wasn't even winded. But the girl wouldn't last much longer. "Wait, stop." She pulled Pixie to a halt. "Just tell me what you know. I can take it from there."

Her leopard was already stirring, pacing, thirsty for a good hunt. Hailey's fingers and toes itched, her eyesight shifting rapidly, but she didn't even notice through the dizziness. She *wanted* to run. She *wanted* to scent the air, lock on to a target and track it.

And when she found it, she would make it hurt.

Pixie's eyes filled with frantic tears. "I don't know! Everything is such a mess, I can't sort through it. I see Jer, I see you, and everything else is just chaos. And so much anger. God, I'm drowning in it!" She clutched her head, pulling on her hair. She'd tear it out by the roots soon.

Hailey covered the girl's hands with her own. *All the power in the world, contained in thought.*

Pixie gave a wet snort. "Hunt's so full of shit."

Hailey smiled crookedly. "I thought so, too. Now I need you to focus for a minute, okay? I want you to show me what you saw."

Pixie shook her head. "That's so not a good idea."

"We don't have another option." Pixie wouldn't be this freaked out if the situation wasn't serious. Jeremy was a trained agent, and both he and Pixie were telepaths. Pixie had to know he was capable of getting himself out of trouble. Which meant that, for whatever reason, this time he couldn't. "I can take it," Hailey said, hoping it was true. "I've dealt with some pretty messed-up shit lately."

"Not like this, you haven't," Pixie said gravely. Whatever it was she'd seen had shaken her badly. She took a deep breath and jumped up and down, shaking out her hands as she blew it out. "Okay, okay. No other options." She met Hailey's gaze, looking far older than she really was. "This won't be pleasant. You better brace yourself."

"Noted."

"Close your eyes."

Hailey did. She waited for a picture to take shape in her mind's eye. From Jeremy's previous forays into her head, she had a pretty good idea of what to expect. But this wasn't Jeremy, and Pixie didn't have a picture to show her.

What she got instead was a torrent of them. Chaos swirled inside her head, images, sensations, and random thoughts flashing past at the speed of light. For a split second, about half of those pictures crashed together into a bigger one, then shattered again to swirl madly. It happened several times, and each time it did, Hailey could make out more of what they built together.

Her stomach did a nasty dive. "What is this?"

"It's you," Pixie said. "And somewhere in there, it's Jeremy."

"Where is he?"

Pixie had to be gritting her teeth when she said, "I don't know! I tried so hard to make some sense of it, but it's like a recording. I can't alter it. All this stuff is just passing through, and there's no filter to it whatsoever. *Nothing* is retained, so I have nothing to focus on."

She wasn't making any sense. Hailey didn't know squat about telepathy or how it worked, except when it came to her and Jeremy.

From what she'd seen, the person who took him was nothing like them. Hell, Pixie couldn't make sense of it, so what chance did Hailey have? Already her head throbbed from the psychic invasion, and the virus spreading through her body wasn't helping. Hailey's heartbeat was ridiculously fast and irregular, her blood pressure fluctuating so much she could feel it. When it went up, her skin throbbed as if it would explode. When it went down, she got so dizzy and lightheaded, she felt that a single step would send her sprawling. "What was he doing before this happened?" she asked, making herself focus on the conversation. "Where was he? Do you know that?"

The vision blacked out, and Hailey opened her eyes.

"He was waiting for you at the Patio," Pixie said.

Hailey's heart raced. *What the hell was he doing there two hours before we were supposed to meet?*

"Did anyone see him?"

Pixie nodded. "Plenty of people. But then they just… didn't. It's like he disappeared from right under their noses."

Hailey took a breath to steady herself. "Okay. I want you to go back to the lab and tell Amelia what you told me. She'll take care of you. Call Hunt, tell him he might be needed. After his litter is born." Of all the times to start having pups…

"Hailey. There's more."

"What is it?" It couldn't be worse than this.

"I think he's killed someone."

I stand corrected.

– 24 –

Whispers dragged him out of the darkness. Gray ghosts slithering through his mind. Disturbed laughter, and through it, a litany of mumbles he didn't understand. Jeremy slammed his mental shields into place, shutting out the nightmare he'd somehow managed to wake from. He shuddered at the cold silence left in its wake.

His head pounded and his stomach roiled. The bastard had given Jeremy a concussion. Just great. Slowly, carefully, he raised his head. His vision swam as he opened his eyes, but thankfully it wasn't long before it settled. Good thing, too. The way he was leaning, tied to the wooden chair, an inch farther, and he would have fallen over.

A figure came toward him, a shadow against the light filtering in from the covered window. Jeremy made out a long coat, a head and arms. Human, then. "Are you awake?" It was a man.

Jeremy squinted, trying to make out the features of his face, but it was pointless. The more he tried, the more his head hurt. "Yeah," he said.

"Good," his abductor replied. And then he swung a haymaker at Jeremy's jaw.

His head lolled again. The chair had to be much sturdier than he'd thought, because he still hadn't fallen over. *Pretty stars…*

His captor braced his foot on the edge of the chair and pushed it over onto its side. Jeremy crashed, and dust clouds floated from the ground. *So much for that thought.* He coughed, eyes watering. Was that a potato sack in the corner?

This had to be a barn or storage of some kind. That narrowed down the possibilities to just about three hundred different places in Amberley alone. The window was covered with drapes. It was translucent enough to allow light through, but Jeremy couldn't see anything outside to orient himself.

Focus. Any little thing helps. Put the pieces together. Dirt floor and rafters above him meant a one-story building. He smelled the dust, dirt, and something… organic. Like vegetables. Potato sack in the corner. Jeremy rolled his head to get a wider view of his surroundings. There were more of those sacks but no tools. This wasn't a farmhouse, then. He was in town. *Which* town; now that was the bigger question.

Sight, smell, touch, taste, sound.

Jeremy closed his eyes to better focus his other senses. He tasted a faint tang of blood. Nothing interesting there—it was his own. It messed with his sense of smell, though. He wouldn't get any more clues from his nose. As for sound…

His abductor paced. His clothes rustled, but his footsteps fell silent on the dirt floor. Beyond that, there was a quiet hum of activity outside. It was far. They weren't by the square anymore. At this distance, even if he screamed, the chances of someone hearing him were slim. It would just be background noise. Easily screened out by busy people.

That was about all he had to work with. It wasn't enough. He might have to use telepathy to get out of this. *That* was risky in the best of conditions. But now, with a concussion and a crazy person who'd almost sent him into a coma once already, it seemed safer to take his chances and see how the situation would develop from here.

"Who are you?" he asked, keeping his voice slurred. Not that it was so difficult. His mind might be recovering quickly, but his body was significantly lagging behind.

The abductor chuckled. "I am no one." He said it like some clever inside joke that Jeremy was on the outside of.

Well, he wasn't. *Arthur Glenn.* The name came to him like an echo of his own voice. The spectator. A man lost in the world because he wasn't part of it. *No one, indeed.*

Jeremy groaned. "No offense, but I'm not really a big fan of bondage unless a really hot female is involved." *Hmm.* Something new to explore when he saw Hailey again. And by God, he *would* live to see her again. "If you could just—"

Arthur's boot slammed into his midsection so hard, his spine hurt. "*Shut up!*" he hissed. "You think this is a game? You think you can just waltz in and take her from me and I'll just sit back and let you?"

God, he was going to throw up. Or pass out. Possibly both. And the confusion wasn't helping. What was he talking about? Jeremy tried to ask, but couldn't find his voice and couldn't inhale to try. He shook his head instead.

Aw shit. Bad idea.

Arthur backed up and breathed in deep, as if to center himself. Then he went back to pacing.

Jeremy coughed weakly and fought to regain his breath little by little.

His head now felt as if someone was trying to shatter it with a hammer. *What the hell…?* He relaxed his shields the smallest bit.

Pixie's frantic emotions crashed through and nearly made him pass out again. She was so scared; he'd never seen her that scared in all her life. She was crying and shaking; she was cold, but her hands were burning, holding something hot. His sister was screaming at him, and her presence in his mind obscured everything else. It seemed safe to let her in a little more.

The moment he did, her words flooded his mind, shouted sentences in no coherent order. Chaotic thoughts in a terrified mind, trying at the same time to reason things out, calm herself, get through to him, and who knew what else.

It felt that she'd been yelling for so long, she didn't even realize he'd finally heard her. —*Pixie,*— he said.

The noise stopped completely.

And in that silence, the whispers rose again. Jeremy bit down on his tongue to distract himself while he performed some serious mental gymnastics to close one channel while keeping the other open. It was like trying to patch a leaking dam with chewing gum. It held in some places, but only for a moment before it all burst through again.

But if he shut down completely, he'd break contact with Pixie, too.

—*Where are you?*— Her words came through broken up, and she had to say it several times for Jeremy to get the message.

—I don't know,— he said. *—I'm on the ground at the moment. Can't see out the window to narrow it down. All I see is sacks of potatoes.—*

—That describes every cellar in Amberley!—

—Yeah.—

Pixie was pacing now, all business. She did that when she had to distract herself from something unpleasant. The little general. Jeremy almost smiled. *—Okay, is anyone with you?—* she asked.

—You could say that.—

—What does that mean?—

—Trust me, sis, you really don't want to know.—

Pixie stopped. He felt her mind go blank. Some whisper of a memory passed between them, too faint to make out, but whatever it was, it frightened her. *—Is* he *with you?—*

—Yes.— He showed her everything he saw, but omitted the other senses, including telepathy. It was very little to go on. Arthur Glenn was still no more than a shadow. Jeremy didn't even know what the guy looked like. He'd never be able to pick him out of a crowd.

—God, Jer, you have to get out!—

—Why?— Being kidnapped was bad, but not bad enough to elicit that kind of response. Used to be his sister had more faith in him. Unless… *—What are you not telling me?—*

Hesitation. Reluctance. Stubborn refusal to answer. Pixie was talking to someone now, screening her words from Jeremy and just leaving him with an impression of physical conversation. Thank God, at least she wasn't by herself.

—Is Hunt with you?—

No answer. More conversation. Then a sigh. Pixie came back subdued and sad. *—Hunt is with Dara. She's in labor.—* Well, that explained why the shifter wasn't busting in the door and coming to rescue his sorry ass. Jeremy would bet that an army wouldn't be able to tear Hunt away from his mate now. And for the next year or more. *—I didn't want to tell you,—* Pixie continued, *—because you need to not freak out right now, but Amelia says I should tell you everything so you know what you're dealing with. For the record, I disagree.—*

—Just tell me already.—

Another sigh. *—Mrs. Dunworth is dead. And not just dead. He…*

did things to her.—

Vague memories surfaced and began to take shape even while Pixie still talked. Images not from his own mind, but Arthur Glenn's. Mrs. Dunworth looking up at him with wide eyes; her scream cut short. A quick thing, to silence her. The rest of the process took a few minutes.

Gleaming claws slashing across, digging deep, tearing skin and everything underneath.

Blood. *Christ, there was so much of it.*

And afterward… *relief.*

Jeremy sucked in a breath. "You sick son of a bitch," he said, heedless of his own predicament.

In his head, Pixie was yelling for him to shut up, but he couldn't.

Arthur Glenn stopped pacing.

"What could that poor soul have possibly done to you? How the fuck do you even begin to justify killing an innocent woman—a grandmother, for God's sake!"

"*I* didn't kill her," Arthur replied calmly. "*You* did."

Pixie must have heard. Jeremy felt her consciousness fade slowly, flowing in a different direction, using him as the divining rod. Aiming at Arthur.

Sheer panic made Jeremy slam his shields back into place to cage her in. She couldn't go there. Not ever. Jeremy would die before he let her get lost in that chaos. "What are you talking about?"

"All this time," Arthur said, "all I could do was manage the effects. But now I can get rid of the cause. I can save her." He was so damn composed, almost giddy. Like someone who'd racked his brain over a puzzle so long, he could hardly believe that he'd solved it.

Jeremy couldn't see his features, but knew he was the object of whatever epiphany this guy had just had. It chilled him.

Arthur came closer and crouched in front of Jeremy. Still too dark to see his face, but the sickening tone of his voice was plenty. "You're the demon," he whispered, like it was some big secret and he was being naughty telling him. "It all makes sense now. Why she's been running, why she's been acting strangely, why she doesn't remember me. You're to blame for all of it."

He pushed to his feet and Jeremy had to crane his neck to look up at his face. A little light caught him just enough for Jeremy to make out his nose.

"When I kill you," Arthur said, before he turned his back on Jeremy, "she'll be free."

~

The moment Hailey entered Amberley, the stench of fear and blood overwhelmed her senses. Her body ached from the run, but rather than suppress her leopard side, it seemed to excite it more. She was fighting herself now not to change. Her cat lashed out, tried to gain dominion. Hailey had to brace herself against a building to keep her balance.

Whatever ground she and Amelia had gained fighting the effects of the virus seemed to be reverting now that she wasn't constantly getting some treatment or another. The dizziness was back full force, and after the mad run to Amberley, she was starting to shiver again. Not from fever, though. The patches along her spine worked like magic for that.

The leopard was frustrated at her weakness. If she could talk, she would probably be using any and every method possible to make Hailey let her out. The virus didn't seem to be affecting her; but then, it affected the body, not the mind. The animal couldn't—or wouldn't—comprehend that.

Hailey decided to name her Hellcat. Seemed fitting. The leopard didn't exactly follow any rules; she was a persistent little monster, like a little devil whispering in her ear that she could do better. The only reason she wasn't winning was that she was still separated from Hailey somehow. Possibly by that mental block Hunt was talking about.

The block that was quickly deteriorating. Hailey was getting more and more of Hellcat invading her thoughts and senses. Even as she shook and shivered, the virus raging through her body, her senses were in overdrive. She could see minute details from fifty feet away. She heard quiet sobs from inside the houses around her. She could smell the blood that had already been cleaned away.

And she could tell *when* it had been cleaned away, and where the body had been taken.

Hailey distinguished between the scents of fifty different people and could trace those scents to where they were now. It was amazing. Like seeing color-coded lines drawn in the air... except with her nose.

But more than that, there was a sixth sense she had no name for. Hailey felt the way she imagined a predator felt during a hunt. Her body was primed for attack, yet leashed somehow, humming with energy that would be explosive when set loose. Part of her thrilled at that, anticipated that moment. But the excitement was contained by tremendous focus. It had to be. Hellcat thirsted for blood, wanted to feel flesh tear beneath her claws, wanted to hurt something. Hailey wasn't sure she disagreed.

Did that make her a monster?

No, was her almost immediate answer. This wasn't something she did for pleasure; it was self-defense. Survival. Hunt had said that Jeremy was her anchor. She believed it now. If having him around had calmed the beast inside her, having him gone now drove it insane.

And that gave it strength. Hailey's control was slipping. Every time she shivered now, she felt fur itch just beneath her skin. She could no longer tell whether the aggression she felt was her own or Hellcat's, and she didn't really care. She *needed* Jeremy back. If anything happened to him, if she found him in anything less than perfect health, the person responsible would know pain unlike anything he could ever imagine.

Stop it! Can't think like that. Can't let the beast win.

Hailey closed her eyes and concentrated on her other senses. *Focus on the hunt, not the kill.* Slowly, little by little, Hellcat listened. The sensory overload rose to a crescendo in her head, but somehow Hailey managed to make sense of it.

She followed the voices first. People were still milling in the streets; remnants of the celebration that was supposed to be going on even now. Hailey could taste the excitement still lingering in the air. But it was now mingled with other, less appetizing emotions.

She followed a sobbing voice to a window. There, she casually leaned her back against the wall and listened.

"I can't believe she's dead," the woman was saying.

A man was there, trying to comfort her. "I sent my boy to fetch her husband."

"Oh, God, her children!"

"Easy now. Just breathe."

"But her body… who could have done such a thing?"

"Looks like wolves. I thought we took care of this last winter. They must have found a way around the fence."

"No," the woman sobbed, and there was force behind her tone now. "This was no animal. Animals don't come near crowds, and they sure as hell don't kill so quietly. *Someone* would have heard her screaming."

The best detective minds in major cities hadn't been able to come to that clear a conclusion. Hailey was surprised and impressed by the woman's deductive reasoning skills. But it made a sort of sense. It was easy to get lost in big, crowded cities. People fell through the cracks every day; they just disappeared and were never heard from again. Most went unnoticed. A single body turning up in the midst of everyday city life wouldn't have raised an eyebrow.

So what if there were claw marks? Maybe a stray dog. Maybe someone with costume claws and a grudge. One dead person. And hundreds of thousands of citizens in need of protection. No one would look too closely unless someone ordered it. And for a handful of nobodies, who would bother?

But here, there were no cracks to fall through. Here, everything was seen and heard. Here, it was easy to spot the monster.

Hailey left the grieving woman's window and made her way around the crowd to where the body had been found. The smell of fear was strongest here, and it took her a while to tune it out so she could focus on the others. She smelled blood and death, dozens of people who had been there since the murder. But no Jeremy.

Hellcat reveled in this. It was a game with a prize at the end. Hailey knew better. Jeremy hadn't been taken to tea and cookies. Every second wasted here could mean his death.

She needed Pixie. If anyone knew whether or not Jeremy was still alive—

—You called?—

Damn telepaths… *Is Jeremy still alive?* She thought it without emotion, all business, predator on the hunt. It wasn't personal. She just had her prey to stalk and kill in unimaginably painful ways. But that could wait. It had to. If she let herself think about anything other than the hunt right now, she'd never find him.

—*Yes. He's awake, but he doesn't know where he is, and he shut me out. The bad guy is with him… someone called Arthur Glenn. Do you know him?*—

The name didn't ring any bells.

—*Well, he knows you.*—

Whatever. *I need a clue here. Nothing in this place smells familiar. I need a place to start.* At the very least, she needed Jeremy's last known location.

—*Hold, please.*—

Hailey wanted to growl.

—*Did you check the Patio?*— Pixie asked.

Of course she had. That was the first place she'd checked. There were too many people even now to make anything out. *Trail was cold,* she told the girl.

—*Okay, he refuses to tell me anything. Said to tell you to stay away.*— *Oh man, I'm gonna kick his ass so much when I find him…*

—*Yeah, whatever,*— Pixie retorted. —*Circle the square. That's the last thing I managed to pull out of his memories. Somewhere near the stage was where he was taken.*—

Hailey went straight for the stage. It was empty now, with just an overturned throne and some confetti on the ground. She hopped up there and looked over the town square.

This was impossible. She could see at least a hundred places from which a person could be taken unnoticed. In a crowd, a thousand. If there'd been a commotion, like, say, when the body had been found, he could have been standing right in the middle of the damn stage and no one would have noticed him being taken.

—*Just focus,*— Pixie said. —*You have five senses, use all of them.*—

She could do that. *Okay. Shut up for a second,* Hailey told her. She needed to concentrate. With her eyes closed, she could sort through the scents better. Stuffy perfume… an older female. The scent came from the throne. Hailey hopped down off the stage and crouched low. More people, now mixing with manure and piss. Fantastic.

Hailey pushed to her feet and inhaled deeply.

There! Just there; just a hint of something familiar. It wasn't Jeremy. It was blood.

Hailey followed the scent away from the square and into an alley. Blood. Just a little. Maybe a few drops. Not enough to be seen readily, but enough to give her a trace to follow. It enraged Hellcat and the leopard went off the deep end.

Hailey fell against the wall and slid down to the ground, her mind in a haze of feral tumult. She couldn't hope to pierce through that rage.

The world spun around her and all she could do was hang on, wait it out, and hope to hell she didn't start to change. Her leg muscles jumped, Hellcat asserting herself and demanding Hailey move. Hailey held her ground. Braced herself and gritted her teeth against the torrent of adrenaline-laced aggression.

When she couldn't stand it anymore, she screamed inside her head so loud it gave the leopard pause. In that split second of silence, Hailey shoved Hellcat back into the dark cave and sealed it shut. *My mind, my rules.* She knew it wouldn't hold. Every second was precious now, so she pulled herself back up and curled her fingers into tight fists to make herself focus again.

She could see marks on the ground. There were footprints in the dirt. Men's shoes with a smooth, worn bottom. Loafers of some sort.

Hailey's mind picked out the design the shoe had imprinted into the sand and looked for more of them. The tracks led farther away from the square and seemed to circle around in some parts, but Hailey was able to pick up on the scent and follow it when the tracks were unreliable.

When she reached the edge of town, the stomped dirt road ended in tall grass of a field and the trail just… disappeared.

No! How was that possible?

Hellcat wanted out. Badly. But the leopard must have learned her place because she didn't demand or attack. She… pouted.

What the hell do I do now?

—*Hold on,*— Pixie said again. Hailey was getting used to the girl talking in her head by now. A scary thought.

Why isn't Jeremy talking to me? She'd have thought it would have been him in her mind, giving orders.

—I'm keeping him out.— Pixie was sad.

What? Why?

—Because he's being an idiot. He doesn't want you to look for him, and if I let him into your mind, he'll try to make you go back. It would be painful. For everyone involved.—

That just figured.

—Okay, your sister's here, doing some fancy thing with the computers. She says there was a taxi there not too long ago. It's a long shot, but she can get it to repeat the trip.—

Send it.

—She also says not to do anything stupid. You need to come back to the lab for your last shot.—

Hailey ignored that.

The taxi took its sweet time getting there at minimum speed. It left Hailey with nothing to do except think. Restless, furious, scared, she paced and growled. Her teeth started aching, and her fingers itched. Fangs and claws. Should she test them out? *Could* she?

Yes! Hellcat wanted that. That was a good plan. Hailey was going crazy doing nothing. *Don't think. Just shut down. Focus.*

Easier said than done. She needed something to focus *on.*

Hailey decided on her right hand. She closed off her mind as best she could, shut out all external stimuli, and just focused on her breathing. Breathe in. Breathe out. See her skin change color. Breathe in. Breathe out. Watch fine fur erupt along the back of her hand. Breathe in, breathe out. Feel bones shift to make a paw.

It hurt. So much so that she thought her bones were shattering all at the same time. Sensing an opening, Hellcat sprang forward, driving the change further, fighting to be let out. Hailey's paw flexed, fur spreading up her arm to her elbow. Her eyes watered, but she bit back any sound and tried to breathe through it. She fought Hellcat back into submission, taking the pain and shoving it out of her mind as best she could. Tears leaked out of her eyes, but she was winning.

Fur receded back to her paw. Breathe in. Breathe out. Reverse the bone shift. Breathe in. Breathe out. Her human hand was back. Stiff and bruised, but whole.

Just in time for the taxi to arrive. Weak and shaken already, now

Hailey had to pull herself up into the transport.

—*Hailey!*— Jeremy's voice in her head startled her just as she was perched on the edge of the cabin in the precarious position of being neither in nor out, and she fell flat on her back. —*Stop,*— he shouted. —*It's you he's after. Go back. You have to go back!*—

Hailey felt him try to manipulate her, like snakes twisting in her brain. She couldn't keep from crying out; he'd momentarily replaced her control with his.

Then he was gone, and Hailey was left gasping on the ground.

—*Whoops,*— Pixie said. —*Sorry about that. Tiny slip. Won't happen again.*—

Hailey picked herself up and crawled into the taxi. *What did he mean, it's me he's after?*

—*Nothing,*— Pixie said. —*Just go get my brother.*—

Her head was pounding. It didn't bode well. She checked the navigation screen and manually raised the speed to maximum. When the taxi took off, Hailey was thrown back against the seat.

A muscle spasm made her torso go rigid like a statue. Her body, from her knees up to her shoulders, was one giant charley horse, and while it lasted, she couldn't move at all. It ebbed slowly, leaving her stunned and trembling. Even Hellcat was surprised. *What the hell was that?*

No time to think about it now. The taxi was nearing its destination somewhere in English Village. She had a to-do list now and worrying about side effects wasn't high on it at the moment.

Task 1: Find Jeremy.

Task 2: Kill the bastard who took him.

Those were her highest priorities.

Anything after that was a bonus.

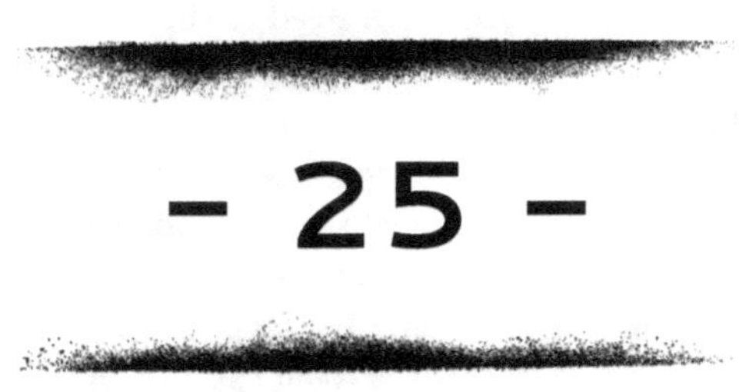

– 25 –

"You can't just kill me."

"And why not?"

Good question. *—Pixie! Damn it, get Hailey back to the lab.—* She was letting Jeremy sense just enough to know that Hailey was on her way, but he couldn't do a damn thing about it. And now on top of that, Pixie was ignoring him. *—Are you trying to get us both killed?—*

No answer.

Shit.

Jeremy twisted his hands behind him, trying to loosen the rope binding his wrists. Knots weren't exactly his specialty. The more he struggled, the tighter the knot seemed to get. And he didn't just have his wrists bound at the back of the chair; the rope was somehow looped *through* it so he couldn't even move away from the damn thing.

"Your silence is answer enough," Arthur said. "I knew you'd be a coward."

The guy was polishing his claws for some kind of sick poetic justice. He actually had claws on a thick leather glove. It looked heavy and stiff, but sturdy. And the added weight would make each point slide through flesh like butter.

The glove, the demon references, his obsession with Hailey…
Christ.

The animal attack files mentioned microscopic traces of metal in the wounds. The medical examiners had written it off as coincidence;

all attacks had taken place in large cities, in or near the industrial districts where air pollution could easily have coated the ground. Metal coats animal claws, which then transfer traces to the victims' wounds.

It was a logical assumption. The same way a blindfolded person touched an elephant's trunk and called it a snake. Occam's Razor dictated that the simplest explanation was most likely the correct one. Except it didn't explain the lack of saliva in the wounds. Not a trace. Not on any of the victims.

That's what he'd been coming to tell Hailey in the first place. The reason the investigation was stalling was that no one could identify the animal responsible for the attacks. There were only claw marks, always inconclusive as evidence, since there were a number of things that could inflict such damage. But animals didn't just rip into their prey and run. And they certainly didn't exist in a vacuum. An animal would have left clues, some kind of DNA or organic material that could narrow the search down. Saliva, hair, dirt to point to its previous location—something.

A dozen police officers in different districts, on different worlds were investigating this case. How the hell could all of them have overlooked that? Jeremy knew the answer. The police were trained to see what was there; to look for the smallest clues and give them meaning. More often than not, they didn't even notice what *wasn't* there. And he'd grown so complacent in his new, quiet life, he hadn't noticed either.

The clues he'd been missing this whole time fell into place. This was the killer the police were looking for. The blood trail leading to Hailey—it was *following* her. Because Arthur followed her wherever she went. It was a compulsion to him, his obsession demanding that he stay close. His life had no meaning without Hailey.

And everything he did, he did for her.

Jeremy remembered the night of the procession on Reynard Colony. Hailey had sensed a threat even then. She'd scented another, a stalker, following her from world to world. She'd been afraid. The son of a bitch had been trailing her, killing innocent people and making it look like Hailey's handiwork.

If Hailey found out…

He had to do something.

"You can't kill me, because I am a demon," Jeremy said, pulling the lie out of his ass. From there, it just rolled off his tongue as if he'd rehearsed it. "All your toy will do is kill this shell and set me loose. You think your pretty girl is troubled now? Wait until I settle in her mind completely. She's strong, that one. I could do well with such a vessel."

The sound Arthur made as he came to his feet was pure madness and rage. He kicked viciously at Jeremy's head, but Jeremy managed to twist just enough so that the blow caught his shoulder instead and dislocated it instantly. Still, better his shoulder than his skull.

"*I will kill you for this!*" Arthur was shaking now, and when he screamed at Jeremy, his words were barely discernible.

Jeremy forced a laugh, but it came out pained. "You can't win," he said. If he could just break the chair somehow, get loose, he could get out of this.

Arthur screamed again, then turned away. He was almost hyperventilating though making an obvious effort to compose himself. One shaking hand smoothed back his hair in a compulsive gesture. "I will protect her," he said quietly, more to himself than to Jeremy.

When he faced Jeremy a long moment later, there was no more rage. Just cold, calm malice. He pulled Jeremy up, righted the chair. With his hands on Jeremy's shoulders—*Christ, that hurt!*—he spoke as if nothing had happened. "You will not touch her again, demon. I will keep you here as long as it takes. I will beat you, cut you, burn you… whatever I have to do. And eventually you will tell me how to kill you. By then, you'll be *begging* for death. Of that, you can be certain."

Note to self: provoking a mentally unhinged serial killer—not a good idea.

Clearly, logic wasn't getting him out of this, and playing into Arthur's delusion was just making a bad situation far worse. Jeremy was running out of options here.

A piercing scream shattered through his mental shields. Female. In such pain, Jeremy felt it too, and screamed with her. Everything turned black, and he couldn't see Arthur anymore, but he heard him drop to the ground.

Hailey!

But it wasn't her. Not Hailey.

Dara.

Something was wrong. The birth was taking too much out of her; she was projecting everything, and not just to Jeremy, but to everyone capable of receiving the signal. Everyone she'd created a connection with, or had ever touched telepathically. Pixie would feel this. So would Hunt and Amelia, and many others here.

The connection severed abruptly, leaving him cold.

Arthur struggled to his feet. "More of your *tricks*?" he growled. There was far more energy in his voice than seemed to be in his body. He was unsteady, stumbling to his chair.

Jeremy ignored him. He searched for any hint of a connection with Hunt and called out to him. —*Is Dara okay?*—

The answer was wordless, terrified.

No, Dara was not okay.

Jeremy broke off contact. There was nothing he could do now, for either of them.

Arthur reached for his glove, put it on. His hands were shaking enough that it took him a couple of tries to get it right. He tightened the straps and rested his hand on his knee for a moment as if he was too weak to hold it up for long.

When he looked Jeremy in the eye, it was with such depth of hatred that there was no question as to what would happen next. The claws caught what little light there was and gleamed.

Keep fighting, or give up?

Jeremy let his mouth pull into a sneer. "Didn't like my gift? Just a hint of what I am capable of. What I can do to you. And to her."

Arthur rose from his seat, came forward with slow, unsteady footsteps. He never even blinked as he raised his gloved hand; never made a sound, except for his heavy breathing. Jeremy didn't dare lower his shields completely, but he did relax them a little.

A tingle of fear raced up his spine and exploded in his head like fireworks. "No," he whispered. Not because of the glove. He didn't give a damn about that. *No… not now. Not here.* —*Run!*—

The glove rose an inch more and came down.

"What did I miss?"

The tips brushed across Jeremy's shoulder, barely catching on the fabric of his shirt. Arthur stared wide-eyed at a point behind Jeremy, his mouth hanging open.

"Get. Out. Of. Here," Jeremy ground out. Arthur was volatile. Unstable. He could turn on Hailey any second. Especially if she provoked him.

"Hailey." Arthur breathed her name in benediction. Jeremy wanted to kill him just for looking at her, talking to her. "It's you."

Rule number one when dealing with obsession: never, ever put the obsessed in the same room with the object of their interest. In Arthur's mind, he and Hailey were meant to be. He was blaming Jeremy for Hailey's indifference, because if not for that, she would surely fall into his arms in gratitude.

If that illusion broke, if something caused Arthur to lose faith in that, both Hailey and Jeremy were as good as dead. Hailey didn't exactly play nice. "Damn it, get out!" he snapped, unable to turn his head enough to look at her.

She ignored him. "Yeah, me, who'da thunk it?" Her tone was completely dry and uninterested, and Arthur's brows twitched in a quick frown.

Not good! Pixie was still blocking his path to Hailey. Jeremy couldn't warn her telepathically and he couldn't do it aloud. Not without provoking Arthur more. "Are you fucking deaf?" he yelled, his helplessness and his fear for her making him reckless. "*Leave!*"

Arthur backhanded him with that damn heavy glove. Jeremy's head snapped to the side and dropped forward again. He tasted more blood.

"Stop that right now!" Hailey ordered. He felt her come closer with silent footsteps. Jeremy fought past the pain, the pounding in his head, and reached out to her again. A smooth barrier reflected his thoughts back to him. He tried again and again, seeking other paths. Pixie's shield around Hailey was flawless. She wouldn't let him through.

"Why?" Arthur asked, sounding genuinely perplexed.

Pissed off beyond reason, Jeremy did something he never thought he could do: he lashed out at his own sister, hurt her just enough to make her back off. He heard her cry of startled pain before her shields around Hailey gave way.

Pixie would never forgive him for that. Just like he wouldn't forgive her for letting Hailey put herself in danger for him, spurring her on to do it.

With the shields down, Jeremy was finally able to connect to Hailey. Shock stilled him. Her mind… her body!

She was fighting so hard to keep steady. Her heart was racing out of control. Jeremy had no idea how she was keeping her breathing even. Looking through her eyes…

—*God, baby, what did you do?*—

"I'm trying to save you," Arthur was saying.

Jeremy felt, rather than saw Hailey shake her head to get him out. The state she was in, even that small movement made her sway on her feet. Jeremy wouldn't budge. —*You have to get out of here. He's dangerous!*—

Shut up, she bit out. She'd noticed the glove. Jeremy felt her jaw begin to ache and throb.

"And you've done a bang-up job so far," Hailey told Arthur. "Kudos. Nice claws, by the way. Now back off a little, yeah?"

Seeming confused, Arthur obeyed. Jeremy didn't have to see his thoughts to know the man was in awe. He'd dreamed about talking to her directly.

—*Hailey…*—

She didn't answer. Jeremy was shivering, mirroring her body's response to whatever she'd injected herself with this time. He felt how weak she was. The world moved around him, making him feel seasick. She walked with her head high and her back straight, but one of her feet was dragging slightly. Jeremy wouldn't have noticed, except Hailey did.

She was very much aware of that loss of dexterity and was making an effort to disguise it. The words *partial paralysis* made him cold with fear, but Hailey just cataloged it in her mind, compensated, and moved on. How was she still standing?

And the leopard!

Jesus.

Hailey touched him, one hand on his shoulder by his neck, the other on his arm. With a wrenching motion, she popped his shoulder back into place. The shock of pain made him yell out. When the stars faded from his vision, he craned his neck to glare at her. "You couldn't have waited for anesthetics?"

"The longer you wait, the worse it hurts," she told him. She spoke from experience. "Stop being such a baby."

Arthur was watching them, mostly Hailey, with something akin to desperation. When Hailey sat on Jeremy's lap outwardly calm as could be, Jeremy thought the man would cry. Arthur didn't know how close Hailey was to passing out. The small sigh of relief didn't carry far enough for the man to hear. The tremble in her limbs, which Jeremy felt to his core, were faint enough not to show.

"Now then," she said, sounding tired. "How come you got my boy here all bondaged and bloody?"

There was a psychotic killer before them, Jeremy was tied to a chair, and Hailey's body was malfunctioning horribly. By all rights, Jeremy should have been terrified—and he was. But with Hailey in his lap, alive enough to taunt the psycho hell-bent on killing him, Jeremy was so damn relieved just to have her close that for a moment he got stupid and let his guard down.

He let himself pretend that everything would be okay, that he could fix what was wrong with Hailey. Keep her from slipping away if he just stayed close enough, held on tight enough. She had one arm around the front of his neck, the other at his back, subtly prying at the rope. He turned his head into her hair and inhaled deeply. God, he'd missed her.

"Am I too late?" Arthur asked, his voice suddenly shaky and unsure. No longer the man in charge, now he seemed more like a defeated hero already mourning the loss of his beloved.

His voice brought Jeremy crashing back to reality. The guy was walking a razor's edge. He could go off at any moment, and the way he looked, he'd either turn those claws on Hailey or himself. Jeremy hoped for the latter.

But in the face of Arthur's vulnerability, Hailey had no mercy. Jeremy felt her shiver, felt the anger in her mind, but didn't know which caused what. "You didn't answer my question," she said.

"Hailey, please," Jeremy said. "I need you to leave." *Don't leave me. Don't die.*

She looked away from Arthur to blink at Jeremy in surprise. Then she put a finger over his lips. "Shh. I got this." She was killing him. The pain was nothing. He didn't fear death, had long ago accepted that he would die young. His affairs were in order; Pixie would be taken care of.

But the thought of Hailey coming to harm—*more* harm… —*Is this what dying feels like?*—

Memories swamped her, and Jeremy along with her. Pain. Unimaginable. Lasting. Body breaking, tearing, ending. She felt everything, remembered it in gory detail. It was a nightmare that used to haunt her night after night. *No,* she thought in reply. *Dying hurts. Being reborn hurts more.*

"Well?" she said to Arthur. "What do you have to say for yourself?"

The rope was coming loose.

"This… *thing,*" Arthur spat, "poisoned you."

Hailey snickered. "He called you a thing."

"Don't," Jeremy warned.

"Too late," she replied, her humor gone in a hurry. *I intend to see this through.* To Arthur, she said, "Explain yourself."

There was a complex dynamic between Arthur and Hailey that Jeremy could only watch, an observer looking at a transport hurtling toward a brick wall, unsure which would remain standing at the end. Hailey seemed a force of nature next to Arthur; she was his reason for living and… his superior. And yet from his shadows of anonymity, Arthur had treated her as a fragile flower in need of his protection.

Was he now finally understanding how unnecessary he was?

What would that epiphany do to him?

"I… I…" Arthur stuttered. "He's the demon. I found him, Hailey. I can free you, and you can be the way you used to be again. We both can. Together."

Hailey stared. "Come again? What demon?"

Arthur looked at Jeremy with murder in his eyes. "You bastard," he snarled. "She doesn't even know."

The rope loosened more, enough for Jeremy to do the rest, although it would take him a minute or two. Hailey, meanwhile, stood from his lap and placed herself between him and Arthur, breaking his stare.

"You talk to *me*," she told him with complete authority.

Jeremy looked through her eyes at Arthur as his face went blank and he blushed. Wait, he was seeing the guy's face?

Night vision, Hailey explained.

Cool. He twisted his hands again, trying to work them free of the rope. But he stayed with Hailey, carefully monitoring her mind and body, ready to step in if she needed it. He wanted to already, but she was stubbornly hanging on to her independence.

Hailey grinned inwardly at his attempts.

"I was there," Arthur said unsteadily. "I was always there, and you never knew it. I was there the night you got possessed. I... felt the demon take over you, and I saw what it did to you. Your hair... it used to be so beautiful."

Another shiver made Hailey sway slightly. Her knees were weak, and she backed toward Jeremy, just enough to be able to lean against him a little. Enough to steady herself, without revealing a weakness. "You were there?"

Arthur nodded eagerly. "And I was with you ever since. Helping you. I... I couldn't see the demon." He was grasping for words to explain, but looked so excited to finally be able to tell his story. "But I could feel him. I could draw his evil into me and..." Something must have shown on Hailey's face, because he broke off. "Hailey?"

She knew. Jeremy would give anything to spare her this. From the moment she'd seen the glove, Hailey had suspected, but hadn't wanted to believe. She had no choice now. "Why?"

Arthur chuckled as if he thought her adorable. "I love you," he said. "I've loved you since the moment we met. Everything I did was for you."

A stranger was telling her that he loved her. That his every action had been for her. The flood of images Pixie had shown her came back as a vague memory. An entire life centered around someone else. Such blind devotion.

So many bodies...

"Not for me," she said with difficulty.

"Yes, of course for you," Arthur Glenn insisted. "Everything for you. If he slaked his thirst on others, he wouldn't hurt you. I was protecting you!"

"*Shut up!*"

Arthur jerked at her shout, grew pale.

His words... He believed what he was saying. The elusive stalker, the scent following her from world to world, always there, no matter how far she went, how well she hid.

The bodies!

Innocent people she'd met or simply made eye contact with. People she'd passed, bumped into, *looked at* from across the street. *I've learned not to look.*

Not well enough. More kept dying. More turned up as nothing but lifeless shells, desecrated by a sick man's obsession.

The fear that she might be responsible had always been there, a kernel of self-doubt. Hailey had thought she was a monster, that she'd unleashed one by doing this to herself. So much regret and fear she'd had for herself.

And all this time she'd been right?

—*No.*— Jeremy's voice whispered through her mind. —*You are not to blame for any of this.*—

Can't show weakness. There was another life hanging in the balance. And this one she could save. *Have to. Be strong.* "Don't you *dare* lay this at my feet." Her words were strong; her voice wasn't. She leaned harder against Jeremy, needing his support, feeling unworthy of it. Stained.

Feeling weaker by the second. No pain this time, but she felt herself begin to slip away.

—*Hailey!*—

Nothing she could do.

So many people dead, killed in horrible ways.

"*You* did this," she said. "You... followed me from place to place and *killed* people who had absolutely nothing to do with me!" Hellcat rallied at this, growling her support. There was vindication in that, which Hailey wanted to feel, too. She shut down her empathy and channeled her wrath. It made her heart pump a little stronger, gave her strength enough to stand on her own and advance on Arthur.

"I had to! It would have killed you." Arthur backed away a step. He tried to look at Jeremy, but Hailey blocked his view. That visibly enraged him.

—*Don't push him,*— Jeremy warned. He was still struggling with the rope, which he'd somehow managed to tighten again. —*Just stall. We'll get out of here and let the cops deal with him.*—

Too easy. He didn't deserve that.

—*Fuck deserve! We're on our own here.*—

All the more reason to get on with it. No one was coming. Not in time.

"Let me kill him," Arthur said, eager to prove himself. "Just let me break his neck and you'll see that I'm right. You can be free, Hailey. Don't you want that?"

"No one did this to me," she said, throwing caution to the wind. Hellcat was sharpening her claws on the inside of Hailey's brain. She wanted out, wanted to take her revenge. She understood things now, like pride and reputation—she had those and this person had stained them. Hellcat wasn't having it. Oh, she'd take credit for a kill, but not if she wasn't the one to do it. "Nothing possessed me. I changed because I wanted to. I left because I wanted to. Do you understand that?"

—*Hailey, stop, you're going too far.*—

"Is your sick, self-centered mind even capable of comprehending what I'm telling you?" Her voice broke; she was losing control of her body, and for once, she welcomed it.

"*Hailey!* Hailey, look at me," Jeremy was saying. She could scent his fear, feel the tension in him as he fought to free himself. For her sake.

But this was her mess to clean up.

"Everything I did was of my free will, and I would do it again in a heartbeat, even if it killed me."

Arthur was shaking his head. "No. You could never… This isn't you!"

"You want to see the real me, Arty?"

His eyes widened at the nickname.

—*Don't!*— Jeremy shouted in her mind, and out loud, "Hailey, just stop for a minute." His chair creaked. He was chafing his wrists raw with his struggles and the scent of it made Hailey's eyes glow silver. She met Arthur's gaze head-on, refused to let him look away.

"You want to see what I've made of myself? I'll show you."

Jeremy stopped fighting. He went completely still behind her.

"But if you want to see the real demon, get a mirror. The only evil here is you."

"Hailey," he sobbed.

—*Hailey,*— Jeremy echoed him. Out loud, he said, "Hailey, don't do it."

"One of us won't be walking out of here," Hailey told Arthur. "And if that happens to be me, then that will be your fault, too, Arthur Glenn."

"Hailey, *no!*" Jeremy redoubled his efforts, and she scented fresh blood. She heard his heart racing, beating so strong. It gave her strength she didn't have. "Please, don't do this," he begged. "You can't!"

"I did it for you," Arthur said. He was weeping now.

Livid, Hailey felt her teeth sharpen and grow. "You forced me to do this."

"*No!*" Jeremy screamed, but it was too late.

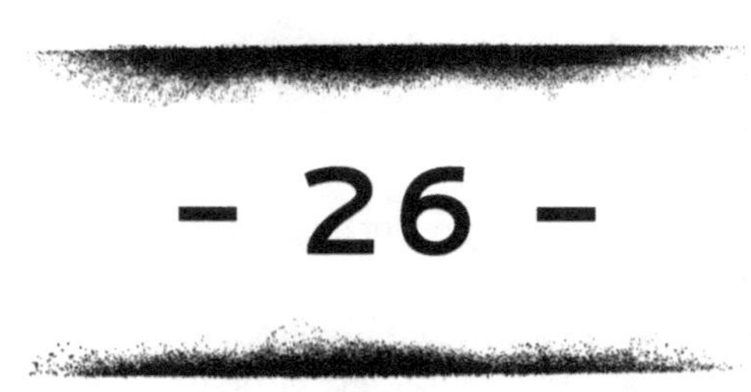

– 26 –

Hailey was beyond hearing him. Sharing her mind, Jeremy became deaf to the outside world right along with her. Too late to pull out; he couldn't break the connection now. He felt the leopard meld with Hailey's mind. She'd named it Hellcat. It liked that name.

Hailey's back bowed, and a growl tore out of her chest. Jeremy howled with her. He felt the wrenching pain, the dizziness as she dropped to her hands and knees. Her clothes were constrictive but couldn't hope to contain her change.

Jeremy felt as if it were him changing; his muscles stretching and his organs rearranging themselves until he thought he would throw up his innards just to get some relief. He felt his upper lip split and the bones in his face become malleable. Unlike the rest of Hailey's body, her head didn't break and snap. There, mercifully, the transformation was smooth and he only felt a slight ripple.

But then her spine began to lengthen. Jeremy didn't know how she wasn't curling into a ball of misery yet, but Hailey stubbornly stayed on her feet—*paws*—and endured the pain that would have killed a lesser creature. Her strength amazed him.

And it was still her. Hailey didn't disappear beneath the leopard's consciousness. She was right there with it; there was no more barrier between them. Two separate beings merged together so that when Hailey raised her head, the leopard's consciousness was only a split second behind her. And then there was just Hailey, with only the strongest of what the leopard had to offer.

She wasn't fighting it anymore, wasn't afraid of it. This was the transformation she'd wanted from the very beginning. It had just taken her this long to fully accept it.

Clothes tore, fur covered her nakedness, her shape steadied and solidified, becoming something other than human. It was a wretched, painful, beautiful thing to witness. Because at the end of it, she was still alive.

He didn't know how long it took, but by the time Jeremy was finally able to see through his own eyes, the snow leopard stood before him, pissed off like nobody's business, glaring death at Arthur. Her massive tail swung left and right, battering Jeremy's legs, but it was intended as a love tap to reassure him.

"Hailey?" His wrists were bleeding behind him, but the pain of his injuries was nothing now. After Hailey's change, he hardly felt his shoulder, and all that remained of his concussion was a little dizziness. But he knew Hailey could smell the blood. It angered her even more. Jeremy wrestled with the rope again, gaining very little ground, watching Hailey stalk her prey. "Hailey, want to help me out here?"

She refused to be distracted. The connection between them hadn't severed. He felt her lips draw back to show off her fangs. Hailey didn't growl, or roar, just stared with those piercing silver eyes. She was Death and she knew it. She wanted Arthur to know it, too.

"I did it for you," Arthur sobbed. The heavy glove was still on his hand, but it was down at his side now. He was broken, far too shaken to do anything with it; he wasn't even running or trying to defend himself, though he had to know he was about to die.

Jeremy tugged at the rope one last time and finally it gave way. He pulled his hands free and quickly went to work on the ties around his ankles. Hailey was beyond caring now; he had to be her conscience. She might not forgive herself if she took a life. He didn't want that for her. "Hailey, look at me."

The tail swung again, harder this time. It hit him in the head, nearly knocking him over in his condition. For a moment his vision blurred, but he persisted.

"He's not worth it, do you hear me?" When his vision cleared, the world was unsteady again. His stomach roiled, and he had to sit up to keep from vomiting. Concussions sucked major ass. For just a second, Jeremy hoped Hailey would beat the shit out of Arthur, but he wanted her to keep him alive long enough for Jeremy to do some beating of his own.

Then he woke the hell up and reminded himself what was at stake. —*You don't have to do this.*—

Her head whipped around, and she snarled at him. *Shut up.*

But that split second was enough for Arthur to come to his senses. He darted around her and ran for the door.

The absolute worst thing he could possibly have done—run from a predator.

Now there was no stopping her, though Jeremy still tried.

Hailey gave chase, slipped right through Jeremy's fingers and knocked him over. The chair broke apart and the legs snapped off, allowing Jeremy to get to his feet.

Just in time to watch Hailey kill a madman.

Hailey tackled Arthur to the ground. He hadn't even made it to the door. She sank her teeth and claws into him, just enough to get a grip. She didn't want to kill him yet, only toss him around a little.

Jeremy saw her intent. He knew what would happen if he didn't do something. For her sake, he tried to pull her off Arthur. He might as well have tried to move a rock. Hailey reared and shook him off without ever pausing in her attack. When she dropped back to all fours, she did it with all her weight, right on top of Arthur's chest, knocking the breath out of him.

Her claws tore at his clothes, scoring skin, but still not enough to truly injure. She grabbed onto his arm and tossed her head. Arthur followed like a rag doll, sliding a couple of feet away from the door. Jeremy heard his arm break with a snap. And then Hailey was on him again.

Only this time, some last dreg of self-preservation made Arthur swing his arm. Those sharp steel claws cut across Hailey's neck and shoulder. She reared and fell away sideways, landing on her paws. She shook her head, and Jeremy knew there was no more helping Arthur. If he tried to get between Hailey and her prey, she would kill him, too, on principle.

—Hailey…—

Jeremy had never heard a sound like the one she made then. It was pure animal, instinct, and the drive to kill. Bloodlust like nothing a human being could ever feel. Not like this.

Arthur was scrambling for the door again, and Hailey allowed him to get out. Head canted low, she followed slowly, stalking, letting him think he was getting somewhere. She was toying with him. Jeremy followed, hoping to hell no one came around to see this.

His fears on that score at least were unnecessary. They were on the outskirts of English Village and there was nothing around except for storage houses. No one would be coming. No one would see Arthur Glenn's demon turn on him.

He was desperate now, headed for town and people. But in his panic, he forgot the most important thing: he was nobody.

Somebody *killed those people,* Hailey growled at Jeremy.

Jeremy's mind turned cold. Images of ravaged bodies, teenagers torn and bloody, pale and still in death filled his mind's eye. Families who would never know what happened to their loved ones; families who would never get justice. This was for them, as much as for Hailey.

Jeremy took a risk and sent a short compulsion into Arthur's mind. One-way road—one message out, but nothing back in. He sent a thought, nothing more. To remind Arthur what he was: invisible. Even if he found people, no one would help him; no one would even see him. Jeremy quelled Arthur's will to run, but inertia still kept him going.

When he rounded a corner to get out of sight, Hailey jumped onto a barrel, and from there, up to the roof of a house. She stalked him from up there, the better able to view her surroundings.

Jeremy followed more slowly, staying with her in her mind, looking through her eyes. He smelled the fear Arthur exuded like an invisible trail. It made him so easy to track.

He stopped on a crossroad, indecision about to become his downfall.

Hailey rolled onto her back briefly, then rolled back to her paws, keeping low to the roof. It wouldn't be long now. Jeremy came in sight of Arthur and picked a barrel to perch on. He made himself known by clearing his throat, but his face was a death mask, never letting

Arthur see how much he hated him. For everything he'd done, and then some. Jeremy hoped there was a hell and that the man would burn there for all eternity.

"You!" Arthur snarled. "It's all your fault!"

Jeremy didn't even bother reacting, just calmly held Arthur's gaze.

Arthur charged him with a maddened yell, and Hailey launched off that roof and bore him to the ground with the full force of her impact. This time she didn't pull any punches. Or claws. When she ripped into him, flesh and bone gave way. Arthur's screams were quickly silenced when she pierced his lung, but he suffered for a long time before Hailey allowed him to die.

Even after his heart had stopped beating, Hailey stood over him, her nose to the back of his neck as if waiting to see if he would rise again. When she lost patience, she took his neck into her jaws and snapped it just to be sure.

Jeremy watched it all with the eye of a detached observer. He felt nothing to see Arthur die. And when Arthur was dead, he felt neither anger nor relief.

A man was dead; a murderer and psychopath. The world was better for it, and tomorrow the sun would rise brighter and warmer.

But today wasn't over yet.

Finished, Hailey thought, and the sheer weariness in her mind-voice brought Jeremy to his feet. He split his focus between watching her body and looking into her thoughts, already going to her with his heart in his throat.

As the adrenaline drained out of her, Hailey swayed on her paws. She was visibly shaking, tripping as she left her kill for other beasts and headed toward Jeremy. She was whining softly. They weren't sounds she was used to making, but they said far more than words ever could. She couldn't even get halfway before her legs gave out and she had to lie down.

Jeremy was with her before she even touched the ground, hardly daring to breathe. "Hailey?" Her eyes were darting left and right as if she was dreaming. When he looked through her, the world twisted and spun. Her eyes wanted to roll back in her head. She was so weak, and so cold…

Patches gone, she kept thinking. It made no sense to him, but it had to be bad. When he slid his hand beneath her head, he felt her burning up. Her nose was hot and completely dry. Was that bad? She wasn't a dog, but still…

"Hailey, I need you to tell me what to do. Do you want to change back? *Can* you change back?"

Time…

That was a question. "What? Who cares what time it is?" Her eyes rolled back briefly. "Hailey! Stay with me. Talk to me. What do I do?"

She didn't stir.

—*Pixie, I need you to get Amelia here* now.—

—*She's on her way.*—

Hailey's paw touched his knee and slid off. She tried again and managed to keep it there, but he felt the effort it took her. Jeremy covered her paw with his hand to take the strain for her. "Stay with me, baby."

—*What do I do?*— he asked Amelia.

Keep her conscious, came the curt reply. She was racing toward them, the scientist's logical mind warring with a sister's frightened heart.

"It's okay. You're going to be okay. You hear me? Hailey! You can do this, just listen to my voice."

So… tired.

"Don't you dare leave me now. Talk to me. What's my name? Where did you go to school? *Hailey!*"

I'm sorry.

"No!" He let go of her paw and shifted to cradle her head on his lap. He stroked her fur hard to get her to focus. "I found you across a galaxy. I can find you wherever you run to. I'll drag you back here one way or another, so just do us both a favor and *stay with me,* damn it!"

The world swayed, rocking Hailey like a cradle. It was soothing. She was too tired to shiver anymore. The sun warmed her, and Jeremy's voice was like a lullaby. There was no more pain. Her eyes wanted to close.

So tired…

Amelia? On her way? What was the time?

—*Who cares?*—

Time meant nothing now. Breathe in, breathe out. Let it go. Jeremy was scared; she could scent it. His hands shook as he stroked her fur. It was stained with blood, but he didn't seem to mind that. He'd seen her kill someone, and he wasn't running away.

Why wasn't he?

Too late. Far too late for anything. Hailey understood so much more now and she would never get a chance to do anything about it.

Jeremy was with her. She loved him.

She wanted to cry.

But leopards don't cry.

Angels standing over her. Her guardian; her avenger. *Jeremy.* And another one. Beautiful glowing creature with pale hair, blazing in the dusk. *Is this it?* Where would they take her? Not good enough for Heaven. Not anymore. Hell, then?

Voices. Yelling. Whispering. Singing to her. Beautiful songs made of heartbreak and sorrow. A lullaby to sleep forever and dream of strange things.

Like people changing into animals and weird worlds where they didn't have washing machines.

Thoughts growing hazy. Was it getting dark already? So much to say, so much to live for now.

Too late. Fading… Fading…

So this was what dying felt like…

– 27 –

She dreamed she was running. On all fours as the leopard, running so fast across the meadow that everything was a blur except the majestic mountain range to her right. And she wasn't tired at all. It felt like heaven. Hailey raised her head to the sky, closed her eyes against the bright sun, and just… breathed.

It was the light that teased her awake. Her eyelids fluttered open, and she squinted up at the sky. The sun wasn't directly above her, but it was bright enough that gazing up at the blue felt like looking into eternity.

Was she dead? Was this Heaven?

Hailey turned her head to look around. Two feet from her bed sat Hunt, smirking at her.

Definitely not Heaven.

"Are you going to call me an idiot again?" she said, annoyed by how weak and scratchy her voice sounded. "Because I think I can take you now."

Hunt got up with all the grace of a sixty-eight-year-old arthritic. "I'll give you this, you got guts," he said and poured a glass of water.

When he offered it to her, Hailey didn't move to take it. "Poison?"

He rolled his eyes. "Vitamin-enriched water. Amelia said you need to drink this for at least a week until you get your strength back."

"Instead of *food*?" That was so not going to happen.

"Just drink it, will you?"

She crossed her arms, refusing to take the glass.

"Don't make me force it down your throat."

Because he looked like he would do it, and probably enjoy it, Hailey took the glass. "Where is Amelia, anyway?"

"She's with my mate and children."

"Everything okay with them?" Not that she cared. The shifter was an asshole, and as far as she was concerned, he could just drop dead. But maybe his mate wasn't so bad. And children definitely needed a mother *and* a father. Even if the father was an asshole.

"Dara's still weak," he said, and she could hear in his voice just how much that worried him. She almost felt bad for him. "The labor was hard on her and she lost a lot of blood. She's here now. Amelia's keeping a close eye on her."

"And the hell spawn—I mean children?"

He glared. "My son and daughter are just fine. They're with their mother. Where I should be, instead of babysitting a pain in the ass like you."

"So why are you here? Go. Really. I can take care of myself just fine."

"Yeah, and you got a stellar track record to prove it," he muttered.

It was Hailey's turn to glare. "Don't make me get up to kick you out." Her hands were whole, her arms worked, she didn't have any broken ribs, and it felt like she still had use of her legs. All in all, she seemed to be in one piece. But she was so damn tired. Her arm was weak just from holding a glass of water.

"Don't provoke me, female. I'm trying to mend bridges here. And I'm not exactly known for my goodwill."

"What bridges? What, are you high or something?"

He sat back down with a frustrated sigh, and rubbed his face. When he'd finished whatever ritual he needed to perform to face her again, he said, "It's like this. Amelia is busy with my family, Pixie went on walkabout to give Jeremy some space, and your new boyfriend has been talking to officials and giving interviews for the last two weeks. They're throwing parties and shit for the new hero of Torrey, and if you ask me—"

"Which I didn't."

"—he's enjoying it just a little too much. And seeing as that is all the family and social circle you have, and I owe Amelia for looking after my family, I'm stuck here with you until someone comes around to replace me."

There was dead silence after his speech.

Then Hailey tilted her head at him. "Are you always so talkative and incomprehensible?"

"It's part of my charm," he retorted.

Hailey snorted. "Like you actually have any."

She knew he was snooping around in her head again, because in true telepath fashion, he cut straight to what she was most likely to pay attention to. "You've been out of it for two and a half weeks. Your heart stopped twice during that time, and if it weren't for your sister and all this fancy machinery, you would be dead now."

I died twice? Creepy.

"By some miracle, you managed to pull out almost completely unscathed. Congratulations. Everyone else can't say the same. Yes, the virus did its job. You can shift all you want and it won't kill you. But just so you know, it'll feel like dying the first hundred times or so."

Yeah, she was intimately familiar with that particular brand of pain. "So I died twice, and came back from the dead stronger. Good deal in my book."

"And that's all you really care about, isn't it?"

"Watch your tone."

"Do you even give a damn that your sister hasn't slept more than three hours a night since your little escapade? Or that you're the reason that Pixie and her brother, who under normal circumstances would die for each other, currently aren't talking? Or hey, how about that your recently dead admirer followed you here and brutally murdered an innocent woman?"

The glass shattered in her hand, shards digging into her palm. What she still had ahold of, she hurled at his head. She didn't say anything. Couldn't even begin to find words harsh enough to toss at him. The monitor next to the bed started beeping like crazy, probably because her heart was racing and she wasn't breathing fast enough to keep up with it. Her teeth were clenched so hard that her jaw muscles ached, and her eyes stung with tears.

Hunt's shoulders slumped, and he hung his head. "I'm sorry. That wasn't fair. I know you had nothing to do with the guy."

Funny thing was, he actually sounded sincere. But her heart rate still wasn't going down.

Hunt looked up at her. His eyes flashed to the screen and back to her. "It wasn't your fault," he said. "You have to know that much. He was crazy. You couldn't have stopped it from happening."

That was it? His big consolation speech? *You're not to blame because you're clueless?* God, she wanted to hurt him so badly. She wanted the psycho back alive so she could rip him apart again. And she wanted to take her time. "Get out," she managed to growl.

He looked as if he was about to argue, but changed his mind. "Good-bye, Hailey," he said as he walked out the door.

When he was gone, Hailey brushed the glass shards off her bed with an angry swipe of her arm, curled up in a ball, and had herself a good cry. Her hand was bleeding, but she didn't feel the pain. She cried for all of those people who wouldn't be coming back to their families because of one sick man with an obsession. She cried for the nightmares and sleepless nights, for the life she'd had and for the one that might have been. She cried for herself, and Amelia, and the relationship they could have had.

But most of all, she cried because she could. While no one was around, she could let herself hurt without hurting others anymore.

She cried so long that she ran out of tears. Though sobs still made her shudder, her eyes were all dried out. Amelia had put her in a room with a glass roof. Hailey could see when the sky above her darkened as evening approached. The sun's dying rays painted the tiny clouds deep purple and red against the pale blue, and it looked to Hailey like blood.

Would she never be rid of it?

For the first time in her life, she felt completely and utterly alone. And the sick thing about it was that a small part of her thought she deserved it. She removed a stalker; got rid of a murderer.

She had killed a man.

Hellcat didn't understand her remorse. The leopard was content now, free of her cage. She remembered a man; how he'd invaded her territory and threatened her mate. Her memory was selective, apparently. Hellcat had gotten rid of a threat. That was all she cared about. Her den was safe and so was everyone in it, and that was as it should be.

Little by little, Hailey felt herself begin to agree with her. It gave her a measure of relief to let go of the guilt, but her human side stubbornly held on to the remorse. Hailey hoped it would fade in time. Maybe when she stopped seeing blood every time she closed her eyes she could let it go and move on.

She wanted Jeremy. Where was he?

Giving interviews and attending parties, Hunt had said. Hailey hadn't really expected him to sit by her bedside all this time, but some concern for her welfare would have been nice. If nothing else, she had saved his life.

He'd told her he loved her. She vaguely remembered him telling her that as she lay dying. And before, in her dream, too. Did he think she wouldn't remember?

Jer? she called tentatively, then waited in pensive silence for an answer.

Nothing.

If souls could ache, Hailey's did. She craned her neck to look at the monitor. All vitals showed stable; her internal injuries were mended. Hailey felt weak, but from all appearances she was healthy. Except that, from all appearances, she'd been in a coma for two and a half weeks. That really sucked. It meant her body would need time to recover, a process she wasn't looking forward to in the least. But hey, with the regenerative agent working properly, she could probably cut down on recovery time significantly.

Too bad it only worked on the body, not the mind.

Hailey couldn't remember the last time she'd been this tired, physically and in every other way. Exhaustion was pulling her back to sleep before it even got dark outside.

But she wasn't ready to check out just yet.

~

"Agent Calen! Agent Calen! What led to your discovery of the criminal?"

Jeremy was nearing the end of his patience. Another press conference. It felt as if there'd been hundreds of them already, always the same. A crowd of reporters jostling and shouting, trying to get his attention just so they could fire questions that had already been asked and answered dozens of times. He was sick of it. His shoulder ached, his telepathy was still going the subtle kind of haywire in crowds, he missed Hailey like a phantom limb, and there seemed to be no way to shake these jackals.

—*Pain sells,*— John said in what Jeremy figured was supposed to be consolation. —*It's like watching a train wreck. It's horrible, but you can't look away. The public eats it up, the stations cash it in. They'll want to milk this for all it's worth.*—

His boss and mentor had taken a break from his busy schedule to come here as an official cover story. With John MacMurphy, the director of Earth's Special Unit, in the picture, no one asked about how Jeremy had gotten onto the case. No one cared about a missing persons investigation. What they wanted was to tell people that a dangerous criminal had been caught and no longer posed a threat to society.

And show as many gory pictures as they possibly could.

There, at least, they were shit out of luck. Jeremy had savored telling the first group of reporters that the bodies of the criminal and his latest victim had already been taken for medical examination and no reporters would be allowed near them.

"Through teamwork and collaboration with the police departments," Jeremy said, repeating a rehearsed line yet again, "the Special Unit became aware of certain factors in the case, which ultimately led us to Torrey, following the suspect's movements."

"How did you know who to watch?" a woman asked. It wasn't her turn, and she got a lot of dirty looks for speaking up.

"By comparing notes from each individual case against arrival and departure times to and from the cities. As you can imagine, it took quite a lot of work. The Special Unit would like to convey our gratitude to everyone who helped us in this investigation."

—*Very diplomatic,*— John said.

—Maybe they'll lay off and go bother someone else for a change.—

"If the entire Special Unit was involved," the first reporter said, "why were you the only one present at the scene? You were the only agent on the planet."

That was new. "Torrey is my home," Jeremy answered. He didn't have much more to add to that.

"I believe," John cut in, "that Agent Calen is being modest. Naturally, when we discovered that the suspect was heading to Torrey, we immediately dispatched several agents and informed Agent Calen of the situation in full detail. He was our eyes and ears here until the other agents arrived. It was purely by a stroke of luck that Agent Calen happened to find the suspect so close to his home."

"Still," the reporter insisted. "Don't you think it's a little suspicious that the suspect came to this specific village, was found by Agent Calen, and attacked him, supposedly sustaining a fatal injury in the process?"

"If you do your due diligence," Jeremy said, his temper spiking, "you will find that the shuttleport outside of Amberley is the largest on this particular continent, and the only one equipped to support inter-world travel. Torrey's not exactly a tourist hub."

"Oh, I have done my homework," the reporter said, "and it seems that *your* travel itineraries match up to the suspect's very well. In fact, your arrival on Torrey preceded the suspect's by a day or two, isn't that true?"

Jeremy saw red. He wasn't usually a violent person, but at this particular moment, he wanted to rip the reporter's tongue out to shut him up. He crushed the now empty paper cup in his fist. It was all he could do. He had to keep his face impassive, but his hand was concealed by the podium. Jeremy imagined that the cup was the guy's throat.

John nudged him aside and took the podium. "As we said in our official report, and in answers to the media, the chase after this dangerous criminal was a team effort. What you have so astutely discovered was our effort to connect with different precincts and compare notes. At the time of Agent Calen's return to Torrey, the trail was cold, and we had no further leads. Agent Calen returned home to address a personal issue, and it was purely by chance that the suspect happened to follow."

The reporter spoke again, but Jeremy didn't hear him anymore, or anything else that followed. He'd had enough of this circus. And from the looks of it, Amberley shared his disgust. The residents were relieved that their community was safe again, but no one wanted this kind of attention.

The town still mourned the death of one of their own, and the media with their constant questions and complaints about the lack of amenities reminded them of it daily. The town market was almost empty most days and there was talk of cancelling the Baroque Bash in English Village. Amberley and the surrounding villages were in a crisis like they'd never had to deal with before.

When John announced that he would answer no more questions, the reporters went wild, shouting a dozen more at him. Jeremy just turned and walked away. It was either that, or dive in there and start busting heads. With his arm still in a sling, that was probably not a good idea.

—*I don't remember you being this temperamental,*— John said. He wasn't following, but taking another way around town to lead the reporters elsewhere.

—*A lot's happened in the last five years.*—

John chuckled. —*Far more has happened in the last five weeks, is my guess.*—

Jeremy rubbed his jaw. He was outside Amberley now, taking the slow way home, walking. He needed time to breathe and cope.

—*Don't worry about the reporters,*— John told him. —*I'll get one of the others to cover for you. We'll talk it around somehow. They won't get anywhere near the Chase sisters.*—

—*Thanks,*— he replied. But that wasn't his only worry. —*How's Pixie doing?*— His sister hadn't talked to him since he and Amelia had brought Hailey back to the lab. She was staying at Hunt's castle now, planning to go see the world or something. She didn't answer his calls and she'd shielded her mind against him. It was the first time he'd ever been so completely cut off from her.

—*Confused,*— John said. —*She knows what she did might have been questionable, but she stands by her choices. At the time, there really wasn't anything else she could have done.*—

—She could have not *sent Hailey to her death.—*

—Yes, well, she was trying to save you.—

Jeremy groaned and sat down hard on a log next to the road. God, this was a mess.

—Bottom line is, she knows she hurt you. She had her priorities and didn't realize that they might have needed to shift. She needs some time to adjust, is all.—

Jeremy had no idea how to deal with that. As an external observer, he probably would have told himself to give her time. They'd been together constantly since before Pixie could probably remember. Maybe she needed this time apart to figure out who she was, and how she fit into this world.

But as an older brother, all he wanted was to have his baby sister back safe and sound. He wanted to drag her back by her ear and lock her up until she was at least twenty-two. He could just imagine how well *that* would work.

The sun was going down. The sky faded, and what few clouds there were became fiery hues of red, purple, and orange. They looked like Hailey's rosettes to him. If he looked hard enough, he could almost make out the shape of her leopard face in the patterns.

She'd died twice.

Jeremy had felt her heart stop beating almost as soon as Amelia had injected her with that final serum. She'd been dead for five goddamn minutes before Amelia managed to bring her back to life. Barely. He didn't remember how long it had taken them to get her into the taxi and back to the lab. Probably wouldn't want to.

Watching Amelia chemically induce Hailey to change shape back to human had nearly killed him. Conscious, Hailey had a modicum of control over the shift. She could steer it and slow it down or speed it up. Unconscious, her body did whatever the hell it wanted to. By the time Hailey had completed the change to full human, she'd been in no better shape than that very first night, her body black and blue from internal bleeding, numerous broken bones, and bloody tears tracking from her eyes.

She'd died again seven hours later. For nine and a half minutes. Which would make it a total of three times Hailey's heart had stopped since she'd changed herself. Another little factoid he hadn't known until Amelia had told him. The very first time Hailey had died had been moments after she'd injected herself with the virus five months ago, and the only thing that had saved her life had been the regenerative serum kicking into gear inside her.

—*Stop thinking about it,*— John grumbled. —*I'll have nightmares for months as it is.*—

—*Can't.*— For the rest of his life, he would remember how it felt to watch her slipping away and be completely helpless to stop it.

—*You'll get over it.*—

—*What?*—

—*Okay, maybe not get over it, exactly,*— John said. —*But you'll appreciate every moment you get with her even more. Unfortunately, nothing does a better job to remind us how precious life is, than death.*—

Jeremy respectfully expelled his mentor from his mind and got to his feet. He had four more miles to walk. He was only going home to shower and change his clothes before he went back to the lab. Hailey was doing better. Her body was healing, and the bruises were finally beginning to fade. Amelia had high hopes that she would wake up soon.

He wanted to be there when she did.

– 28 –

"What do you mean, she's gone?"

"Hailey Chase is not in the facility," the computer repeated. Jeremy was going to smash it to pieces. All of it. The computer, the equipment, the whole damn building. Starting with whatever was emitting that automated voice that refused to give him information.

Hailey's room was empty. There was glass on the floor and a few drops of dried blood on the sheets. The covers were hanging off the edge of the bed, the monitors were turned off, and the patches that used to be attached to Hailey's chest and arms were stuck together and tossed into the trash.

Not exactly what Jeremy had expected to find.

"Locate Amelia Chase."

"Dr. Amelia Chase is in room 202. North Wing. Second floor."

That was just down the hall. Jeremy ran the few yards and banged on the door with a curled fist before he barged in without waiting for an answer. "*Ame—*" he yelled before he spotted her by the window, "*—lia,*" he finished at a more reasonable decibel level.

She blinked up at him. "Come in," she said dryly. "Something I can help you with?"

"Where's Hailey?"

She set down the notepad and took her feet off the coffee table. "What do you mean, where's Hailey?"

"Did you move her to another room?"

Amelia shook her head. "Locate. Dr. Hailey Chase."

"Doctor?"

"I submitted our research on managing the virus's side effects to a medical board in her name, and they awarded her an honorary medical degree. All she needs to do is take a written exam and pass a test on a cadaver and she'll be a fully licensed research MD like me."

"Dr. Hailey Chase is not in the facility," the computer said.

"That is, of course, if she doesn't disappear again," Amelia added and got to her feet in a hurry.

Jeremy followed her out of the room and down to the main floor. "She's got to be somewhere close by. Tell me you implanted a tracking chip in her ass this time."

"Not exactly, but if I adjust the scanner's range, I should be able to locate her." In the center of the facility was a giant lab with a lot of medical equipment and computers. Amelia went to the largest computer and typed in command after command, swearing at the results that popped up on the screen. "She's not here," she said after the last string of curses.

"Yeah, I got that," Jeremy said. He should have seen this coming. Hailey wouldn't have stayed put to save her life. When it came to running, she was an expert at finding a loophole and sprinting for freedom. "Just expand the range to all of Amberley and the surrounding area."

"No," Amelia said. "I mean, she's not on Torrey."

Jeremy's shoulders slumped, and his gaze turned up toward the heavens. "You have got to be shitting me."

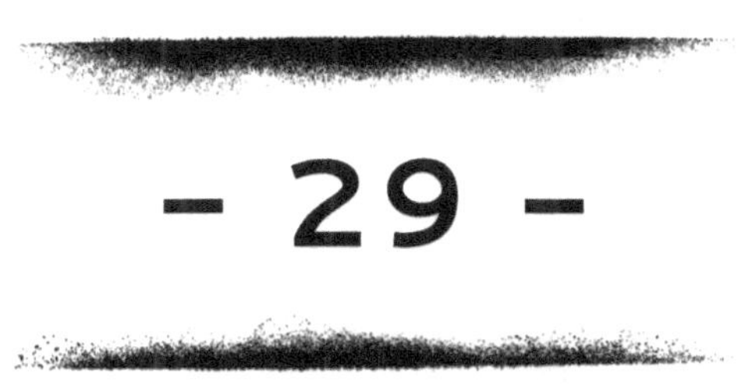

– 29 –

September 19, 3032 – Lotus Three

The Beach wasn't so much a town as it was a sprawling beach resort. An island in the clearest, most beautiful shark-free ocean known to man. The water was a glistening green, and all sorts of colorful fish swam in it. There were coral reefs circling the island about fifty yards from where the waves broke on the beach, palm trees scattered here and there for shade, little huts with bars offering every refreshment and drink known to man.

It was a sandbar, really. Only bigger, with a strip of green running down the middle of the snowy white expanse of beach. The best a guest could hope for in terms of accommodations was a hammock strung up between the palm trees. Maybe an extra one to serve as a roof when it rained.

This was as cheap as it got on Lotus Three and it was leagues beyond five-star resorts on other planets. People didn't come here to sightsee or hold business meetings. They came to surf, and dive, and sunbathe. And for that, Hailey didn't need a hotel room.

She was actually tanning. Oh, she'd missed the sun so much! Now that she didn't have to worry about sprouting fangs and claws or a coating of fur every few minutes, she could just lie back and enjoy. And the best thing about this was that The Beach offered complimentary sunblock. The stuff was amazing. It adjusted to the skin and let just enough sunlight through to tan but not burn.

So someone like Hailey, who had begun to blend in with the sand here, didn't have to worry about looking like a lobster at the end of the day. She could fall asleep, wake up hours later, turn over, fall asleep again, and she wouldn't burn.

That was pretty much what she'd been doing ever since she got here. It was the best therapy ever. Hailey now had her healthy tan back, and she loved it. She adored being on the beach, listening to the waves hiss in and out, even the chatter of other people.

It was as close to Heaven as a woman like her could get. Absolutely perfect. Except for the times she thought of a certain telepath and got that achy hollow feeling in her chest and craved a giant bear hug, she was getting along swimmingly. Her body had healed in record time, she hardly thought about the psycho anymore, and she could just enjoy being free.

All on her own. By herself. Alone.

At first, she'd had a little trouble relaxing, kept feeling exposed, but that had faded in time. She still felt that something important was missing, but Hailey was almost certain that sensation would go away at some point, too. She was fully prepared to move on with her life.

She deserved it. After all Hailey had been through, she was looking forward to a little peace and quiet. Some quality alone time. R&R without anyone stirring up trouble in her mind, or making up outrageous fantasies that made her toes curl and her body respond whether she was awake or asleep.

Yep, solitude was nice. Really, it was.

She'd started making friends again. There was a group of college graduates she'd met just this morning. They were a handful of twenty-somethings celebrating their entrance into adult life and they'd invited her to a bonfire tonight. Hailey planned on attending with glee and enthusiasm. Just thinking about it made her all giddy and excited. She couldn't remember the last time she'd been to a bonfire.

Around noon, Hailey went for a dip in the ocean to cool off. Hellcat might be completely integrated into her now, but she was still a creature of cold climates. She got cranky if she didn't cool down every so often.

The water felt like heaven. Hailey swam for a while up and down the beach, even dared to go up to the coral reefs, but without her snorkeling gear she couldn't fully appreciate its beauty. A wide circle to the reef and back. That was her exercise for the day. When she swam back to shore, she felt like stretching and purring at the same time. Her bikini was hot pink today, ensuring that every male eye in the vicinity turned her way at some point. Many of them tended to stick, and she'd get a whiff of desire carried on the breeze.

Normally that would be a good thing. Great, even. Now it irritated her. She licked a fang, pondering what to do next. Her stomach felt not full. Not a dire need for food, but Hellcat got fussy when she was peckish.

On the other side of the island was a shack that served the most amazing seafood. She went there. No more nuked meals for her—*ha!* She dined on world-class cuisine these days, ironically, for about the same price as a prepackaged meal. Why couldn't she have found this place earlier?

The bartender-slash-cook saw her coming from a ways away and smiled in greeting. "So you're back again," he said, giving her a once-over. As usual, his gaze touched first on her breasts, then on her ass, then trailed back up to her hair, as if it bothered him. It was an annoying habit of his, and even though he never said anything about it, Hailey was offended that there was something about her he didn't like—and that it was something she thought of as one of her better features.

As far as men went, Marco was on the steamalicious side of the spectrum. Long, sun-streaked hair, player smile, ripped arms and abs, and most definitely a flirt. Add his dreamy accent to the mix, and a girl was liable to melt. When he wasn't making a face at her hair, thinking she wouldn't notice. Still, he was no telepath.

Hailey straightened in her seat as if she'd been goosed. By that, she of course meant that he didn't invade her privacy whenever he pleased. It was nice to actually get to talk to a guy without him already knowing everything she was going to say. Who cared if she had to explain some things several times before he got it? That was part of the fun of holding a conversation.

And as an added bonus, she could keep her secrets undisturbed and

just enjoy him lavishing her with his steamy looks and saucy remarks.
    Except…

As much as she enjoyed hearing what Marco said to her, Hailey
sensed the script behind his words. He didn't flirt because he liked
her, necessarily. He did it because she was a female wearing a bikini
in his presence. It made her feel kind of cheap. And he definitely
did not inspire any toe-curling fantasies. What was up with that?
It wasn't like she was looking for a happily ever after here. Hell, she
wasn't looking for anything at all. But if she happened to come across
a willing, steamy one-night stand, she wasn't going to turn it down.

In theory. In practice, Hailey was pretty sure she actually *had* turned
down *several* willing, steamy one-night stands recently. She might be
a little rusty in her flirting skills, but she was pretty sure that when
someone said, "I know this amazing place with a hot spring," it wasn't
an invitation to go sightseeing.

Marco's eyebrows quirked down for a quick frown. "Something
wrong?"

I'll say! The damn telepath wasn't even here and still he was messing
with her head. It didn't take a PhD to figure out why she was turning
down perfectly good studs left and right. None of them were Jeremy
Calen. How screwed up was that?

Hailey made herself smile. "Nah, just a bit too much sun, I guess."

"Ah," he said, a man who must have heard that ten times just today.
"There's room back here by the grill, if you want to duck in for a while.
Although it does get a bit… *hot*, if you know what I mean."

Oh, the lost art of punning. She hadn't missed that at all. "What's
on the menu today, maestro?"

He grinned, not in the least affected by her lack of interest. "For
you, I got something special. Paulo over there decided to do squid
day today and forgot to tell his meat guy. So I have a pound of the
freshest steak you've ever seen."

Meat. Her mouth watered for a bite of juicy steak. Maybe a baked
potato and a fruit cup to go with it. Side of succulent telepath and a
bottle of bold red wine… *yum.*

God, what was it, snow leopard mating season again? Exactly how
many did they have? And why couldn't she have latched on to someone

easier to deal with? Like Marco here.

Marco was giving her a strange look. If she didn't knock it the hell off with the daydreaming about the telepath, she'd scare off her social circle again. "You know, sometimes you look so beautiful to me; your eyes… they glow."

Gulp. She forced a chuckle. "You're such a sweet-talker," she said, and did that girly, halfhearted, limp-wristed slap on the shoulder thing she'd used to be so good at. "Steak sounds like just the thing today. I'll have that."

Strong male arms slid around her waist, shirtsleeves rolled up to the elbow. On her high stool, she might as well have been standing. She felt his chest vibrate against her back when he said, "Make that two."

No. Way.

Hailey twisted around, wondering if this was heatstroke or just a stroke of good luck. *Bad luck, damn it! Remember? This was supposed to be vacation party time, celebrate life to the fullest, escapism at its best? No guests invited?* Yeah, and just like everything else in her life, it was working out exactly as she'd wanted.

Or was it?

Jeremy looked like he hadn't shaved in days—*damn*, it was a good look for him. Hellcat liked it, too. She was making purring noises in Hailey's head, pretending that she was rubbing her face against Jeremy. God, she was so easy!

"Hello," Jeremy said, grinning like he'd just won the lottery.

"Not possible," she said.

He scowled. "You of all people shouldn't be so quick to judge things possible or not."

Marco made a sound of enlightenment, so out of place in a surfer dude, it was almost funny. "I see now why you resist me. But he would not mind if I borrowed you, no?"

Hailey knew he was winking and smiling that player smile again by the annoyed look on Jeremy's face. "He most assuredly *would*. In fact, he would go so far as to beat the shit out of any guy who so much as looked at her inappropriately. *Comprende?*"

Hellcat thrilled at the territorial display. Even Hailey couldn't say she was unaffected. She breathed in the scent of him, feeling about ready to swoon. She'd missed that scent. Her eyes grew heavy-lidded, and she couldn't keep from leaning into him a fraction of an inch.

"*Sí*," Marco said. "I'll go make the steak now."

"Good idea," Jeremy muttered. When Marco disappeared into the kitchen, Jeremy's expression smoothed and he smiled at Hailey again. "Now then, where were we? Oh, yes. Want to explain to me why you ran again?"

"Well, gee, I guess it's sort of in my nature," she said, but her heart wasn't in it. Her voice was way too breathy to pull off indignation. Then she frowned. "Actually, it's in my name, too."

"Chase," he said. Then, to himself, "Right. We'll have to fix that."

Hailey shook herself. No way was he just strolling into her life now, when he couldn't even have been bothered to come see her at the lab. "What are you talking about? And why are you here? Another contract for the good Dr. Chase?"

He took a breath to say something, then just grinned. "I suppose you could say that."

"Well, you can tell her to find herself another guinea pig. Thanks for the save, but I am done and *done* with needles."

"I'm not here for Amelia," he said.

"Oh? What, then? You decided it was time for a vacation?"

"Maybe."

"And just happened to end up in the same exact nowhere location as me."

He shrugged. "It was either this or Everest Bay. My travel agent got me a deal."

It was the sort of comeback she would have delivered. So completely out of character for him, she didn't know what to make of it. He looked different. More at ease, almost lighthearted, as if some great weight had been lifted from him.

Even as she stared at him, grasping for something to say, he smiled wider, his eyes twinkling. Hailey shook herself and scowled. "Stop looking at me like that!"

"Like what?"

Like you're Prince Charming and I'm your happily ever after. "Like you don't plan to look away any time soon."

"Ah, my stubborn, sexy, pain in the ass, beautiful Hailey," he said. His arms tightened around her, almost pulled her off her stool, leaving her no choice but to lean on him in a very awkward position. "There's nothing else here worth looking at."

"You're going to make me fall." *Really?* That was the best she could come up with?

"I would never let you."

"Sometimes you have to fall to learn how to get back up again."

"Sometimes it's okay to let someone catch you."

This conversation was veering off into the absurd. "Seriously, if I end up face-first in the sand, you're a de—"

"Marry me."

Hailey's jaw went slack. She stared into his smiling eyes, more blue than black in the bright sun. He didn't look away, or even flinch. He actually looked *amused.*

She was forgetting something… what was it?

Oh, yeah. Breathing.

Jeremy nudged her chin. Hailey closed her mouth, but that breathing thing still wasn't coming to her. She pushed away from him enough to straighten in her seat. "I almost wish I was a telepath, too," she said. "I can't begin to imagine what you could be thinking to say that."

Jeremy sat on the stool next to hers and took her hands into his. "Let me show you."

She felt him enter her mind like a physical caress. Hellcat curled up to him immediately, and while he greeted her, he did something probably only another telepath would understand. Whatever it was, her eyesight went wonky, the entire world shifted, and then she was looking at herself through Jeremy's eyes.

It didn't last long. This wasn't what he wanted to show her, although he did take a second to appreciate the way she looked in her tan and mini bikini. Then he closed his eyes and built an entire world for her. Beaches and mountains, lush valleys, dense forests, towns and cities filled with smiling faces, but that was all just backdrop. The main scene taking place was a house. Just a house, with flowers in the garden and on windowsills, cozy rooms inside with a fireplace. *A home and hearth.* A warm place to come back to at the end of the day.

And the two of them.

The tranquility of the picture shattered into thousands upon thousands of scenes of them together, laughing, smiling, fighting, sleeping, dancing, traveling, making love, yelling the lyrics to a very loud song; all the little things and the big ones, with friends and on their own. Hailey saw a snapshot from their wedding, lovingly framed and displayed in a place of honor on the fireplace mantle. In it, she wore a white gown but no veil, her hair pinned in an intricate knot at her nape. Jeremy held her off balance, leaned back against his arm. They were smiling, gazing into each other's eyes.

The emotion of that picture was so powerful, so cherished, it almost felt real to her. She could almost remember that day with its hassles to get the last-minute details squared away, and the nerve-racking walk to the altar, the indecision and need to flee, which she stamped down almost completely by the time she came within Jeremy's reach and he took her arm and looped it through his. Oh, how well he knew her.

But that moment, just as the photographer had captured it, was what held her captive in the imagined memory. If something as incorporeal and incomprehensible as love could ever be given shape, she was looking at it. It was there, in the possessive hold of Jeremy's arm, in the tenderness of his smile, in the heat of his gaze. And she could see all of those things mirrored in herself.

Alone or not, parents or not, it didn't matter. That was why, of all the images he'd shown her, this was the one that stuck. The variables were endless, and that was all right. As long as the constant remained: Jeremy and Hailey together.

The image came closer, grew larger until she could distinguish the millions of pictures that made up that magnificent mosaic. Jeremy showed her an entire lifetime, fragmented into moments, flying by so fast, and yet each held some significance. Nothing was trivial. Each built on the next, all of them tying together in an endless chain of a sense; a feeling of such depth and width that it overwhelmed everything else. It said, *I love you.*

He showed her Hellcat, to tell her that just as the leopard had become a permanent part of Hailey's life, the both of them had become a part of his. And he couldn't get them out of his mind if he wanted to.

He didn't want to. His life had changed enough that it wouldn't make sense now without them in it.

Hailey felt him squeeze her hands. She hadn't even realized she was clutching his so tightly. *Foolish,* she thought to him. *To stake so much on another being. To be so completely dependent on them for your own happiness.*

—*Call it a leap of faith,*— he replied. She was leaning toward him and felt his raspy cheek against hers. His mouth was next to her ear, but she didn't hear what he said, only what he thought. —*Don't be afraid of this,*— he told her. —*I don't need you to catch me. I just need you to leap with me.*— At her ear, he whispered, "So we both can fly."

Hailey returned to herself, dizzy and disoriented, with Jeremy the only point of focus. Her anchor. "From anyone else," she said, "that would have been such a sappy line."

He quirked an eyebrow. "But not from me?"

Hailey shook her head. "That's what's insane. You actually mean it."

"So what do you say? Want to get hitched?"

Yes. Yes! YES!

Wait, we just decide that quickly?

Oh, who was she kidding? She was in the most beautiful place in the universe, something she'd dreamed about for months and years, and still, if he didn't take it back in the next five minutes, she would leave it all in a heartbeat and move into a concrete cell if that's what it took. "Well, Hellcat is all ready to jump on the happy joy-joy band-wagon," she said dryly.

Jeremy laughed. "She has good taste."

"Try not to be so smug about it. She's just horny."

He was still grinning, but now his blue-black eyes began to smolder. "Funny thing I've noticed about your Hellcat. She's not really a separate entity anymore. She's you. She thinks what you think, feels what you feel… even what you try to hide."

Hailey blushed. *Not like I'm known for my self-control.* Even *before* she'd amped up her animal id to the max. That was probably it, anyway. If she just studied her blood some more, she'd probably find the underlying reason for her persistent… preference to one male in particular.

—There is absolutely a reason,— he said. *—It's been studied for centuries. Has a name, too: love.—*

Occam's Razor, she retorted. Just for the hell of it. *It's far more likely that I'm just horny and you're the most qualified to give me what I need.* Of course, he already knew otherwise. Damn telepath.

—And you know I'm always happy to oblige, baby.—

The pet name made her snicker.

"So where does a guy go to get some privacy around here?"

Marco emerged from the kitchen and set two plates before them. "There is a lovely spot to the north," he said, smiling big and waggling his eyebrows at Hailey. "Not many people know. I told you about it, remember?"

Jeremy's grin turned into a snarl. "I'm going to kill him."

Hailey bit back a laugh. That jealous streak of his was adorable. "Hmm, bloody murder, or an early wedding night," she said and hopped off her stool. "Tough choice."

When she turned north and started walking, swaying her hips for good measure, Jeremy was less than a split second behind her. "So where are we going?" he asked, openly projecting his refusal to go anywhere that jackass cook suggested.

Hailey just smiled. She turned to him and snatched him close for a kiss. His arms came around her, so tight, her feet left the sand. It was the kind of kiss that happened in movies and books. The kind that left her breathless, and dizzy, and hot. A perfect ending to a love story, but it was only the beginning.

Where were they going?

When Hailey's feet touched sand again and she looked at the man she loved, who loved her enough to go chasing her across the universe, Hailey answered simply, "Heaven, as far as I'm concerned."

The End

ALIANNE DONNELLY was a wordsmith long before she became a reader. Driven by an insatiable curiosity about everything from history and mythology to science and philosophy, she grew into a fiction writer who hates coloring inside the genre lines. Her books all have elements of romance, with different series sorted under paranormal, science fiction, fantasy, and erotic. And then there's *Wolfen*…

Alianne lives in California, doing hard time in a corporate 9-5, while secretly scribbling away any chance she gets. She loves pizza, hiking, and avoiding small talk, and hopes to one day win the lottery jackpot. To find out more about Alianne's books and works in progress, visit her website at AlianneDonnelly.com.